Death and the Runaways

Books by Heather Redmond

The Dickens of a Crime Mysteries

A Tale of Two Murders

Grave Expectations

A Christmas Carol Murder

The Pickwick Murders

A Twist of Murder

The Mary Shelley Mysteries

Death and the Sisters

Death and the Visitors

Death and the Runaways

Death and the Runaways

Heather Redmond

kensingtonbooks.com

This book is a work of fiction. Names, characters, businesses, organizations, places, events, and incidents either are the product of the author's imagination or are used fictitiously. Any resemblance to actual persons, living or dead, events, or locales is entirely coincidental.

To the extent that the image or images on the cover of this book depict a person or persons, such person or persons are merely models, and are not intended to portray any character or characters featured in the book.

KENSINGTON BOOKS are published by

Kensington Publishing Corp.
900 Third Ave.
New York, NY 10022

Copyright © 2025 by Heather Redmond

All rights reserved. No part of this book may be reproduced in any form or by any means without the prior written consent of the Publisher, excepting brief quotes used in reviews.

Without limiting the author's and publisher's exclusive rights, any unauthorized use of this publication to train generative artificial intelligence (AI) technologies is expressly prohibited.

All Kensington titles, imprints, and distributed lines are available at special quantity discounts for bulk purchases for sales promotion, premiums, fund-raising, educational, or institutional use. Special book excerpts or customized printings can also be created to fit specific needs. For details, write or phone the office of the Kensington Special Sales Manager: Attn. Special Sales Department, Kensington Publishing Corp., 900 Third Avenue, New York, NY 10022. Phone: 1-800-221-2647.

Library of Congress Card Catalogue Number: 2025934265

KENSINGTON and the K with book logo Reg. US Pat & TM Off.

ISBN: 978-1-4967-4906-2
First Kensington Hardcover Edition: August 2025

ISBN: 978-1-4967-4908-6 (ebook)

10 9 8 7 6 5 4 3 2 1

Printed in the United States of America

The authorized representative in the EU for product safety and compliance is eucomply OU, Parnu mnt 139b-14, Apt 123
Tallinn, Berlin 11317, hello@eucompliancepartner.com

July is so ripe
Love tangles under willows
Hush! Feel hearts breaking

Cast of Characters

Mary Godwin*	16	Child of fame, a writer
Jane Clairmont*	16	Mary's stepsister
William Godwin*	58	Mary's father, a philosopher
Mary Jane Godwin*	48	Mary's stepmother
Percy Bysshe Shelley*	21	Atheist, lover of humanity, democrat, poet
Winnet Davies	18	A cheese seller
Branwen Davies	18	A fish seller
Denarius Fisher	30	A Bow Street Runner
Reverend B. Doone	24	A clergyman
John Griffith	48	A cheesemonger
Cleda Griffith	56	A cheesemonger
Hubert Asquith	45	A professor of natural philosophy
Irving Bryan	50	A secretary
Gideon Wharton	45	A constable
Humphry Davy*	33	A natural philosopher
William Godwin the Younger*	11	Mary's half brother
Fanny Godwin*	20	Mary's half sister
Charles Clairmont*	18	Mary's stepbrother

*Real-life people

"Nothing is so dangerous to the progress of the human mind than to assume that our views of science are ultimate, that there are no mysteries in nature, that our triumphs are complete and that there are no new worlds to conquer."
—Sir Humphry Davy

"An old alchemist gave the following consolation to one of his disciples: 'No matter how isolated you are and how lonely you feel, if you do your work truly and conscientiously, unknown friends will come and seek you.'"
—Carl Jung

"[H]er soul, susceptible of the most exalted virtue and expansion, though cruelly nipped in its growth, thrilled with delight unexperienced before, when she found a being who could understand and perceive the truth of her feelings, and indeed *anticipate* them...."
—Percy Bysshe Shelley, *St. Irvyne*

Chapter 1

London, Monday, June 20, 1814

Jane

Hyde Park's summer heat had tormented us for more than two hours by the time the artillery's royal gun salute began to sound twenty-one times, announcing the arrival of the Prince Regent and his party. Mary and I were attempting to keep ourselves cool among the trees, while listening to our fellow bystanders' discussions about the Definitive Treaty of Peace with France, but my brother Charles and his lady friend gamely tilted their straw brims against the heat and leaned against the fences, doing their own inspection of the troops within our eyeline.

While smoke puffed over us, graying the blue sky and covering the scents of earth and grass with that of gunpowder, I daydreamed a bit about traveling to places we'd heard so much about but couldn't visit. Now the war with France over. When would our adventures begin? My thoughts were interrupted by cannon fire, and then a band began to play "God Save the King." All our brave soldiers in their colored coats and white breeches did complicated things with their guns. Charles, in front of me, didn't move a muscle, so drawn was he to the manly display, but the sharp-nosed young lady with him, who looked vaguely familiar, though I couldn't place her, plucked at his arm and spoke in his ear, restless in the heat.

I had not known my older brother was courting. Charles had never been of much interest to me, at least not since my mother had married William Godwin and I'd acquired Mary, just six months older, as a stepsister. Charles's taste in females had apparently settled on the neat-as-a-pin type. Carefully constructed light brown curls danced around her temples, a straw bonnet hiding the evidence of whether her hair was naturally curly or not. Her sprigged muslin gown hugged her body more tightly than what I might have chosen, but it set off her straight, boyish figure well.

Over the rustling of leaves, I heard someone say fourteen thousand troops and officers had combined on the vast, hot fields of Hyde Park today. The twenty-six hundred horses underneath officers and cavalrymen, which our neighbor had reported on previously, made themselves evident to my nostrils.

I counted off the third volley of cannon fire. Next to me, Mary held her hands over her bonnet, looking cross from the wave of percussive sound. Even that expression could not diminish the fairy beauty of her face, so different from my darker skin and eyes. I pulled a twig from her fine red-gold hair, then turned back to the field. Enthusiasm did not exactly bubble forth from my breast, either, since we had seen the royal party at the theater recently. Distinguished personages had been in London for quite a while now, and they had hangers-on, some of whom I knew to be dangerous.

Mamma and Papa had hoped many of these deep-pocketed, consequential people would enter the doors at our Skinner Street bookshop or, even better, take tea with us in our private rooms. But it had been weeks since we'd had a visit from anyone with the funds and idealism that might send coins dropping into the outstretched hands of my mother and stepfather. That they desperately needed the coins had kept us out of sorts. Papa had been extricated from the grasping hands of the moneylenders only by merest circumstance, and we were all waiting for the next disaster.

Mary's hands dropped to her waist when the cannons stopped sometime later, the royals having progressed down the endless lines of men, reviewing the troops. Plumes waved merrily above the smoke as the personages rode along the field. They were little more than stick figures to me. Stick figures with money, which I desperately wanted to figure out how to liberate from their pockets. Drums and music still played over the sounds of the horses' equipment, keeping our attention on the field.

My avaricious thoughts were interrupted by newer sounds. I looked up, then turned as branches cracked, leaves fell, and a boy cried out.

An older man pulled the spindly lad from the bush under an oak tree and roughly dusted the back of his coat. "Did ye break any bones, Jimmy?"

The boy, half a dozen years younger than me, shook his head. One glance at the man's face made him hang his head low.

The man glanced around, his expression calming as he saw so many gazes looking in his direction. "Don't climb that tree again," he cautioned. "Have some sense, lad. The upper branches are weak."

The boy bit his lip, then nodded.

I turned back when Mary sneezed.

"The smoke is so thick I can't see the trees on the other side," she complained. "Why did we come today? I have such a headache."

"I thought you could write a scene like this for your novel *Isabella, the Penitent; or, The Bandit Novice of Dundee*," I explained, mentioning her manuscript in progress. Her heroine was named after Isabella Baxter, Mary's friend who lived in Scotland. Mary wanted to be a writer like Papa and her late mother, Mary Wollstonecraft, and I aimed to encourage her. I liked it when she read to us. "It can't all be chasing mummies and lovemaking."

She began to argue with me on that point, but her voice squeaked into a cough. Giving up on speech, she threw up her hands and went to stand next to Charles. I stayed in the shade.

Two foreign crowned heads rode by, along with a crowd of men in the uniforms of their home militaries. I recognized the rulers as Emperor Alexander of Russia and King Frederick William of Prussia, who was accompanied by his two handsome young sons, but Mary merely brushed off the dust graying her white skirt and didn't look up. I counted to amuse myself. More than three hundred men were in the royal party, all of them with full pockets. Any one of them had the power to save us at Skinner Street. I didn't want Papa to have to go to the sponging house, then debtors' prison.

When the shouts of onlookers to the royals died down, I heard the young lady with Charles suggest he find her some lemonade. He turned and saw me. I knew by his wild expression that he didn't have so much as a tuppence with him. Neither did I. He had been educated expensively for his role in the family business, unlike me, but he wasn't paid much for his time in the warehouse, and I wasn't paid at all for my work in the shop. He'd have to find a way to court without spending anything, but I didn't know who would want him. I suspected Miss Neat as a Pin wouldn't stay for long. She already looked almost as disgruntled as Mary.

In fact, while I watched, Charles's companion suddenly swayed. Clutching her belly, she crumpled. He swore, crying,

"Miss Davies, Miss Davies," and grabbed her under the arms. Mary had been paying more attention than I expected. She snaked her arm around the girl's waist, and they helped her down to the packed dirt so she could lean against the fence.

An older woman clicked her false teeth, then came toward Miss Davies with a bottle. The woman helped Miss Davies drink until some of her color had been restored. She drank so greedily from the bottle that water dotted her prominent nose.

The serene weather and warm sun did not help with the dust. Miss Davies coughed from her low vantage point. She reached into the pocket of her apron and pulled out a bundle and handed it to the older woman, who unwrapped it and nodded, then returned to her party, leaving the bottle with Miss Davies.

I glanced curiously at the object and saw it was a small round of cheese. I admired Miss Davies for having taken matters into her own hands. I knew who she was now, a shopgirl at the local cheese shop, who was familiarly called Winnet by the owners, a married couple.

The boy who had fallen laughed loudly behind me. I turned back to him and saw that a young man with sunken cheeks had come around the tree. That round of cheese would benefit him more than the comfortable lady who had offered the bottle. He, after he had some attention on him, pulled a deck of red-and-green abstract design-backed cards from a bag he carried, then shuffled them with theatrical flourishes. They looked like a deck I had seen the French émigrés playing with at the Polygon when we lived there.

Mary joined me in the shade, and we both gazed upon the magician, drawn toward the unfolding drama of the cards. His expressive, bony face, capped by lank, dark locks, matched his body, though his clothes looked quite new and maintained for someone who probably made little coin.

"Choose any eight cards," the magician invited, moving the cards with lightning speed through his fingers.

The boy fell back, but his older male companion stepped up. "What's the trick?" he growled.

"No trick, no trick. One penny to play," the magician said with a broad grin that exposed his crooked lower teeth, all huddled together in that narrow jaw.

"How do I win?" the man asked.

I clutched Mary's arm, excited. I hoped the magician would lure the man in.

"If I can trick you out of a card, you'll have tuppence. But it's one penny to play." The magician let the cards fall like a waterfall through his fingers.

The boy squeezed the older man's arm, urging him on. The man tugged on his graying beard; then his hand went under his coat. He produced a penny and set it on a waist-high branch, his fingers leaving it only slowly.

Quick as a blink, the penny vanished, replaced by the cards, spread across the branch.

"Count them if you like," the magician said. "All fifty-two are there, gentlemen and ladies, but we only use eight for this experiment."

"Which eight?" the man asked, more eager now that he'd committed his penny.

"Your choice, sir. Pick them out. Then we'll see if I can make it disappear."

"I'm a carpenter, son. Good with my hands," the man growled.

The magician nodded solemnly and sucked in his lower lip before saying, "Very good, sir. Eight, any that you choose, sir. Let's not keep your audience waiting. They want to see if they can beat me, too."

"I'll beat you myself if you cheat," said a rough-looking individual on my other side.

The magician laughed merrily. It seemed very practiced, an act he'd perfected.

The man chose his eight, and soon they were spread out on

the branch, the others having vanished. The magician flipped the eight into his palm; then the cards flashed as he shuffled them until they were back on the branch, facedown.

"Pick one," the magician invited. "Show your boy, or the crowd, but don't show me, no, sir."

The man put his hands over the cards, then hesitated, looking like a fortune teller himself. Finally, he plucked up his choice and turned it over under the boy's nose. They nodded at each other.

"We'll lose it in the cards," the magician said. He deftly flipped the remaining seven into his hand, then held them out. "Push it in, sir, and don't let me see."

I watched breathlessly as he shuffled the eight cards again. Here would be where the trick came in, but I'd probably never see it.

"I have no idea where the card is now," the magician said in a breezy tone. He started flipping up cards. "Is this yours? Is this?" He kept going until there were four and the man had nodded.

"I'm going to give these to you to protect," the magician said, all business now. "Place them between your palms, sir, just like so."

"I'll give them to the boy to hold," the man said gruffly.

The boy grinned and held out his palm. The magician placed the flat package of four cards on his hand, and the boy clapped his other hand like a clamshell over the cards.

The magician set the last four cards together on the branch. "Let's see what happens!" He muttered something in Latin, I thought, then passed his hand over the cards and snapped his fingers.

His little crowd pushed forward, closing in on the branch, as the magician turned over his pile.

"That's my card!" the man said. "How did you get it?"

The boy cried out and opened his hands. Three cards fell to

the ground. He sniffed hard, tears welling up in his eyes. "I didn't let go, Grandfather, I swear!"

"I know you didn't." The old man squared his shoulders. "Well done, sir. You hornswoggled me good and proper."

The magician nodded and held out his hand for the cards. The boy picked them up from the dirt and handed them over. The magician sighed and pulled out a handkerchief to wipe off the dust.

"Let's go again," another man said. A lady clung to him, some years older than us, avarice in her eyes. "I'll bet I can beat you."

Mary loosened her arm from mine and turned. I looked back and saw my brother had his finger in Winnet Davies's face. What was going on?

I stepped forward to hear Miss Davies's rather shrill words.

"I would do anything for a pretty dress," she said.

I frowned. No one in our household was buying pretty dresses right now. Mary's expression matched my own.

I suspected the relationship wouldn't last long, but she didn't seem like a good match for our household in any case. We were a family of thinkers, readers. Our entertainment was our little brother, Willy, giving speeches that Mary wrote from his cut-down pulpit, not the careless delights that a cheesemonger might enjoy.

Mary's expression pinched as the girl's tone became increasingly whiny.

"Why on earth do you think she expects Charles to buy her a dress?" I asked. "That is utterly inappropriate even if they had been courting for some time."

Mary shrugged. "I cannot say."

"You must have an idea." Behind me, the magician's patter began again. Someone else must have offered up their penny.

"Maybe he damaged her gown in some fashion," Mary said, passing her hand over her eyes.

"Are you not well?" I asked. "Don't you want to discuss how to turn Miss Davies into a villainess for your book? A mad abbess, perhaps, or an innkeeper in collusion with Diego, the mummy master?"

"I have a pain behind my eyes. The sun is most bright, and the dust is terrible." She squeezed her eyes closed.

"I expect there is nothing much more to see," I said. "If you do not want to watch the thousands march away."

She yawned. "I snuck out last night, and I am feeling the effects."

"Without me?" I asked.

She smiled. "Shelley invited me to see his friends at Old Bond Street."

"Without me?" I repeated stupidly. The anarchist poet Percy Bysshe Shelley was my friend, too. Why wasn't I included? I wanted to pinch Mary for sneaking out and not bringing me along.

"They are publishers," she said. "I must meet such people if I'm to sell *Isabella, the Penitent* one day."

"You have to finish writing it first," I snapped. "Did you have too much wine?"

She nodded, then licked the side of her mouth, as if still tasting it.

I considered her. "You do look a little green." I glanced past her to Charles, who was throwing up his hands, intent on Miss Davies. "Oh, well. Let's go home without Charles."

Mary nodded, wincing. "I don't want to listen to them argue all the way home."

I sat up the next morning when a stray ray of sunlight snaked between the curtains. It was Tuesday, but it felt like a holiday after the events in Hyde Park all day and night yesterday. We'd taken our youngest brother, Willy, to see the mock Battle of Trafalgar on the Serpentine at 8:00 p.m. When I went to the window, I saw the street was very quiet, but then all of London had been celebrating the night before.

After putting on my wrapper and tying garters over fresh stockings, I tiptoed down to the parlor to do my vocal warm-up exercises without disturbing the house. Mamma didn't have the coin for my singing lessons anymore, but I was determined to keep from losing progress. I knew it would be a challenge with no pianoforte in the house, but at least I could sing, and my pitch was good.

Once I had rehearsed for forty minutes, I went back up and took my clothing into Mary's room so she could help me dress. She was not there, however. My fingers tingled as I forced down my outrage. Had she sneaked out with Shelley again?

I knew she had not gone out since I woke. Only one door connected the entire building to the outside world, and it was in the small front hall between the parlor and the bookshop.

I went back down, then took the steps to the basement to have Polly, our kitchen maid, help me dress. She had the fire going already. Mary, by all rights, should be in the kitchen, as well. Mamma had assigned Mary to manage the cooking once she fired our cook a couple of months ago, but she was not very keen on it.

"Where is your sister?" Polly asked as she pulled the drawstrings at the back of my gown closed.

"I don't know," I admitted.

"I'll need help with the breakfast," Polly said. "There aren't enough hands to do the work here. Your parents expect breakfast on the table as soon as you've opened the bookshop."

My ears perked up as I heard light footsteps on the stairs, followed by a heavier tread. Mary appeared in the doorway a few moments later, holding a basket. Behind her came our friend Shelley, always welcome at Skinner Street because he had promised to support Papa in his old age, due to being his disciple in the anarchist philosophies of Papa's bright youth some twenty years earlier.

Shelley, the grandson of a baronet, stood tall and broad shouldered, though he didn't eat enough to fill out his rangy frame. He had wavy sandy brown hair and large blue eyes that drew a person in. His fingers were habitually ink-stained, since he was quite the poet, and his overall demeanor positively bubbled with energy and ideas.

We all doted on him. My oldest stepsister, in fact, twenty-year-old Fanny, had been sent away to Wales to work as an unpaid governess due to her unrequited love for Shelley, a married man. Fanny's loss had caused great difficulties in our household, but our parents saw the punishment of the unwanted exile as just. If nothing else, her honor was being protected.

I didn't see what use honor was, however. We were not young ladies of the nobility. We didn't even believe in marriage. Such things were artifacts of the church and the government and had no place in our lives.

"What do you have?" I asked Mary.

"Sour gooseberries." Already dressed, she wore her favorite tartan dress, which she'd made during her time in Dundee, Scotland. I hated the loud fabric, but she liked to look original.

Shelley certainly didn't seem to dislike it. His gaze on her was frankly admiring.

"What good are those when I have breakfast to get on the table and you aren't here to help?" Polly demanded peevishly.

Mary frowned at her. "The good is that they are free. We can make jam or a tart with them. Shelley saw some bushes with ripe fruit a few blocks north of here, and we had to get them before the squalid children did."

I pulled the basket off her arm. "That's all very well, but, Shelley, you need to leave. It's too early for you to be here. Don't cause a scandal."

Shelley laughed. "I can do no wrong in dear Godwin's eyes."

"Do you want to work in the bookshop with me this morning?" I demanded, setting the basket on the scarred wood worktable.

Shelley mimicked writing in a ledger, then laughed. "Your mamma would not like it, for I would sell seditious pamphlets to infants."

"It's going to be a dreadful day with the heat," I said, knowing he wasn't joking. He'd turn the children of the upper classes into atheists if he had access to them. "Mary, hurry up and help Polly. I'll wake Willy."

"Why do either?" Shelley asked, then quoted from a poem I knew well. "'Come forth into the light of things, let nature be your teacher.'"

"Don't Wordsworth at us," I snapped. "You don't even like his poetry, and if you aren't intimidated by Papa, Mamma is another story."

"I'll make you a cup of Papa's special coffee," Mary offered.

I threw up my hands and went upstairs. Mary had the sense of a goose where it came to Shelley. She ought to be happy to hang about St. Sepulchre, where the curate, who set a fine table, was desperate to court her. Not that I believed in marriage, but at least it would get her out of the house, one less mouth to feed. Maybe I'd have my singing lessons back if she were gone.

Upstairs, I did not hear Charles snoring as usual when I walked by. I went into Willy's room, where the air was heavy with the onion-scented smells of the eleven-year-old boy on this summer morning. After I opened the curtains, I pulled back his covers and tossed his shirt, trousers, and waistcoat at him.

"Hurry up, sleepyhead."

Willy stuck his tongue out at me.

I made a face. "Clean your teeth before you come down. Your tongue is white." I flounced out of the room, then decided to make Charles get up. He should be more eager to get to the warehouse to earn his daily bread if he was courting so seriously that the girl was asking him for dresses.

When I opened the door, however, I didn't hear him breathing. I opened the curtains and looked at his unused bed, the coverlet was pulled up over the pillow. Not only was he not here, but it didn't look like he'd slept here, either. No body smells, no dirty clothes.

I shrugged and went downstairs. I'd found myself becoming quite efficient in the weeks since Fanny had been sent away. She'd been the early riser who kept the household running. I didn't like housekeeping, but it was better than cooking.

In the bookshop I hadn't been able to see how breakfast went for Polly, but she seemed calm enough as she placed small glass cups of gooseberry fool in front of each of us at the end of luncheon.

"The fruits of our labor?" Shelley inquired.

Papa looked confused, and my eyebrows elevated. I did not think Shelley should push his luck so far, wealthy or not, but Papa's expression relaxed the second he dipped his spoon in and took a bite of the cream, egg, and sugar-infused fruit. Mamma merely emptied her cup and asked for more. Mary said nothing but looked serene.

Polly bobbed a curtsy and dashed out. She had no fear of the children of the household, but Mamma was another issue. She slapped and pinched.

"We were speaking about alchemy," Papa said to Shelley, his spoon forgotten in his half-eaten cup.

Willy carefully slid the cup to him, but Papa didn't even notice.

"Indeed. I have made a study of it since my youth," Shelley said, rather loftily for one who was twenty-one.

"Papa took me to hear Sir Humphry Davy speak a couple of years ago." Mary set down her spoon. "He made quite an impression on me."

"He has proven that electricity can break items into their base components," Papa said.

"Could they be rebuilt into something different?" I asked.

Shelley chucked me under the chin. "Would you like to turn that muslin gown into silk?"

"La," I said with a snort. "I have a silk gown already."

The dining room door banged into the wall as Polly dashed in. Mamma looked up, no doubt hoping for her fool, but the kitchen maid didn't have anything in her hand.

"Constable Wharton is here," Polly said, then quicky bobbed a curtsy. "Mr. Godwin, he'd like to see you right away."

Mamma pushed herself to her feet, then went to the wall behind the door to make sure her expensive wallpaper had not been damaged by the doorknob. She ran her hand down the wall as Papa rose.

"Did he say why?" Papa asked. "Some trouble in the neighborhood?"

"I don't know, sir." Polly twisted her hands in her apron. "I don't like it."

"I'm sure it is not your place to like it or not," Mamma said acidly, then went through the door.

Papa followed her.

Willy finished eating Papa's fool, then glanced around the table for any other remains of the treat, but we had all cleaned our shallow cups.

I bent my head toward Mary. "We should listen."

She nodded and rose with more natural majesty than Mamma possessed. After leaving the males, we crept down the passage and went to the top of the stairs so we could hear voices in the front hall.

Papa had already greeted the neighborhood constable before we came into earshot. "What brings you here on a Tuesday afternoon?"

"Godwin," the constable said. An older man, but not in his decrepit years, he had an air of authority, augmented by good relationships with the local inhabitants. "I am sorry to say, sir, but I have a summons for Charles Clairmont to appear at the inquest this afternoon for Winnet Davies's death."

My mouth dropped open, and I clutched Mary's arm. She put her hand to her eyes, as if shielding herself from the news.

"Shocking," I mouthed. Why, we had seen her only the afternoon before.

"Who is this person?" Mamma inquired in a tone that spoke to shock equal to my own.

"She works in the cheese shop down the street from you," the constable explained.

"Why is my son being called?" she asked.

"He is a known associate of hers, Mrs. Godwin. Seen with her just yesterday, in fact."

"Nonsense," Mamma said. "He is not in the business of befriending shopgirls."

"He was with her in the vicinity of Hyde Park."

"Charles was there with his sisters, not some girl," Mamma said. She screamed my name.

Mary held me back for a couple of beats, then released me so we could both go downstairs.

"What is this about?" Mamma demanded.

I felt very small and young all of a sudden. I glanced at Mary for support. She sighed and spoke.

"We were with Charles," Mary said. "But Miss Davies did join us."

"I recognized her from the cheese shop," I added.

"When did you last see her?" the constable asked.

"We left them at the park," I said. "Mary and I came home alone."

The constable nodded, as if to agree that this matched his information.

"What happened to her?" Mary asked.

"Miss Davies was found dead at first light this morning at

the site of the former Tyburn gallows. Hanging below a tree branch."

"That's three miles from here." Papa shook his head. "How unfortunate, but Charles had nothing to do with the situation."

The constable regarded him with watchful eyes. "She was with child, according to an examination."

I gasped, remembering the boyish figure. Then Mamma's voice rose. "What is going on?"

"We were all together yesterday afternoon," I said. "She looked slim to me."

"The doctor would know best. Did anything memorable occur?" the constable responded.

"She wanted a new dress," Mary said. "I remember her talking about it."

Mamma's shoulders shook. "This has nothing to do with our household, sir. My son is just nineteen."

"Where is Charles?" Mary asked. "Jane, you said he wasn't here last night."

Mamma hissed.

"His bed," I said meekly. "Not slept in."

Mamma glanced at me. "Keep your thoughts to yourself, girl."

"What if Charles is dead, as well?" Mary asked. She looked at the constable. "Are you sure he wasn't there, in another tree perhaps?"

Mamma's fingers clenched into a fist. I hoped she didn't lose control of herself in front of the constable. She'd already been in the lockup once this year, and she had a terrible temper.

"Surely we should be more concerned about Charles's safety than whether he was involved in Miss Davies's death," Papa said. "Indeed, Constable Wharton, I am disappointed in your approach."

"It didn't occur to me that he would not be at home," the constable said, his natural dignity undisturbed. "I want to clear this up as much as you do, Godwin."

"We can't help you," Mamma said.

"You aren't harboring him?" Constable Wharton asked sternly.

"No, we are not," Papa said. "He has missed two meals now."

The constable nodded. "Then I will take my leave, but as soon as he reappears, have him find me at the watchhouse."

Mamma marched to the door and held it open, her mouth in a tight line. The constable hesitated, then slid around her and returned to the street. She slammed the door behind him.

Mary winced, then went down the passage to the kitchen. It would be the best place in the house to conceal herself. I went into the bookshop to hide behind the counter.

Chapter 2

Mary

Mary rarely thought Jane should envy her, but as she sat at the kitchen table peeling potatoes that afternoon, she much preferred her lot in life belowstairs to sitting in the parlor with Mamma.

If Fanny were home rather than in Wales, they'd probably be looking through pattern books, choosing what they'd make when they next had money for fabric. Fanny needed new things because what she'd left in her room had been steadily pilfered these past weeks due to one misfortune after another.

Mary's hand shook all of sudden. She stabbed her knife awkwardly into the potato and steadied her right arm with her left. Her skin itched, a ghost of the affliction that had plagued her when young and was resurrected under stress. Her mind slid through uncertain waters. What had happened to Charles? With Fanny gone and Charles likely murdered, she was now the oldest child in the house. Yes, Charles ate a lot, but he toiled in the publishing business. He knew rather a lot about it, having apprenticed in Edinburgh. Practical to a fault, he didn't like it much, but he knew more than Mamma and Papa both about a well-run publishing concern and had helped ensure Mamma had the business on a sound financial footing, even though it was too late to restore Papa's resources. The rest of Papa's creditors would come soon, like the dogs of hell they were, to undo the work of the Clairmonts.

Poor Papa, not cut out for this life. She imagined him young, with a pen in his hand and that beloved serious expression across his brow. Deep thoughts flashing through his mind, the energy to work unceasingly and change the world with a new philosophy animating him.

Now not in the best of health, he spent his energy trying to solve the failings of a decade ago. He'd wanted to find a partner for the business, but no one had wanted to join it, and no surprise. They were a bad luck family, and Shelley was their only safeguard from abject disaster.

Polly slid up to the table. "There's a bit of ham left for dinner. Mostly fat, to be sure."

"Have you thought of any new butcher's shops we can try?" Mary asked. "Is there anyone who will give us credit tomorrow?"

Polly rubbed her nose on her apron. "I hear there is a new shop up north of Smithfield Market. Meat should be fresh given how close it is."

"Try opening an account there," Mary said. "Tomorrow."

"Washing day tomorrow." Polly sneezed.

Mary picked up her knife again. "Then we'll dine on eggs and cheese. We can get them cheaply enough."

"Your father," Polly started.

"Washing day," Mary said. "He'll have to understand, and it buys us a day before we have to find meat again. His stomach should thank us for the good plain fare."

"Will you gather berries again?"

Mary nodded. "I'll try, but it's a long walk to good bushes."

"Free, though," Polly said. "I'll toast the bread. It's stale, but it won't matter once it's been through the fire."

Footsteps clattered in the passage, and Jane walked in.

"You're wanted upstairs, Mary," she said, her eyes very wide.

Mary glanced at the dark curls falling out of Jane's pins and the damp summer's high color on her cheeks. "Why did you run?"

"That Bow Street Runner is upstairs. Mr. Fisher." Jane gulped in air, then belched in unladylike fashion. "Faith, but he's terrifying."

"He's rough," Mary suggested. "Like his creator did not quite finish cutting him out of marble."

Jane nodded agreement. "What has gone wrong now to bring Bow Street to our door?"

"Charles," Mary said.

Jane shook her head, sending her curls dancing. "No. Listen, Mary. He wants you, not Papa."

She didn't like the sound of that but tossed her apron on the table. "Put the potatoes I finished in water, will you, Polly?"

"Do you want tea?" Polly asked sourly.

"We don't want to encourage him to stay." Mary shrugged and went to the water butt, then ladled water into a cup. "I'll bring him this."

Mamma sat with Mr. Fisher in the parlor. He looked very large on their sofa. Mary had seen him a few times now, and he never ceased to make her shudder. Massive shoulders and a broad body completely filled every inch of his garments, causing his buttons to strain. He had a low brow, dark hair with red highlights, which glinted hellishly when he took his hat off.

Mary curtsied awkwardly and held out her cup. "It's a hot day. I thought you might need some water."

He smiled at her and took it.

She thought of a wolf when his teeth flashed. Surely, she had never seen him smile before. In fact, she might never have seen him without his hat. He looked no less intimidating without it, though. He had been a part of making arrests at the bookshop before and wore his natural authority easily.

"We've been discussing your stepmother's experience in the lockup," Mr. Fisher said, looking at Mary over the rim of the cup as he put it to his oversize, very red mouth.

Mary glanced at Mamma's pale face. Was Mr. Fisher subtly threatening them? "Have you learned something about Charles?" she asked.

Mr. Fisher tilted his head, but Papa came in before he could say more.

Mary wrapped her hand around her father's arm and rested her head against his shoulder.

"What can we do for you, Mr. Fisher?" Papa said genially. "I second my daughter's question. We would be very happy to hear any news about young Charles."

Mr. Fisher set down the cup, empty now, then stood. He immediately commanded the room, being at least a foot taller than even Papa. "I will be happy to understand what this concern is about Clairmont, but I am here only to make a confession."

"A confession?" Mamma said behind him. Her voice shook a little. He had terrified her, showing up like this.

"Yes, ma'am. I confess I have a desire to court Miss Godwin."

"Fanny?" Papa blinked. "You wish to court Fanny? But she is in Wales presently. You cannot see her until she returns, though I will be happy to write her with this most interesting news."

Mary squeezed his arm. He sounded rather pleased. Well, why not? Fanny could marry a man with steady employment. She was a deeply practical creature and would be happy to keep his buttons secure. "How nice," she said, "but I must return to the kitchen."

Mr. Fisher shook his head, the fiery tips of his hair catching at his sharp chin. "No, Miss Mary Godwin is who I mean. My fascination for you has existed since I first came into the family bookshop in May."

Mary stiffened. Her fingers slickened against Papa's sleeve. Not her. Oh, he couldn't mean her. He must be close to twice her age.

Papa pressed her hand between his arm and body. "I am afraid, Mr. Fisher, that you have come at a difficult time. Why don't you return tomorrow, have dinner with the family, perhaps?"

Mr. Fisher frowned. "Can I be of assistance? What is this matter with Clairmont?"

"He never returned from Hyde Park yesterday. He was there with the girls and a local shopgirl," Papa explained.

"She was found dead this morning," Mary added. "Murdered."

"Do they think Clairmont did it?" Skepticism was visible on the rough features. "I never thought he had that much sensibility in him, though anyone could be a killer under the right circumstances."

"I think he's dead," Mary said. "But no one wants to listen to me."

"He is not, miss!" Mamma said in a near shout. "How dare you?"

"It's better than thinking he's a murderer," Mary shot back. "Don't you think? He will have gone to his reward, rather than suffer here."

Her father shifted. She knew her words might hurt him. An atheist like him might well think a man alive and in prison better than to be dead, but to sit in a dank cell and fear the noose? That sounded worse than death to her.

Mr. Fisher reached out with one of his massive hands and patted her shoulder before she could shrink away. "There,

there, Miss Mary. Why don't you hire the Bow Street Runners to find him?"

Papa shook his head. "I do not presently have the coin."

"That is unfortunate, Godwin." He searched Mary's eyes. She held her ground, though her chin trembled. "Aye, I will accept your kind offer and return for dinner tomorrow. When do you dine?"

"Five o'clock, sir. We do not keep society hours," Mary said.

"Very good." Mr. Fisher inclined his head, then left.

The family seemed to Mary to be suspended in time until the front door closed. Then Mamma stirred first and pushed herself off the sofa, groaning.

"We cannot afford the expense of feeding him," she snarled.

"We have no choice," Papa said. "We may yet need to ask for his help."

"He showed no willingness to offer it for free," Mamma said.

Mary let Papa's arm drop. She clenched her jaw to stop the trembling. After she lifted her chin, she said, "There will be scant dining tonight, but Polly will try out a new butcher tomorrow so that our table does not embarrass us." She went out of the room, and neither Mamma nor Papa stopped her.

They were at lunch on Monday when the front door opened and closed. Jane had left the dining room door open so she could hear any foot traffic and run back downstairs if needed.

Mary glanced up from her cheese and bread. Thoughts churned in her brain, affecting her stomach. They were all dull with worry. "I'll go."

Jane said nothing, just took a large bite of pickle.

When Mary reached the front hall, she found Constable Wharton. Not an imposing sight, he had a stoop, which meant they were nearly the same height.

"Miss Mary," he said, his tone kind and weary all at once.

Mary crossed her arms. "Do you have news about Charles? He didn't come home last night."

The constable pressed his lips together and nodded. "I bring a warrant for Charles Clairmont's arrest since he didn't appear at the inquest."

"I see." Mary made a show of looking alarmed, though how could it be otherwise? "I assure you, the family doesn't know where he is, but everyone besides me continues to think he's on the run rather than deceased."

"Do they think he killed Miss Davies?" the constable asked.

"Of course not," Mary said stoutly. "You mustn't think of him like that. He's not violent. Miss Davies was greedy, though."

"What do you think happened?"

"I suspect she had another man, one who could buy her the things she wanted. She asked Charles to buy her a dress, which is laughable. He didn't have the money."

"He could have been stealing from your business," the constable suggested.

"I heard him refuse myself," Mary said. "No, she had another man somewhere, and that will be who killed her. I'm just afraid he killed Charles, too."

"You're bound to protect him, Miss Mary. He's your brother."

"Stepbrother," Mary corrected. "I wouldn't lie to you, Constable Wharton. She was a greedy girl, and Charles did not have the coin to keep her."

"He might have become angry at her demands," the constable suggested.

"I've never seen anger in him. He's more of a complainer." Mary forced her hands down to her skirts. Never in her life had she imagined begging for Charles's life in this manner. She felt little but indifference toward him, but he wasn't a killer. "Listen, Constable. Someone hanged that girl. That's not some sort of accident. It's vicious and depraved. I know Charles. He's not one to exert himself."

Constable Wharton rubbed his chin. "It isn't for me to do anything but attempt to arrest him." He held out the piece of paper. "When he comes home, if he does, he needs to turn himself in at Bow Street. Or, if you prefer, he can come down to the watchhouse, and we'll escort him."

Mary took the paper. "Yes, sir. You can set a watch on the house, if you want, to look for him. You know we've only one door into the street."

She offered the paper to Papa when she returned upstairs. He read it over, rubbed his glasses clean with his handkerchief, then read it again before handing it to Mamma.

Tears welled up in Mamma's eyes as she perused the writing. "I never thought I'd see the day."

"Charles is innocent," Mary said. "Jane and I both heard her trying to get money out of him. He said no. She'll have gone to find another source of money, and that's who killed her."

Mamma's lips trembled violently. "Then where is he?"

"He must have seen something and run away," Jane said.

Mary and Papa shared a glance. She knew then that he thought like she did. The oldest son of the house was dead. Willy, seated next to Mamma, as self-absorbed as his older half brother, had the platter in his hand and was scraping the last bits of ham fat onto a slice of bread.

Mamma pushed back from the table and stood. Her hand clenched; then she pointed at Mary. Mary sat up in her chair. What nonsense was this?

"You, girl. You make nice with Mr. Fisher."

"Why?" Mary asked.

"To keep my boy safe. The Bow Street Runners are powerful."

Next to her, Jane nodded violently.

Mary glanced at Papa, who also nodded. She wished she was perceived to have as much value to the family as Charles, but the world didn't work that way. The hopes of the firm were on his shoulders, not hers. Mother, with her dreams of female education, was long dead, and this version of the Godwin family had left her principles in the eighteenth century.

Mary rose from the table. "I'm not hungry."

She heard the scrape of her plate moving across the table as she walked out. Willy, probably, parasitically taking what remained of her food. In her room she pulled a copy of *A Vindication of the Rights of Woman* from her trunk under the bed. She'd taken it from a bottom shelf in the bookshop years ago, but no one had ever noticed it was missing. Though she needed to return to the kitchen, she couldn't help closing her eyes and turning the leaves. She ran her finger down a worn page until it scratched the paper, then opened her eyes. "Strengthen the female mind by enlarging it, and there will be an end to blind obedience," she whispered, reading the text.

The words gave her strength. "Oh, Mother. *Please help us. Help me.* You cannot have wanted this life for me. You must have imagined a life like yours with Papa. Separate intellectual lives, a coming together for communal family raising. Not this. Cooking in a basement for a woman who slaps and pinches me." She bent her head to the page and kissed it with reverence, then closed the book and hid it away.

"It doesn't smell fresh," Mary said early that afternoon, while Polly unwrapped a fish she'd talked a street merchant into selling her, since she'd had no luck at the butcher's.

"Of course it doesn't," Polly said in her most exasperated tone. "I told you what I paid for it. We'll bury it in a garlic sauce. It will last a few hours more."

"I don't want to make everyone ill," Mary protested. Maybe someone, but definitely not everyone. "We have enough problems as it is."

"I'm just glad it's enough," Polly said. "If Charles was here, I'd have needed a second fish."

Mary sighed. "Even so, you'll be eating bread and bacon drippings for dinner tonight."

Polly shrugged. "Fine with me. I don't want to eat this."

Mary slapped the fish down on the table and began to butcher it. She chopped off the head and sliced the belly open, wondering what Winnet Davies's child had looked like inside her, an uncomfortable thought. She could not have been far along, since she had had no hint of a stomach under her skirts.

Mary tried to recall what the cheesemonger had been wearing. Nothing flashy. Light blue cotton. Possibly with a mended tear up the side of the skirt, but nothing that looked too obviously damaged, nothing that made her look less than she was, a shopgirl in search of a husband.

Mary had just bent to the work of deboning the fish when Jane came into the kitchen. She made a face when she saw what Mary was doing.

"Wash with strong soap, Mary. Your beau is here."

"What?" Mary set down her knife.

"The Bow Street Runner is here." Jane held out her hands, arms straight, and rocked from side to side.

Mary frowned. "What are you doing?"

"Imitating him. He thrust some flowers at Mamma."

Mary sighed. "He must be dreadfully nervous if he looked like that."

"I'd be nervous if I were you. Do you think he'll try to kiss you?"

Mary shuddered. "Not if he's bringing flowers to Mamma. He's aiming for a proper courtship."

Jane snorted. "Reel him in, Mary. Make him help us with Charles."

"Why would I want to sacrifice myself to do that? You are one thing. He really is *your* brother."

"He's been yours since you were a child," Jane pointed out.

"Mamma made sure to treat Fanny and me differently," Mary said. "Have the sense to recognize she created the chasm between us, not me."

Jane's lower lip trembled. "Not between you and me. We're the same."

Mary stared at her. Did she not see how differently she was treated?

She needed to find a way to keep her distance from the Bow Street Runner, without infuriating Mamma. Doing her best to get the smell of fish off her hands, she scrubbed until her fingers stung, then pulled off her apron. Luckily, she hadn't worn long sleeves, so her clothing remained spotless. "Peel potatoes, Jane. We always need more. And you, Polly, finish with the fish."

She went up to the parlor. Mr. Fisher stood next to the unlit fireplace. Mamma sat on the sofa. Motes of dust danced in the rays of light streaming in through the window, catching the planes of his face. His jaw seemed so elongated that it didn't quite match the rest of his skull. But then he shifted, and everything worked together again, if not in a handsome manner.

Why couldn't she have a beau with the uncomplicated good looks of a man like Shelley? Mr. Fisher had announced himself as her beau, but what she and Shelley had was different, sacred. A poet pledging allegiance was of finer stuff than this.

Mary bobbed a curtsy to Fisher as he turned to her, feeling formal and intensely awkward.

He didn't smile. She suddenly had a flash of paranoia. "What is your motive, sir?"

"What do you mean, Miss Mary?" he asked in a gentler tone than she was used to. His voice was deep, and she'd never heard it soft before.

"Charles hasn't come home, in the first place," she said, folding her arms. "You've never seemed interested in me until now, though we have met multiple times. Has someone hired you to look for him? Winnet Davies's family, perhaps?"

Behind her, Mamma sucked in a breath.

He shook his head, the sunrays highlighting the fire in his

hair. His hair didn't match the rest of him. It had an appeal that was quite separate, as if it should have been on another head. "I assure you that I have not been hired to hunt for Charles."

"Why now, then?"

He backed into the mantelpiece. The candlestick rocked. "I could not very well court a girl whose mother was in the Bow Street lockup. But that nonsense is done with. I went away for more than a week—into Essex, chasing a runaway butler—but I'm back now. I couldn't stop thinking of you."

He took a step toward her, but she shrank back. Maybe Jane was right. Perhaps his style of wooing was a bit rougher than she'd expected. Had he ever done this before?

"Prove your regard for me by finding Winnet Davies's killer to relieve the pressure on my household," she said, holding steady. "You cannot possibly think I can focus on anything else right now."

Mamma blew her nose into her handkerchief.

His head tilted as he regarded Mary. "I'd never thought you liked that part of your family much."

Mamma gasped at the rudeness.

"What do you know of that?" Mary asked, even more wary. "You do not know me at all."

"Very well." His tongue, thick and meaty, darted out to lick those unnaturally red lips. "To business, then. What would you want me to do if it turns out young Clairmont killed Winnet?"

Mamma squeaked, but Mary said what she thought. "You are no fool. He is most likely dead."

He moved his jaw from side to side. "I have the afternoon free."

"Very well, then," Mary said, forcing herself to sound pleasant. "You know my charge."

His lips turned up very faintly. "You need to accompany me on the quest you have set for me."

"Why?"

He gestured. "I have to learn his haunts. Who can acquaint me of them best but you? I know well you roam the streets whenever you can."

She watched those massive hands swing toward her, then retreat. "How do you know that? You've only seen me here and at the lockup."

"I've seen you more than that." One eyelid half closed. Was he winking at her?

She wanted to curl into a ball at those words. Had he been watching the house? She closed her eyes. "I will need a chaperone."

"When are you not with Jane?" he asked.

She clenched her jaw. So that was something, then. He did not watch her closely enough to see her with Shelley. "I'll ask Jane to join us."

She waited, but Mamma didn't protest, so she fled the room, then returned to the kitchen. Jane had finished peeling the potatoes and was wiping her hands dry.

"You have to come with us," Mary said.

Jane settled her apron against her hips. "Where are we going?"

"I don't know. Wherever Fisher thinks there is information, I suppose." She threw up her hands. "Mamma said nothing. She just sat on the sofa like a lump of butter."

"She was letting him court you."

Polly turned toward them, dropping garlic cloves on the table. "Are you being courted again? My, you have a lot of suitors."

Mary's face grew hot. "I do not."

"The kitchen girl at the vicarage says the curate wants you for himself," Polly said, then brought the flat side of her knife down on the cloves to separate them from their skins.

Jane snorted. "We would finally see you grow fat."

"At least I'd never see a kitchen again," Mary said. "They have an expert at the vicarage."

"Why don't you take him seriously, then? A man of God would make a good husband," Polly suggested.

"You know how Papa feels," Mary said vaguely, then took Jane's arm and towed her upstairs.

"Imagine being hitched to Reverend Doone for life," Jane said. "Faith, we wouldn't be able to stay friends with Shelley."

"I won't," Mary protested.

"What about Mr. Fisher?"

"I doubt Shelley would like that, either," Mary said. "You know that he's under suspicion because of his writings. He wouldn't want the daughter of Godwin and Wollstonecraft married to Bow Street."

"When Shelley is supporting us, he might have a say, but he hasn't given Papa a penny yet."

"It should be resolved by the end of summer." Mary squeezed Jane's hand.

When she and Jane went into the parlor, she found Fisher still standing by the fireplace, as straight as a poker. Mamma had taken up a magazine. Was she pretending to be invisible?

"We can go," Mary said. The scene might have been humorous if she'd liked the man.

His tailcoat flapped against a deck of cards on a little table next to the fireplace. Cards scattered onto the rug.

"I'll get them," Jane said, then crouched on the floor to pick them up.

"It's no problem. We ought to keep them in a box," Mary said.

"Do you like to play cards?" he asked.

"Indeed, who doesn't?" Mary asked, though she'd rather read or write instead. Jane and Fanny often played silly card games with Willy while she curled up on the sofa when it was too cold for walks.

Jane rose and slapped the cards down on the table.

"You missed one," Mamma said, pointing beneath the table.

Jane sighed and dropped to her knees again. Mary gestured to Fisher and went into the front hall to pull her bonnet from its peg and put it on.

"It's a lovely warm day," Fisher said when she reached toward the next peg. "You won't need a shawl."

Just to be contrary, Mary wrapped a light one around her shoulders, anyway. Jane came out from the parlor and grabbed her own bonnet.

"Where are we going?" she asked, taking off her apron.

"We should trace the victim's life. Often, the question of who committed murder lives within the victim's history, even within their personality." Mr. Fisher stared at her.

"She was a grasping sort," Mary said.

"Greed will get you killed," Fisher said.

"It's a good thing we were raised not to want things." Jane grinned and linked her arm around Mary's.

"The cheese shop?" Mary asked. "Is it open, given what happened to their shopgirl?"

"Even so. No doubt the owners live above it, just like you live over the bookshop," Fisher said. "We will make our inquiries, unless you would like to walk somewhere else? The Charterhouse Gardens, perhaps?"

Mary held back a shudder. They went there with Shelley regularly. She would not want to defile the place by trysting there with Fisher. "We must remember Charles. If he is dead, the story of why lives within Miss Davies's life, not his."

"Don't say such things," Jane cried. "I can't believe it. I would know."

Mary squeezed Jane's arm to her side, but she didn't offer pointless words of comfort. If he was alive, why hadn't he come home? He hadn't been out trysting with the girl. She was dead, after all.

The cheese shop was only a two-minute walk from the house. Fisher went right up and tried the door, but the knob didn't turn. "They could be working, even if it isn't open. Where do they get their cheese?"

"They make it," Jane said. "I think they get their milk from Smithfield Market. I see milk cans being delivered on carts from my window sometimes."

"They won't give us credit anymore. When we had a cook, she could manage them, but they are difficult," Mary said.

Fisher shifted and looked through the front window with his hat tilted down to block the light. "Someone is inside." He banged on the window.

The sudden noise made Mary jump. Jane squeezed her arm. After a few seconds of waiting, a black-haired man came to the window. Very tall but slim, other than a belly that pushed his waistcoat out from his tidy coat, he filled the window vertically but not horizontally. Fisher gestured at the door, and the man opened it.

"We aren't open," he said, his eyes moving up and down Mary's and Jane's bodies in a way that made Mary uncomfortable.

"I'm Fisher from Bow Street," their companion said. "Might we have a word?"

"What are you doing with the Godwin girls?" the man asked. He pushed graying dark hair out of his eyes.

Mr. Fisher raised his heavy eyebrows. "They are helping me with my inquiries regarding Winnet Davies's death."

"Who hired you?" the man asked suspiciously. "Bow Street doesn't work for free."

"I'm not at liberty to say," Mr. Fisher said smoothly.

Mary recognized the accomplished falsehood. She had never thought about what a part of his job lies must be. His voice was rough like his body, but his mind worked in a well-oiled fashion. He could be a character in a book. She'd have to add a Bow Street Runner to her cast of characters in *Isabella, the Penitent*.

The man sighed. "I'm John Griffith, the owner here. My

wife and I are just doing a spot of cleaning before the week begins." He stepped back so they could enter.

Mr. Fisher's shoulders were so wide they filled the doorway. He didn't think to let the girls go through first. "Your wife?"

"Cleda," Mr. Griffith said. "She's in the back, bloody woman."

"Why do you say that?" Mr. Fisher asked.

"We ought to be out enjoying the day, not doing this, but she moves slow as a horse on the way to the glue works."

"I understand that Winnet Davies worked here? Isn't that the reason you are closed?" Mr. Fisher asked.

"We had to close for a few hours to catch up on our chores," Mr. Griffith said, seeming to deliberately misunderstand.

"What does that matter?" Mary asked.

He pulled a handkerchief from his sleeve and blew loudly into it. "She was a pretty girl. We kept her out front serving customers. Not like my wife." He pulled a face.

A woman came out of the back. She wore an apron with streaks of dirt on it, and her hands looked rough. She had deep circles under her eyes, and her hair had more gray in it than her husband's did. Mary guessed she was half a decade older than the man. "What's all this about, then?"

Fisher reintroduced himself.

"Why are you wasting your time here?" she asked. "The girl didn't get herself killed in the shop."

Mary cleared her throat. "We could purchase some cheese, if it would help. We aren't trying to waste your time."

Mrs. Griffith snorted. "On credit?"

"That's the way business is done," Mary said. "We've lived on the same street for years. I'm sure our cook had an account with you."

"Certainly, before she and your mother were in trouble with the law." Mrs. Griffith snorted again. "No credit for the Godwins. You're a dangerous lot. Reputation for not paying bills."

"We always pay our food bills," Jane said indignantly. "We have to eat, don't we?"

"I saw that girl of yours buying fish from Bill this morning, instead of going down to Billingsgate like a sensible person. She'll poison all of you. That fish isn't fit for cats." The cheese maker chortled.

Mary's face flushed hot. "Do we have an account with you or not?"

"You owe me five shillings," Mrs. Griffith said. "Not a crumb of cheese will leave this shop until you pay it. Your mamma has no interest in paying her bills, whatever she tells you girls. That Miss Fanny Godwin is the only one of you with any sense, but since she's been gone, your reputation in the neighborhood is even worse."

"What about Miss Davies's family?" Mr. Fisher said, changing the subject. "Did she have any?"

John Griffith scratched his cheek. "She did. A twin sister, though they didn't look much alike."

"No, they do," Mrs. Griffith contradicted. "Different noses, that's all. Easy to tell them apart, but very similar."

Mr. Fisher put his hand into his coat and came out with a sixpence. "I'll take a small round."

"It should go on their account," Mrs. Griffith said doubtfully.

"He's not in our household," Mary said, horrified.

"He's being polite," Jane said. "Think about how much he must eat."

Mr. Fisher side-eyed Jane, but she looked at him with her hands clasped under her chin. Mary heard her sister's stomach rumble. She must hope the treat was going immediately to her belly. But Mary wasn't impressed. She remembered her father's common statement that before he had children, he wanted for nothing and easily paid all his bills. Mr. Fisher had extra coin now, but that meant nothing when it came to a future with him.

"Fetch him a nice round of that cow's milk cheese," Mrs. Griffith ordered her husband.

After he disappeared, Mr. Fisher asked her, "What's the sister's name?"

"Branwen."

"Where can I find her?" he asked.

"At Billingsgate fish market." She fixed her gaze upon Mary. "You'd do better to direct your girl to shop there. She's acting a fool. Though I can't be surprised, given the state of the household."

"I'm not used to ordering a servant about," Mary explained.

"You'd best become used to it, before the girl robs you blind," Mrs. Griffith said. "Not born to it, I suppose. Common and putting on airs. No better than Miss Davies, I suppose, with her end, a bellyful and all."

Mary drew herself up, ready to spring herself at the loathsome woman. Jane pulled her back just as Mr. Griffith came in with a small round wrapped in paper.

"There you go, sir," he said pleasantly, handing the round to Mr. Fisher. "Thank you for the trade, but remember we aren't giving credit to Runners."

"You'll open to Bow Street," Mr. Fisher said laconically. "I'll be back."

Mary knew in that instant that Fisher suspected one or both of the Griffiths of Miss Davies's murder. Why? Her mind worked over the puzzle as she and Jane followed him back to the street. Mr. Griffith was lustful. He'd stared at both of their bodies. Had he done the same to his shop assistant? Had Mrs. Griffith been jealous? She had a character full of spite.

"Hateful woman," Mary muttered as soon as the door was closed behind them. "Wasn't Papa a minister, his mother from a wealthy family? Wasn't Mother a respectable governess?" She started to get worked up again, raging internally, though she tried hard never to let her feelings show, lest Mamma attack her for the crime of anger.

Mr. Fisher put his arm out to stop her as soon as they had left the cheese shop windows and were in front of a blank-faced warehouse.

She put her hands into fists. He raised his heavy brows and stepped back. "What is wrong, Miss Mary?"

"She was so incredibly vile!" Mary exploded. "How dare she deny us credit? We have standing in this neighborhood."

"They are in turmoil themselves," Mr. Fisher said. "Lest you forget that one of their own was murdered. They are fearful and unsettled."

She sniffed. "Does everyone know that debtors' prison is on the horizon for my father?"

"It might not be," Jane said. "He has saved himself before."

"We are running out of options, Jane," Mary said. "And now Charles gone, too? Who is going to manage the publishing business? You and Mamma do all you can. Papa won't do it."

"It may be time to let it go," Mr. Fisher said in his rough voice.

"Whatever do you mean?" Mary swiped at her eyes. They were still dry, but they prickled.

"I can take care of you." He smiled, exposing large, square teeth.

"We barely know each other."

"Mary is used to suitors she has already shared a household with," Jane said with a smirk.

Mr. Fisher frowned. "What, Charles?"

"No, no," Mary assured him. "I lived with a family in Scotland for a time, and some of the menfolk in that family made offers, but Papa did not think it wise."

"They would have kept you there," Mr. Fisher said.

"Yes. But I do not think I would go back there now."

Mr. Fisher pushed out his chest, making him look even more massive. "I can take care of you."

Mary watched the buttons on his waistcoat strain and wondered how much they could take. "I know nothing about you," she said.

"I saw where a Bow Street Runner lived once," Jane said in an artless tone. "It wasn't very nice, just a sort of room at the top of a stable."

"I have two rooms with proper walls and a door," Mr. Fisher said.

"We live in a house." The breath seemed to catch in Mary's chest. She pressed her hand to her breastbone, pushing the bubble of worry down.

"I expect my rooms are nicer than your house," Mr. Fisher said. "The walls are dry, for one thing, and the floors don't list. I have a salary, and a reward each time I finish a case. I'm good at my job, and I can give you a nice life."

"It isn't polite to insult our house," Jane said, puffing out her cheeks.

"He's not incorrect, however," Mary said.

He seemed to take her defense of him as permission to continue. "People call me Fisher because, well, it is my name, and because I fish London for criminals. But I am Denarius Fisher. I'm named for an old Roman coin that has been my family's good luck piece for centuries. I'd give it to you, Mary, to wear as a necklace, so you can have our good fortune, too."

"Fanny is the oldest," Mary said faintly.

"I want you." He stared at her, his bald words hanging in the humid air.

His brow hung low over his deep-set eyes; then his face widened again into brutally carved cheeks. He was monstrous. She'd never seen anyone so tall or broad outside of a circus. The thought of those hands touching her terrified her very soul. She'd die in childbirth if she married him. His child would not fit inside her.

She put her hands to her waist, pushing her tears down like her breath, deep inside, where no one could see them but her. "I am only sixteen. You shouldn't say such things to me. You need to speak to Papa."

Jane's hand slid into hers. Mary turned away. She and Jane walked toward their house and went in, leaving Denarius Fisher in the street.

Chapter 3

Jane

I jumped when the front door opened behind me. My hand fell out of Mary's. I could see she was near tears from the strain of Mr. Fisher's romantic suit. Poor Mary, always so desired by men.

Mr. Fisher came in, stirring rage in me.

"Can't you see you should leave us alone?" I demanded. "At least until you speak to Papa. You can't speak of bedchambers and walls to her."

"Where is your father?" he asked, relentless. "I'll speak to him right now."

My lips parted as a small squeak erupted from Mary. Papa was the only man in the house, with my brother gone. We were quite defenseless, as Papa was quite elderly and not in the best of health. I pushed Mary to the stairs, my only thought to preserve her dignity before she broke down entirely. "Go up and find him." I stood at the foot of the staircase, blocking it, while she ran up, not looking behind her.

"Do you really think so badly of me, Miss Clairmont?" Mr. Fisher asked, his hands swinging loosely at his sides.

I felt like a child in front of his bulk, though I was taller than Mary. "Why must you do this now, with our household so in disarray?"

"Do not blame me. Given my regard for your sister, I am compelled," he replied.

I narrowed my gaze, trying to think of something to make him think of us instead of just himself. "You do a dangerous job. A criminal might come after my sister if she were connected to you."

"They seem to come after her, anyway," he said in a wry tone.

"You are old enough to be her father. And we don't believe in marriage in this household," I retorted.

"I am not as old as you think," he said. "Your mother and stepfather are wed. They certainly believe in it."

"Only because of the pressure of society." I sniffed. "Mary's mother married Papa to make her legitimate, to save her from the world. As things change, it will be unnecessary. I never plan to marry."

"Then it is a good thing I am not trying to court you."

"Why not?" I demanded hotly.

"You speak your mind even more often than Miss Mary," he said, then glanced away from me.

My blood boiled, for I knew he had insulted me. Before I could say anything about it, Mary came down. She stopped on the stair above me and looked over my head, speaking formally. "Papa is not at home. I think you should go, Mr. Fisher, though I do appreciate you paying the call with us this afternoon."

He inclined his head and thrust the package of cheese into my hands. "Have a nice evening, girls. I will call again soon."

As soon as he was gone, I darted forward and turned the lock.

Mary half collapsed onto the stairs, looking bereft. I put the cheese in her hand.

"It's an odd courtship gift. You'd prefer a book, I know." I shrugged. "But we will enjoy eating it."

"Yes," she said in a faint voice. "It will get us through a day or two, unless he is invited to dine with us."

I worked my mouth, feeling terrible for her. "What are you going to do?"

She shook herself, as if shaking off water like a street dog in the rain. "We need to find Branwen Davies, the twin who hated Miss Davies, according to Mrs. Griffith."

I understood she was putting her marriage problem into a box and tucking it away for now, so I let her change the subject. "She said Branwen is said to sell fish in Billingsgate Market. It's only a little over a mile away. Do you need to stay to work on dinner?"

Mamma came in from the bookshop. "Is Mr. Fisher gone?"

"We told him he should speak to Papa," I told her.

Mamma's eyebrows rose, giving her a speculative mien. "Has he proposed marriage already? My, he's eager for a taste of our Mary."

My sister's cheeks flushed scarlet at the crudeness.

"Nearly," I said.

"We want to go to the fish market," Mary said through clenched teeth.

"Why? I checked on the kitchen, and Polly has fish stew in the pot already."

"Mamma, we went to the cheesemongers," I said. "Look." I pointed at the bundle in Mary's hands.

Mamma plucked it from her and unwrapped it. "Oh, how nice. Are they giving us credit again?"

Mary looked up, her eyes dull. "Mr. Fisher bought it."

"Such a kind man. I always thought so. Is he offering you credit at Billingsgate as another courting gift?"

"No," Mary growled. "But Mrs. Griffith said Miss Davies has a twin sister and she works there. I thought we ought to go speak to her, for Charles's sake."

I would have laughed, for Mary would likely not lift a finger for Charles. She just didn't want to go near that foul fish in the basement. At least Polly had had the sense to make stew, where it would be boiled into submission and the stench would meld into the other ingredients.

"A twin sister, eh? I agree we should go. I'll speak to the porter," Mamma said, then walked away.

Mary and I shared a glance. "She's worried about Charles," Mary said.

I nodded. "All three of us together outside on a Tuesday afternoon? It's unheard of."

Mamma came back a couple of minutes later and fetched her bonnet. Mary and I still had ours on. Mary was fiddling with the banister, making a loose spindle squeak. The whole house was decaying without a known owner who would fix it. And charge us rent.

"We could go to St. Pancras next. I believe there is open space next to my mother," Mary said in a careless manner, making the warped wood squeak again. "Or nearby, in any case. When Charles is found, he could be buried next to my mother."

"How dare you, miss!" Mamma shrieked. She barreled forward and used the full force of her arm to slap Mary across her back. "How dare you suggest Charles is dead!"

Mary lost her balance and fell onto the banister. The weak baluster cracked and fell out of the rail. She groaned low and straightened up. When she turned, I saw deadly rage in her eyes. "I am being realistic, madam," she said, hunching her shoulders. "I offer nothing but kindness in suggesting a resting place near my dear mother."

"I am as close to a mother as you will ever find in this life, girl. Mind your manners. My son is not dead."

Mary stayed stony-faced but didn't respond. She stretched her shoulders back, then rubbed her collarbone. I could feel her pain. Why couldn't Mamma control her anger better? Because she didn't want to, I supposed. I didn't think even indifferent Charles would want his disappearance to play out in violence, but what could I do? Promote a marriage that would allow Mary to leave but would kill her all the faster?

I rubbed my hands together. I attempted to break the tension. "We should find Branwen Davies right away. I bet the coroner didn't call her to the inquest. They always overlook women."

Billingsgate Market, effectively out in the open just north of the Thames, always felt like a brawl in motion, with foul-mouthed fishwives shouting at each other and the customers, while enormous fish were tossed around and wrapped. Though the overall scent was wet and maritime, at least the fish and other seafood for sale were much fresher than what was being offered around Snow Hill.

"Where do we go, girl?" Mamma demanded.

"I—" I hesitated and looked at Mary.

"I expect Mr. Fisher would ask at each shed and booth until someone recognized the name," Mary said, batting at a fly.

A droplet hit my hand. I looked up and saw the sky had filled with clouds. People began moving toward the piazza to the west, the only covered structure in the area.

"Less people to ask questions to, girl." Mamma towed me to the table of the first booth.

A woman stood behind the table, using a cleaver to remove the heads on fish. She glanced up when we approached, then held up the silvery body of the fish she'd just beheaded. "Sixpence, madam. Good eating. Just came in on the boat today."

Mamma glanced at Mary, who responded with a poisonous glare.

"Charles," I whispered frantically to Mary, not wanting my brother's fate to be lost in the everlasting battle between them.

Mary sighed. "We are looking for Branwen Davies. Do you know her?"

"Works out of the shed with the red paint," the woman said. "Are you certain you don't want this fish? Good deal."

"I would love to purchase your fish if only I had the coin." Mary stretched her thin lips in a false smile.

Mamma pulled me down the row until we found the red shed. Mr. Fisher's hands might be massive, but Mamma had the strength to leave bruises with fingers alone.

Inside the shed, the air was thick with years of fish-gut odors. Two buckets, nearly full, to the left of the door did not bear investigation. In front of us was a table, with three workers busy behind it, wrapping fish.

Mary marched up and said, "Branwen Davies?"

"Not 'ere," said the sole woman. Her forearms were as wide as my upper arms. She didn't look up from her wrapping, just finished it and pushed the package toward the waiting customer, then slapped another whole fish down on the next sheet of newsprint.

"Where can we find her, please? It's urgent."

"About 'er sister wot's been found dead?" the woman asked.

"Yes," Mary said. "We didn't know Miss Davies had a twin until today."

"Not a close famb'ly," the woman said. "She's got a room in the garret of the last house behind the piazza."

"The houses that the roof is attached to?" Mary asked.

"No, the row behind it, the brick uns." She pushed another wrapped package forward.

"You're very neat," Mary said. "I'll be sure to shop here when I can. Thank you."

The woman nodded without looking up. Mamma grabbed Mary's arm as soon as she came close enough, and then the three of us went back into the rain, linked together like a sea creature.

The moisture seemed to push the fishy air ever deeper into our nostrils. This late in the day, the ground was littered with detritus, which needed to be swept toward the wharf and down into the river. I was happy to walk past the piazza, head hunched so that the rain hit my bonnet instead of my face, and around it to the next row of houses.

The brick row was four stories high, but without the wash lines and railings on the roof that the piazza row possessed. It still smelled like fish this close to the market, and I could hear at least a couple of women shrieking as we went into the last house.

Mamma grunted as we stood at the base of the staircase and looked up the steps.

"It's no different than going upstairs at Skinner Street," I said, shaking her free so that she couldn't lean on me.

When we reached the top of the house, I realized the air smelled more of dirty linen than of fish, finally. Three doors indicated at least three different apartments. I took charge. "Let's each knock on one."

Mary and Mamma went farther down the passage as I knocked on the first door. No answer there, so I joined Mamma at the middle door, but before her knock was answered, the door at the back of the house opened in front of Mary.

The girl who opened it looked very like Winnet Davies, though her nose had a slim tip instead of a bulb. Her hair was held off her face by a band, with a bun in the back, but was the same color as her sister's. She did not have the neat appearance of her sister in dress, though. Her muslin gown had stains and less skillfully repaired tears. Unlike her late sister, though, she had a sensual air about her rather than a grasping one.

I waved off the elderly woman who opened the door in front of me and went to stand next to Mary, Mamma close behind.

"I can see you are Miss Branwen Davies," Mary said. "I am sorry about your sister. Do you know anything about the whereabouts of Charles Clairmont?"

The girl looked at me, then at Mamma.

"Please, I am looking for my son," Mamma said in pleading tones, quite unlike her.

The girl wrinkled her nose rather pertly, then stepped back and gestured us in. Once the door was closed, I stood in front of it and surveyed the room. It had two windows, which lit up the space in satisfactory manner. Smaller than I expected, it contained a bed and a spindle-legged table with two chairs. There were boxes and pegs on the wall. I could smell a chamber pot under the bed. And on the bed? There sat my brother, alive and well.

Mamma cried out and rushed toward him. He allowed her to gather him into her arms, though his lower legs became tangled in the blanket. Mamma sagged as she took on too much of his weight.

Mary's eyebrows were near her hairline when I glanced at her, though I detected surprise rather than disappointment in her expression. For myself, I had known, somehow, that my brother still lived.

Looking at Miss Davies made me awkward. "Thank you for keeping him," I said.

"I don't expect you know there is a warrant out for him?" Mary's tone was laconic.

"Why?" Miss Davies asked.

"He was meant to testify at the inquest and didn't show up."

Miss Davies shrugged. "He didn't know anything about that."

"What did he know?" Mary asked. "We saw him with your sister. She wanted money from him."

"They were courting?" I asked.

Miss Davies shook her head. "No, he is mine, not Winnet's."

I blinked. "Then why did she go with him to the troop review?"

"I had to work, and she didn't. I met him when I was through, but he was hot and tired, so we didn't stay at the park. We came back here."

"When did you learn about what happened to your sister?" I asked.

"It was in the newspaper the next morning." Miss Davies rubbed her nose.

"You did nothing?" Mary asked.

She bared her teeth. "What could I do? I'm sure that John Griffith took care of her."

"The cheesemonger?" I asked, shocked.

Miss Davies held out her hands. "Who else? She lived with them, you know. Who else would have the strength to force her into a noose?"

"Why would he do something like that?" I asked.

"She had a bellyful." Miss Davies glanced away and licked her lips. "I expect it was his."

"Drowning would have been easier," Mary said, not speechless from Miss Davies' shocking speech like I was. "Hanging is a dreadful business. Newgate Prison is just across the street from us. The gibbet is barely out of sight of our windows."

Miss Davies's expression continued to darken. "He's the only person I can think of who would want her dead."

"She seemed greedy," Mary said.

"I know. She was always like that. I think she expected Charles to take care of me and her both? But we aren't even betrothed."

"He's only eighteen," I said, finding my voice again.

"Nearly nineteen and finished with his education, but still,"

Miss Davies said. "I'm smart enough to be in no hurry. I don't ask him for a thing."

I knew she couldn't, for Charles had nothing. She might be smart enough to hold on to him.

"Here," Mamma said, thrusting a purse at Charles.

Mary gasped with outrage. I grabbed her arm, knowing how angry she must be that Mamma had had money all along and hadn't bought fish for the household.

When he took the purse, Mamma said, "Stay hidden in case someone tries to arrest you, son. Constable Wharton is sniffing around. You can't come home."

The words had extra significance to me, after Mamma's recent time in the Bow Street lockup. She knew exactly what Charles faced if he sneaked home and the watch saw him.

Miss Davies put her hands on her hips. "I don't feel it's safe myself to go to the cheese shop. I might do a mischief to that man if I have to see him."

"Understandable," Mary murmured.

"You need to collect Winnet's possessions for me from the Griffiths," the girl said. She stepped close to Mary and looked down at her, then thrust her finger at Mary's nose. "There are forty shillings hidden somewhere in her room. I want every single coin or else."

Mamma charged toward her and smacked her finger away from Mary. "My daughters will not be abused over some likely fictitious coins. You collect your sister's possessions yourself, if you have the right to them."

"I'm protecting Charles now," Miss Davies said. "You don't want me to leave him alone."

"You must leave all the time," Mary said in her habitual tone of exasperation. "To work, to purchase food. You can go to the cheese shop."

Mamma glanced at Charles. He didn't move. "Stay here,"

she said to him. "I've given you money for food. The girl can buy it for you."

She grabbed my arm and removed me from the room.

"Will you come back?" I heard Charles say.

"You don't want us leading a constable to you," Mary said, then sidled past Miss Davies and moved to the door. Just as she was about to join us in the passage, she stopped and said, "You didn't do it, Charles?"

I couldn't see him from my angle, but Mary looked satisfied enough with his silent reply. Then, in the doorway, she stopped again. "What about you, Miss Davies? Did you kill your sister?"

Something hit the wall next to the door, but Mary didn't flinch. "Such a child," she said. "Well, did you do it? I can ask loud enough for that tenant next door to hear."

"I didn't kill my twin," Miss Davies said angrily. "How dare you!"

Mary stepped out, shutting the door behind her. She glanced at me. Mamma grabbed her before I could say a word and marched us both to the steps and did not stop until we were back in the road.

The rain had stopped. The ground had been dry enough that it had not turned to mud, just ceased being so dusty. My shoes sank into the dirt a tiny bit as we walked toward home, but I'd be able to brush them clean easily enough.

"The pair of you need to find Winnet Davies's killer before Charles is arrested," Mamma said.

"Us?" Mary said with a snort. "Madam, I am in the kitchen all day."

"You are nothing of the sort, and it is summer now, anyway," Mamma said. "It is easy to find food in the summer, and we can eat cold plates without taking a chill. Polly can do more."

"That girl would feed you poison and not bat an eye," Mary said.

When I gasped, she said, "Not like rat poison. Just bad, cheap food, like that ghastly fish. She has no discernment."

"That I agree with, after smelling that fish," I said. "But might it be the fact that she has no money? Why is it that you have money for Charles, Mamma, and not us? We need to eat, too. Mary is spending her time picking berries since they are free, not dawdling in the sunshine."

"Send Polly to pick them," Mamma said, ignoring my concerns. "I am very concerned, girls. Branwen Davies might be the killer and could scapegoat Charles."

"She said she wasn't," Mary said airily.

"I don't think much of that claim, but I also don't think Charles is that bad of a judge of character," I said.

Mamma, either hungry herself or a little concerned about our complaints, stopped at a cart full of sandwiches as we were coming up the road to Skinner Street.

Mary pulled me aside. "I admit I am a little disappointed that Charles was found alive and that the situation is so prosaic."

I understood her point. "You will have to find drama elsewhere."

She grinned at me. "A dramatic retelling of the event, you say? Let me see. We shall call it, *Charles, the Feckless; or, The Unlucky Lover of Skinner Street.*"

> "*A Romance; in which is depicted the wonderful Adventures of Charles, son of London, who was diverted from the track of virtue by the untimely death of a young cheese seller, who was hanged from a tree, the victim of deadly violence, and, after Charles left the safety of his humble home, was kidnapped by the dastardly villain, a twin of the deceased, so she could obtain the person of a most indifferent beauty.*"

When she paused for breath, I giggled. I couldn't help it. How droll she was. "Go on, Mary, do."

Mary took a theatrical breath. "*How he was discovered, despite the dark blankets he sheltered underneath, by his young sister, who had been tormented by their same relative; and the particulars of the means by which the sister caused the body of Charles to be conveyed in a sleep to the perfectly dreadful enclosures, where he was forced to toil in a dark warehouse, having lost his love, though attended by a dastardly servant, who afterward betrays him to his beastly mother, in the madhouse of which he is confined and suffers torture; and how, to escape from thence, he assigns over his soul and body to his sister, who is ever faithful to him, even unto her ignominious death, shortly followed by his own.*"

"Goodness, that sounds very similar to the stories you have spun before," I said.

She waved her hand. "There is a formula to it. I shall not write this one. It isn't original enough for me. But I have to gain experience, and from each story idea I come up with, something can be learned."

"You do make the point that he might be better off relaxing in Miss Davies's bed than returning home," I said, feeling quite grown-up to speak of other girls' beds so calmly.

"I daresay," she agreed.

"Could you change the end so I'm not dead, too?" I asked, hearing my voice quaver.

"Of course. How about '*and how, to escape from thence, he assigns over his soul and body to his sister, who is ever faithful to him, even unto her escape to Switzerland, shortly followed by his own fortune made*'?"

"Ooh, I like that," I praised. "Do let's go to Switzerland and help Charles make his fortune."

Mamma came back with a package large enough to contain

sandwiches for everyone. My eyes feasted greedily on the sight, for the walk had made me hungry.

"No need for the kitchen tonight?" Mary asked lightly. "Shall I go out sleuthing?"

"On the contrary, you can come up with a soup to go with these sandwiches," Mamma said.

"We have fish stew," I pointed out.

Mamma shuddered. "Polly can eat that. No, a nice beef broth sounds perfect. You must have some bones in the kitchen."

Mary sighed. "But then I won't be hunting for the killer."

"I'm sure you'll have to think it through first, consult those notebooks you are always scribbling in," Mamma said. "You, O Mary the Boastful, ungrateful daughter of Skinner Street."

I positively cackled at the setdown, even though it did come from Mamma. She had her moments of humor.

Mary looked sour when we went in our door. She went straight down the passage to the kitchen without even taking off her bonnet.

"I hear voices in the bookshop," Mamma said to me. "Go attend our customers."

I took care of the pair of tutors who had come in, looking for books and supplies for their students. Mamma had never come through the bookshop to return to her office, so I told the porter he was in charge again and escaped the house when they were gone.

I wanted to see Shelley in his new rooms, less than half a mile away from the house. He'd moved from his publisher friends' abode in Old Bond Street to Fleet Street on his own. I wondered if his wife had given him funds before they had argued, since otherwise he wouldn't have been able to afford it. His father had quite cut him off, which was dreadfully insulting of him. But Shelley had told us he couldn't force his father to come to sensible terms while his grandfather, the baronet, still lived.

I hunted for the address, which I found above a newspaper office, and left the house before anyone could notice. Not many minutes later, I knocked on his door.

Shelley opened it after a few seconds. He had a banyan over his shirt and waistcoat. I'd never seen him so informal before, and it gave me quite a turn.

"Jane!" he exclaimed. "Have you and Mary come to pay me a visit?"

"Just me. She's in the kitchen, trying to turn old bones into soup."

He gave a theatrical shudder. "How vile."

"Are you liking it here?" I asked.

"Louder than I'm used to, but I sleep well enough." He shrugged. "I live in my thoughts."

"Speaking of thoughts, I have some about Mary's situation," I said. "I have news about that other sibling of mine."

He promptly stepped back. When I went in, I saw a place not much better furnished than the last poet's bachelor abode I had been in. I expected the place had been let furnished, for I didn't think Shelley possessed anything but a chest of books and some clothing.

"What is it?"

"I'm worried about Mary and Charles," I said.

"You say you have news of him?" He poured me some beer from a cask into a chipped mug, then topped off his own.

I took a deep drink. I needed it after the walk. The dust had already risen again. "You remember the Bow Street Runner Mr. Fisher?"

"Who could forget him? I'm tall enough, but he—" Shelley gestured above his head. "And broad enough, but he—" He threw out his arms, spilling half his mug. The smell of beer instantly flooded the room as the plank floor absorbed the liquid.

"He's come courting. He's interested in Mary."

Shelley's expression went blank. He set down his mug. "By Jove, you have to be joking."

"He's very serious. Can you scare Mr. Fisher off? He's terrifying."

Shelley collapsed into an armchair. The cushion sagged alarmingly. The chair needed restuffing.

"Say something," I begged. "How about alchemy? Could we transmute substances to make money for the family? I'm afraid Mamma and Papa want to marry Mary off to save money."

His chest rose and fell. "She makes them money, between cooking and the bookshop."

"I run the bookshop almost alone now," I boasted.

"Well, alchemy," he said. "It would cost money to make money. Davy's battery at the Royal Institution consists of two thousand voltaic piles, an enormous expense."

"That doesn't help."

"No. This is science, not magic. What all of you need is outside employment, unless Godwin can get something new written. He can still make money, if not what he commanded at the height of his powers."

"He's always working on something."

Shelley ran his tongue over his upper lip. "And how about you? The bookshop doesn't bring in enough trade to waste your efforts inside it. I've always thought your mother could manage it herself."

"I have lost my singing lessons, due to the expense."

He considered. "I could teach you Italian to help your opera singing. That is a possible job for you."

"With a life like that, it is well that I don't believe in marriage," I said. "But learning Italian might help me with singing or to find a governess position."

"Speaking of governesses, is there any word from Fanny?"

"Yes, we did have a letter saying she'd arrived in Wales. She said the children are very sweet. But, you know, they aren't paying her."

"I hope she has the presence of mind to at least ask them for a letter of reference before she leaves. That is some kind of coin."

"You are right, of course," I agreed.

Chapter 4

Mary

Mary heard the front door open as she carried up the tureen of pale beef broth. She'd done her best, but the bones she'd had available had not offered much flavor. She had, however, come up with a very satisfying fantasy of Charles and his lady love escaping the constables to head for Calais and freedom. It might even be possible, given the end of the war, but Charles shouldn't go anywhere with Miss Davies until he could be certain she wasn't a killer.

Then again, he could know the truth. If they'd truly been together all night, she couldn't have done anything to her twin.

Jane came in, untying her bonnet. Mary's heart thumped when she saw the tall, handsome man coming in behind Jane. "Shelley!"

"Good evening," Shelley said, offering her a dazzling, conspiratorial smile.

"There's nothing for you to eat," Mary said. "We have ham sandwiches, fish stew, and beef broth."

"Just have Polly bring up some extra bread and cheese," Shelley said carelessly, tossing his hat onto a peg.

"Cheese." Mary remembered. "Yes, we do have that. A very good point. Go down and get it, would you, Jane?"

Mary went upstairs, Shelley close on her heels. When they entered the dining room, he plucked the tureen from her hands and set it on the table, then pulled her close.

"Shelley!" she cried, blushing.

"Oh, sweet Mary," he whispered. "You smell like a cow, but I almost like it on you."

"Better than rotten fish," she said. He nuzzled her neck, sending sparks of light all the way to her fingers and toes. "You mustn't make love to me."

"My marriage is finished. Harriet and I are done. She's nothing but a sister to me now, like Jane." His nose rubbed against a sensitive tendon, making her gasp. "And you've that foul beast Fisher stalking you like a rabbit in the grass."

"He is approved by Papa." Her voice came out breathless, as played out as the bones in the stock. She closed her eyes as Shelley's hand moved up and down her back. How heavenly to be in this man's embrace. She allowed him to cradle her, and she fit so neatly in his arms, as if they'd been made to come together. "What am I going to do?"

She looked up at him, then realized she'd placed her mouth just a fraction of an inch from his. His breath, bitter with hops, blew against her lips.

Squeaking hinges gave the alarm. Mary pulled away. Polly came in, carrying another bowl with the stew, fragrant with enough garlic to hide the foul scraps of fish.

Before she set it down, Mamma and Papa entered with Willy. Shelley was greeted enthusiastically. As soon as Jane arrived, the round of cheese on a plate in her hands, they all sat.

It seemed that Jane's and Mamma's appetites were restored, for as soon as Shelley served himself first, as guest, and then

Papa and Willy took rather small amounts of the offerings, they both attacked the ham sandwiches and the cheese.

Mary decided to try the fish stew. What did it matter if it made her ill? She ignored the cheese, not wanting to eat what Fisher had offered for fear it would somehow enchant her, and took the last of the sandwiches.

Halfway through the meal, Papa looked at the table with confusion. "You have scarcely eaten for days, Mrs. Godwin. I am glad to see you are feeling better."

Jane rolled her eyes at Mary. They both knew Mamma had a frequently replenished box of shortbread in her bedroom.

"I am. Thank you, Mr. Godwin," Mamma said.

"Have we an update about Charles?" Papa asked.

"I have asked Mary to continue our investigation," Mamma explained. "We must have faith in her."

"Is that why you purchased these sandwiches?" Papa queried. "I thought we agreed having Mary cook would reduce expenses."

"My son is important, as well, do you not think, Mr. Godwin?"

Mamma's cool tone made Mary's blood boil. She knew where Charles was. Why was she effectively lying about Charles's whereabouts to Papa? How dare she? Papa must know everything. He was head of the family.

As soon as dinner was over, she pretended she hadn't heard Shelley and Jane talking about a walk, as they often did.

As if falling in with her plans, Papa turned to her after setting his napkin on his plate. "Come to my library for a moment, Mary."

Mamma didn't look up from her second slice of gooseberry tart. "Go on, then. I plan to enjoy this."

"It's very tasty, Mary," Willy said, then inserted the last bite into his mouth. "Charles will be sorry to miss it."

Mary smiled faintly, then followed Papa out of the room.

Charles would eat very well indeed on the money Mamma had given him.

Papa led her into the study, then went to the windows and pushed back the curtains to allow in the light. "I do like this time of year. It saves on candles. You did not want to walk?"

"Later," she said. "The stew is resting uneasily in my belly."

"It was heavy on the garlic," he agreed, stopping in front of her mother's portrait, which he kept in his library as a sort of shrine. "Your Mamma had a minute to tell me that Mr. Fisher has made an effort to court you."

Mary worked her jaw from side to side. "He was kind enough to buy me a small round of cheese when the Griffiths wouldn't give me credit today."

"They have never been the best neighbors," Papa said. "I noticed that you did not eat any of that cheese tonight."

She glanced down when his attention finally moved from her dead mother to her.

"You must allow Mr. Fisher to court you," he said gently.

"Why, Papa?" Instinctively, she reached for Papa's arm and clung to it. "He's so dreadfully tall and large. He quite dwarfs me. It's frightening."

"Think of him as a protector. He could save the family."

"He doesn't have the coin for that," Mary said, scorn lacing her voice. "A round of cheese sufficient for a couple of days is not an answer to our problems."

"Because of his position," Papa said with sweet patience.

How far Papa had fallen since his youth to see a Bow Street Runner, a tool of the government, as a protector. She wanted to soothe him. "I'm intelligent enough to help us. I want to write books and articles as you do, Papa. That's a better use of my time than cooking. You've made a living out of such things, and so can I."

"You are sixteen and a female," he said, not unkindly. "Mr. Fisher can protect you, and us. Don't you want a family of your own?"

"What good is having one when all they do is lie and eat?" Mary asked.

Papa slid her hand off his arm and went to his chair behind his desk. "What do you mean?"

"We know where Charles is hiding. We found him today, and Mamma didn't tell you. That's why her appetite is back. Her mind is relieved, and she gave him money."

He paused, then folded his hands on the top of his desk. "She has made the best decision she could, no doubt. The great model of the affection of love in human beings is the sentiment which subsists between parents and children. She could not do nothing for the lad."

"Is it the best decision when it might send you to the sponging house?"

"It is not so bad as that. Those peculiar arrangements after Mr. Cannon's death bought me some little time to come to terms with my other creditor. And Shelley assures me that his post-obit loans will be resolved soon."

"I do not think Mamma should hide anything from you," she said, feeling stubborn.

"In her judgment, speaking in front of Willy would not be appropriate. She'd have told me in her own time." He rubbed his hands together. "Now, Mary, what do you think happened to Winnet Davies? To what solution has your fine intellect attached?"

Mary smiled and sat in the chair on the other side of his desk, then leaned forward. "Charles is with Branwen Davies in her room by Billingsgate Market. We didn't know Miss Davies had a twin. She's a grasping sort, who demanded we collect her twin's belongings from the cheese shop for her."

"How odd," Papa said, rubbing his chest. "Why would the Griffiths surrender the dead girl's possessions to you? That is for her sister to accomplish, assuming she does not have parents living."

"Branwen Davies probably killed her sister for the forty shillings she demanded we procure for her from the cheese shop."

"Do you think Charles's judgement so bad as all that?" Papa asked.

"She's more attractive than her sister was," Mary offered.

"Many a young head is turned by a pretty girl," Papa admitted. "I prefer a handsome woman myself, but I understand it. Shelley is quite susceptible, I believe."

"His wife is rather beautiful," Mary said as casually as she could.

"If you think Charles is hiding with the murderess, then we must prove you wrong or right," Papa said. "You shall keep up with your kitchen duties, but if there is to be some expense to your effort in uncovering the truth, so be it. I had rather eat a sandwich in June than let Charles be blamed for the girl's death."

"Yes, Papa," Mary said. "I will do my best."

Mary felt very thoughtful as she peeked into the dining room. Polly had her arms full of plates, so she helped carry the rest of them down to the kitchen.

"They didn't like my stew," Polly whined.

"I ate it." Mary felt her stomach rumble and walked outside at a rapid pace.

When she returned from the garden, she met Jane and Shelley as they were entering the front door.

"We went out for a walk without you," Jane said self-importantly.

"I had things to do," Mary said.

"I'm going to read in the garden," Jane said. "It is too nice to stay inside. Shelley?"

"I'll be out in a minute," he said.

Jane smiled and ran upstairs to fetch her book.

When she was out of earshot, Mary said, "Papa wants me to figure out who killed Miss Davies."

"Any ideas?" Shelley asked.

"Her twin," Mary said. "I want to see what she does, but of course, it's been hours since we were at her room already."

"People skulk about after dark, particularly when they want to hide something. Why don't we go to her rooms at dusk and keep an eye on them for a while?"

Mary nodded. "I'm sure Charles won't venture out until the sun has set. That's hours away still, since the summer solstice was just yesterday."

"I promised our friends Hocke and Corn that I would stop in and listen to their new verses this evening. Why don't I meet you at your door in a couple of hours? We'll go over to Billingsgate together."

Mary nodded. "Should I bring Jane?"

"I don't think she is best suited to quiet watching," Shelley said.

Just then footsteps clattered above. Mary laughed. "I agree. I will see you then."

She went up to Willy's room, crossing Jane on the steps, and played marbles with him for a while, then made him read to her from a Juvenile Library title, *Tales from Shakespeare*, while she sewed up the never-ending tears on his sleeves. She also replaced two missing buttons, all the while wishing Fanny were here to lighten the load.

"When can I read your book, Mary?" Willy asked, closing the Shakespeare, while she put everything back into her sewing box.

"It's not finished yet," Mary admitted. "I have too many distractions these days."

"That isn't good."

"No. I was just thinking how much I missed Fanny."

"She shouldn't live here, though. She's all grown up."

"Where else do you think she might live? In a fairy circle?" She leaned over and wiggled his ear. "Maybe we should all go live on the tops of mushrooms."

He flopped down on his bed, making the ropes squeak.

Mary glanced out the window at the sky. "Why don't you wash up? Then you can play with your soldiers until dark."

Willy flopped over and pulled his box of tin soldiers from under his bed. "Is Charles going to come home soon?"

"Very soon." She kissed the back of his head, then went out.

In her room, she changed into her black silk gown, all the better for skulking in on a summer's night, then pulled out a pencil and her notebook.

Diego and Fernando fought with swords by moonlight quite satisfactorily while the sun descended in London. Poor Isabella lay on a blanket in a swoon, awaiting either the hero or the villain. Who would get to her, and which one had the antidote for the poison she had taken to save her maidenly innocence from Diego?

When the light was nothing more than a whisper of color on the horizon and a graying blue above, Mary left her room and went downstairs, hugging the wall preventing the squeaky stairs from alerting anyone. She had a pocket pinned to the inside of her dress. She took the key to the door from its place in a drawer in the front hall, then safely tucked it in the pocket as soon as she'd locked the door behind her.

Shelley stepped up to her. "Good evening."

Mary smiled and put her bonnet on. "We are a respectable pair. You even have a hat."

"I know you have certain standards, my lady." He lifted his top hat and bowed.

She giggled and bobbed a curtsy. "Now what? We walk down to the market?"

He nodded and tucked his hand into her arm. "We'll be a courting couple, just out for a stroll. Don't be alarmed if I pull you into a dark corner and hug you close. It's how we hide."

Her cheeks heated as they moved up the street. "I wouldn't mind that, in any case."

"No? Oh, my sweet Mary." They hadn't gone more than a

dozen steps when he stopped and pulled her against a warehouse wall.

"It's too close to home," she whispered but then saw around his shoulder that someone had just opened the door of the cheese shop.

She and Shelley flattened themselves against the wall, too late to take any more precaution than that.

How she wished they had gone out fifteen minutes earlier. Surely that was Branwen Davies. Had she gone to demand her sister's possessions since Mamma had refused the task?

That had to be John Griffith at the door. Yes, because a lantern in the shop betrayed his height, and in any case, he was the only man on the premises.

Three men walked down the street, but they didn't have their own source of light. Shelley clutched Mary's hand but didn't move her. Hopefully, they hadn't already been detected.

At the shop, Mr. Griffith handed the woman a bundle, larger than the one containing the cheese that Mr. Fisher had bought. Mary had so many questions. Had this been arranged? Was that small lump all the possessions that Winnet had, she who was so greedy for a dress?

One of the passersby broke into song, preventing Mary from hearing anything said at the shop. Then Mr. Griffith shut the door, leaving the woman and the bundle in the street. She held it against her, like it was something precious, and hurried up the street, away from the bookshop.

Shelley counted to ten under his breath, just loud enough for Mary to hear, then squeezed Mary's hand and started to follow.

Mary hoped they were following the right person. If she passed under a source of light, they would know. Still, it didn't really matter. She was out on a fine summer evening with her hand in Shelley's. Perfect happiness reigned. Even Charles was not so badly off, snug in Miss Davies's room, with Mamma's coin undeservedly in his pocket.

They passed along the outer edges of Smithfield Market. The

scenery did not improve as they moved into the bad neighborhood on the northern edges.

Eventually, their quarry stopped at a tavern. She had crossed a street to get there, while Mary and Shelley had hung back on the other side of the narrow road. A lamplighter lit torches on either side of the door. Mary saw a boar's head on the sign above the door and imprinted it on her memory.

Shelley tugged her into the shadows of a decayed house. They watched the woman peek into the tavern, her entire upper body disappearing into the dark doorway before she straightened.

"It's her," Mary whispered when Miss Davies stepped back. "We were right." A raindrop hit the exposed tip of her nose.

"She's trying to get someone's attention." Shelley squeezed her hand, then released it to put his arm around her shoulders. He pulled her closer against the dank wood wall of the house. Shutters covered the window overhead and protected the backs of their heads from the drips of rain.

Someone appeared in the tavern doorway. It didn't appear to be the man she waited for. This one walked to the corner of the building and fumbled with his clothing. Mary averted her eyes as nature took its course.

A few seconds after that man had returned inside, another set of shoulders filled the doorway.

"Here we go," Shelley whispered as the man exited to stand next to Miss Davies.

They were close enough to the torches for Mary to see the man hand Miss Davies a long box, some two and a half feet in length, in trade for the bundle she had carried from the cheese shop. Torchlight glinted on brass fittings on the box.

Shelley's hand tightened on Mary's shoulder. Her shawl scraped and caught on splinters on the wood wall as he pulled her down the street away from the tavern. She could feel the tension in his arm, rigid against her shoulders.

When they had crossed another street, moving rapidly enough that it was all she could do not to turn her ankle on the cobbles, Mary asked, "What's wrong? Shouldn't we follow them?"

Shelley growled. "That was a gun case. I'm taking you home."

"We need to know what she's doing," Mary protested. "Charles is mixed up in it."

"No," Shelley insisted. "I don't want you involved with violence. I'll try to find her when you are safely home."

"You might not be able to find her again. I'll keep my shawl over my head."

"No. You'll go home." He pulled her down a street on the edge of Smithfield Market. At least the flies had gone to bed at this time of night.

"I cannot help but admire your protective instinct," Mary said breathlessly, having to trot to keep up with his long limbs.

"You are everything to me," he said simply. "There, you are right down the hill. Run along, and I'll go back and pick up the trail before it is too late."

She turned to him and caressed his cheek almost before her brain had commanded her fingers to touch him. A gossamer stroke, then she let her hand drop and ran down to the house, praying no mischief would come to this golden man.

Chapter 5

Jane

I stood in front of Shelley's window the next morning, before the bookshop opened, as we had agreed, so he could begin my Italian lessons.

"Why do you look so tired?" I asked.

He was slumped in the room's single armchair, unshaven, with reddened eyes. "I was up late last night chasing shadows for your brother."

"Do you know who killed Miss Davies?"

"Not yet, but her sister appears to be up to something dangerous."

I blinked. "Should we tell Charles to leave her?"

Shelley yawned. "There's no real reason to think he's in danger in her bed, but he would be in danger for certain if he left."

"It's a complicated situation, and meanwhile, his work isn't being done, which means even less money in our coffers." I sighed.

"He'll end up in the lockup if he leaves. There is no version of the story in which he returns to work, Jane," Shelley said, rubbing his eyes.

"Then I may need to find a singing job," I said. "I could work in the bookshop during the day, then perform opera at night, I suppose."

"Unlikely," Shelley said. "You cannot be up half the night, then open the bookshop in the morning, but it is not as if you have so much trade. The porter can handle it."

"I must do something."

"I agree. Let's work on pronunciation. You don't really need to speak Italian, just have a sense of how it sounds. I know rather a lot of Mozart's *Don Giovanni* by heart. Let's work on that."

He recited lines. For half an hour, as the sun rose in the sky, I forced my tongue to roll the letters and moved my mouth as he did.

Eventually, I developed a cough and needed to wet my throat. Shelley didn't even have a water can, just the pitcher he used for washing up and an old wine bottle, both empty. When he had fetched water, I leaned against the windowsill and drank from the bottle. It felt decadent, despite the mundane contents.

"Would it not be easier to turn the contents of this small bottle to liquid gold?" I asked after I'd drained half the contents. "Why can't there be truth in alchemy?"

"Many have tried to transmute items into gold over centuries. It is only charlatans who have claimed to do it."

"Kings get money somehow. Generals and such, too. Maybe someone does know how to do it, but only the already rich benefit."

He chuckled and set the pitcher next to the fireplace. "For me, alchemy is how your voice sets the very air on fire. That is your wealth, that beautiful voice of yours. You can make money with it."

I smiled. Neither Fanny nor Mary had such an instrument as mine. Mamma could barely croak out a tune. My voice must have come from my Swiss side. "Do you think I can sing in the great European capitals some day?"

"Such vanity, Jane," he admonished. "You will have to work very hard."

"I am not afraid of hard work."

He nodded. "I know you and Mary work very hard. Not like my wife, who has servants for everything."

"At least she has the money for them. It must be nice. It seems the older I get, the more Mamma and Papa lose any help they have to keep our household going."

He shrugged. "It is no matter to me. My wife and her sister have returned to Bath. I will not see their allowance now."

"They left their father's house?"

He nodded. "It is at an end, the marriage, you know."

"That means you won't be able to see little Ianthe," I said, troubled by that.

"Bath isn't so very far. Harriet and I get along very well, but she is nothing but a sister to me. She doesn't have the fire to learn like Mary, and you. In truth, you, Jane, are my only friend now."

"Not Mary?" I asked, my heart thrilling.

He put his finger in the air. "My heart belongs to Mary. You will be another sister to me, and my good friend."

"I see," I said, not really seeing at all. "I think I can sing for a little longer. Then I need to be back at Skinner Street for breakfast."

After breakfast I followed Mary down to the kitchen with a tray full of dishes. We'd managed to clear the table between the two of us.

"Thank you," Mary said. "But you'd better open the bookshop."

"I have important news," I whispered and bent to speak close to her ear. "Guess what Shelley told me?"

Mary scoffed and waved away my breakfast breath. "It can't be anything important. I saw him only twelve hours ago."

I narrowed my eyes mysteriously. He spoke to me in confidence, as well, not just her. "Do you know Mrs. Shelley has left town?"

Mary's strawberry-blond eyebrows pulled together. "Yes."

I clapped my hands together. "Aren't you happy? Harriet Shelley and her mercenary sister are gone from London."

Mary smiled and set dishes in the sink. "Yes, it is good news. That sister of hers can't keep conspiring with Mamma to separate Shelley from his family fortune."

"But in the same way, Shelley can't get ready coin from his wife." I handed her a bowl. "I wonder how he can afford his rooms."

"I think he sees his mother sometimes when his father is away. It is dreadful that they don't give him a regular income." She scraped bits of oatmeal from bowls.

"What are we going to do about Charles?" I heard footsteps on the stairs and assumed it was Polly returning from wherever she had been hiding, but then Mamma came in.

"I could scarcely eat a bite, worrying about Charles," Mamma said. "Mary, fry up some bacon and take it to him. Some bread, sandwiches."

Mary laughed. "Madam, we have no bacon or ham. You gave him money that you had hidden away somewhere. We possess none for the feeding of this household. Why do you think you ate fish stew and oatmeal for breakfast?"

"Hasn't Papa given you the household money this week?" Mamma asked.

Mary frowned. "He has never given me money for the household since I have been running the kitchen. I scrape by with whatever you give me."

She grabbed the back of Mary's head. I could see her fingers tighten on the knot of hair pinned there. Mary winced. "I will take no sauce from you, girl. Make Charles some fresh oatcakes, then. Give him the rest of that gooseberry jam you made. It will have to suffice."

"But I want to eat the jam, Mamma," I cried. "I work too hard to dine on oatmeal and nothing else."

She let Mary go and pinched my cheek. "Your brother is in trouble, and we have to sacrifice for him." She tightened her fingers until it hurt, then released me and left the room.

I clapped my hand to my cheek. Tears fell from my eyes.

"Here," Mary said and pulled my hand away so she could set a cool, damp cloth against the pinched skin. "And here I thought I took the brunt of her anger."

"We don't matter. We're only girls," I moaned. "Why should he get the jam? All he's doing is relaxing in some harlot's bed."

Mary rubbed the back of her head with her free hand. "I agree he should pay the price for his own romantic entanglements, but you cannot think Miss Davies's death is in any way his fault. He is innocent of that."

"Mamma gave him money already." I pushed Mary's fingers aside so I could hold the cloth myself.

"I know, but she's greedy." Mary shrugged. "At least we get to go out of doors."

"Why do you think Papa hasn't been giving you the household money?" I asked.

"Because he hasn't got any. Or because Fanny used to ask him for it so very sweetly and gently, and neither you nor I have got her manner."

"I miss her," I said. "I didn't think I would, but I do."

"She is dull, but a good sort," Mary responded. "Now, go earn us a few shillings in the bookstore while I make oatcakes."

* * *

I didn't manage to quite make it to a shilling, but I sold a sixpence's worth of pencils and paper by the time Mary came up with a basket of food.

I told Mamma we were leaving. She merely adjusted her green visor and told me to get the porter in from the warehouse, where he was apparently attempting to do Charles's job.

After that, we were finally ready to walk to Miss Davies's lodgings. We hugged the sides of buildings, both to stay out of the dust and to be mindful of anyone who might be following us. Though the watch worked at night, a beadle or constable might be about.

We had no trouble accessing the house. "It would be better if the outside door had a lock," I said as we climbed the stairs.

"These are too-poor accommodations for that," Mary opined. "Only such as a girl alone can afford."

"Can you imagine making enough as a girl to be able to afford a room to yourself?" I asked.

"You have a room to yourself," Mary said. "Only imagine being paid for a day's toil in the bookshop and there you go."

I'd have retorted something back about free choice and liberty, but then we were at Branwen Davies's door. That was locked, I discovered as I turned the knob, so I knocked.

Charles eventually answered the door, unshaven and with a hunted look in his dark eyes.

"We should have brought you a razor rather than food," Mary said.

Charles opened the door a few inches wider and gestured us in. After he shut it behind us, he said, "I wish you had."

Inside the air smelled close and fetid. "Isn't there a window you can open?" I complained.

"I don't think I should be seen. There's only supposed to be women in here."

Mary handed him the basket and pushed the one window in the room up. "Duck as you pass by."

Charles nodded as he lifted the cloth draped over the basket. "Jam and oatcakes?"

"We have no money for meat, I'm afraid," I said. "Papa hasn't been giving Mary the household money."

"It is one thing after another, isn't it?" Charles broke a cake in half and unstoppered the jam jar to scoop out a dollop with his finger.

I licked my lips, wishing he would share, but I knew he wouldn't. "Where is your lady love?"

"At work." He returned to the bed. "And she's not my lady love."

I noted that he'd walked right past the window. *Idiot.*

"Not now or not ever?" Mary asked.

"It was fun at first, but I'm frankly afraid of Branwen now."

"Why?" I asked. "Didn't she spend the money Mamma gave you on food?"

He stuffed the rest of an oatcake in his mouth and chewed. "I didn't give Branwen the money. We had food at the time."

"And that angered her?" Mary asked. She gave me a look as if to say she'd been angry about that. I agreed. Charles should have given Miss Davies the money when she left this morning, to bring food back at least. He simply never showed consideration for anyone, especially us girls.

"She was in a rage after she went out last night," he explained. "She slapped me when she returned."

I examined his face and saw no sign of a red mark, such as the welt I could feel on my face, thanks to Mamma's pinch. "Not very hard."

Charles curled his upper lip at me, then stuffed another oatcake in his face from the basket on his thigh.

Mary sat next to him on the bed. "Shelley and I went out last night. We thought to come here, but then we saw Miss Davies at the cheese shop."

I snarled at her. "You didn't invite me."

Mary shrugged. "The more of us there were, the less we'd be able to avoid notice."

I crossed my arms over my chest and went to look out the window.

"What was she doing there?" Charles asked.

"It was complicated," Mary admitted. "At first, we thought she was gathering her sister's belongings, since Mamma said we wouldn't do it."

"Makes sense, but why would that lead to me getting slapped?" Charles demanded.

"Mr. Griffith gave her a small bundle, not even large enough for a spare set of clothing, though I don't suppose a shopgirl has many possessions. But then..." Mary paused.

I threw up my hands and turned around. "Then what?"

"She went to a low pub north of Charterhouse, and she traded the little bundle for a box." She paused until I squealed in outrage. "And guess what?" Mary asked, her eyes wide.

"What?" Charles asked.

"It looked like a gun case, Shelley said." Mary held out her arms. "A little under three feet long and less than a foot wide, with brass fittings."

"Sounds like he was right," Charles said. "Though that doesn't mean there was a gun in it."

"What use would your Miss Davies have for a gun case?" I asked, irritated at being left out from all the drama.

"Did it look heavy? Or empty?" he asked.

"Is it here? We could open it," I said.

He shook his head. "She didn't bring it back to the room. She was empty-handed. We said a few words. She slapped me, then went to bed."

Mary considered him with narrowed eyes. "There were a few words first? Is that why she slapped you?"

He colored. "Perhaps."

"She'd been in too bad a mood to want your advances at any rate," Mary said.

"I don't want to be here," Charles whined. "I would flee to France if I had the coin. Would Shelley lend me the money?"

Mary snorted. "He has nothing until the loans are finalized, and all that money is going to Papa."

"Hopefully, the matter will be resolved soon, before it is too late for Papa's freedom," I said dutifully. I didn't like our chances of surviving with only Mamma at home, in a bad mood, and Papa gone. At least we wouldn't lose the house. The business was in Mamma's name.

"I hope Papa will give me funds from the loan so I can run away," Charles said. "I've always dreamed of leaving the British Isles."

"Haven't we all?" Mary said.

"Why don't you take me with you when you go, and we can visit Switzerland to see the homeland of my father," I suggested. "Two could travel as easily as one."

Charles sniffed and stuck his finger into the jam jar. "I'd do better on my own. I'm a fugitive, you see."

"I don't care about that," I retorted.

"Don't be such a chucklehead, Charles. You're hurting Jane's feelings. What does it hurt to say she could come? You're only dreaming."

"I wouldn't want a sister to keep track of," he said and licked his finger.

Mary pulled the basket from his lap. "You are helpless and are being taken care of by women right now. You had better reflect on that."

"I'll be fine," Charles said loftily. "I can make my own way."

I wondered how. "Are you going to marry Miss Davies?"

Mary chortled. "How naïve you are, Jane. He's just said he wants to get away from her. Look at Mamma. Do you want your brother marrying someone with her violent tendencies, whatever the provocation?"

"I was only asking." I held out my hand. "Why don't you give us the money Mamma gave you, Charles? We can get food and cook it for you."

He leaned back on his elbows. "No."

"Fine." I flounced to the door. "Mary, lock up that window again. It's time we left. I remember a tutor from a good household said he was coming in this afternoon to stock a schoolroom."

Mary shut the window with a bang, using one hand, then walked out behind me, the basket on her arm. When we reached the street, I rummaged in the basket as she groused at me.

"One oatcake left," I said. "My, he's greedy."

"Split it up," she ordered. "I'm hungry after all this walking and arguing."

I did not disagree. We made good time on our return to Skinner Street, and we even had a taste of the last bits of jam that clung to the nooks and crannies of the jar. Mary went back to the kitchen to see what she might find to prepare for lunch, and I went to the bookshop. The porter was itching to see me return, for a letter had come instructing us to deliver a nice set of Juvenile Library books to a house in Mayfair.

I sent him off once I'd wrapped the package, then leaned against the counter, thinking. I had not yet changed my pose when the front door opened.

A moment later monstrously large shoulders filled the doorway in the bookshop.

I straightened. "Mr. Fisher."

His forehead creased as he raised his brows. "Where is Miss Mary?"

"In the kitchen, of course, trying to sort out a midday meal."

"Could you get her? I'd like to speak to you both."

I frowned at him, for there had been no time for Mary to organize the kitchen. I slid around him without saying a word and went downstairs, wondering over his tone. He'd sounded stern, more like his Bow Street persona, which I remembered well, than the eager suitor he'd been of late.

"There's nothing to eat yet," Mary said when I walked in. She and Polly were huddled over a substantial bowl of eggs, with a small bottle of milk to one side.

"Where'd you get those?" I asked. "They will make something nice to eat."

"She traded the rest of that cheese for them," Mary said. "I can't decide if it was a good bargain."

"We'd have had only one more meal of the cheese, but it's two meals' worth of eggs, more if we mix it and make cakes," Polly said with a stubborn jut of her chin. "I grew up poor. Unlike old Thérèse, I know how it's done."

"It's true that we can make cheese again from the milk, anyway," Mary said, straightening. "What is it, Jane? If you've been working more than fifteen minutes, I've turned into a turnip."

"Mr. Fisher," I said. "And no roses in his eyes, either."

"Who is dead now, I wonder?" Mary muttered. She cast off her apron, and we went up.

Poking her head through the bookshop door, she said, "Why don't we go into the parlor, Mr. Fisher?"

I wondered if Mamma would appear, but she didn't stir, so I followed Mary into the parlor. Mr. Fisher gestured us to sit, then towered over us, ignoring Mary's request that he take a chair.

He laced his fingers behind his back and announced, "I know where Charles is."

Mary lifted her chin, but I saw the wobble. "How?"

"I followed you and Jane this morning. I knew your leaving was odd. You both have too many duties to be wandering around with a basket."

"We have food to purchase," she said.

"Polly usually does that, and indeed, she went out with a basket, as well," Fisher said.

"Haven't you better things to do than follow my household around town?" Mary asked, steel in her voice.

I envied her that hardness, given how fearsome he was. Which was not to say I'd have avoided snapping at him, but it would have been out of bravado more than anything.

His bloodless lips curled at the corners. "I will arrest him if you don't say yes to my marriage offer."

"Why would you arrest Charles?" I asked stupidly. "He didn't kill that cheese girl."

"He has a warrant out for his arrest. I'm paid to retrieve such men."

"He's just a boy, really," Mary said. "An ungrateful lump of a boy at that. I don't care."

"Yes, you do!" I jumped up. "Mary, please. He's my brother."

"He ate all the jam," Mary said, her tone implacable.

"He's frightened. That Miss Davies is no good, besides. He's in awful trouble, Mary."

"Why should I sacrifice myself for him?" Mary asked. "That is what is at stake here."

"I'd sacrifice myself," I said in noble tones.

Mary rolled her eyes.

"Your decision, Miss Mary?" Fisher said.

Mary considered him. "Even if Charles is dreadful, I know Papa depends on him."

I squeezed her arm. Of course it came down to Papa. It always did for Mary. "See, you have to say yes. It doesn't really matter that it helps Charles."

She sat very still for a moment. Her cheeks paled, as if the sun had gone out of them. "Call the banns, but I don't want to see you in this house again today."

"I'll give you time for a meal, but then I will be back. I want to hear exactly what young Clairmont has said to you. You can go with me to the vicarage." Mr. Fisher sketched a beastly bow, then walked out without saying another word. Though I thought I heard him whistling in the street once he left the house.

Mary turned to me, her gaze intent. "We have only a couple of weeks to figure out how to escape this marriage. I'll die, Jane, like Mother did, if I have to bear that man's child."

I glanced over her slim form. No, she was not made for a man like that. It would have been better if he'd chosen me. "Pray to your God, Mary. If he exists, you need him now."

Chapter 6

Mary

Papa and Mamma had gone upstairs after they ate their egg and oatcake luncheon, leaving the rest of the house to Mary and Jane to run.

Mary clicked her tongue against her teeth when she realized how untidy the bookshop had become since she'd been banished to the kitchen. She began to straighten the books; Jane followed her with a feather duster.

Mary's pulse leapt in her neck when the bookshop door opened, but the first time, it was merely the porter. Jane put him to work cleaning up the pencil box. Children always broke the leads.

The next time the door opened, however, Mr. Fisher entered. Her betrothed. She shuddered at the thought as she peered around a bookcase. Her thoughts flashed to Shelley, his blue eyes intent on her. Oh, to be wed to a man like him instead. She did not even know if the Bow Street Runner would appreciate a writer wife. Would he ban her from doing what she loved? He would have that power over her, damn him.

She must insist Papa wring certain concessions out of Mr. Fisher before they wed, if indeed it came to that.

"I did not think I would find you here," Mr. Fisher said, straightening his enormous black tailcoat. He'd shined his boots since she had seen him last. Did he feel like he was going a-courting, even though he'd blackmailed her into it?

"My duties were here before our cook went away," Mary said.

"Now I never leave," Jane said pertly as she walked past to shake her feathers in the street.

"It will be nice for you to have to manage only two rooms." His gaze drifted around the bookshelves.

Mary looked down and saw she had a line of dust right across her bosom. She batted it off her apron. At least she knew something made him uncomfortable, though whether it was untidiness or her body was still in question. "Do you have a fireplace?"

"I do, yes. You'll be able to cook. I will fit it out for you with everything you might need as a wedding present."

Her breath curdled in her chest. "That sounds like a gift for you, sir, for surely you want to eat."

"Chophouses and taverns are all very well for me, but you can't eat in them," he said, not offering her any concession.

She bobbed a curtsy. "How kind you are, to not let me starve."

Jane came back in just as Mamma appeared from her office. "Are you two alone without a chaperone?" she asked, playfully waggling her finger.

Mary pointed to Jane.

"I was just shaking out the duster, Mamma, but now I have to go out with Mary."

Mamma smiled coquettishly at Mr. Fisher and made a shooing motion. "Go, go. I will watch the shop."

Mary snatched off her apron, sullen comments filling her mouth but thankfully not escaping. Mamma really wanted to remove her from the household. Did she think Polly would work harder if she were gone? Maybe the maid would start receiving the slaps and pinches that Mamma saved for her stepdaughter now.

The trio went out onto the street. Mary pulled on her bonnet as the sun assaulted her eyes. Two horses, looking unkempt with untidy manes, pulled a wagon past, fouling the street as they went. Her skirts would be covered with dust by the time they crossed the street. She'd never been less eager to leave the house. If only she could have had assurances from Papa. Not only was marriage to Mr. Fisher an assault on her liberty, but it also meant death.

"Shall we go straight to the church?" Mr. Fisher said, displaying a little less confidence than usual. "Or the vicarage?"

"I think we should go to the cheese shop," Mary blurted.

Mr. Fisher tilted his massive head. "Why?"

"We have windows overlooking the street," she said, pointing up. "I, er, Jane and I saw Miss Davies and Mr. Griffith at his shop last night. He gave her something bigger than her hands, but it didn't look like enough to be Winnet Davies's belongings."

"What does any of that matter?" he snapped, then smiled politely at two servant girls who appeared around the corner.

"Is this the bookshop?" one asked. "We have to pick up a parcel for our mistress."

"Just go in and to the right," Mary said. "Mrs. Godwin will help you."

"She traded her bundle at a tavern," Jane said, jumping in as if she'd really been there. As soon as the door shut behind the girls, she added, "For a gun."

His chin tilted down. "A gun?"

A street seller stared at them as he passed by, pushing a cart of men's hats.

"A case," Mary said in an admonishing tone, smoothing her glove over her fingers until they settled into place. "Really, Jane. We have no idea what was in it."

"But you said—" Jane retorted, then stopped when Mr. Fisher gave her an odd look.

"It did *look* like a gun case," Mary admitted.

"Very well," he said and pointed down the road.

They walked the few steps to the cheese shop and went in. Mrs. Griffith stood behind the counter, looking harried as she dropped coins in a box. A matron was gesticulating at her while a very young child sucked a stick of candy into a sliver, holding on to her skirt. Mary edged around a wide-hipped woman in a gray dress, a large wheel of cheese in her arms.

The matron finished her business and turned away. The child walked right into Jane. When she pulled back, the candy was sticking to Jane's skirt.

"Bother," Jane exclaimed. "It's half a week until washing day."

The woman wrenched the child away from Jane as soon as he ripped the candy from her skirt.

"I am sorry, Miss Clairmont," Mrs. Griffith said in an exasperated tone. "These young women. They do not understand the proper care of infants."

"Do you have children?" Jane asked.

"No." Mrs. Griffith shuddered. "We were not blessed."

"Where is Mr. Griffith today?" Mary asked.

"Well," Mrs. Griffith said, instantly becoming more cheerful, "he is supervising the dairy. We have been honored with the commission to make cheese flecked with gold for White's Club, who are catering the grand ball celebrating the Duke of Wellington at Burlington House on July first."

"How wonderful," Jane exclaimed. "Real gold?"

Mary felt a cold shiver go down her spine at the sound of the avarice in her stepsister's voice. Jane had *issues*.

"Indeed. We had to procure it special. The cheeses are so lovely, creamy white, and the gold leaf is flecked on it."

"It sounds delightful," Mary said. "But we are here on a much sadder mission. Miss Branwen Davies asked if we could bring her sister's possessions to her rooms by Billingsgate Market. As you know, we are acquainted with the Davies family."

"I heard, as your brother has a warrant out for his arrest." Mrs. Griffith smirked.

"Not for murder," Mary said quickly. "Only he is out of town and didn't know to appear at the inquest."

"Humph," Mrs. Griffith said.

"Bow Street would appreciate your assistance," Mr. Fisher said.

"I really can't leave the counter," she said.

He dropped sixpence onto the counter. "Perhaps you could fetch me some good white cheese along with those belongings?"

The cheese seller snatched the coin and dropped it in her box. "Right away, Mr. Fisher." She vanished into the back.

"That will be delightful," Jane said. "The cheese you bought for Mary is already gone."

"Have you eaten nothing else?" Fisher asked. "Is the household on that lean of a footing?"

"No," Mary said. "Our maid foolishly traded a large amount of it for other food. I cannot understand why she thought she had the right to do it."

"What did she trade it for?" He crossed his arms over his massive chest, straining the seams of his jacket.

Seams Mary would have to mend soon if she couldn't find a way to escape. "Eggs and cream."

"I see. Did she get a good deal?"

Mary crossed her arms. "Perhaps? I'm new to managing a kitchen, and she did it while I was busy elsewhere."

"You will have a lot to learn as a young wife." He leered at her.

She went to the counter, ignoring him, though her heart thudded precariously in her chest, and peeked into the back room. The sweet, sour, milky scent of cheese strengthened. A long wooden table centered the industry in the rear. Two young women worked there with bowls, using wooden spoons to cut curds. They were pretty, with round rosy cheeks and light brown hair mostly hidden under starched white caps, and might remain so if their work was always so light. Were they sisters? Another, narrow faced, with luxuriant black hair, was squeezing a knot of cheesecloth, her body bobbing back and forth as she forced liquid into a bowl. Two older women, bare armed and muscular, cranked butter churns along the wall. Mr. Griffith, at a separate, smaller table, used tweezers to place what was probably the gold leaf on finished rounds of cheese.

Mrs. Griffith came onto the landing at the top of the stairs that were in one corner of the shop. Mary retreated from the counter.

"They have quite a few employees here," Mary said to Mr. Fisher. "I wonder why Miss Davies worked in the front instead of in the kitchen."

"Here we are," Mrs. Griffith said, handing Mr. Fisher the cheese and Mary the bundle. "This is what is left of poor Winnet's earthly life. You'll tell her sister we are sorry, I hope. We don't like her in the shop, because she always smells like fish, and the customers don't like it."

Mary opened the bundle and found what she expected. A change of clothes, some underthings, a Bible, and a few hygiene items. "Miss Davies told us to look for forty shillings. She was very certain her sister had that in savings."

"If she did, it's under a floorboard or such." Mrs. Griffith shrugged. "I'm no thief. Don't need to be."

"No, madam," Mr. Fisher said, taking the items from Mary. "It's a prosperous business, you have. But that money would mean the world to a fishmonger."

"I understand that, sir, but this is all that was in her box. Likely one of the other girls in the room took it. I'm surprised that hairbrush was still there. It's quite nice."

"Thank you," he said, then took Mary's arm and escorted her to the door, Jane trailing behind.

"I wonder what Branwen Davies picked up from Mr. Griffith, since Winnet's things were still there," Mary said.

"Something worth trading for a gun case," Mr. Fisher said. "And that's not forty shillings."

"I'd have to agree," Mary said as they passed the first warehouse. "A cheap case would be one thing, but this one had brass fittings." The door to Skinner Street came next, after they passed the bow window of the shop. She wished she could go inside, slam the door on her betrothed's face, and not depart again until Shelley came to take her for an evening walk.

Mr. Fisher, seeming to not notice her inner turmoil, worked his jaw from side to side. "Well, then, we did what you'd asked." He handed Mary the cheese. "Take that to your kitchen and then let's go to St. Sepulchre. I assume you want to be married from there."

"We often go to St. Paul's," Mary said. At least it was a slightly longer walk.

"That's not your parish, miss," he told her. "Be reasonable."

"What about yours?" she asked.

"St. Paul's, Covent Garden."

The other St. Paul's, then. "Is that where your rooms are?"

"Indeed, right near Bow Street. I was destined for the work." He smiled at her for the first time. She found him alarming, a wild animal ready to devour her.

"What are you going to do with Miss Davies's things?" Jane asked.

He sighed and handed them to her. "I'm sure you'll be seeing your brother soon enough."

Mary could not begin to understand the man. He used their knowledge of Charles as a threat yet suggested they return? Every man wanted something unfair from her, except Shelley. Without saying anything more, she went into the house.

Jane spoke, but Mary blocked the noise from her ears and went to the kitchen, where she plunked the cheese down on the table.

Polly had the stewpot on the table, an unusual sight. Water steamed from it. "I thought I'd use the eggshells to give it a good scour."

"We really are out of food," Mary said. "I never thought to see that pot empty."

"What did you bring home?"

"Mr. Fisher brought me cheese again," she said.

"When is the wedding?"

Mary shrugged. "I am dawdling here, but next I go to the vicarage to order the banns called."

"You'll be gone by midsummer, then," Polly said. "Then I'll have to do everything myself."

"One less mouth to feed."

"You don't eat enough to matter."

"Why don't you leave?"

"My wages are still paid. As long as that continues, well, it's quiet here." Polly gave her a crooked smile.

Mary nodded. "Would you want to go with me if Mr. Fisher gives me funds for a maid?"

Polly shook her head. "That would be a step down in the world for me, no offense, miss."

"I understand," Mary said. "Don't trade away more than

half of that cheese, please. If he wants to dine with us, I had better have it on a plate."

"I could get some cockles," Polly said thoughtfully.

Mary nodded. "If you see Mamma, do try to get some money from her. Tell her you don't even have money for vegetables, much less meat. She obviously has some tucked away."

"Not your father?"

"Don't you dare," Mary said. "He's not to be bothered with domestic concerns."

Mary smelled rich stew and fresh cake as the housekeeper opened the vicarage door. Jane's shoulders relaxed as she took a deep breath.

"The vicar, please?" Mr. Fisher said. "We have business with him."

"He's away, sir. Dying man in the parish," the woman said, rubbing the enlarged knuckles of one hand with the other.

"We should return another time," Mary murmured, delighted at the prospect of being turned away. Maybe she should talk to Papa about the finances.

"Reverend Doone must be here," Jane said. "It smells like you've been cooking luncheon for him."

The woman's face wreathed into happy wrinkles. "Indeed. There is a man who appreciates the domestic arts. Will he do as well as the vicar, sir?"

Mr. Fisher nodded. "He would be fine. Thank you." He took Mary's elbow and escorted her in.

Jane followed, looking enchanted, the traitor. Mary enjoyed the aromatic delights of Reverend Doone's table as much as the next person, but his longing glances he cast in her direction when she called on him made it difficult to actually dine.

"I'll just be a moment, sir." The housekeeper went upstairs.

A couple of minutes later, they were admitted into the congenial upstairs parlor of the vicarage. Mary fondly remembered the first time she'd seen it: a cheery fire, a table well set with delightful treats, and the rosewood cabinet she admired, full of pretty teacups. Though she might not covet such things for herself, she enjoyed looking at them. Her heroine, Isabella, must have a room like this, but would it be better to make it a prison or a refuge?

"Miss Mary Godwin," Reverend Doone said, rising. He straightened his coat over his abundant frame. Crumbs fell to the carpet. "And Miss Clairmont. I do not believe I know this gentleman."

"Fisher. Of Bow Street," said their companion, doffing his hat.

"Ah, I have heard Constable Wharton mention the name," the curate said. "Will you take tea with me, sir? And your delightful companions?"

Mr. Fisher glanced at Mary, seeming less self-assured for once.

"They set a perfectly brilliant table at the vicarage," Jane said encouragingly.

The curate chuckled and stood, his chair creaking.

"Why is it that the vicar goes to the side of the dying and not the curate in this parish?" Mr. Fisher asked.

Reverend Doone spread his chubby-fingered hands apart. "It all depends on income, you see. If they are poor, I am sent. If they are wealthy, he goes. He also prefers to attend at Barts, as he has dear friends there."

"It makes sense," Mary said, sitting where he gestured. Jane followed suit.

As soon as the men were seated, the curate said, "Do you know, Miss Mary, that our housekeeper has finally finished her magnum opus?"

"What is that?" Jane asked. "A very large cake?"

He winked at her. "No, a book of flower pressings. Do you enjoy such things, Miss Mary? It is quite lovely. She has an eye for color and pattern."

Mary could not answer, because Mr. Fisher rudely interrupted. "I need you to arrange the banns for our wedding."

The curate's jaw dropped. "Miss Clairmont is to be wed?"

"Miss Mary," Mr. Fisher growled. He put his massive hand on her shoulder possessively.

She had to adjust herself to take the awful weight of it.

Reverend Doone bristled. "Are you already married, sir, like that ghastly Shelley? A wife in the country somewhere, perhaps? Or in some sort of care?"

"I was born in Covent Garden," Mr. Fisher said. "I am free to wed. Miss Mary has done me the honor of accepting me."

The curate stared very hard at Mary. She kept her expression blank. "She is too young for marriage. I believe I can speak for the vicar in this and refuse you, with all due respect, sir. You aren't even of this parish."

Mr. Fisher puffed out his enormous chest. "The age of consent is twelve for marriage by banns, and besides, her father is allowing the wedding."

"I see." The curate rose and went to his desk. His quill went into his inkpot, and he scribbled a note, then blotted it and went out.

"What is he doing?" Mr. Fisher asked, but neither girl answered him.

Jane jumped up and went to look out the window. Mary scooted her chair far enough away from him that he took his hand off her shoulder.

"He wouldn't actually get you that flower-pressing book," he said.

"Why not?" Mary asked. "We are quite friendly with the reverend."

"Why?" he retorted. "He is obviously not so friendly with that poet who is always lurking around Skinner Street."

"They have a difference in theological opinion, as I am sure they are entitled to," Mary said. "But there is no malice in it. He is really very kind."

"He seems very intent on you."

"I am not meant for a curate's wife, if indeed he could even afford to wed," Mary said.

"He thinks you too young, in any case."

Mary permitted herself a small smile. "There is that. If only you agreed. Perhaps an engagement until I am seventeen, at least? My birthday is August thirtieth."

"That is more than two months away."

"It would be for the best." Mary hesitated. "I would have time to bring Fanny home from Wales. You would not deny me the comfort of my older sister at my wedding, I trust?"

"The sooner you are wedded, bedded, and out of mischief is my opinion," Mr. Fisher said. "Your father said I can have you, and that is good enough for me."

Mary pressed her lips together as emotion welled in her breast. How could he be such a beast? Had he no human emotion?

The curate appeared at the door, huffing a bit and holding his chest. He stepped in, the housekeeper behind him. She set a tea tray on the table with a fat-bellied pot and slices of seedcake.

"I wonder if I might consult with you on your recipes?" Mary asked as the housekeeper straightened. "I am soon to be running a little household of my own, and you make such delicious things."

The woman smiled at her. "Of course, Miss Mary. I would be pleased to help you fill up your notebook." She bobbed a curtsy in the curate's direction and left the room.

"How nice," Mr. Fisher said sourly.

"You should be glad," Mary snarled. "Your diet will be rich."

"Will you?" Reverend Doone said, gesturing to Mary.

She nodded and stirred the leaves in the teapot, then strained tea into each of the green and pink teacups the vicar so prized after Jane retrieved them from the cabinet.

By the time they were finished, the flavor of the tea a little soured by the reverend's pained looks in Mary's direction, the housekeeper had appeared again with a note on a salver. Mary recognized her father's handwriting.

"Very good," the curate said after perusing it. "We will call the first banns of matrimony Sunday next week. Let us see, it is the twenty-third, so that will be July the second, I believe. Would you like me to notify your parish, Mr. Fisher, or will you also be calling on your vicar there?"

"This Sunday," Fisher said.

"No," Reverend Doone said in the firmest of tones. "You must give seven days of notice before the banns of matrimony are called. Shall I write?"

"It's St. Paul's, Covent Garden," Mr. Fisher told him. "Please write, but I assume Miss Mary would like to be married here."

"You will have to consult with the vicar as to the date," Reverend Doone said.

"As long as the first banns are called."

"On the second of July," the curate said pleasantly.

Mary cleared her throat. "Thank you. I am sure Mr. Fisher needs to return to his duties at Bow Street. I must attend to my family. I instructed our maid to procure food, and we need to prepare it."

"I hope you were inspired by your visit here," Reverend Doone said.

She smiled at him. "It is always a pleasure to dine with you, sir."

When they reached the street, she wondered where a Bow Street Runner out-of-town assignment was when she needed one. If only she could rid herself of the man, for as long as possible, really. She preferred the priest's petulance to Fisher's stoicism. At least the priest was educated. Whoever would have thought Reverend Doone a better matrimonial choice? But then he wouldn't come with the exceptional housekeeper. She belonged to the vicar.

Mr. Fisher left them at the Skinner Street door, saying he would return for dinner.

"What does he think he's going to eat, I wonder?" Mary snarled when he had gone out of view.

"That cheese?" Jane asked.

Mary nodded. "I told Polly she could sell half of it to get cockles or eels or something. Why don't you see if you can get some money out of Papa?"

"What about you?" Jane undid the ribbon on her bonnet, even though they were still outside.

Mary's resolution, newly formed, firmed. "I'm going to talk to Shelley."

"I want to go," Jane insisted.

"I need a minute's peace," Mary said. "Can't you see how difficult a position I'm in?"

"What can Shelley do about it?"

Mary put her hands on her cheeks. They felt hot, and she was cross and fearful. "I don't know. Maybe he can reason with Charles."

"Yes, I see your point," Jane said, opening the front door. "Godspeed."

Reason with Charles. Reason with Charles. If Mr. Fisher had nothing to blackmail her about, could the wedding be stopped? The words resounded like a drumbeat in her head the entire way to Fleet Street.

Thankfully, Shelley opened the door when she knocked at the top of the stairs. His handsome face creased in welcome. "Mary, my dear! Are you and Jane come to pay your first duet of a call?"

She shook her head. "It is only me. Is that enough?"

"Mary." His voice deepened. "My heart. Come in. Of course."

Jane had said he had two rooms. Inside, the first room felt very plain, though not cheerless. The single armchair blazed in red velvet, and the window had curtains in the same fabric. A rickety table piled with books and papers waited next to the chair, and a faded hearthrug brightened the fireplace. The mantelpiece was crowded with bottles and half-burned candles, and she saw some chemical equipment on another table in the corner.

"Are all these things yours?" she asked.

He buttoned his coat. "Only the portable items. The furniture came with the rooms."

She nodded, then felt her lips tremble. He put his hand on her shoulder. His fingers, so light and delicate, seemed to break her more than Mr. Fisher's heavy grip. Tears built, then flowed down her cheeks.

"Oh," Shelley whispered, then wrapped his arms around her.

She clung to his waist and rested her head on his heart. He smelled like lavender soap and sweet sweat, a scent she would remember forever. How familiar it seemed, though she'd known him only some part of three months. "I cannot bear it, Shelley. I am breaking."

"What is going on?"

"Blackmail, sir," she said without lifting her head. This close, she could smell the starch on his shirt. She breathed in the sensation, cool fabric from his waistcoat scratching her cheek, the scent of the warm linen and man underneath. "I have to marry Mr. Fisher of Bow Street, or he will tell the coroner where Charles is."

"Why do you have to sacrifice yourself for him?" Shelley sounded disgusted. He set his cheek on the top of her bonnet. Her head vibrated as he spoke. "Why, your papa let his own wife go to the lockup a few weeks ago."

"I think Papa wants me gone from Skinner Street, perhaps before he is arrested himself." Her words sounded broken even to her. "First, there was all that nonsense with my Scottish suitor, and now he has flung me at Mr. Fisher with only the slightest provocation. If his creditors get him, he'll lose everything, even his precious library."

He rubbed his cheek against her bonnet. "You have no interest in the marriage? He has a good job. Bow Street, though dangerous, I suppose."

She squeezed his waist. "You have seen him. He is monstrous in appearance. I would die. He needs a giantess to bear his offspring."

His chest moved as he laughed. "Ah, Mary. Women can survive much, but I do see your point. Do you like him?"

"No," she said, outraged. "The only nice thing he has done is buy me cheese, and that was only to get the Griffiths to talk. What was he going to do, carry around cheese all day? Do you know? Even Reverend Doone doesn't want me to marry Mr. Fisher."

"Even a fool can get the time right twice a day," Shelley commented. He pushed her away gently, then moved his hands under her bonnet, up the back of her neck. She looked up at him. "Remember this. Your heart is free regardless of what happens."

"My heart is not free," she whispered.

"No?"

She shook her head, staring into his eyes.

"Ah, sweet Mary." His mouth came very close to hers. "I have some thoughts about that scribbled somewhere, yes."

"Tell me. I want to hear the words." Her head spun with the taste of his breath in her mouth.

He loosed one hand from her skull, picked up a notebook behind her, and read.

> *Mine eyes were dim with tears unshed;*
> *Yes, I was firm—thus wert not thou;—*
> *My baffled looks did fear yet dread*
> *To meet thy looks—I could not know*
> *How anxiously they sought to shine*
> *With soothing pity upon mine.*

She smiled. "How could you not know?"
He continued.

> *To sit and curb the soul's mute rage*
> *Which preys upon itself alone;*
> *To curse the life which is the cage*
> *Of fettered grief that dares not groan,*
> *Hiding from many a careless eye*
> *The scornèd load of agony.*

He broke off. "It is not yet complete."

She felt transported. "Shelley, we are both so oppressed. You by your marriage and me by my betrothal. We must be each other's support."

He set down the notebook, his nostrils flaring. "This Fisher is an oppressor."

"Yes," she agreed. "But did you really write those words about me?"

He smiled, his hand slipping down her neck. "Of course, dear Mary."

She shivered. "You have a golden pen. Mr. Fisher, he is . . .

he is iron, just some base metal, not shiny and delicate like you." Now with his wife far away in Bath, the Shelleys had been broken into their base elements. Could he not be reconstituted into another family to form a new unit? Could he somehow be hers?

How could she think to marry Mr. Fisher? How could she think positive thoughts about Reverend Doone in Shelley's charismatic presence? No, she was all his. She must be.

But they had so much to worry about. She forced herself to think. "Can Charles doom my family?" she asked, stepping away.

He shook his head. "Charles is nothing. It's his lady love who concerns me."

"He is scared of her now," she observed.

"What could this young woman do that might impact the Godwins?" Shelley mused. "I'll try to find the man from the tavern that Branwen met."

"How is that possible?"

He sighed. "I will start at the tavern. He might be known. There aren't many who deal with guns, assuming that was what was in the case in the first place."

"Be careful. You said it was too dangerous for me."

He nodded. "I am not a stranger to guns, as you know. It is no wonder that I needed them in Wales but not here. I have one, though, in my bedchamber, under the bed, just in case."

"Creditors have followed you from Wales to here, so violence could follow, as well," Mary agreed. "Vigilance is important."

He nodded. "Do not let Mr. Fisher press you overmuch. We will free you from him somehow."

"The banns will be called a week from Sunday," she warned.

He smiled. "We have weeks still. Anything might change in weeks. Be strong, my dear."

"I will try." Her voice trembled.

"I know you will. Now, you had better go, before your father grows angry with me. I do not want to be denied a place at your table." He touched her cheek.

"He loves you well, and your money even more, I am afraid," she said pertly. "Fear not that."

Chapter 7

Jane

My brain had been overtaken by thoughts of cheese, hearty and melted over a slab of bread toasted on the fire. A salad of field greens, gooseberry tart. In truth, I'd be lucky to have a cold slab of cheese and nothing else, for Mary had been busy and Polly didn't have the nerve to demand household funds from my parents.

The church bells began to sound. Five o'clock. Time to lock up the bookshop and go to the dining room.

I took the cash box from its hiding place under the counter and quickly compared the contents to my ledger, which I handed over to Mamma at the end of each day for further accounting.

When I noticed I had been writing in pencil instead of ink since a schoolmaster came in for a fat set of copybooks and five bottles of ink, I pulled out my quill, ready to remedy that. Somehow found myself rubbing out the penciled number and writing in a lower one. A sixpence went into the hidden pocket under my apron. If Papa wouldn't give Mary money for food, then this sixpence might be all that lay between me and starvation. It would buy enough oatmeal to get us through a couple of weeks.

I didn't feel bad at all. In fact, my heart rate did not increase as the street door banged. I calmly wiped my pen and stoppered the ink. Perhaps we were getting some last-minute trade before I locked the door.

When I went to the door, though, only Papa and some men stood there, so I returned for the ledger and cash box and walked them to Mamma's office.

She opened her big drawer, and I dropped them in.

"Papa has two men with him, one tall and one short, both of middle years," I reported.

The corners of Mamma's mouth turned down. "What does he think we are going to feed them, I wonder? I had Polly worrying at me today, demanding coin."

"Mary and Polly cannot feed us on air," I said, feeling bold, as Polly had been for once.

"Nor can we dine on food going into strange men's bellies." She pulled off her visor and tossed it onto the desk. "These household concerns will drive me mad. As if I have nothing else to do."

"Fanny should return to take up the role of housekeeper," I suggested. "You and I are both working women."

"The household is not so large. Mary can do it."

"Not without money," I protested. "Come, Mamma. If Polly is left to do the marketing, she will kill us all with spoiled meat."

"I had strong words with her about the fish stew." Mamma rolled her eyes. "I was in the garden half the morning after she served it the second time."

I knew she meant the outhouse. "And Papa's stomach is so very delicate."

"It is indeed. Which is why I gave her five shillings to stock up the larder properly." Mamma growled low. "Who are these men your papa has brought home? Do they look prosperous?"

"The shorter man has a very bright red coat that must be freshly dyed."

"That could mean anything."

"He has a good hat," I added. "The older, taller man looks rather threadbare in green."

Mamma rubbed her hand over her eyes. "Not promising in the least, but not likely to be moneylenders."

My ears pricked up at the sound of the bookshop door opening. Mamma shooed me away.

"There you are, Jane," Papa said as I came toward him. "This is the bookshop, gentlemen, and my daughter Jane Clairmont."

I curtsied to the two men, who looked around curiously. "I was just about to close up the shop, sirs, but I am happy to attend you. Did you have a particular title in mind?"

"Your father invited us to dinner, Miss Clairmont," the younger man in the bright coat said. "I am Dr. Hubert Asquith, professor of natural philosophy."

When he said nothing more, Papa said, "And his assistant, Irving Bryan."

"I did not know we had company this evening," I said as the older man inclined his head.

"I met these gentlemen, natives of Bath, I believe, while out taking a walk," Papa said genially. "I am sure we will have a most stimulating conversation."

Mamma came out of her office and was introduced. She told me to tidy up and left with them. I delayed as long as I could, and sent the porter home when he appeared.

When I went into the front hall a couple of minutes later, both Shelley and Mr. Fisher were there. I had not heard the door, so distracted was I by irritation at Papa's foolishness.

"Good evening," Mr. Fisher said politely. Shelley merely grinned at me.

"Papa brought home dinner guests. Have you heard of Dr. Hubert Asquith, Shelley?" I asked.

"No. Who is he?"

"A professor of natural philosophy," I explained.

"That could be anything from a true man of science to a mountebank," Mr. Fisher said.

"I'm sure Bow Street can sort it out over dinner," Shelley said with a smirk.

"Were you invited to dine?" Mr. Fisher asked him.

"I am allowed to treat Skinner Street as if it were my home," Shelley said. "I am Godwin's disciple, you see."

Mr. Fisher stared hard at him, but Shelley's natural geniality was so evident that the stare soon softened, despite the constant rumor that Shelley was known to the Home Office. Personally, I had never seen him do anything the least seditious, but I hoped they would keep the dinner conversation to science, just in case.

We went up. I pulled two extra chairs from the wall and reached for additional place settings from the sideboard so that everyone could take a seat. Papa had two wine bottles uncorked already as Shelley held out my chair for me. At the sight of our party of three, he went right to work on a third bottle. I added up figures in my head. I should have stolen more than sixpence, given the way Papa was behaving. Mamma insisted on pouring and filled the glasses only a third of the way, but I knew that would not do any good. Gentlemen were experts at keeping their glasses refilled.

Willy came in, followed by Mary and Polly with a tureen of steaming seafood-scented soup, not so heavy on the garlic this time, and a plate of bread, along with the full round of cheese. I was surprised to see the cheese had lasted this far into the day.

Mamma's mouth went tight at the parsimonious fare, but I

noted Mr. Fisher sat up even straighter in his chair. I had judged him so tall that his head could have reached the candelabra, but that was mere fancy.

"Go and prepare the second course, Polly," Mamma instructed. "Mary, sit down." She smiled at the strangers. "Mary is practicing in the kitchen for her nuptials."

It confused me that Mamma had not pegged these gentlemen as I had. The professor had announced no affiliation with a university, which would have legitimized him, and his assistant looked quite downtrodden. Her worry over Charles had clouded her judgment.

Polly bobbed, looking very confused. Mary gave her a wide-eyed glance, then sat down. I suspected the rest of the coins Mamma had given Polly to last for days would now be spent on this one meal.

We passed the soup around, then the bread and cheese.

"So kind of you to give Mary this little betrothal gift," Mamma prattled.

"The soup is excellent," Mr. Fisher praised, gazing in Mary's direction.

"Soup is one thing, but Miss Mary's beauty and intelligence are unequaled," Shelley said, with a wink in my direction.

"I am a lucky man indeed," Mr. Fisher said, then stuck his spoon back in the bowl of soup, which I was sure Mary had nothing to do with.

"We have been talking about alchemy and the work Sir Humphry has been doing with batteries," I prattled, wondering what sort of natural philosophers these men were.

"Ah, alchemy," the professor said, with a wink in my direction. "You have to be an adept to uncover those secrets, my dear."

"Do you know anything about the batteries?" Mary asked politely. "I do hope Papa will take me to another lecture someday soon."

"I know they come at great expense," the professor said, waggling a finger in her direction. "But money is never the purview of young ladies. It is not a delicate subject."

"I work in our shop," I said. "And Mary does sometimes. We definitely concern ourselves with coin. Otherwise, our customers would take our books for free."

"We cannot have that, clearly, miss," the professor agreed.

Polly struggled into the room with a plate of sliced potatoes in one arm and a bowl of sausages, likely meant for breakfast, in the other. She set them in the middle of the table and departed.

"Very nice," Professor Asquith murmured and stuck his fork right into a sausage.

His assistant followed suit, the professor's action seeming to have given him permission. He ate hungrily, like a man who had not enjoyed a full meal for some time.

"What sort of experiments have you embarked upon?" Mary asked after Shelley toppled a potato's worth of slices over the smeared remains of bread and butter on his plate.

"Bring me a candle, pretty lass," the professor said, with a twinkle in his eye.

Mary, frowning, did what he asked. He handed her his empty plate and centered the candlestick in front of him on the tablecloth.

"Watch closely," he said, passing his fingers through the candle flame.

We all leaned in except Mary, who was plunking his plate on the sideboard. He reached into his waistcoat and pulled out a piece of paper a couple of inches in length.

"Observe," he said, passing the paper through the flame. It went up in a little puff of smoke, but when his fingers were on the other side of the flame, he held a shiny coin!

"There," he said, an expression of satisfaction on his florid face. "A bit of gold for you."

I held out my hand, thinking he would give it to me, but it

disappeared back into his waistcoat before I could even examine it.

"Ah, you're a conjurer," Mary said. I could hear the sour tone in her voice, but I was rather enchanted.

"Not at all. I am working on a subscription to improve on the voltaic battery," he said complacently and poured wine into his glass. "But one has to sing for their supper, no? It does no harm to provide a few tricks to enchant pretty girls."

Mary's tone went acid. "Before you ask their parents for funds to improve your personal finances?"

"Mary," Mamma snapped. "Go down and see what is keeping Polly from bringing up the dessert." She smiled falsely at Mr. Fisher. "I do hope one of Mary's famous gooseberry tarts is on the menu."

Shelley licked his lips and grinned at Mr. Fisher. "Something tells me she has been too busy to collect any more berries."

"More's the pity," Mr. Fisher said, giving Shelley a wolfish look in return. "But next year I look forward to tart season in our rooms."

"I do enjoy considering the matter of alchemy," Papa said, as if none of the preceding conversation had taken place. "I worked through the likely consequences of obtaining mysterious wealth in my novel *St. Leon*."

"Fascinating," Mr. Bryan said. "I hope to turn my hand to a novel one of these days, when I have the time. I would like to read your work."

"I am curious myself," the professor said.

"We have it in stock," I promised. "If you produce that gold again, I will run down and find the volumes for you."

"You will find them highly illuminating about the state of Europe in the sixteenth century," Papa said and began a discourse about the Camp du Drap d'Or, where the young kings of France and England spent a vast sum to show off to each other.

"You wish to turn my coins to knowledge, eh?" the professor said.

"Please," pleaded Mr. Bryan with a curious sort of desperation. "I would love a pattern to follow for my own future work."

"It examines how dangerous the aristocratic notion of honor is," Papa said expectantly.

The professor, with an air of great forbearance, reached into his waistcoat, then handed the coins over to me. I jumped up from my seat and trotted down to the bookshop.

Mary met me in the front hall. "What is all this? You look painfully eager."

"Professor Asquith gave me coins for *St. Leon*," I explained. "At least we had some payment for the meal."

"I am afraid it is some kind of scheme. Such men always want twenty-pound subscriptions for this and that. He may press Papa for something now."

I leaned over the bowl of strawberries in cream that she held. "Well, Papa doesn't have twenty pounds," I said. "Let us just be happy for this sale." I sniffed at her and went into the bookshop to find the four volumes and make sure they were free of dust.

Had we experienced a week of activity in one day? When I woke, it was only Friday, and I had to open the bookshop. Mary came in, sunk into a predictably foul mood, to help me dress. I assisted her with a few fastenings, as well, then went to Mamma to retrieve the keys to her office. I had left Professor Asquith's coins in the drawer under the counter in the bookshop, and I confess I was half-afraid that they had been magicked away somehow. I chided myself for my silliness when I found them still there, and put them on Mamma's desk after I updated the ledger.

We made it all the way through our breakfast of oatmeal and

the remaining scraps of cheese, the sausages all being gone, of course, before disaster struck.

Mamma was debating whether Mary or I or both should attend upon Charles with food we did not have when a loud knock came at the street door.

Papa consulted his watch. "Go down, Jane. Customers this early? A good sign."

I flew downstairs and opened the door, hoping for more sales, but instead I saw Constable Wharton, looking grim under a couple of days' worth of whiskers, and Mr. Fisher, with his harsh-faced Bow Street Runner expression in place on his forbidding face.

"S-sirs," I stuttered, my good mood faltering. Glancing between them, I asked, "Should I get Papa?"

"Summon all, Miss Clairmont, now, there's a good girl," the parish official said.

I hesitated. "Should I bring tea?"

Mr. Fisher shook his head. I bit my lip and ran back upstairs, my speed still present, if not my gaiety. I surveyed the group. Everyone was already dressed for the day.

"Mamma, Papa, you need to come down."

"What is it?" Mary asked.

"Constable Wharton is here," I managed.

"Charles?" Mamma's eyes went wide. She rose, her napkin dropping to the floor.

I shifted uneasily. "I don't know. Mr. Fisher is with him."

Papa stood and squeezed Mamma's shoulder. Mary took a last, deliberate bite of oatmeal, then stood. Our parents went out, while Willy remained seated, wild-eyed.

"Go up to the schoolroom," I said. "Your tutor will be up soon."

"Is Charles dead?" Willy asked, the words all the more poignant given they were spoken in his child's reedy voice.

I shook my head. "No. I would know." I went to him and

wrapped my arms around his shoulders. Mary followed me and came to stand on Willy's other side.

Our brother sighed. "I should not like to be all grown up."

"Time passes whether we like it or not," Mary said gently.

"We will never be all together again, will we?" Willy said softly.

Mary forced a smile. "Maybe for my wedding, but perhaps never all under the same roof."

"This has been the oddest summer," I added. "But Mary left and came home in the spring. Indeed, we all travel. I expect we will all be seated around this table again very soon."

"Humph," Mary said. "Run along, Willy. If Mr. Fisher is here, I need to be present."

As soon as he went up the stairs to the schoolroom, we went down, ignoring the dishes for now. I hesitated on the landing, my old trick of listening just out of sight under consideration, but Mary sighed and grabbed my arm.

We went into the parlor. Mamma was on the sofa, Papa next to her, while the men stood at the fireplace. Mary did hesitate then at the doorway. The difference between Constable Wharton, kindly, elderly, and stooped, compared to Mr. Fisher, so tall, so broad, so carved out of granite, was astounding. Fear caused tense lines in her body.

The constable nodded at us. Mr. Fisher merely stared.

"What is the news, Constable?" Mamma said. She wrung her hands.

"Your demeanor is alarming, sirs," Papa added. "Pray do not wait another moment, upon this mother's tender heart."

I glanced at Mary, waiting for a derisive noise, but her gaze was fixed on her betrothed. I knew then something very bad had happened.

"Is it Charles?" I cried out. "Please, tell us."

"No, Miss Clairmont," Mr. Fisher said. "It is Branwen Davies, in fact."

Mary reanimated then. She went to the back of the sofa and put her hand on Papa's shoulder. "She has died?"

Constable Wharton nodded, a faint smile of gratitude on his face for the conversation having begun. "Branwen Davies's body has been found hanging from the same tree where her sister was discovered."

"How dreadful," Papa said, the words muffled by Mamma's shriek. She burst into tears, a bubbling, frothing mess of them.

"Mamma, please," I said, rushing forward. "Charles is well. We know where he is."

"Do you?" Constable Wharton asked, his eyes narrowing.

"Hold up," Mr. Fisher said, glancing at him. "I know where he is, as well. It is no mystery."

"Have you eyes on him? Is he innocent of this?" the constable asked.

"That I cannot say," Mr. Fisher admitted. "He is not in your parish."

"I have a warrant for him. Enough of this protection of the boy. We will get him this instant," the constable said.

"Go with him," Papa said, turning to Mary.

"Yes, sir," she said, then pulled me into the hall. By the time we had our bonnets on, Mr. Fisher and the constable had joined us.

We went into the street, Constable Wharton firing irritated questions at Mr. Fisher but ignoring us, which was fine with me. I wondered how Mary felt about marrying a man who had surveilled her. It made me nervous, but women chose their husbands less often than was desirable. I wholeheartedly agreed with Papa's criticism of the marital state in his books of twenty years ago.

"What are your thoughts, Miss Mary?" Mr. Fisher asked when the constable had finished venting his spleen.

"I want to know what was in that possible gun case," she

said. "Charles told us it did not come into the room he shared with Branwen Davies."

He nodded. "That could be crucial to the matter. I do wish I had spent the night watching the building."

"No one paid you to do it," Mary said.

"No. I pursued a thief most of the night, a jewel thief."

"Were you successful? I thought you looked tired," she commented.

"I had some three or four hours of sleep before the boy came to call me to the watchhouse." He bared his teeth at her. "The reward for the capture will pay for the outfitting of your kitchen, Miss Mary."

"Perfect," she murmured softly. "I am glad you were successful."

"The jewel thief might end up being my brother's cellmate," I said sourly. The scent of fish grew in my nostrils, though we were a bit behind the fish market.

We went up the stairs to Miss Davies's rooms. Mr. Fisher knocked on the door, then unlocked it with some curious apparatus when no one answered, ignoring the constable's gasp.

Charles was not at the rooms when we entered. The room smelled sour and felt hot, but it was still except for a row of ants crossing the floor, focused on a small puddle of ale.

I stared at the tousled bed as the men walked through the small space with intent expressions.

"Are you going to claim he is dead again, Mary?" Fisher asked.

She shrugged and flipped back the covers, increasing the animal smells. "He was not when the first sister died. But he could have been kidnapped. I cannot imagine he is involved in whatever the sisters were doing."

"I will have to speak to the men at the watchhouse for St. Magnus the Martyr," the constable said. "Hopefully, there is someone there at this time of day. See if these Davies sisters are known in the neighborhood."

"Good idea." Mr. Fisher glanced at Mary. "I think we had better speak to the Griffiths again."

"I agree," said my sister. "John Griffith may hold the key to this puzzle."

Mr. Fisher flung open the trunk at the foot of the bed. I took that as a signal and went to my knees to hunt under the bed. Mary went to the cupboard and rummaged through it.

"This isn't good news," she said.

"What?" the constable asked, his hand in a pile of newspapers.

"There's two pounds here and some loose change in a pot. This must be her life savings, and it's still here."

"We know Miss Davies is dead," the constable said in a condescending tone.

"Yes, but Charles has been alone here for days. He'd have found the coins," I said, understanding. "Why didn't he take them if he fled?"

Mary nodded. "Why indeed?"

Mr. Fisher said nothing, just moved furniture around and kicked at the floorboards to see if any of them hid a hidey-hole. We found nothing, and I was too worried about my brother to enjoy the search of a dead girl's room.

"What should we do with the money?" Mary asked.

"I'll take it," the constable said. "I'll speak to the coroner about it. Someone will have to notify her heirs, if she has any."

"Charles might know," I ventured, then subsided at Mary's gaze.

"Is there anything of your brother's here?" Mr. Fisher asked me.

"It doesn't look like it."

"Very well. Let's lock up and be on our way," he said.

We left the constable hunting for a landlord to make sure the room wasn't rented to someone else right away, and headed toward the cheese shop.

I didn't dare ask if Mr. Fisher was going to buy us more cheese, since he must know it had been mostly consumed during the impromptu dinner party the night before. A gentleman would simply offer, knowing that, though I supposed Bow Street Runners were not gentlemen.

"Are you well?" he asked Mary as she trudged through the dust next to him.

"Of course not. Our fears about Charles are utterly renewed," Mary said. "What is going on? Why did these sisters both die?"

"We need to look closely at the persons they have in common," Mr. Fisher said.

"Charles, of course," Mary said.

"And according to you, John Griffith," he suggested.

"Oh." I stopped in the street, right in front of a butcher shop.

"Chicken would be perfect for dinner," Mary said sourly, glancing at the plucked fowl lined up above the shop window.

"Yes," I agreed. "Do you think Mr. Griffith killed the girls?"

"We know Branwen Davies thought so," Mary said. "Because of the pregnancy. There's no reason we know of for him to have killed her, too."

"It could have been in a passion," I mused. "She abused him for what he'd done to Winnet Davies, and then he killed her, too."

"No one drags a living person all the way to Hyde Park for a murder of passion," Mr. Fisher said.

"Mr. Griffith would have a cart." Mary tapped her chin. "Did Miss Davies have any head injuries, as if she was knocked unconscious, or had she been tied up?"

"I don't know much of anything yet," Mr. Fisher said. "I also don't know if she was with child like her sister."

"I don't think she was, at least not by Mr. Griffith," Mary said. "She did not have the demeanor of someone who'd learned she'd been betrayed by her own sister or lover."

"What is most likely?" I asked.

"That the tree was a meeting place for the sisters," Mr. Fisher said. "That both of them went there of their own free will for unknown purposes and were captured and strung up there."

"Then Branwen was attempting to finish some work Winnet had begun?" Mary asked.

He nodded and opened the door of the butcher shop. "Or was forced to attempt it."

After he bought us a plump chicken, we went to the cheese shop. Mary seemed pleased with the gift. She said little, but I could see the hint of merriment dancing around her mouth and eyes.

When we went in, there were three customers ahead of us and a buzz of interest in the shop. I heard a matron gossiping about the gold-dusted cheese. We did not often receive such elevated trade in this neighborhood, except at our own house.

Mrs. Griffith, looking harried, sent us into the back when she saw Mr. Fisher.

"Where is your master?" Mr. Fisher asked one of the dairy maids, who was busy separating cheese from whey at the long table.

"Upstairs." She pointed.

Fisher took Mary's arm, and we went up the steps in the shop. We found Mr. Griffith sitting at a desk in an open room that had more steps, probably going up to the living quarters. He had a ledger open and a quill in his hand.

He glanced up at us. His look of concentration dropped from his whisker-bound face when he recognized Mr. Fisher. "What do you want?"

"Where were you last night?" asked the Bow Street Runner.

"In my bed," Mr. Griffith said. "I have a nearly fatal amount of work to do here, with the special orders. I worked, I slept, and here I am at work again. What is all this about?"

"Don't be cross with me, sir," Mr. Fisher said. "Branwen Davies is dead this morning, hanged from the same tree where Winnet Davies was discovered."

Mr. Griffith dropped the quill, his features slackening. Ink dribbled from it onto the ledger, but he didn't look down. "Branwen, as well? Such foul news."

"Who can vouch for you?" Mr. Fisher asked.

"I wish I could say my wife, but I am very afraid Cleda is the murderer and is trying to frame me," said the cheese shop owner.

"Why?" I asked, shocked.

"She wasn't in bed when I woke up just before dawn."

"Neither of you has an alibi," Mary declared, interpreting his words.

He nodded, then looked down and startled when he saw the mess he'd made of the ledger. He attempted to blot it with his handkerchief, which only spread the stain. He left the handkerchief in the puddle and dropped his head into his hands.

With his head down, we could not truly discern his expression. Mary and I glanced at each other; then she spoke.

"What did you give Branwen on Wednesday night? You were observed handing her a bundle."

"Winnet's things," he said, not lifting his head.

"The bundle was too small for that," Mary said coolly. "I am here with the law, sir. Tell the truth."

Mr. Griffith set his elbows on his desk and lifted his head. "Wednesday?"

Mary nodded. "That is the night you were observed interacting with her."

Color flooded his cheeks. "I—I had an arrangement with both girls. It is embarrassing to admit, but I was paying for Branwen's sexual favors with cheese."

My eyebrows flew up. How could Charles have been courting a girl with such low morals? Did he know any of this? Free love was one thing, but using one's body for trade was another. I knew that females were forced to such measures at times, but Miss Davies had both employment and a courtship. Why would she take money for carnal relations?

"You think your wife killed Miss Davies because of your relationship with her?" Mary asked.

He nodded, a perfect picture of misery. Really, I wanted to comfort him, but the thought that he was merely a good actor stopped me. "Did she know for certain? Your wife, I mean."

His lips trembled. "I don't know, but she is so harsh with me that I must assume it. I cannot think of a time she ever seemed to notice, but how I wish . . . well . . ." He subsided.

"I recall our conversation with Miss Davies," Mary continued, a cold expression on her face. "Did Winnet really have forty shillings of savings?"

"Yes, she did," he admitted.

"What happened to it?" Mr. Fisher asked.

"I found the money after she was murdered, and felt justified in keeping it," Mr. Griffith said, staring at nothing. "I assumed she'd probably been stealing cheese and selling it, to have obtained such an amount."

Yet Miss Davies had even more coins in her cupboard, I remembered. But I had no reason to believe both girls hadn't worked hard for years and had sold their bodies on the side, too. They could have amassed such small fortunes easily enough since they had not succumbed to gin or laudanum.

"You are a thief," Mr. Fisher said, putting his hands on his hips. "I shall turn you over to the parish authorities."

"She would have made me her heir if she'd thought of such a thing," Mr. Griffith said. "Their parents are dead. They had no other siblings."

Mary's eyes bulged at the foul words. I was more curious

than angry. Did one's employer inherit if no family remained? I'd rather have thought the king would get it all.

Mary, less curious and thoughtful, took my arm and marched me down the stairs. We went directly out of the shop to the street. I did not blame her. Mr. Griffith was completely vile, whatever the legal issues.

Mr. Fisher came out a minute later. "That is a low character."

"Agreed," Mary said, hugging her chicken.

He looked up at the façade of the shop. "What does that say about the people around him?"

"That includes Mary, your betrothed, and me," I said. "We live just down the street. Maybe you'd like to cancel the wedding now?"

Fisher tilted his head at me, then lunged at Mary and pulled her into his arms right on the street in front of the cheese shop windows.

Mary went pale, lolling like a rag doll in his massive arms. I put out my hand, afraid she was going to swoon.

"The future Mrs. Fisher is a woman above such behavior," he said.

Mary untangled herself from him more gently than I would have. "I do hope our friend Shelley can learn what was in the box Branwen paid for with the cheese. Whatever it was, it probably led to her death."

Chapter 8

Mary

Mr. Fisher's talk of attending poor Branwen Davies's autopsy had Mary and Jane scurrying back into their house alone.

Mary brought her chicken down to Polly, and they made quick work of cleaning it, then built up the fire and placed it on the roasting rack.

"We have not had such a meal in quite some time," Polly said.

"Luncheon will be late, but the results will be worth it," Mary said. "I will go up and tell everyone to delay an extra half of an hour before going in to dine."

As soon as she reached the front hall, a knock came on the door. Most people knew to enter, since they were going into the bookshop, but when she opened the door, she found the conjurer's assistant, Irving Bryan, rubbing his hands down his worn coat.

"Mr. Bryan," Mary said. "May I assist you?"

"I would like to call upon your esteemed father, if I may," he said, his eyes shifting from side to side. He rubbed his nose and left it looking very red.

Mary gestured him in. "Please wait in the parlor. I do not know if Papa is upstairs, but I will see." She went up and knocked on her father's study door, hoping Mr. Bryan could be sent off before he was invited to luncheon.

Papa said, "Enter," so she opened the door and saw him at his desk.

"Two things, Papa. Luncheon is delayed, and Mr. Irving Bryan is here to see you." She considered her poor father, who looked quite gray in the late morning light. "Do you want to see him?"

Papa pulled off his glasses and rubbed the bridge of his nose. "I did not think we would see those men again. They were not what they had represented to me."

"It's only the assistant here. He is agitated."

"Don't call us to dine until he leaves," Papa said, rising.

"Yes, Papa," Mary said, relieved. "Mr. Fisher bought me a chicken this time."

"I thought him a good man, and he is proving to be so." Papa smacked his lips. "Soup with the carcass, I think."

Mary winced. She knew something about soup making, at least. A messy process to ladle off the fat and pull the bones and gristle out, but as a reward for the toil, delicious.

Papa rose and patted her cheek as he went out. She followed him down the stairs and hovered in the doorway while he greeted the assistant and took a seat on the parlor sofa.

Mr. Bryan rubbed his hands down his tailcoat again. He glanced at the fireplace, as if hoping to see a cheery fire, but no one other than the exceedingly wealthy lit a parlor fire in June. "Thank you so very much for condescending to see me, sir."

"Please, be seated. I have a few minutes only," Papa said without offering any refreshment.

Mr. Bryan took a straight-backed chair from a corner of the

room and flicked out his tails, then sat. "I have had a most disturbing morning, and I come to you for advice, sir."

"Pray tell," Papa said.

The assistant put his head in his hands for a moment, reminding Mary of Mr. Griffith, though his hands had not trembled like Mr. Bryan's did. "To be frank, sir, and I am sorry to have to admit it to such an esteemed personage like yourself, but in a word, I was sacked."

"Sacked," Papa said, shifting uncomfortably. "You mean to say you have lost your position with that, er, professor of natural philosophy?"

"He is a conjurer, in truth," Mr. Bryan said, waving his hands in front of his face in the manner of a magic trick. "Additionally, I am sorry to say that Professor Asquith is a mad drunk."

"He imbibes overmuch?" Papa said. "It is a problem of the age, is it not?"

The assistant leaned forward. "He has a taste for French spirits, sir."

"The war is over." Papa shrugged.

Mr. Bryan lowered his voice. "Before that, sir, when such things could not be possessed legally. I know the professor is mixed up in 'French' affairs."

Mary, leaning against the jamb, could hear the special emphasis he placed on the word 'French,' but she had no interest in politics.

Her mind wandered to the kitchen and her duties as the wretched man continued to speak. What would her allowance be for household purchases in her new surroundings after the wedding? The house was inadequately ventilated, and she already felt she could smell roasting fowl wafting up from the kitchen. A shudder overtook her at the thought of doing all the cooking in a two-room apartment. It would constantly stink of whatever she cooked. And Fisher, she would smell him all around her, too. A man who regularly attended autopsies would have hegemony over her body?

She put her hands to her mouth to muffle a cry. How long would his adoration of her last once they were wed, given how cutting his remarks about everyone else were? She was no household angel. It had only been recently that she'd been forced into a more domestic fate. Before their cook had been sacked, she'd worked in the bookshop. She didn't even have a receipt book of her own.

Unexpectedly, her father rose. "Excuse me." He went out the door and smiled weakly at Mary. From his posture, she could see he was heading to the garden. Poor Papa and his stomach troubles.

Mary spoke. "I am sorry, Mr. Bryan. Papa is unwell. I think you should go now."

"I thought . . . Mr. Godwin," he started, then rose from the chair.

She came forward. "We cannot help you, as we are in difficulties ourselves."

"With the war over, there are not going to be any jobs for an older man like me," he said hoarsely. "All those soldiers will be in London, looking for work."

Mary desperately hoped he would leave before her father could return and react as he did in such situations. Her pulse leapt when she heard footsteps in the hall, but it was only Jane who peered in.

"I don't know what sort of work you know how to do," Mary said, "but we don't have any work here."

"In the Juvenile Library?" he suggested.

"My brother will be back soon," Jane snapped.

Mr. Bryan looked confused. At least Mary took that as a sign he was oblivious to their current troubles.

"We don't have any openings. I'm sorry," Mary repeated.

"If you are truly desperate, I expect there is always work at Smithfield Market."

"Or Covent Garden," Jane said. "There are all kinds of people who do tricks and things there."

He stared at them both with a kind of numb expression; then his nostrils flared into a sneer. "I should have known Godwin was nothing but an empty promise. Spends all his money on his pretty young misses, I expect." He stalked out of the room.

As soon as the front door shut behind him, Mary and Jane stared at each other. Mary spoke. "It's for the best. Papa would listen to his sob story and give him money. Even if he's angry, it's best that he's gone."

"He's not one with any influence," Jane said agreeably.

Mary nodded. "Where are we going to hunt for Charles next?"

"Mamma is making a list of everyone he knows," Jane said. She hugged her torso. "You thought he was dead before. You don't think so now?"

Mary patted Jane's arm. "That is the point. I was wrong before. He seems to have a knack for survival. But I would dearly love to know the sequence of events. The gun case never turned up in her room. Her money was still there, which makes me think she had no notion her life was about to be stolen."

"No sense of danger," Jane agreed eagerly.

Mary put the chair Mr. Bryan had used back against the wall. Mamma came into the parlor. "What is going on?"

"Papa had a caller, but he had to answer a call of nature, so we talked Mr. Bryan into leaving," Mary explained.

"That man from dinner?"

Mary nodded.

"Very well," Mamma said with a sigh.

"We thought we should look for Charles," Jane ventured.

"Where?" Mamma asked.

"Did you make a list?" Mary inquired.

"One never realizes how little one knows about one's children's lives until a moment like this," Mamma said. "I know I have heard of him meeting schoolfellows at the Coopers Arms in Covent Garden."

"Can you think of anyone he would know in the Poplar neighborhood?" Jane asked. "I learned how he met Miss Davies at the cheese shop, but we don't know how he ended up courting her sister."

"He probably met her there, too," Mamma said.

"We should ask Shelley," Mary said. "He knows the haunts of young bucks."

"Charles would know everywhere Shelley goes, since they've talked about all sorts of places at dinner," Jane said.

"I believe Shelley is in Fleet Street right now," Mamma said.

"That is true," Mary agreed cautiously. "Before, he was in Old Bond Street with his publisher friends, the Hookhams."

"Charles would know them, as well, because of his work," Jane mused. "I know he's sold our books to their circulating library. I've heard him mention going to the Literary Assembly."

"How could he afford that?" Mary asked. The Assembly contained subscription rooms with periodicals and reference books, also owned by the Hookhams, who had one of the largest circulating libraries in London.

"They probably let him in as a professional courtesy," Jane said.

"It would be easier to start there," Mary said. "They might have more ideas."

"I agree," Mamma said. "Thanks to that chicken, Polly can manage on her own today. You and Jane go together. I don't think you should be out walking alone right now. Who knows what mischief is focused around that cheese shop?"

"We want to eat, too, Mamma," Jane said, shocked, as if she couldn't imagine that Mamma wanted that bird for herself.

Mamma pulled a couple of small coins from her pocket. "You can buy something to eat while you are walking."

"Not cheese," Mary said, glaring at Mamma as evilly as Mr. Bryan had at her.

Jane shook her head so fast that her cap slid over one eye. "A ham sandwich or a pie. Thank you, Mamma." She snatched the coins and pulled Mary away.

They pelted into the street before Mamma could change her mind and headed to 15 Old Bond Street in the hopes that Shelley's friend Mr. Thomas Hookham, Jr., could advise them.

Mary found an orange in the road, dropped by someone moving produce from the warehouse next door. She peeled it quickly.

"It's a good sign," Jane said. "I'm sure we will find Charles now."

"That's ridiculous," Mary said, carefully putting the peel into her pocket for use later. She tore the fruit in half and gave one portion to Jane.

About halfway to Old Bond Street, they came across a street seller with fresh ham sandwiches, the third vendor they had considered. Jane paid and took the food.

"I have become quite a domestic," Mary said, accepting her half of the sandwich with thanks. "I know what fresh ham looks like now."

"That is all to the good. I cannot imagine how much meat Mr. Fisher must consume on a daily basis."

"Pounds and pounds," Mary said, admiring a hat in a milliner's shop window.

"You are going to have to be very careful to avoid being burned," Jane said, biting into her half of sandwich. "You'll have to cook over an open fire with fewer kitchen tools than you have at Skinner Street."

"I am careful now." Mary narrowed her eyes. "You can't think I'm really going to marry him."

"What choice do you have?" Jane asked.

"I'll think of something. I'm not willing to die young. My mother would want better for me than that." Mary broke off a piece of crust and nibbled on it, then focused her entire being on her food, ignoring Jane's other comments as they walked.

Finally, they were in front of the buildings that housed the Hookhams' literary enterprises. Jane pointed. "Let's try the periodical room first. Maybe there is a porter who will speak to us."

They weren't allowed into the room, but the dark-skinned man who guarded the front entrance told them how to access the domestic space where the Hookhams resided. They went through a lending room and up some back stairs until they reached the doorway to the Hookhams' private residence.

A maid opened the door, once again illustrating how much more successful the Hookhams were than the Godwins.

"We are Mary Godwin and Jane Clairmont," Mary said. "Is any of the family at home?"

"We have pressing personal business," Jane added.

The maid let them in to the tidy front hall. It had a mirror facing the door, over a table with a silver tray holding cards. Oilcloth covered most of the floor. Mary could see through the open door to the parlor, with its large painting of a lake surrounded by parkland over the fireplace.

"We should have a circulating library," Mary said with envy as the maid went to fetch a member of the family.

Jane nodded. "Everything here is on a much nicer scale. This part of town is so much more luxurious, besides."

Mary nodded. "Yes, they get trade from more than just the governesses and tutors and such, who are the majority of our customers. Actual people of consequence come in here to read or even shop. I hate that Mamma pushed us into Skinner Street, where gentlefolk do not like to go."

Jane sighed, then looked at her hands, as if wondering where her long since consumed half sandwich had gone. Mary could do with more food herself. Would the Hookhams provide tea?

As they waited, Mary considered the grisly situation. Two girls dead in the same manner. They were connected to two men, John Griffith and Charles. What had led them to their ends? And where was Charles? He looked far more suspicious. Mr. Griffith had not fled his job and home. There was the matter of his wife to consider, too. But Charles was a careless young man. Had she ever seen him passionate about anything? He had been about six when their parents married, already resigned to the wandering life of his mother. Though he and Fanny had much in common, they had never bonded, not like Jane and Mary. Their different sexes kept them apart. Even now Charles was treated like an adult, and Fanny more like a child, but to what end? He was no mature man.

"What are you thinking about?" Jane asked. "I'm hoping they serve us cake. Shelley must have found a good table here to have stayed so long."

A door above them opened and closed. Footsteps sounded on the stairs. Mary and Jane both looked up. Instead of Thomas or Edward Hookham, a decade older than both Mary and Jane, Charles himself walked down the stairs, brown hair unruly over his brow, wearing a rust-colored coat Mary didn't recognize.

Her mouth dropped open when Jane cried, "Charles!" and ran into his arms.

Charles wouldn't normally have appreciated such an embrace, but he greeted Jane warmly, patting her back.

"How did you come to be here?" Mary asked incredulously.

"How did you find me?" Charles asked over Jane's head. He blew a strand of her dark hair away from his mouth.

"Just a lucky guess," Mary explained. "We didn't know how to trace your footsteps, so we thought about where Shelley lived last. If you'd actually been with him in Fleet Street, he'd have sent us a note."

Jane let go of her brother and straightened her bonnet. "Why didn't you write us? The Hookhams would have sent someone."

"I came here only this morning," Charles said. "When it was still dark, very early. I didn't want to be seen."

"Why?" Mary asked. "What happened? Branwen... Well, do you know what happened?"

"I know she's dead." Charles went a little green. "She'd been saying such bizarre things, and then when she never came home last night, I knew the same thing had happened to her as to Winnet."

"Exactly the same thing," Jane emphasized.

"The Tyburn Tree isn't far from here," Mary said. "We aren't so far from Hyde Park." That fact was not in his favor; nor was the fact that he'd said he had made sure to come here unseen. Still, the killer could not be Charles, whom she had known for a dozen years. She'd fed him, washed his clothes, dined with him.

"I didn't kill Branwen," Charles said stoutly. "I know it looks bad, but I swear it wasn't me."

"Of course not." Jane's voice cracked a little. She put her arms around him again, though he didn't respond in kind this time. "You aren't a terribly angry person. I'd have trouble believing you were passionate enough about anything to murder someone, much less do what happened to the Davies girls."

"What kind of bizarre things did she say?" Mary asked. "You said you were scared of her."

Charles pressed his lips together.

"Can we sit down?" Jane asked. "Puzzle this out?"

Charles sighed and stepped away from Jane, then led the way into the parlor.

"The bellpull is just there," she said helpfully.

"I am a guest. I wouldn't dare, Jane," he admonished.

Mary sat in a well-cushioned chair, happy to have that much comfort. Her face felt hot, and she dearly wished for at least a glass of water, but Charles couldn't risk being demanding, for fear they'd ask him to leave. She didn't even know why Shelley had moved along to Fleet Street.

The maid reappeared just as Jane dropped onto the velvet-covered sofa next to Charles.

"Would you like anything?" the maid asked him.

"Do you have lemonade?" Charles asked.

Jane sat forward eagerly.

"My sisters are parched. I know it's an imposition."

The maid's pale face remained impassive. "I am sure it can be managed, sir." She went out.

"How nice." Jane bounced a little.

"Back to business," Mary said, giving her a severe look. How much of a child she still was. At least Charles seemed to understand the gravity of the situation. His skin hadn't much more color than that poor, thin maid's.

Jane shushed her. Mary bristled indignantly, until Jane mouthed, "Not until the lemonade comes."

It irked Mary that she could understand Jane's mouthed words, but she let Jane offer a litany of sisterly questions. Had he left anything behind at Miss Davies's rooms? Was he sure Mr. Fisher of Bow Street hadn't followed him here?

Charles said so little in response that Mary's suspicions did not subside in the least.

The maid came in with a tray of lemonade and, gloriously, seedcake. A knock came on the front door, and she jostled the tray. Liquid trickled down two of the glasses. She apologized and went to the door.

All three of them instantly snatched up the glasses, ignoring the droplets, and drank deeply. When Mary lifted her head, she saw Shelley coming in. She jumped up.

"Mary, my dear!" he exclaimed, dropping his hat into the maid's hand and coming into the parlor.

"Did you send word to Shelley?" Jane asked her brother.

He shook his head. "But it stands to reason I would come here. They are the only people I know with a spare room."

"Indeed," Shelley said. "Spare rooms are not thick on the ground, though you always have a place on the hearthrug in front of my fireplace."

"Thank you," Charles said.

Mary held up her lemonade. Shelley took it and nearly drained the glass. When he handed it back to her, she put her lips to the place where his had been, and drank the last drops. They smiled at each other.

"Shelley is here now, Charles," Jane said severely. "You must know more than you are saying."

"I expect he knows who killed Miss Davies," Mary added. "Why don't you tell us, Charles? Be honest."

He shook his head violently. His glass slipped down his fingers, but he tightened his grip and saved it, then tilted the rest of the contents into his mouth.

Shelley gave him a shrewd look. He had a pleasant mien in general, but keen brilliance hid underneath. "I think he knows what has happened but is too scared to tell."

"That is unwise." Mary gestured Shelley to sit in the chair next to hers. "Mr. Fisher has his eye on you, and he is no fool."

"He's a fool for you," Jane said tartly.

Mary tightened her shoulders and glanced at Shelley.

"I have news," he said.

"What?" Mary asked.

"The man from the tavern who spoke to Branwen and handed her that case is indeed a gun seller."

"She traded cheese for a gun?" Mary asked, incredulous. "What kind of cheese would be worth that much?"

"Gold cheese?" Jane asked. "I mean, we know they have a

supply of gold. What if they lied about using it and were just using, I don't know, paint or something?"

"Do you know anything about the dealings in the cheese shop?" Shelley asked Charles.

"No, I don't think so." His voice held the disinterested tone Mary knew so well. "We would go there, Willy and me, because they'd give him free tastes of cheese. I met Branwen there. She did deliveries for them sometimes for extra money. They have a lot of customers who want the cheese to be delivered to them, taverns and such."

"Did you hear about them selling anything but cheese?" Shelley asked.

"What, you mean like milk and cream?"

"Like guns," Mary said.

Charles shook his head and grabbed a piece of seedcake. The girls followed his lead.

"I wonder what Branwen did with the gun case." Mary considered. "Or maybe she didn't really do anything with it, but it was taken when she was murdered."

"But Charles said he never saw it at her rooms," Jane said. "She must have taken it somewhere that night, when Shelley took you home because of the danger."

Charles swallowed a huge bite of seedcake. "You are wasting time asking me questions. All I know is that I met a girl to have fun with, and then she became troublesome, and I didn't want to know her anymore."

Shelley raised an eyebrow. "My good sir, that is quite a story unfit for court. You must understand that if the authorities find you, you are headed for the lockup and a murder trial. Your parents cannot afford to aid you. Indeed, your stepfather's history may harm you. Surely you can see that you have to help us help you."

Charles's mouth turned down in a mulish expression. "I must insist I know nothing."

Mary felt the bit of seedcake, which was rather stodgy, lodge itself somewhere above her stomach. "Jane and I are kept too busy to save you, as much as Mamma wants us to help. We still have to run the bookshop and the kitchen."

"I cannot help you," Charles muttered, staring at his hands.

Shelley rose and held out his hand to Mary. "Very well, then. Stay indoors. If Fisher has not yet found you, we will not aid him or any of the bailiffs of the coroner's court."

Chapter 9

Jane

I saw no point in leaving the rest of the seedcake for Charles, so while Mary and Shelley said their goodbyes to Charles, I hid the rest of it in my handkerchief.

Shelley laughed at me as soon as we reached the street. "I saw that, you little thief."

"It's not as if they would have put it back in a box for the family," I said, not offended.

"No, but that skinny little maid might have eaten it."

"I expect she's not allowed to," Mary interjected. "Otherwise she would not be so thin. Do you think she is being mistreated?"

"I never saw any sign of it," Shelley said. "What do you think of the situation?"

"Very bad," Mary said. "We have to be careful. I always feel a shivery sensation at the back of my neck now. I'm afraid Mr. Fisher is following me."

"He might be," I said, wondering why Shelley needed to fear Mr. Fisher. "Bother."

"He can't follow me and you both," Shelley said mysteriously. "I suppose I will have to do some investigating."

"You already have been," Mary said. "Did you talk to the gun seller? Does he know where Branwen was supposed to take the gun?"

"Not yet." Shelley tilted down his hat to block the sun. "But I must, no?"

"I'm afraid so." Mary fiddled with her bonnet brim. "We should see if we can get a look at that fancy cheese and see if gold is really on it."

"We don't know how much they had." I stared at a fruit seller passing by, willing fruit to drop from the cart so I could have a treat. "What good would that do?"

"If it isn't gold, that tells us something. I bet it would tell us that one of the Griffiths killed the twins, for instance."

"Mary is right," Shelley said, dodging a man carrying buckets in both hands. "If the gold is there, we need more information. If it isn't there, that's enough to tell someone like Fisher."

I took Shelley into the bookshop when we arrived home. With few customers, we spent the afternoon laughing and practicing Italian. Shelley couldn't stand still. He roamed the shelves so continuously that I handed him the feather duster, though he had no idea he could clean the books with it. Still, it amused me to see the grandson of a baronet holding a maid's tool.

Eventually, we got down to business and discussed what we should say about Charles. I had a brilliant idea. Shelley seconded my notion, and I handed him paper and quill. He handed them back to me, suggesting I knew my brother's handwriting better than he did, so I went to work.

As soon as I had locked up the bookshop at the end of the day, Mr. Fisher came in the front door. "Are you invited to dine?" I asked.

He nodded. "Good evening, Miss Clairmont, Mr. Shelley."

Shelley lifted a languid hand from where he leaned against the table in the front hall.

I heard rattling below. "Let us go up," I invited. "I think the food is coming."

"Did you have a good day in the bookshop?" Mr. Fisher asked from behind me as we went up the steps.

I didn't know if he was being sarcastic because he'd followed us or if he was genuinely curious.

"Not very," I said. "A poor day for customers."

"Unfortunate," he responded.

"The business is profitable," I assured him. "Mamma works hard to make all the pieces fit together."

"She has an unusual mind for a woman," Mr. Fisher commented.

"She gets her labor cheaply," Shelley said from behind me.

He made a fine point, but as best I could tell, debt brought down our household, not the business. We did not live within our means, even if the numbers balanced in Mamma's office.

Nonetheless, I could not help sighing with pleasure as I entered the dining room. Every bit of it had been furnished to taste and for pleasure, from the Greek-style wallpaper to the upholstered seats on the sturdy, gleaming chairs.

Papa came in, making the conversation instantly genial. Mamma, huffing and puffing from her walk down the street from the warehouse, followed Mary and Polly, who presented a golden roasted chicken that had apparently not been consumed for luncheon, cabbage, and potatoes. They had also made oatcakes with a bit of honey from somewhere, which made Shelley happy.

We fell on the food with relish.

"A most excellent chicken," Papa praised. "Your cooking skills are improving, Mary."

She smiled serenely, but before she could speak, Mamma let out a choking cry.

"What is it, Mrs. Godwin?" Papa asked.

Mamma sniffed and covered her mouth with her napkin. "I cannot enjoy this food without knowing if Charles has anything to eat tonight."

Mary smacked her lips at me, and I remembered the delicious taste of the lemonade and seedcake this afternoon. Charles, as always, was fine. But then Shelley kicked my foot under the table, and I remembered our plan to outwit Mr. Fisher.

"We had a letter from Charles, Mamma, while you were at the warehouse," I revealed, pulling my forgery from my pocket.

"F-from Charles?" Mamma repeated tremblingly, then took a deep sip of her wine.

I opened the letter. "That pitiful Mr. Bryan was sacked, remember? It turns out that Professor Asquith offered Charles the position as his secretary."

Shelley snatched the forgery out of my hand. "Will you look at that? He's gone to Bath with the professor. That seems sensible, to leave London until the Davies twins' murderer has been uncovered."

Mr. Fisher held out his hand and took the letter, clearly skeptical. I held my breath while he perused it.

"We don't know who we are dealing with, Mrs. Godwin," he said. "Given the chance he is being held against his will somewhere, would you say this is your son's handwriting?" He handed Mamma the letter.

She looked it over, then ran her finger over the signature. I prayed her finger did not lift up with ink on it, though I had blotted the letter well. Thankfully, her finger was clean. "Yes, it looks like Charles's writing. Messy, but he may not have had a proper writing desk."

I winced. I had left rather a large stain over the professor's name because I'd pressed the quill too hard.

"Give it here?" Mr. Fisher took the letter, then closed his

eyes for a moment. "He has a position here, in the family business."

Mary frowned at him. "He can't come home, not while the troubles continue. Our Shelley learned today that Branwen Davies had some kind of interaction with a gun seller. Did you learn any more, Shelley?" She fluttered her lashes at him.

He shook his head. "I spent the afternoon in the bookshop."

"Why?" Papa asked. "You could find texts of more value upstairs in the library."

Shelley inclined his head. "I was helping Jane."

"With sales?" Mamma asked.

"Dusting," Shelley said. He quoted his own poem, saying with great hilarity, "'Must putrefaction's breath/ Leave nothing of this heavenly sight/ But loathsomeness and ruin?'"

I giggled. "The shelves were a bit dusty. At this time of year, it seeps through every crack."

Papa looked between us, a frown on his face. Then his mild gaze turned to Mamma, and they seemed to share some silent communication. I didn't like it.

The dining room door opened. Polly came in, bobbed, and said, "Mr. Fisher, sir. There is a man at the door for you."

He wiped his mouth and stood. "Excuse me." He followed Polly out the door. Not knowing the language of the stairs, he generated every grinding, squeaking, irritating noise from them as his heavy tread went down.

I rose and went to the window. A boy walked two horses in the street.

"What is it?" Mary asked.

"I don't think he's going to come back."

Mr. Fisher appeared in the street and mounted his steed, needing no help given his height. Another man, more wiry and somewhat older, used the help of the boy's laced hands to get into his saddle; then the men rode off, the boy running behind.

"I wonder what they are chasing," I mused.

"Not Charles," Mamma said. "The man who came wouldn't know about the letter yet."

"He took the letter with him," Shelley said.

I didn't think it mattered, because it wasn't as if they had any writing of Charles's to compare it to. Anyway, Bath was hours from here. "Maybe he'll be too busy to keep looking for Charles, with this new matter."

"Why would he have been looking for Charles in any case?" Papa asked. "Bow Street hasn't been hired to look into the Davies murders."

"They are orphans," Shelley said. "But this matter of the gun seller troubles me. I would like to know what they were mixed up in."

Papa nodded. "I understand your concern, but we must focus on the post-obit loans."

"Of course, Godwin," Shelley agreed. "For the sake of your family. Who knows what additional funds will be required to rescue Charles from his enemies?"

Papa's expression shifted slightly. I knew he didn't want to go to a sponging house and then to debtors' prison. He might not survive long in such conditions, not having the money to fit his prison room out comfortably. He would place Charles's issues above his own, though, and endure what he must.

"I wish we could all go to Switzerland," I said.

"That is a rather sudden thought," Mamma said.

"Would it not be nice to have a little shipwreck?" I asked. "Have nothing to concern us but survival, like that translation you and Papa have been working on?"

"The family is Swiss," Papa said. "They were shipwrecked on an uncharted island."

"'By break of day we were all awake and alert, for hope as well as grief is unfriendly to lengthened slumbers,'" Mamma said, quoting from the book. "If only our troubles energized you girls first thing in the morning, as theirs did the Robinsons."

I wanted to snap back, but I didn't dare. Mary looked to be having as much trouble holding her temper as I was.

"Fresh air is quite enervating, I find." Shelley leapt from his seat. "Mary, Jane? Why don't we stroll? Your permission, Godwin?"

"I don't want the girls calling on gun sellers," Papa warned.

"I don't even know where the man lives," Shelley told him. "I spoke to the tavern owner where that transaction took place and could do no more than ascertain his profession."

"Then where will we go?" I asked.

"To find some amusement," Shelley said carelessly.

"St. Pancras?" Mary asked, dropping her napkin onto her plate.

"Covent Garden," Shelley said.

I had no idea what his intent was, for we tended to avoid the place due to certain unpleasant experiences there earlier in the month. Still, I was up for something fun, and as long as we kept our wits about us and didn't allow ourselves to get separated, it would probably be safe.

"Bring Willy," Mamma said. "He could use some fresh air, as well."

"Very well," Shelley said. "Come along, lad."

The four of us pelted down the stairs, making nearly as much noise as Mr. Fisher had earlier.

In the hall we passed Polly, who looked disgruntled that Mary was leaving without first helping in the kitchen. Sometimes I didn't think our maid quite knew her place. Or it could simply be that she was more used to Fanny, who was more dutiful than us younger girls.

"I am in a poetic mood," Shelley announced, grabbing Mary's hand once we were out of sight of the house and twirling her around.

"'Who would "go parading"/ In London, "and masquerading,"/ On such a night of June/ With that beautiful soft half-moon,/ And all these innocent blisses?/ On such a night as this is!'" he cried.

Willy laughed as I reached for him and twirled him around, as well. "In another year you will be too tall for me to do this."

"Then I will spin you instead," he promised. "Did you write that, Shelley? It is pretty."

"Wordsworth," Mary called over her shoulder. "He does have his uses."

We sped through the streets, raising dust. I paused at one point. "We have to avoid Bow Street," I reminded them.

"They would not have brought horses if Fisher was going there," Shelley said. "He's gone out of town for some purpose."

The summer crowd made it feel like midday instead of evening. We avoided the theaters and went into the market. Coffeehouses, taverns, and stalls all did brisk trade. There were men dressed as clowns, advertising a circus, and jugglers, too. Ragged, sometimes barefoot boys ran through the crowd, calling among themselves. At least some of them would be pickpockets, after handkerchiefs and coins. I had neither, so I didn't worry about them.

I saw small groups of clerks and shopgirls, out for the air, and even a couple of pairs of women with visibly dampened skirts, showing off their wares. I did admire one woman's diaphanous veil, which cascaded down the sides of her face in place of a bonnet. Willy kept Shelley busy with questions.

"Why are we here?" I asked Shelley. "Is it really just for fun?"

"Yes," he said. "Watch your brother, Jane. I want to have a word with Mary."

She smiled at him, and just like that, I was invisible. I took Willy's hand, and we took a tour of the food sellers around the square.

"Can we buy anything?" he asked. "The food at home has not been very nice lately."

"It was tonight, but no, we can't afford anything." I brightened. "Keep your eye on the ground. Maybe you'll find a dropped penny."

Willy squealed and immediately focused on his feet. I had to lead him around, for he was paying no attention.

I was considering a very nice-looking display of oatcakes with jam when Willy let out a squeak and scrabbled in the dirt. "Did I find something good?" he asked, holding his find out to me.

I stared at the strange coin. "République française," I read. "You found a French coin, Willy. One franc."

He shrugged. "You can keep it."

I stared at the emperor's head. "Thank you." I tucked it carefully into my pocket, disappointed it was nothing we could use to buy oatcakes.

When I rotated Willy to another direction, an older boy looked straight at me and smiled. "Step right up, pretty lady."

I glanced around, but then he pointed at me and winked. I could not resist such an invitation.

"What are we doing?" Willy asked as I tugged him up to the folding table the boy stood behind. I giggled as the boy doffed his ragged cap with a flourish. His black hair was matted from the heat, and he smelled of sweet oil.

"Play with me," he invited.

"We don't have any money," Willy said.

"It's an easy game," the boy wheedled. He tapped the three tiny pewter cups on the table, then turned them over and showed us the marble underneath the second one. "Watch."

We were transfixed as he slowly moved the cups around. Willy pointed at one when he stopped, and the boy turned over the cup. The marble dropped out. Willy caught it before it rolled over the table.

"Ready to try for real?" the boy asked, taking the marble back and flipping the center cup over it, then turning over the other two.

Willy licked his lower lip. "I can do it, Jane. Can I have my coin back?"

"It's a French franc," I said. "What does this boy want with a French franc?"

"Show it to me," he said.

Willy nodded, so I held it over the table. The boy put his hand over mine, then slowly slid the silver from my hand, his fingers touching mine. He grinned slyly at me, and I flushed from the attention.

Then he tossed the coin into the air. It spun and dropped back into his hand. "I'll give you a penny if you win, young man, or keep this for myself if you lose. Fair?"

Willy nodded. I didn't argue at the waste, for what could we do with a franc? The boy slid his cups slowly enough. I kept my gaze tightly on the movements of his hands. As soon as he stopped, Willy chose the one on the left.

"I concur," I said, sure we were right.

And we were! The boy growled, "Crickets," very irritated, but then his grin reappeared on his full lips. "I lost a penny, boy. What's your name?" He produced the penny and handed it over.

"Willy," he said.

"And your pretty sister? What is her name?"

"Jane," Willy said with a roll of his eyes.

I wondered if we had fair value for the franc, but then a penny could buy a treat.

"Your turn," said the boy, dropping the marble into the pewter cup and flipping it down, then setting the others on each side.

I didn't notice Willy leaving my left side,. The cups began to move. I was sure I could track the cups; we'd won before. The boy moved them slowly enough.

"What's your name?" I asked.

"Jack the natural philosopher," he said, then moved the cups just a little faster.

I still had it, though; I knew I did. When he stopped, I pointed to the one on the right. "That one?"

He smirked and turned it up. Empty.

"No," I gasped. "What happened?"

He turned over the middle cup, then with a flick of his wrist, spun the marble into the air, then caught it again. "That's a penny, miss. I should have had it from you before."

"I don't have a penny. I told you, we only had the franc."

He tossed it at me. "The boy has the penny. Get it for me."

Tucking the franc away, I looked to my side, only then realizing Willy was gone. I turned in a circle, then saw him at the oatcake seller, stuffing a jammy cake into his mouth. The ungrateful little beast hadn't even thought to save me a bite.

"He must have spent it," I said, furious. "But I never agreed to any bargain."

Jack shrugged. "You chose. You owe me. I'll take your wrap or your shoes."

"Absolutely not," I spluttered, outraged. "You can have the franc back."

"I don't want that Frenchie coin." He reached over the table and pulled harshly at the ribbons on my bonnet. "This, lass. You don't want to get on my bad side."

My lips trembled. "My mother will be furious."

He shrugged and held out his hand. "Then you shouldn't have played."

Eyes full of tears, I pulled off my bonnet, noting the ragged ends of the straw, and threw it at him. It was on its last legs, anyway, but I couldn't afford another. I ran to Willy and yanked him away from the oatcake seller, wishing I could slap him, but the fault was all mine. He was just being a carefree boy. I should have known better.

I looked for Mary, wanting to pour out my stupidity to her.

She could be nice when I was truly sad. I saw her, arm in arm with Shelley, laughing over some private amusement. How dare they have a good time when I'd just been humiliated?

I marched up to them, pulling Willy along, and stopped their perambulation. "You need to do something," I told Shelley. "I've just been cheated."

When I turned to point to Jack the natural philosopher, he and the table had vanished.

Mary had a vague, infatuated look on her face, but Shelley frowned at me. "What do you mean?"

"That boy took my bonnet!" I recounted the adventure. Willy laughed at me.

"You shouldn't have spent the penny," I scolded.

"It was mine," he said and wiped a bit of jam from the corner of his mouth, then licked it off his finger.

"Why didn't you fight back?" Mary said, finally joining the discourse. "Snatch it out of his hand?"

"You should not have given it to him," Shelley corrected. "Next time, if there is one, call for help. He had no power. He was a charlatan."

"Gambling is a gentlemen's game," Willy added.

"Yes, it is tied into the notion of honor, which your father has exposed for the horror it is in his *St. Leon*," Shelley said.

"It is best not to interact with the unscrupulous in the first place," Mary opined. "Who is more visibly unscrupulous than a street gambler?"

"I won," Willy said with a giggle.

"He was enticing the bigger prey," Shelley said with a stern expression. "Do not worry, Jane. We will find you a new bonnet."

"It was going to rags, anyway," I said, mollified by his promise.

"That's your fault for being untidy," Mary added.

"Fanny always fixes things," I complained.

"She isn't here. You can't let everything go. The next thing you know, your hems will be dragging." Mary took a deep breath. "Have some pride."

"Well," Shelley said, amused, "I was actually told to be on the lookout for a conjurer known to perform here, a known associate of the gun seller, but we haven't seen anyone doing magic tricks tonight, have we?"

"You didn't tell us to look for such a person," I pointed out.

"I will now."

"I thought you would naturally be drawn to such amusements," Shelley said with a glance at Mary.

She smiled at him. "You stayed with the Hookhams for some weeks. How long will they house Charles?"

Shelley grinned foolishly at her. "Until they need their extra bed for a planned guest. I had to leave because some uncle came for a brief visit."

"Why, Jane, did you tell Fisher at dinner that Charles had gone to Bath?" Mary asked.

"It just came to me because of Mr. Bryan's call at Skinner Street."

Mary said, "Mr. Fisher is no fool, generally, and, despite his size, has proven himself adept at secretly following us."

"Charles cannot stay hidden for long," Shelley said. "Unless he remains upstairs at the Hookhams' rooms. We must ensure that he does so. I will drop by. No one would remark upon it."

"Mr. Fisher has likely left town, anyway," Mary said. "We may all have a respite from him."

"But that is also a respite from him learning who killed the twins." I shaded my eyes from the sun since my bonnet was gone. "Which leaves Charles in danger. I'd rather have Mr. Fisher in London."

Mary shuddered. "Never say that."

"I believe he is a good Bow Street Runner at least."

Mary bared her teeth at me as soon as I spoke. "Leave off, Jane."

* * *

The next morning I darted into the passage outside my room when Mary passed by on her way to the kitchen, and pulled her in to help me dress.

"You'll be back in time to open the bookshop?"

"I will do my best," I said. "But I must have a summer bonnet. Even Mamma must see that."

She sighed right in my face. "What she will see is what a fool you were to lose it. Let Shelley pay for it and don't bring it up to Mamma."

When we went down and unlocked the front door, we found Shelley in front of the house already. He gently caressed Mary's cheek, rather shocking to me, though no one was in the street quite yet, but then he held out his arm to me.

"Ready to bonnet shop?"

"Yes, sir. Thank you," I said, feeling happy at the early morning adventure. Usually Mary sneaked out, not me, so this was a nice change. "I hope we can pick berries on the way back."

Mary gave Shelley an achingly soft look and went back into the house, then shut the door gently. I hoped she'd leave me some breakfast, for I feared Shelley's largesse would not get us far.

"I thought we could walk over to High Holborn," Shelley said. "There are establishments for ladies in the area, and I've seen some peddlers who might have what you need."

"I do think some ladies make straw hats at home and sell them," I agreed, touching my cloth cap self-consciously. "I had the one I lost for so long that I can't remember where it came from."

He tilted his head. "Let's go before your mother notices."

"I have a couple of hours. My main worry is finding anyone about to sell to me."

"Poverty is a tough master," Shelley said. "We should find someone."

We walked past our warehouse, then the one that often held oranges. The sweet scent attempted to combat the animal smells from the market, though I sometimes thought it attracted just as many flies.

Next came the cheese shop, then another warehouse and a seller of scientific books. We passed Fleet Prison. One of the debtors was already in the iron cage outside. I could hear him call, "Remember the poor debtors." I could not imagine Papa being reduced to such a state. I clutched Shelley's arm and tried very hard not to think about it. Feeling the warmth of his arm underneath my fingers made me relax.

I collided into someone and bounced off them and back to Shelley. He pulled me into a one-arm embrace to stop me as I pressed my hands to my chest to stop my fast-beating heart.

"I do apologize," I said. Then when I looked up at the someone, I recognized John Griffith.

The girl with him sprung away from his side, where she had been rather snuggled up. Had she been holding his arm like I had held Shelley's? I recognized her as the narrow-faced, black-haired girl from the dairy room in the back of the cheese shop. She wore a tightly molded military-style navy jacket that cut right at her waist, allowing the long length of her legs to sweep out her skirts as she walked. Easy for other things, too, I thought, judging from their furtive expressions.

Mr. Griffith cleared his throat and attempted to pass on after giving the girl a warning look. She didn't move.

Shelley smiled politely at her. "Lovely day, miss."

In response, her lips began to tremble and her eyes filled with tears. I didn't know what to say to her, so I merely edged around her.

"On your way to work?" Shelley asked.

She moaned and put her hands over her eyes. I could not think of why. It wasn't as if we had any power over her.

"Do you need an escort?" Shelley asked politely.

She shook her head, her eyes still covered.

I took Shelley's arm. "I have to work, as well." He allowed me to pull him on.

"I wonder what his wife thinks of his behavior," I muttered once we were out of earshot. "How much cheese is he offering these girls when she isn't looking?"

We looked at each other, both of us taken aback by the strangeness of my words, and began to laugh.

"It's a tough life on all sides," Shelley said when he had sobered. "Cheese notwithstanding. They need to separate. How can Mrs. Griffith want to be with a man who chooses his lovers from amongst their employees?"

"He did claim his wife is killing them," I said. "Perhaps a quiet poisoning of him is next."

"Many a husband has ended his days that way, in such a manner that no medical man can discern," Shelley said.

We arrived in High Holborn Street and stopped in front of a corset maker's establishment. I would not have minded shopping a bit, but the items were so expensive that Fanny wore her late mother's old stays, and I wore some of Mamma's old stays from twenty years ago, re-formed to my shape.

The tradespeople who served the street rather than the shops were on the move. In Covent Garden the flower sellers and food merchants would already be doing a brisk business. We walked the street, passing two sellers of handkerchiefs, all likely stolen merchandise, and a man who had a cart of used shoes. Shawls, ribbons, then finally, as we were coming up to Chancery Lane, we saw a girl with a tray of trimmed straw bonnets.

I immediately exclaimed over the one with cunning silk violets, though they would probably release their dye at the first hint of moisture in the air.

Shelley attempted to negotiate with her, but she knew the worth of the bonnet's excellent appearance, and she brushed us off as soon as a woman came up with more coin than us. I lost the bonnet with violets to her, and the girl had nothing not already expensively trimmed.

"There must be someone selling used bonnets," Shelley said. "Another part of town."

"Even half that price is more than you have," I said mournfully. "Must you give Papa everything that comes from the post-obit loans? It will just go to old debt."

"I begin to think otherwise," Shelley said, a concerned look on his pleasantly handsome face. "I am appalled by the conditions you and Mary are forced to live in. However, I do not want your father to go to debtors' prison, either."

"The decision will be difficult, but I do hope you make the right one." I squeezed his arm and bounced on my heels, my voice rising with every word. "Look what happened when those disciples of Mary Wollstonecraft came with largesse. Did her daughters reap the benefits? Indeed not."

I had worked myself into a little frenzy. A woman drinking at a coffee stall looked at me disapprovingly. I stamped my foot and turned around, then headed for home.

Shelley pulled me to a stop when we saw a temporary stall. "Scientific equipment. Look."

"If we can't afford a bonnet," I started.

"Yes, yes." Shelley had his head over the bits and pieces of scientific paraphernalia already.

"I have crystals of nitrate of ammoniac," the man behind the table said in a confidential tone. He gave me an oily wink.

I didn't like him or his purple-striped waistcoat. All too much flash for my taste.

Shelley fingered a green silk bag.

"Properly oiled," the man said, pushing the bag and a small pouch toward my friend.

"Do you have a mouthpiece?" Shelley asked.

The man opened a box, then set a fancy metal tube next to the bag.

They quickly made a deal. Shelley could have afforded my bonnet, after all, I realized, if that woman hadn't chosen my favorite one. I should have bargained for one of the others.

Shelley rolled everything up and put it under his coat. I followed him as he started back toward Skinner Street.

"Jane, you still need a bonnet," Shelley said in my ear as I lifted my skirts to cross the dusty road.

I expected his pockets were to let now. "I'll take one from Fanny's room."

"Her possessions have been thoroughly pilfered during her absence in Wales?" Shelley commented.

"Exactly the point," I said. "The state we are in. What is she going to wear when she returns?"

"We will figure something out. I will bargain with your father. For now, we can have a bit of fun tonight."

"What did you buy, exactly?"

"The ingredients for a favorite experiment of Sir Humphry," Shelley explained, sounding exceedingly pleased with himself. "I have a mind to replicate it."

Chapter 10

Mary

Since Shelley and Jane had gone out on a mysterious errand, Mary had left on her own to source free food.

She'd taken her notebook, since she hadn't been able to progress on *Isabella*. Horrible thoughts washed over her every time she set pen to paper. If only that horse Mr. Fisher had ridden off on kept going, taking him far away. She wanted to push Denarius Fisher onto an iceberg and set him afloat, never to be seen again. Perhaps Diego should be a more imposing villain, with Mr. Fisher's heavy brow and thick, coarse eyebrows, or there could be another villain with power over Diego, a master villain.

As she walked home, her basket half-full with chickweed, sorrel, and elderflowers, along with the berries, free except for her labor, she realized something discouraging about her novel. She did not have enough plot, not really. The addition of a master for Diego could bring the plot to a climax most deliciously.

* * *

After Polly served lunch, Mary told Polly to go find credit wherever she could get it and not return home without meat. That bought her time to work on a new scene toward the end of her book. She'd write the climax first, a battle between Diego, Denarius, and Fernando. If Papa agreed to try to sell the book for her when she was done, she'd make a fresh copy with a new name for the master villain. Or perhaps not. He should know how she felt about her betrothed.

Fernando, on the other hand, had understanding blue eyes and flyaway golden-brown hair. Well made, with a careless attention to appearance, and he almost never wore a hat.

"You must do better," Mamma chided at the end of dinner.

Mary regarded her coolly over the greasy plate that had held just four narrow sausages supplemented by greens cooked in their fat. "Polly found credit where she could. This is what we are reduced to, unless you are willing to give me more funds."

"I am tired of your complaining," Mamma said. "We have larger issues in this household."

"Than your stomach?" Mary said, feeling daring with Shelley in the room. "I quite agree, madam."

Mamma rose, bumping the table, her ink-stained hand closing into a fist. Papa put a hand on her arm. She stared at him. Some silent communication passed between them; then Mamma took her seat again.

Shelley cleared his throat loudly.

"What is it?" Papa asked, as unperturbed as if his wife hadn't just been about to perform violence against his daughter.

"We found a stall this morning when we took a walk," Shelley said. "Fancy a little experiment, à la Sir Humphry?"

Papa leaned forward. "What is it?"

Shelley produced a large silk bag, as large as his head, a tiny pouch, and then finally a metal tube with a valve. Jane's expression went sour.

"What is wrong?" Mary whispered in her ear.

"This is what was purchased instead of my bonnet," Jane said.

Mary understood Jane's upset, but then she'd lost her bonnet from her own stupidity and here was Papa, happy for once because of Shelley's idea to buy him a treat instead.

"Ah." Papa smiled. "Crystals of ammonium nitrate?"

"Indeed. Why don't we make nitrous oxide? We could all use a laugh."

"A laugh?" Mary asked.

"These are the tools to make a sort of gas that causes euphoria," Papa explained. "Sir Humphry has experimented with it. I believe it is harmless."

"Not Willy," Mamma said.

Willy made a face. "Can I have shortbread from your box?"

Mamma waved him away, and he ran out of the room before she could qualify the amount of the pilferage.

"What is needed to perform the experiment?" Mary asked.

"We need something to hold the crystals while they heat," Shelley said.

"It is a dangerous process. We cannot heat the crystals above four hundred degrees, or they will explode," Papa warned.

"I have seen it done before. I can judge it properly," Shelley said.

"Girls, stay well away from the fire," Mamma warned.

"We will want to heat a kettle of water, as well. The gas needs to be sent through water." Shelley pulled another apparatus from another pocket.

"You are well prepared," Mary observed.

He grinned at her. "I have been experimenting since Eton. Shall we begin?"

Mary took Jane's hand and squeezed it. "Lay a fire, will you? I'll go down and fetch what Shelley needs."

She went to the kitchen. Polly sat on a stool, munching on a sausage that looked much larger than what they'd eaten. She must have hidden it. Mary took note, ready to retaliate at the right moment. Servants did not eat better than their masters.

She used the tongs to light a stick from the kindling, then grabbed an empty kettle and a small pot before filling the kettle with water. She then carefully took it all upstairs without speaking to the maid.

Jane looked irritated by the fire. She'd never been much good at lighting them, but her face brightened when she saw Mary's fire stick. They soon had a nice little blaze going.

"Excellent," Papa said, rubbing his hands together. "Now, girls, I want you and Mamma to stay at the back of the room while Shelley and I prepare the gas."

All three of them dutifully moved back. Mamma set a chair against the wall and sat, remarking with irritation that she was sacrificing all her shortbread for this.

Jane squeezed Mary's hand and whispered in her ear. Mary heard only disjointed words since Jane tried to speak low enough for Mamma not to hear. Something about bonnets and violets. More complaining.

"Is this safe for females, Mr. Godwin?" Mamma called as she became bored.

"Of course," Papa said absently, holding a metal item with a handkerchief.

"Careful that you do not burn yourself," Mamma instructed.

"I think I will draw this scene," Mary said. "I will return shortly."

She went upstairs to fetch her notebook and a pencil, her thoughts focused on the scene in front of the fire, one of scientific exploration, a joining of natural philosophers. How many men, from youths to graybeards, participated in these timeless scenes of scientific exploration? Yet the Godwins were makers of words, not substances. Generally, they created out of thin air words instead of gases, but were they really so very different from the natural philosophers? How easily had Shelley shifted from a boyhood of experiments to writing his novels. He had even published his youthful efforts. Could she not do the same?

In her room she chose her writing notebook, not her drawing one. When she came back down, the kettle already hissed steam, and the men's voices were low hums in the air. Jane had her mending basket.

What might be the inner voice of a man who spent his days over a fire, conducting experiments? The words came to her, and she wrote them down. *Natural philosophy is the genius that has regulated my fate.*

Might Professor Asquith so declaim before some sort of charlatan's trick? Where had he gone? For that matter, they had not heard from Mr. Bryan since he had visited in extremis. It seemed that people had continued to appear and disappear this week.

"It will only have been a week tomorrow since we were all in Hyde Park," she whispered to Jane.

"I know," Jane said back. "Two girls dead just a week later."

"Yet Mr. Griffith continues on his immoral path, trysting with the girls in his employ." Jane had told her what she and Shelley had seen.

Shelley cried out in pleasure, and her father's head pressed close to the younger man's, gray hair brushing against soft, dreamy curls. They fiddled with valves while strange smells filled the room.

Mamma muttered to herself, and Jane picked at the armholes in one of Willy's shirts, attempting to lengthen the arms since he was growing again. Mary kept writing, trying to think like a young natural philosopher bent on an experiment he didn't understand. *Sometimes, on the very brink of certainty, I failed; yet still I clung to the hope which the next day or the next hour might realize.*

"I think we have it," Papa said some minutes later, holding up the green silk bag in triumph. They had attached the metal tube to it, regulated by a valve.

"That is all we do," Shelley explained. "Open the valve and sample a bit of the gas."

"A very little bit," Papa instructed.

"What is it like?" Mamma asked.

"It's similar to drinking wine, I believe," Papa said, "for the sort of person who drinks happily instead of becoming melancholic."

Jane shivered next to Mary and dropped her needle.

"What is it?" Mary whispered.

Jane shook her head. "I want to try it." She dropped the shirt, its half-sewn shoulder seam gaping open like a mouth, onto the chair. Shelley helped Jane place the tube into her mouth and instructed her on its use while he opened the valve.

"This is how Sir Humphry experimented before he extended his apparatus," Shelley said.

He closed the valve and steadied Jane. She stepped back and giggled.

"What happens now?"

"It will take effect. Your limbs might feel heavy, so make sure you don't fall."

Jane did an experimental spin. Papa grabbed her. "Now, Jane, don't fall into the fire."

She sat down at the table, her head unsteady on her neck. Shelley helped Papa with the bag, then brought it over to Mamma. By the time Mary took her turn, Jane had risen again and was twirling, raising her arms slowly.

"Heavy, so heavy," she chanted.

Mary finished with the bag, then coughed.

"That was rather a lot," Shelley said. "No twirling for you." He dropped into the chair next to her, put the tube to his mouth, and fiddled with the valve, then inhaled even more deeply that she had.

"Will it help you write?" Mary asked, her head swimming a bit from the effect of trying to breathe through a tube with her nose pinched shut.

"It's possible. Mostly it's just a bit of amusement. An easy experiment."

Papa relaxed into his chair, looking rather undefined to Mary's eyes. Jane grabbed the bag and took another dose. Mamma snatched it away and set it in the center of the table. Then she rotated her head on her neck, a tranquil expression drifting over her features. Both she and Jane giggled, and when Papa saw them, he did, as well. Shelley dropped his head onto his arms, resting on the table. His back moved up and down as he sighed deeply.

Mary rubbed her temples. They ached suddenly. Had she taken too much?

Along the wall next to the fireplace, a candle burning on the mantelpiece cast an unfamiliar shadow. It grew and grew. She wanted to turn away from it, but her torso wouldn't obey. Her fingertips tingled, but her arms felt too heavy to move. The shadow grew arms and legs, a large bulbous head.

It was Denarius Fisher! He was coming toward her, demanding his marital rights.

"Ahhh!" she screamed and pushed backward, but she was still in her chair. The front legs of the chair went up, and she fell back. Her entire body bounced when it hit the floor, but she couldn't lift her arms to protect her head.

Shelley fell to his knees next to her as Mamma and Jane giggled wildly.

"What?" she heard Papa say in a thick voice.

Shelley patted around her head. "Mary? Mary? Are you dead?" He lay next to her and snickered.

She pulled her legs to her body and sobbed. Her limbs moved, even if her fingers still tingled too badly to control them. Her breaths came in pants. What if Mr. Denarius, that was, Mr. Fisher, came toward her? What if he could escape the wall that imprisoned her? She let out a hitched breath. A laugh? Was she laughing? But this wasn't euphoria; it was hell.

Her anxiety mutated into agony. Was she entirely broken? She put her hands to her eyes.

Wait, she'd moved her hands. She fluttered her fingers, then slowly sat up using her abdominal muscles, then held her head in her hands. The room swam a bit. Her head ached quite badly.

"This is lovely," Mamma said.

Mary could sense Mamma's fatuous expression from her position on the floor. Next to her, Shelley patted her leg, his hand warm and not at all alarming. She looked up, heart rate speeding again, and saw the shape on the wall was just a combination of a table and a vase with flowers in it, not Mr. Fisher at all.

A couple of minutes later, she had crawled her way to a standing position. From the floor, Shelley helped right her chair.

He took a deep breath and let it out. "In future, I suggest we stick to experiments with hot air balloons when Mary is present."

Mary tried to nod, but her head still hurt. "I am surprised I had such a strong reaction when Jane is usually the dramatic one."

"Why don't we take a walk to clear your head?" he suggested.

Mary waited for Mamma to protest, but she was pulling the bag toward her, ready to try more gas. Jane, who had partaken again, merely giggled at her.

Mary walked out of the room, followed by Shelley.

"St. Pancras?" he asked. "A long walk will do you good."

"The burying ground?" she asked as they went into the street.

"Of course. I know you feel most at peace there." He smiled at her.

She realized the sky still hung bright blue above them. They'd closed the curtains in the dining room before conducting their experiment. "I feel that I left October and returned to June."

Shelley took her arm and helped her walk down the street. She felt stronger as they moved.

"I don't think nitrous oxide agrees with you," Shelley said. "Though I suppose one experiment could be different from the next."

"I am not so scientific as to explore that for myself," Mary said tartly. "I would rather imagine the results than test them."

"I can understand that. How is your head?" Shelley giggled, a little residual gas still in his system, apparently.

But his laugh made her laugh. She clung to his arm like she was his wife, because she wasn't going to be able to stay upright otherwise. "I am so grateful that you are willing to take me to the St. Pancras burying ground," she pronounced.

"I think we already agreed to that," he said, stumbling over a rock.

They held each other up. "It's important, though," she insisted. "Of everyone, you are the person who truly understands me."

"We are twin spirits," Shelley said. "Aligned in our common thoughts and goals."

"Exactly," Mary agreed. "Nothing can be more important than that."

"Yes." Shelley squeezed her hand between his arm and

torso. Her knuckles dragged against the fine fabric of his somewhat stained coat. She had forgotten her gloves.

Still, she hugged every second of the walk close to her heart. The throbbing in her head didn't matter. Being close to Shelley, this perfect being, was all she wanted.

The next morning, Mary and Jane took Willy to St. Paul's for church services, then quickly returned him to the house so they could meet Shelley. Though she and Shelley had walked alone last evening, it hadn't been proper. She couldn't go out with him alone in the middle of a Sunday, when anyone might be about and might complain to Mamma about immorality and deny them trade.

Mary felt aches and pains in her body still from falling backward in her chair the night before. Her heart lightened, though, when Shelley peeled himself away from the bricks of a house across from Fleet Prison to join them. They walked out to St. Pancras, chatting animatedly.

Mary asked a lot of questions about the experiment the night before and what Shelley had been like as a boy, doing experiments.

"Do you still have all your apparatuses?" Jane asked.

"Some of them," Shelley said. "Shall I try to make you an elixir of immortality, Jane?"

She giggled, reminding Mary of her fatuous laughter of the night before. It made her feel a little ill again.

As they came into the burying ground, Mary begged, "Let us speak of something else."

"It was only yesterday morning that we saw John Griffith with his dairy maid," Shelley said, changing the subject. "I do think that leads us to an inescapable conclusion."

"What is that?" Jane asked.

"That Mr. Griffith is likely the father of Winnet's baby, given his Lothario ways."

"Ah, yes," Mary said. "If learning there was a child on the way led to Winnet's death, what led to Branwen's?"

"She knew something," Shelley said.

"Blackmail?" Jane asked.

"The coins." They all stopped in front of Mary's mother's grave. Mary stroked the top of the handsome monument.

"I could believe she was a blackmailer." Shelley patted Mary's shoulder, seeming to understand her emotion in the moment.

"She sounded impetuous, from what Charles said," Jane added.

"You don't think she'd have had the nerve to try to blackmail?" Shelley asked.

"She'd have threatened violence, I would think," Mary said. "Look at Mr. Fisher."

Shelley's mouth twisted derisively. "What about him? He is nothing to us."

"That's not true, as much as I would want it to be. Last night—" Mary hesitated.

"What?" Jane asked.

"I did not relax and have euphoria with the nitrous oxide," Mary admitted. "I saw him in the shadows, a monstrous version of him."

"Why do you think you are so afraid?" Shelley asked.

"I have to admit he has done nothing violent." Mary stared at the inscription on the gravestone. "Nothing truly, but he is something of a blackmailer."

Jane nodded. "He did use blackmail to get you to agree to the marriage."

Mary shuddered. "That big, clumsy body is very unattractive to me."

"You will not marry him," Shelley promised. "I will speak to your father. We have some pull there."

"We need to ensure he doesn't find Charles again," Mary urged. "Or he can turn him in."

"Charles can fend for himself," Shelley said. "It is not the job of his stepsister to rescue him from his mistakes." He opened his mouth to say more, then closed it, frowning.

Mary looked from him into the stand of willows near her mother's grave. Had she heard something? She strained to hear; then Jane clutched her arm.

"Was that a scream?" she asked.

There was another, louder cry for help. "Someone is in distress," Jane agreed.

Shelley turned in a circle, then pointed. "It's coming from there."

"But that's the marshes," Mary cried, suddenly fearful. She grabbed Jane's hand. Shelley reached for hers, and then they ran, pushing branches away from their faces as they went through the stand of willows.

Mary dropped Jane's hand in favor of attempting to hold up her skirts as the grass and low-lying vegetation under her shoes turned to muck, then mud. The smell of sulphur hung low in the air as the sun warmed the land and water. The cry came again.

Shelley stopped and put his hand over his eyes to survey the landscape. Sunlight dappled the water prettily, despite the sickly green cast to it.

"Where?" Mary asked, looking around frantically.

"It sounds like a child," Jane added.

Shelley turned sharply. "That way." He tugged Mary along in his wake, Jane following.

They came to a bank of a sort of marshy river. Reeds, waist high, waved in the breeze. Mary squinted. Was that a dark head bobbing some tens of feet away?

Shelley swore, an explosion of sound that shocked her. "Help me with my jacket."

She obeyed instantly, reaching for his collar. "Help, Jane!"

Together, they tugged the tight fabric away from Shelley's torso so he could have the full motion of his arms. They helped him with his boots next, but even as they grunted, pulling off the tight leather, the head disappeared.

"Run!" Mary cried, fearful.

Shelley started to move but fell forward. Jane still had one of the boots only half off. He caught himself with his hands, then pushed through the reeds and into the water. "I don't know how to swim," he called. "Get a stout stick ready."

"Go that way," Mary instructed Jane, pointing. Jane went back toward the willows and broke off the thickest branch she could manage.

When Jane turned back, Mary could see the head again. It was so small, it must be a child's. The child flailed around, then went under again. At any moment, they might not have enough strength to stay afloat again. "Please, Lord, protect them," she prayed.

Shelley's distance from the bank grew as he got closer to the child. Mary ran toward them, trying to stay on the dry ground, but there wasn't any. She slipped and slid in the muck, just barely staying upright. She pulled a thin branch off a willow to try to keep herself steady.

Just as the water reached to the level of Shelley's armpits, he drew close enough to the child to start searching.

"I saw him just west of you," Mary cried. Should she wade in, too? She didn't want him to have to rescue her, though.

Shelley went down. Jane screamed from the other side, holding her stout branch. A few breathless moments later, he reappeared, covered in muck.

He pointed.

"I haven't seen the child again, Shelley. Hurry!" Mary urged. She stepped forward cautiously, poking the branch out ahead of her. Mud sucked at her shoes until she knew if she went one step more, water would cover them and they'd be ruined beyond repair.

Jane started windmilling her arms and toppled over into the mud, the branch flying out of her hand.

"Do you need help?" Mary called.

Jane pushed herself up. "No. It's just so slippery."

Shelley dropped below the surface of the water again. Circles of movement spread out from where he was thrashing underneath. Birds flapped their wings and ascended into the wind, cawing at each other. Mary forced herself to ignore them and focus on where Shelley was.

He came up again, his mouth open with the effort to breathe. Jane made her way along the reeds and started coming up to Mary.

Shelley wiped his eyes, inflated his chest, and went down again. Mary held out her hand to Jane. She extended her branch so that Mary could grasp it and pull her close.

"God blind me, what a sight." The smell emanating off Jane was enough to make her nearly gag.

"Mamma will not be best pleased," Jane agreed. "I've never been so filthy in my life."

"Shelley must be exhausted," Mary said, turning back to the marsh. "I haven't seen the child in at least a couple of minutes."

"He's going to drown," Jane said.

Mary pulled Jane close. "How could it even happen?"

Jane sniffed, then sneezed. "Ran after a dog maybe? What would they be doing out here all alone?"

"I can't stand this. Where is he?" Mary pushed both branches into the ground, then pulled them out. She repeated the motions, moving forward. Water pooled between her shoes.

As she was about to take a third step, water exploded out in the marsh. A dark shape appeared; then Shelley came up from the depths. He had the child on his shoulder.

"Got him." He tried to take a step forward, then fell.

Mary started to go forward, but Jane grabbed her around the waist. "Don't do it. It will be over your head."

Mary pressed forward, using the branches. Jane came along in her wake. Mary put them out to strike them into the ground again, but Shelley reached out for the longer one and grabbed it. Mary stepped back, pulling gently, watching to make sure he still held the branch with his one free hand.

He did. "Help me," she urged Jane.

Between the two of them, they helped Shelley come forward until the water lapped only at his knees. Mary dropped the branch and grabbed his arm.

"That's just a baby." Jane gasped. "Where are its parents?"

Shelley stumbled forward. Mary guided him out of the reeds; then he laid the child down. It appeared to be a boy.

"Is he breathing?" Mary asked.

Shelley put his face close to the pale-faced little one's. "No. And we don't have one of those resuscitation kits. What do we do now?"

Mary thought back to diagrams of drowning victims she'd seen. "Massage his back, I think? And he needs to be warmed. All animals need heat to live. We might be able to bring him back to life."

Jane pointed. "There are some logs over there we can use as a bed, above the mud."

Shelley picked up the child again and ran forward. Jane helped him settle the child facedown on the logs, then started rubbing his back. Mary retrieved Shelley's coat and boots. They put the coat over the child and the boots on. The boots covered the entirety of the child's legs.

"I wish we had a flint," Jane said. "How can we build a fire?"

"We can't," Shelley said. "This is a remote area. We need more clothes."

Mary pulled the soaking shirt off the child's body, then draped her light summer shawl over before adding the coat. Jane knotted a handkerchief over his wet dark curls.

"Should I have rubbed his hair dry first?" Jane fretted. "Oh, I just don't know." She patted the child's back. Her hand stilled, reminding Mary of a pointer dog.

"What?" Mary asked.

"I swear he moved, like he was breathing."

"Rub his arms, girls," Shelley instructed. "I'll rub his back."

Mary dropped down in the dirt and began to squeeze the child's dankly cold hands, then run her hands up and down his arms. Jane did the same, and Shelley massaged his back, putting quite a bit of effort into it.

"Yes, I felt it, too," Shelley said. "Keep going, girls."

Mary rubbed and rubbed until she was panting. There was no lack of animal heat in her body. Jane, too, looked flushed.

Then the child coughed and retched, murky water exploding from his mouth. Mary detected a tiny bit of warmth in his hand. "Vital warmth is returning."

Shelley bent over the child's head. "Breathing is an act of combustion. He's with us again."

The child retched again. More liquid flowed; then he began to cry.

"Calm, child, calm," Shelley said. "I'm going to pick him up, girls."

He lifted the child, cradling his head against his chest. Mary stared at the contorted face. All of sudden, the face seemed to change. She recognized her mother's face—the one in the portrait of her, which was the only image of her that Mary had ever seen—on the child. Was this what had happened to her mother when she attempted to commit suicide? How undignified had been the workings on her body as some stranger worked to save her life. Had they ruined her modesty with tobacco enemas and baths, or had she kept some privacy in the process? A wave of vertigo hit Mary, and she stumbled back.

"Mary?" Jane asked. "Mary?"

She blinked hard, trying to restore her vital humors. "How horrifying this all is," she whispered. "How violent is restoring a life."

"It was a heroic effort." Jane worked her jaw.

"Yes, yes," Mary agreed just as Shelley's boots fell off the child.

Jane sprang forward and grabbed the boots before they hit the mud.

"Sit down," Mary said to her hero, "so we can get your boots back on."

Shelley sat slowly. The child cried on, sounding utterly exhausted. Mary and Jane stretched out one of Shelley's legs, then the other, and slid the boots up as far as they would go before they had to tug them up the rest of the way.

Mary exulted in performing this intimate task for him, this savior, this father who had restored a dead child to life. They fit his other boot onto his foot, then helped him rise again. Mary stayed on the side of him with the child's legs, and Jane took the head.

"What's your name, little one?" she asked.

The child cried and hiccupped; then his body convulsed. Shelley easily shifted him so that he could get more of the marsh water from his thin frame.

"He is not well nourished," Mary observed.

"Can you point us to where you live?" Jane asked when the boy had settled down again.

This time he answered, raising a tiny, shaking finger toward Somers Town, an area Jane and Mary knew well from before they had removed to Skinner Street. The girls walked alongside Shelley as his long legs ate up the dirt. Eventually, they came to civilization. The child still didn't speak, but his pointing took them to a cottage that was reasonably well kept, with thick enough thatch to keep out the rain.

A man opened the door when Jane knocked. He, dark haired and lanky, looked at Jane in confusion; then when he saw the boy in Shelley's arms, his gaze went wide in shock.

The boy started to cry again. Mary realized he must be even younger than they had thought, just long limbed like his father. The man took him in his arms.

"What happened?" he asked, his accent French. Immigrants were common in the area.

"We saw him drowning in the marsh over by the burying ground," Shelley said. "He's had quite a lot of water out, but he has yet to speak. There might be more."

"Be careful with your precious one," Jane said. "The marsh water is dirty."

Mary nodded dumbly. The boy reached out and took hold of a hank of her hair. She smiled at him and put her hand around the boy's cold fist. "He needs a fire."

"Can you build one?" Shelley asked.

The man nodded. "*Oui*. We have a fireplace."

Jane helped Mary disentangle herself from the child, and they said their goodbyes. The three of them said little as they returned to Skinner Street. Jane shivered occasionally and rubbed her hands down her arms. Mary tried to tuck her hair under her bonnet, but it kept falling out. She must have lost pins in all the excitement. Shelley plodded on manfully, water dripping into his boots. He could have been a soldier, marching away from a battle in the wars.

Jane shivered visibly as they went past the bookshop windows. She pushed her hair behind her ears.

Shelley patted her back. "You did well, Jane. You'll make a fine mother one day."

She smiled at him, her eyes squinting with pleasure, then went in.

That left Shelley and Mary on the street alone. In unspoken agreement, they pressed themselves against the wall, out of sight of the windows. "Shelley," she whispered. "You are a hero. What you did with that child, resurrecting his little life . . ."

He took her cold hands in his and tugged her away from the windows. "My heroine, Mary. My helpmeet."

She tilted her face up to his. "I am yours, Shelley. There is no better man that exists."

"My love." His breath warmed her cold lips.

She took a step forward until her dress pressed against his damp coat, aching to make contact with him. They shivered together. "My love," she responded. "Forever and now, my love."

His lips met hers, warm despite the temperature of his clothing. She melted against him, artful and untutored. What could he teach her, this amazing man?

His lips slid along hers until they opened. He tasted the warmth of her mouth. She gasped at the indescribable sensations, the meeting of souls.

Then he stepped back, releasing her.

She stared at him and put her hands to her chest. Her breaths came in pants, as if she had run all the way home.

"My darling," Shelley said, "we must not continue so in public, on your very doorstep."

"No one could but understand, in circumstances like these." His chest rose like hers. They were twin spirits, feeling exactly the same thing. How she loved him. She *worshipped* him, her hero. She licked her lips to draw more of his essence into herself. "I must say adieu, I suppose."

He nodded. "You must, my darling girl. For now. But on my life, you will never belong to Fisher."

She opened the door, still looking at him, then took a step in. Her feet stumbled over her filthy skirts. She smiled, lopsided, and closed the door, then carefully went up the stairs.

The realizations, absolute as they were, kept her as off-balance as the weight of the mud and her chilled limbs.

She could not marry a brute when a hero was right in front of her.

Chapter 11

Jane

Monday dawned hot and bright, so much so that my eyes opened as soon as the sun pressed against my curtains. I leapt out of bed and pushed them open. If the child had fallen into the marsh today, he'd have been much warmer. I hoped he did well today and did not take with a fever.

I heard footsteps in the passage and flung open my door.

"You are up early," Mary said, her notebook in her hand. "I thought I could do a little writing before breakfast."

I pulled her in to help me dress, prattling about yesterday's adventure the whole time. When I would have followed her into the kitchen to continue, she suggested I put my energy to tidying the bookshop instead and parted from me.

I did as she suggested, for we three, me, Mary, and Polly, had to do the work of five now. I even swept the parlor, the front hall, and the bookshop free of the street dust that accumulated at this time of year. I counted five dead flies in my tidy pile when I was done. Better on the ground than buzzing around my face.

Happily, we had a fair amount of trade once I had unlocked the doors, though the opening and closing of them, and the windows I'd needed to open, brought in more of the buzzing little devils.

We had a cold lunch of sandwiches and salads. Mamma had become cross enough in the heat that she herself went to walk and came back with vegetation from a market stall.

I was melting in the bookshop an hour later, wishing I had lemonade instead of a flyswatter in my hand, when Shelley came in.

"*Buon pomeriggio, signore*," I said gaily. "May I interest you in a new notebook or pencil?"

"Mamma in her office?" he said with a raised eyebrow.

I shook my head. "I am alone." A fly dove in front of my eyes, and I swatted it away ineffectually.

However, as soon as I said the words, Mary drifted in, as if drawn by Shelley's ever-electric person.

"Mary!" he said in the most thrilling way. He never said my name like that, but then "Jane" was such a dull thing to say.

Color dusted her cheeks as she came forward. "Good afternoon. It is hours until dinner still. What brings you here?" She waved her hand in front of her eyes as a fly came at her.

He poked his tongue into his cheek, his expression uncharacteristically blank for a moment, before his eyes narrowed in determination. Then he thrust a piece of paper into her hands.

"What is it?" I asked.

Mary read aloud, with Shelley pacing back and forth in front of her, in a state of agitation. His hands even went into his hair a time or two, though the flies didn't seem interested in him. One alighted on Mary's cap, though, as if fascinated by her voice.

III
Whilst thou alone, then not regarded,
The . . . thou alone should be,
To spend years thus, and be rewarded,

> As thou, sweet love, requited me
> When none were near—Oh! I did wake
> From torture for that moment's sake.
>
> IV.
> Upon my heart thy accents sweet
> Of peace and pity fell like dew
> On flowers half dead;—thy lips did meet
> Mine tremblingly; thy dark eyes threw
> Their soft persuasion on my brain,
> Charming away its dream of pain.
>
> V.
> We are not happy, sweet! our state
> Is strange and full of doubt and fear;
> More need of words that ills abate;—
> Reserve or censure come not near
> Our sacred friendship, lest there be
> No solace left for thee and me.
>
> VI.
> Gentle and good and mild thou art,
> Nor can I live if thou appear
> Aught but thyself, or turn thine heart
> Away from me, or stoop to wear
> The mask of scorn, although it be
> To hide the love thou feel'st for me.

He gave her the most anxious of stares as she finished and handed the page back to him. They stared at each other. I was distracted from the electricity between them by a herd of cattle passing by in the street. The rail-thin driving boys with their sticks looked exhausted in the heat. I wished they had lemonade, too.

Mary shook her head as in wonderment, drawing me back in. "Oh, Shelley, it is lovely."

I frowned as I considered the poem. "Who are you kissing, Shelley? Isn't your wife still in Bath?"

He turned his head to me, his lips curving. "Why, yes, so she is, Jane."

Mary's color burned hotter. "Poetry is many things, and not always true to reality."

The bookshop door opened. Mamma stepped through, panting hard. A positive swarm of flies came in. I shrieked and began flailing around with my swatter. Shelley clapped his hands, then dropped a dead fly to the floor.

Mamma looked at us in distaste. Only Mary seemed unmoved, though her hands never stopped moving through the air.

"Keep the door open. They'll soon leave," Mamma said. "Get some water, girls."

I did not need to be told twice and darted for the door, dropping the swatter. I didn't stop running until I was through to the street, for the front hall was not much better. Why was it that flies were more tolerable outdoors?

"They are vile," Mary said when she reached me, holding the ribbons of her bonnet. She had a basket on her arm, and I heard the clink of coins in her skirt as she adjusted it. Shelley followed.

"Let's walk away from the market," I suggested.

"Mamma will be cross. I don't think she meant for us to go for long." Mary considered. "But I do need to buy food."

"It is hot as blazes in the bookshop," Shelley said. "I'm with you, girls. Let's find ourselves a peaceful green field." He took Mary's arm and led her toward Fleet Prison. They smiled at each other, as if they were starting a private adventure.

I trailed behind them, happy to be away from the flies, using

Shelley for shade since I had only my cap and it didn't protect my eyes at all.

The crowds were not bad. I expected the women were all doing laundry, as was common on Monday. Mamma would eventually remember the long task and make us start it, or perhaps the heat would make her too lazy today. No fit housekeeper, I, but I'd never been put in charge of the household.

Men loitered around the prison, as they always did, and the taverns nearby. I saw a man stagger out of one and remove his coat before vomiting in the street. Shocking that he would disrobe so, even in this heat.

We passed carts coming to and from the warehouses and even saw a seller of lemonade, a heavy jug on a tray that was suspended from ribbons around his neck. I licked my lips, but Shelley did not produce any coins. Mary needed what Mamma must have given her to feed the family tonight. We would have to find a public water source to slake our thirst.

The light seemed to flicker. I turned my head to the prison wall to settle my eyes and then spotted a familiar table. The young conjurer had moved from Covent Garden to the prison for his latest prey. Grabbing for Shelley, I stopped him in the road.

"It's that boy again," I hissed. "My bonnet thief!"

"You gambled it away yourself," Shelley said calmly, but he stopped.

Mary smiled at him, looking rather dazed. I fanned her with my hand, then took the basket from her and used it to move the air around her face. After a few seconds, she swatted me away. "You can't confront him, Jane. Your bonnet is long gone."

I stared at the young man. I wanted to use the basket like a weapon and sweep that table free of those little cups and that tiny marble before he robbed anyone else. Not a game, that. A casual bystander could never win against a conjurer, one trained to deceive.

My ire, already naturally high because of the heat, caused me to heft the basket. I prowled in the direction of the table. I could ruin his game and free the neighborhood. His ilk belonged in Covent Garden, not here.

I was halfway there when a strong arm wrapped around my waist and hauled me back. "Stop," Shelley whispered in my ear.

Mary pulled me against the prison wall and put her hand over my mouth when I asked what was going on.

She and Shelley passed looks between them. I put my hand over my eyes and squinted. A woman in quite a nice pink dress and a red silk stole had stopped at the table.

"I suppose I don't want to rescue her," I said sourly. An unaccompanied female dressed like that was hardly an honest woman.

Mary gasped as the conjurer reached behind him into a pack and pulled out a long box. She and Shelley nodded at each other as the box moved into the hands of the woman. No game commenced; she merely walked away.

"What are you nodding about?" I asked but was ignored.

"Will she go into a tavern?" Shelley whispered.

"Should we follow her?" Mary asked.

Shelley shook his head. "No, that is my duty. I will not involve you in violence. I still regret Wales and my family being there when I was attacked."

"What?" I repeated.

"What should we do, Shelley?" Mary asked.

"Go back the way you came. Don't let the conjurer see you," he instructed. "I will return to Skinner Street when I have news."

I took Mary's arm, and we walked backward a couple of steps while Shelley crossed the street in pursuit of the woman. We turned around then and went back toward home.

"We need provisions," Mary said. "And since we have coins, we can go to our usual butcher shop."

"We don't have debt there?"

"Where is my head?" she asked ruefully. "No, you are right. He'll take the coins to pay on our account."

"Being poor is vexing," I said, trying to be cheerful. "How much money do you have?"

She didn't pat her pockets, being too streetwise to alert the boys, who had appeared out of nowhere, lest they try to lighten them once they could see where someone kept their money. "Enough for cheese, and we can give that old woman on the edge of the market a penny for some eggs."

"Sometimes she has a bit of meat, as well," I noted. "It's too hot to cook much, anyway."

"I'll make oatmeal cakes, and that will be enough with the eggs and cheese." She rubbed dust out of her eyes. "But I am most concerned about Shelley. This is murder, Jane. The gun moved from Branwen to this conjurer to where?"

"Shelley will see where the woman went," I said confidently, as if I'd understood all along.

We headed toward the egg woman and were able to collect some fresh eggs and a rind of ham, which would flavor stock, for the price Mary wanted to pay. Then we went into the cheese shop.

"Nothing on account," Mrs. Griffith snapped when she saw us. "Where's that man of yours, Miss Mary?"

"We don't know," she said, setting her remaining coins on the counter with an air of having successfully deceived the shopkeeper. "He left with a messenger, and we haven't heard from him since. Bow Street business probably."

Mrs. Griffith swept the coins away. "That will buy you a nice bit of cheese. Good day for it." She reached behind her then set a wrapped round parcel on the counter.

"Only the best for the neighbors," Mary said warily.

"It's nicely aged, this." Mrs. Griffith smirked. "No one will complain. I know your mother sets a fine table when she can afford it."

"The business is profitable," I said sharply. "My mother does very well for us."

"It's too bad your father can't do the same. So many airs that man puts on."

"My father is all that is benevolent and wise," Mary shot back before picking up the cheese and setting it in her basket.

I wondered why she trusted the woman.

"Benevolent and wise don't pay the bills, my girl." Mrs. Griffith sniffed. "The pair of you would be wise to find work that gives you coins at the end of a day instead of stealing your youth. I'm glad you've found yourself a man, Miss Mary, because all that kitchen work is going to coarsen your pretty skin."

She looked me up and down. "Now, you, you've strength about you, Miss Clairmont. You want a job in the dairy, you just let my husband know. He does the hiring."

"Well, we know it," Mary said, a hard cast to her gaze. "Good day to you, Mrs. Griffith. I hope you'll tell us if there is any more to learn about those poor Davies girls."

I pulled her out of the shop and down the street, then gave her a little push toward the stairs once we were inside. "I'm starving, Mary. Something about that cheese shop makes me feel wild."

"Animal instinct," Mary said. "It isn't safe, for all that I don't think they'll poison us."

I had served three customers by the time Polly came in and said lunch was ready.

Mamma appeared at the announcement as if she'd been summoned by a jinni. She pushed her hair out of her eyes, leaving an inky stain on her forehead. "Keep the bookshop open, Jane. It's good trade today." She set a ledger on the counter. "Check these numbers for me while I'm upstairs. It's too hot to think."

"What about me?" I called to her back.

"I'll bring you a plate." The door shut behind her.

I snarled to myself, hoping Shelley would come soon and relieve the monotony. Pacing about the empty bookshop, I did figures in my head. I found two mistakes Mamma had made before she returned with a tankard of water and a plate.

Mamma shook her head when I showed her my adjustments. "Where is your head, girl?" She pointed at the second figure. "Neither of us has this one right." She snatched up the ledger and returned to her office.

I scarfed up the lukewarm food and drained the tankard, thinking it would make me feel better. Instead, I felt faint after eating. The street noise outside seemed to recede, and saliva pooled in my mouth. I clung to the counter. When footsteps sounded, I didn't even look up.

"What is wrong with you?" Mary demanded.

"I don't feel well."

Mary snatched up a book and fanned me with it. The binding had a Roman name on it, some old history tome. "Sit," she said, then disappeared into the recesses of the bookshop.

Mamma came toward me a couple of minutes later. "Has anyone come in since I went to eat?"

"No, Mamma," I said.

She sighed loudly. "Close the bookshop. I don't need you swooning on the bookshop floor."

I instantly felt a little better.

"Go out to the back garden," Mary said. "I'll lock the doors. It's Monday, anyway."

"Set the clothes to soaking," Mamma said.

I'd known we'd have to do it at some point. Limply, I wandered out and started filling the tubs with clothes.

I felt better by the time Mary and Polly came out with baskets full of linens. I had run water over my wrists and temples until I'd cooled down.

"Do you feel up to hauling water with us?" Mary asked, dumping her basket of linens into the dolly tub.

I nodded. "I couldn't bring myself to start the fire out here, though."

"I'll do it, miss." Polly made quick work of the fire while Mary and I hauled water to the big pot over it; then the three of us went into the house.

"Shelley!" Mary said, finding him inside the front hall.

"I thought we could go hide under the willows," he said. "It's very nearly the hottest part of the day."

"We have to haul water to the tub first," Mary said.

"I can assist," he offered. "If it helps you go faster."

"Indeed." She smiled up at him. "Your muscles will be put to good use, sir."

Mary and Polly already had the largest pots and kettles ready on the fire in the kitchen. We poured the boiling water into buckets to get the process underway; then the four of us hauled them to the garden, trying not to slop too much onto the floors.

Even Shelley looked flushed by the time we had poured all the boiling water over the clothing. "I would be happy to wade back into that marsh."

Mary nodded. "I would, as well, if only the water were clear. I liked your idea of sitting under the willows, though."

"I second that," I added, adding in soap from a large glass jar.

We left Polly with the dolly stick after another round of emptying buckets into the garden receptacles and headed onto the street.

Mary stretched her neck from side to side. "I do not see why washing clothes is women's work. It requires a well-developed musculature."

Shelley flexed his muscles, making Mary laugh. "In my idea of an ideal community, men and women would work and study together."

I had a feeling Shelley did not entirely understand the reality of life for the common man. As the grandson of a baronet, he'd nearly always had servants to do the heavy work. His idea of work involved intellect, not his well-developed musculature.

When I looked up from my thoughts, Mary was running her hands over his arm on the street corner, in sight of everyone. I rolled my eyes. We saw bigger muscles passing by every day on the arms of the men who pushed the carts to and from the warehouses.

After a long, hot walk, we reached the St. Pancras burying ground. As always, we stopped at Mary Wollstonecraft's grave first to pay a respectful visit. This time, though, Mary seemed to be paying more attention to Shelley than the monument. I wanted to seek cool air more than anything else.

"It seems cooler in the marsh," I announced.

"The mud, though," Mary protested.

"It might be dryer now. I'm going to go over there," I told her.

"Take your time," Shelley said. "I need a private conference with Mary."

"Under the willows, where we'll have shade," she added.

"Very well," I said agreeably. I could practice my Italian aria if I was out of earshot. My pronunciation was not the best, and I was too hot and cross for a lesson from Shelley today. For now, I just wanted to get the notes down properly.

I walked toward the marsh as they disappeared into the thicket, and began to run scales, warming up my instrument.

Chapter 12

Mary

Mary's legs trembled as the trio walked out of the burying ground. They had been gone too long and would pay the price for it, no matter the monumental events that had taken place in the interim. Polly would need their help with the laundry, and dinner needed to be provided somehow. The work never ended. All they had were these lissome interludes and then back to toiling.

Jane regarded her with narrowed eyes but said nothing. Was her gait as disordered as her skirts? Shelley whistled, clearly in charity with the world, though he stayed at her side instead of bounding ahead of them, as he so often did.

How little it meant, and how much, what she and Shelley had done in the stand of willows, their bed a blanket of soft grass, within earshot of her mother's resting place. She could still feel him in that sacred, secret place in the recesses of her body. Her hero had enjoyed his reward, and she had experienced *him*. Her parents' daughter, how could she better prove it to herself than this, by giving love freely, without any blessing of church and state, which should have no rights in these matters.

The last time they were there at St. Pancras, she had witnessed a near death. Shelley had saved the child. Now she had experienced the start of new life herself, at his hands, in concert with his body. She was Shelley's now, completely his, had come into her feminine time, and Mr. Fisher would get nothing from her.

If she told her loathed betrothed what she had done with another man, he would likely turn away in disgust, he a man who lived by the old rules, which did not control her life or choices. A happy thought, that.

In fact, she could even be with child now. A child who would revere her, like she did her mother. A child who would be dedicated to Shelley, unlike his child with his wife, who scarcely knew her father. She would not go wandering off, leaving Shelley apart from his offspring, but vowed to follow him to the ends of the earth, if necessary, and not make the mistakes her mother had, either, chasing praise from her lover rather than time with him.

The child, her child, would be blessed to be an offspring of Percy Bysshe Shelley. She glanced at him exactly when he looked in her direction. They shared a secret smile that didn't catch Jane's notice. She was licking her lips in the direction of a strawberry seller.

What a child her stepsister was, not a woman like Mary herself. She had secrets Jane could never understand, the secrets and cares of a woman, who even now could not walk in the same carefree manner of a child. Could it be that she had more in common with the Davies sisters than her own sisters? The dead had secrets, as well.

Winnet had been the paramour of John Griffith, likely in

order to keep her employment, rather than due to a great love or a small one. But she had had a child in her, had maybe died for it.

The thought pained her. Mary's fingers brushed against Shelley's, seeking comfort. He clasped her hand between their bodies and gave her a squeeze before releasing her again. He was right to do so. Caution was warranted now. They could not give the game away before she could figure out how to release herself from Mr. Fisher without any violence, especially as Papa had grown conservative in his old age. He did not seem to care about great love anymore, only comfort and complacency.

How frightening it must be to have lived into one's fifties, to have experienced that growing infirmity of age, and to find no end to troubles in the autumn of one's existence.

Winnet Davies had perhaps been cautious with John Griffith, though he did not seem to have that tendency himself, if he was out in the early hours with paramours. However, Miss Davies had been seen out in public with Charles, too. She had not thought to be cautious with him. In Hyde Park, at the review, anyone in London, in the world, really, could have seen her. Would John Griffith have been angry about that if he'd been told? Murderously so?

If Charles was courting Branwen Davies, behind closed doors at least, why did he fight with her sister in Hyde Park?

"We are missing some part of the story," Mary said aloud.

"What story?" Shelley asked.

"Yes, what?" Jane said, stopping and turning around.

She blocked Mary's path, so Mary stopped, too, then pressed herself against a building. The sun-warmed stone against her back was no relief, but a slight overhang of gutter allowed her head to cool a little.

"I was thinking about secrets," Mary said. "Miss Davies's

secret was her relationship with her employer, and also that she was with child. But in public she had an argument with Charles, whose secret was an entanglement with Branwen Davies."

"Who also had involvement with Mr. Griffith," Shelley said.

"And that conjurer." Jane's upper lip curled. "For he ended up with the gun case in some undetermined fashion."

"You are right," Shelley said.

"Which the pink and red woman now has," Jane continued. "Does she have a connection to the Davies twins?"

Shelley ran his hands through his hair. "I don't think that matters. The gun case is now the paramount issue since the twins are deceased."

Mary touched his arm. Odd that the gesture seemed less natural now that she had given her very life to him. "I am sure Charles is keeping some kind of secret. There is also the possibility that Mr. Griffith thought Charles was poaching on his territory, as it were, and killed Miss Davies because of her being seen with Charles."

Shelley nodded at her solemnly, no hint of the teasing, sweet words under the willows. "Then he must be made to talk. Both of them, really, though it will be a tricky matter with Mr. Griffith."

"Will you speak to Charles today?" Mary asked. "Jane and I must return to the laundry."

"I have an appointment this evening, my dears," he said. "Why don't we go see him together tomorrow? Jane knows him better than anyone and will be best placed to make him talk."

"That's true," Jane said with a wink. "I'm not afraid of a little violence in order to get my brother to talk."

When they reached Skinner Street, Shelley separated from them with a bow. Mary felt dazed when the cooler air hit her on the basement stairs inside. She ran her fingers along the wall as she went down. Black spots danced around her eyes from the effects of the sun. She needed to fill her basin with water and douse her head or tie a wet handkerchief over her head before she swooned. Scotland had never felt this hot, even when she and Isabella had gone for long walks.

When she went into the kitchen, she found Polly there.

"What are you doing here?" Mary asked in a temper, too hot to be calm. "Who is doing the laundry, you lazy thing?"

Polly's nostrils flared. "You stink, Miss Mary, and you had better wash before Mrs. Godwin catches wind of what you have been up to."

"How dare you!" Mary cried, though with her dizziness, her voice sank low rather than rose. She leaned against the table. "I've been out in the hot sun, and my head hurts, that is all."

"I wasn't born yesterday," Polly said with a snicker. "What nonsense is this? You have a man out of town, and you can't manage to keep your legs closed. I thought better of you."

Mary drew her hand into a fist. She did not want to react like Mamma would and slap the insolent servant. But for sure, Polly would never have a place with her if she lost her position with Mamma.

She went to the water butt and dipped water into a tankard, poured it over her head, then filled the tankard again and left the kitchen with it, pretending Polly didn't exist.

It hurt to go up the stairs. Her thighs ached, and the space between them, too. Shelley had said it hurt only the first time, which she hoped was true. She had no time for discomfort. But the sublime experience of becoming one with him trumped any of this silly fussing.

She barred her door after she went into her chamber, and drank half the tankard before pouring the rest into her bowl. No water remained in her jug, either. The household was falling apart with Fanny gone.

After she had done her best to wash away the evidence of her love with Shelley and the exertion of the walk, the basin was in a sorry state indeed.

She made a face and poured the soiled water into the chamber pot, which at least had a cover, then flopped down on her bed. Her fingers went to her notebook, a pencil trapped inside it, that hid under her pillow during the day.

She put the pencil to her lips and wrote. *With an anxiety that almost amounts to agony, I wonder if you feel what I do, Shelley. You have infused a vital spark in me. I am newborn, a child, an angel. You are my delight.*

She had not the words to describe their communion. Shelley had a celestial talent for self-expression, and her parentage indicated she could develop the same, if only she had the space to build her talent.

For now, though, she heard Mamma shouting at Jane through the open window. The laundry must be done.

Life had been at a standstill since they'd arrived home the afternoon before. They hadn't finished with the laundry until dusk. Mamma had been furious, and Mary's arm ached with the pinches she had suffered.

For self-protection, Mary had begged enough coins from Papa to buy some decent lamb and had even baked rolls. The ironing had stolen much of her day, so she hadn't been able to forage for greens, but she'd purchased potatoes and strawberries. Polly had taken enough abuse from Mamma herself to be silent through the day.

When she and sullen Polly carried everything up to the dining room at five, she found Shelley seated across from Papa. He smiled at her, lightning quick, before returning his attention to

Papa's discussion about the latest activities of the foreign dignitaries. She knew Shelley wouldn't give anything away.

In fact, Jane was the only one to act like she had a secret. After dinner, she suggested a walk, with a lot of exaggerated facial expressions. Mary remembered well that they were going to confront Charles that night, but she still felt sore and languid after her tryst with Shelley under the willows. Having Shelley so near but so untouchable just made the memories, and the sensations of her awakened body, more intense.

"I'd like some coffee tonight," Papa said, ignoring Jane and focusing on Mary. "It is cooler."

"I'll make it," Mary said, rising, keeping her expression calm, despite the twinge that went through her, then went out of the room and down to the kitchen, carrying the first load of dishes. Why couldn't Jane have a pain in her head tonight and leave her and Shelley alone to do the interview with Charles?

Polly wasn't even in the kitchen when Mary went down, and she'd left a dirty plate from her own meal on the table. Mary set the dishes she'd carried onto Polly's plate, then tossed an apron over her head.

Since Mary couldn't complain to Mamma about her servant for fear of what Polly might reveal, she prepared the coffee herself for Papa, then mixed it with water and a bit of sugar and placed it on the fire to warm.

She poured out the foam a couple of times, then emptied the pan into a tankard for Papa, wondering why Polly hadn't appeared. The servant had better come in to do the dishes soon. Really, she couldn't let Polly get away with this. What did she have to fear from the girl, in truth? Shelley was Papa's disciple and benefactor. Mamma could do nothing worse than she'd already done for fear of alienating him.

Mary felt warmth flow through her body, righteous indignity that needed release. No, Mamma had nothing worse to offer. Did she not now stand in a basement kitchen, over a fire in the heat of summer? She pulled off the apron and wiped her face dry, then drank lustily from the water butt before picking up the hot tankard.

When she went into the passage to get to the stairs, Polly was coming down them, looking furtive.

"What are you up to?" Mary demanded.

Polly made a face at her and said nothing. As she attempted to pass by, Mary grabbed the girl's arm. "I'm not going to tolerate this from you. You aren't being mistreated."

"You can't tell me what to do," Polly taunted. "Or I'll tell Mrs. Godwin what you've been up to."

Mary snorted. "I've thought it through. Feel free to tell her what you think you know about me, but Mamma has a fast hand, and you're more likely to be slapped for insolence than to create any worse trouble." She stared Polly directly in the eye. "Think about what happened to Thérèse before you make any final decisions."

Polly went pale at the memory of their former cook's fate. Mary smirked and passed by. Now she'd made herself safe.

Papa gave her such a sweet smile when she came in that a flush of tenderness filled her heart. Whatever Shelley was to her, Papa surely had pride of place in her bosom. She set down the coffee then squeezed his shoulder.

"My good girl," Papa said with another smile.

Mary sat, then noticed that Shelley did not look pleased. "I'm sorry. Did you want coffee?"

He shook his head, then turned to Jane and started making plans for a walk.

When Papa had finished his coffee, Mamma dismissed them. Mary and Jane took the last dishes downstairs and found Polly scrubbing utensils in the scullery, looking morose. Then they went back up, where Shelley waited in the front hall.

When they went into the street, Shelley took Mary's arm and

marched her around the side of the house quickly, away from Jane.

"I thought you had chosen me," he said. "Why all this affection for your father?"

"What does it matter?" Mary asked, confused by his frowns.

"I need all your love. You know how broken I am, Mary sweet," Shelley expostulated. "I have been betrayed in the most terrible ways. I need to be able to trust you."

"Shelley, what is this concern? Have I not given you all of myself?" Mary asked, her voice trembling. How could she reassure him?

"When your papa asked you to perform a task, you did it without even glancing at me. I am concerned you will choose his needs over mine." Shelley took his hand from her arm and tore at his hair.

Her hand hung in the air for a moment before she lowered it, unable to move without his direction. What had she done to torment him so? "I will not. I would never. I have chosen you, my love."

"What would you do to keep your papa out of the sponging house, I wonder?" Shelley said, his face contorting. "Marry? Give yourself to another?"

"No, no," Mary promised. "I am yours forever."

Strands of his hair drifted in the breeze when he pulled his fingers away. "To keep Charles out of trouble, you agreed to marry Mr. Fisher. What of that, Mary? How can I trust you?"

"You have everything that is me," she repeated. "Papa is happy, laboring under the power of my deception. I agreed to marry Mr. Fisher, but I never will. It is all false. I am entirely yours. Mr. Fisher is out of town and not following us anymore. He does not know where Charles is, and therefore, he has no power over me."

"We should not go see him again," Shelley warned, his brow

lowering. "I would not trust a Bow Street Runner to disregard what he considers his own."

Mary pressed her lips together, tears of frustration welling up in her eyes. "I live under my father's roof. What am I to do about Mamma? I have to keep going through the motions of rescuing Charles from suspicion. Papa expects me to keep her happy."

"Your papa knows so little about what is going on in his household that he isn't even aware of where Charles is now."

Desperation made her words come out in staccato puffs. "I cannot lie to my father. He is the best of men. We would never have met, you and I, if you did not revere him."

"He is a tyrant to his daughters." Spittle flew from Shelley's lips. "You are in a terrible position."

She ungracefully wiped tears from her eyes. "Yes. I don't know what to do."

"You have too many burdens on you, you and Jane both." He rubbed his mouth. "Something bad is going to happen. I feel it."

Jane came up to them. Mary couldn't tell if she had been listening or was entirely oblivious to their heated conversation. "The sun is still oppressive. I almost think I would be better off in the basement, doing the dishes, if I could get the grease off the plates with cold water."

"Hot is best," Mary said. "Cold doesn't work well." Warm, salty tears stung her eyes.

Jane sighed. "Don't cry, Mary. Charles won't like it. Aren't we going to go see him?"

"Fine," Shelley said through gritted teeth. "Let's not say his name in the street. We can simply claim to be visiting the Hookhams."

Jane nodded. "We've got to find that gun case, haven't we?"

"It's the key to the whole thing, I expect," Mary said. "Somehow, it went from Branwen to that conjurer, and Charles said it never showed up in her room."

"She must have taken it to the conjurer that night," Jane offered. "I wonder where he lives."

"We'll make your brother tell us Miss Davies's haunts," Shelley said. "We'll go to all of them and describe him. Someone will know something."

"That's very wise of you," Mary praised, glad the focus was off her again. "Solving murders is a lot of walking around and talking to people. We need more people to investigate."

Chapter 13

Jane

Shelley told me he needed five minutes to consult with Mary about our plan to interrogate my brother, but his throat was parched. Eager to accommodate him, as always, I ran into the house to get him water. When I returned, Mary's face was tear-stained, but Shelley seemed calmer than he had been earlier.

The heat was getting to both of them, I supposed. I felt that way myself as we made our way to Old Bond Street. Shelley had been the sensible one, requesting water.

London had taken to the streets. Straw hats and bonnets were on every head, and women had removed the long sleeves from their dresses in order to stay cool. Men were red in the face, not being able to take off their coats out of decency, but at least many had the money to pay for refreshments. Dozens were huddled around taverns and even more around street sellers, drinking vessels in hands.

When we reached Covent Garden, Mary begged for something to drink. I could hardly swallow for the dust myself. "We're dying of thirst," I told Shelley.

"Wait here," he said and went into a tavern behind a bank of market stalls.

"I really don't like this area anymore," Mary said. "I am most ready to leave London."

"This is where Mr. Fisher was born," I said, spreading my arms. "This is literally where you're going to spend your days once you marry."

She shuddered. "I will never marry him, Jane."

"Of course you will. Papa said so."

She shook her head. "It will never happen. I promise you that."

"You'll be married in a month," I said less certainly. "Will I live with you then? You'll need someone to help."

"Where would you sleep? At least in Skinner Street you have a bedroom." Mary's gaze wandered from me and fixed on a lemonade seller. Next to him, someone was doing a brisk business in sandwiches and another in buns. Children darted around them, kicking rocks through the dust or chasing each other, calling merrily.

I relaxed, for if they turned out to have light fingers, I had nothing for them to steal. "Take me with you, Mary. I don't want to stay at home. I wouldn't be able to bear it."

"You're needed for the bookshop. That is your fate until you find a husband of your own."

"What is wrong with you, Mary?" I said, feeling cross. "I don't want a husband."

"Then working in the bookshop is the best thing for you to do. It's safe. It's indoors."

"It can't last." I rubbed dirt from the corners of my eyes. "The best I can do is gain experience until it all falls apart, and then what? No, I need to go, too. Maybe Charles and I can do something together while you're busy being a wife."

"Where is Shelley, I wonder?" Mary said, turning around. "He should have been back by now." She put up her hand to cough into it; then her eyes went wide.

I followed her gaze. "What is it?"

"That conjurer is back again."

I saw him then. The youth stood behind his little table, his cups set out in a neat row of three. He juggled three marbles while trying to entice a couple of giggling girls into his web. Their bonnets were no finer than mine had been, but a market existed for clothing in any condition.

"This isn't the same part of Covent Garden that he was in before. He must move around a lot." I watched him entice the girls with delicate movements of his hands, growing more agitated with each finger's flutter.

"All the better to run guns through the city. I wonder what they are for?"

"Nothing good." I shivered despite the heat. "What has Charles mixed himself up in?"

"Nothing, most probably. He never saw anything, and it isn't as if Papa's teachings would incite him to violence. He was raised by the mildest man in London."

Better his influence on my brother than Shelley's. Though he had made it clear he didn't want women mixed up in violence, he'd brought it toward him, nonetheless. So had I, in some of my more foolish moments.

Before I thought any further about it, I ran forward, waving my arms. "Get away from him," I called to the girls. "You won't have a fair chance. He'll take your money or your things."

One of the girls glanced toward me. "What?"

"He took my bonnet," I cried. "Don't risk what you can't afford to lose. He's a trickster, a conjurer."

The young man looked me. Mary came up beside me. He blanched; then the marbles and cups disappeared into his coat. The table was in his arms in an instant, the legs folded. He took off at a run, leaving all four of us with our mouths open.

One of the girls turned to Mary. She played with her bonnet strings as she asked, "Why is he afraid of you?"

She shook her head. "I have no idea, but he may be mixed up in bad doings. Anyone like that is just there to take your money. It's how they earn their daily bread."

"It's just a bit of fun," said the other girl, plump and radiant in her corn-colored gown.

"It isn't, though," I explained. "I can't explain, but he might be mixed up in some bad things."

"Like bonnet theft?" The first girl giggled and pulled the other girl away from me.

I shrugged and turned back to Mary. "La, what an odd reaction."

"He might know we saw the gun case, but he passed it off, so what does he fear?" Mary said.

Shelley came out of the tavern, holding a tankard. "It's a weak beer, girls. I tried it myself."

I took it and downed precisely half, then told Shelley about the conjurer. Mary drained the rest, then burped delicately before passing it back to Shelley.

Our friend shook his head. "I don't like this. We should tell Bow Street."

"What good would that do?" I asked. "They only take cases they've been paid for."

"Someone ought to know about guns circulating around London, with the kind of elevated personages who are here right now," Shelley said. He licked his lower lip. "The Home Office perhaps, though they are no friends of mine."

"We could write Mr. Fisher," I suggested. "He could contact the Home Office. I'm sure he'd know the right people."

Mary shook her head next to me. Her color had changed somewhat, growing pale instead of rosy with impending sunburn. I thought she looked ill.

"Have you had too much sun?" I asked.

She let her eyelids flutter down for a moment. "I want no part of Mr. Fisher."

"I know, Mary," Shelley said gently. "But the conjurer's behavior is clear evidence that something untoward is going on."

Mary pursed her lips. "I want to go home. I need to rest. My side hurts."

"You drank too quickly," Shelley said.

"You can go home." I put my hand on Shelley's shoulder. "We are halfway to the Hookhams' house already."

Shelley regarded Mary closely. "Jane, we can't leave Mary alone. Let's take her back. I'll call at Hookhams' tomorrow." He moved away from us, and we attempted to follow.

I had no idea why Mary had begun to walk with short, shuffling steps, but concerned, I put my arm around her and helped her along with my longer strides.

"Did you fall on the stairs?" I asked.

She shook her head. "I have a pain in my side. I just need to rest."

"I hope that beer wasn't bad." I felt fine, though.

We made slow progress through the streets, stopping at a public water source to slake our thirst and bathe our heads. We were nearly dry again by the time we came to Skinner Street, though the sun had visibly dipped on the horizon. Soon the wind would likely pick up and drive the heat from London.

Despite the hour, I saw a tall, bulky man in front of the bookshop windows.

Mary gave a little gasp, and I realized Mr. Fisher had returned to town. We were at the end of her reprieve and hadn't known it.

Still, eagerness filled me, for here we had a professional fighter against crime, and we needed one.

I took my arm from Mary's waist and darted to Mr. Fisher. "Sir," I called. "You have come just in time to hear a curious story."

"What is that?" he asked. His eyes were shadowed with exhaustion, though he'd taken the time to be barbered properly. It spoke well that he would not come to his betrothed's house fresh from the road, or wherever he had been.

"It is a tale of a gun case and a very wicked conjurer," I explained, hoping to entice him, but he said nothing, only stared wearily at me.

As I spoke, Mary and Shelley came alongside.

Over my words, Mr. Fisher exclaimed, "What are you doing out on so hot a night, Miss Mary? You look ready to faint."

She sneered faintly. "Do you think the kitchen any less warm, sir?"

"There is no breeze tonight," he warned.

"The air will move again soon," I said. "Aren't you concerned about the gun case? I know there isn't anyone to pay you to search for it, but you have all those informants, don't you? Someone who can find out the identity of this conjurer and his accomplice, the woman in red and pink?"

"I doubt it would come to much," Mr. Fisher said after he gave me a minute to explain.

"I disagree, sir," Shelley said. "Gun cases usually hold guns."

"Not among the poorer classes. The conjurer likely has a better fence than the woman has access to."

"This case moved from a tavern at Smithfield to Fleet Prison. It has some significance, I am certain," Shelley said, nearly snarling. Even his posture had elongated, and he held his head back, offering some sort of challenge to the wider man.

Mr. Fisher crossed his arms over his massive chest. "Call on your father and acquire some funds to hire me, then, if you think it so important."

"We cannot even afford a bonnet," I cried. "Be reasonable, Mr. Fisher. You know how many royalties there are in London right now. We even had a princess call here at Skinner Street more than once. Who knows what mischief that gun case could bring. Think of England's reputation."

Shelley described the woman in pink and red in detail while Mary feebly waved her bonnet back and forth in front of her sweaty face. Only a poet could have memorized a face and a shape so completely. I did not remember half of the details, though I could give a fair account of the conjurer and did so until Mr. Fisher yawned.

"Stay out with me tonight," Shelley urged. "Jane should take Mary to her rest. The sun has touched her a bit."

Mr. Fisher yawned again. "Fine. I will retrace your steps with you."

"We have seen the conjurer in Covent Garden twice. You know that area. I am sure you will recognize him," Shelley said. "You may already know his history. We'll go to a coffeehouse and wake you up."

Mr. Fisher took Mary's very limp hand in his. "I am sorry you are unwell, Miss Mary. Stay out of the sun tomorrow."

She offered a rictus of a smile back, then pulled her hand from his to take my arm, with rather more strength than she should have been able to summon.

I unlocked the door and took her inside. We went directly up the stairs, but then she stopped on the landing.

"I am so afraid that Papa will force me to marry Mr. Fisher no matter what is happening with Shelley." She pulled off her gloves and put her hands against her breastbone.

"What is happening with Shelley?" I asked, frowning.

"Mrs. Shelley is gone. He said she is nothing but his sister now, like you, Jane."

"They are married, though," I said, confused.

"It's not his child in her belly. Shelley has sworn it, Jane."

I sighed and pulled her back downstairs again; then we went to the basement, to the water butt. I knew she needed a good drink of water. Once she had drunk her fill, I pushed her onto a stool.

"We've known about the baby for a long time," I said, sitting. "And we know Mrs. Shelley travels to London all the time."

"You don't understand," Mary crooned. "We're in love, Shelley and I. True love."

"True love?" I repeated.

"Yes, Jane." Mary smiled, the exhaustion suddenly leaving her face so that only the fairy princess remained. Mrs. Shelley, about Fanny's age, was a true beauty, but in that moment, Mary outshone her. "He loves me deeply, and I have pledged myself to him."

"Then you must be protected," I said, bespelled by her radiance. "I'll help."

"Do you promise?" she asked.

"Of course." I clasped my hands over my heart. "True love. You've never been in love before."

"No," Mary said and took my glass, then drained it, too.

I retrieved the glass from her and set it against my throat. "I must say I am delighted to know that you have thrown off the shackles of conventionality and are acting more in the true spirit of Wollstonecraft's daughter than you usually do. Your love for such an excellent character as Shelley does you credit."

"He is excellent," Mary agreed. "To think of everything he has tried to do for Papa."

"I am sorry we had to send him away, but we would have had to entertain Mr. Fisher if we had not."

"He was acting in my best interest, as always." Mary rubbed her eyes. "I am for bed now, though."

"That would be wise." I set the glasses on the table, then popped off my stool and offered her my hand. "Go to bed, Shelley's true love. He'll want to see you blooming and happy."

"I will only be that once Mr. Fisher is out of my life." She offered me a weary smile, squeezed my hand, and left the kitchen.

*   *   *

Wednesday had been a normal sort of day. I waited for Shelley to arrive to tell us if he'd learned any new information about the gun case and the people involved. Instead, we had a dusting of customers, the usual disaffected tutors and impoverished lady teachers from small schools, buying the poorest-quality ink.

After lunch, the sun came out and made the bookshop very hot, which in turn made me very sleepy. I propped open the bookshop door to the front hall in the hopes that the air would move.

I was yawning behind the counter when I heard a sharp knock on the outer door. Rubbing my eyes, I said aloud, "Don't people know they can just come in?"

I sighed and used the corner of my apron to wipe the sweat off my upper lip while I walked to the door. When I opened it, I found Constable Wharton there.

"Good afternoon." I wiped my hands down my apron, too hot for fear. "What can I do for you, Constable?"

"Miss Clairmont," he said in the formal tone he'd adopted after Charles's troubles began. "Are your parents at home?"

"I don't think Papa is here, but Mamma is in her office. Come through, if you like," I invited.

He came in, taking off his hat, and followed me into the bookshop, then looked around. "I've never been in here before."

"Do you like to read?" I asked, hoping he was in fact literate.

He seemed confused by the question. "Do you have a lending library?"

"No, sir. We carry mostly children's books, and the books wouldn't survive to the next person, so Mamma says." I didn't suppose being a constable paid enough for books. It was too low of a position. I led him through the bookshelves until we came to the office. The door stood open here, as well. I could see the sheen on Mamma's face.

She wiped it with a handkerchief as she stood. "Constable?" Her voice wobbled. "Do you have news about my son?"

The constable reached into his coat. "Do you, madam?"

She shook her head. "I do not know where he is. I had hoped that our family's Bow Street Runner friend might be of assistance, but he was called out of town."

"Mr. Fisher?" the constable asked. "He is in London."

"We saw him last night," I said when Mamma glared at me. "But only for a moment in the street. I don't even know what he was doing out of town."

"Chasing a gang of robbers who had robbed an estate in Essex," the constable said. "Nothing to do with the matter of Mr. Clairmont."

Mamma shrugged. "I have nothing to tell you, sir. I wish I knew he was safe."

The constable pulled his hand out of his coat, clutching a folded piece of paper. "A warrant for his arrest has been issued."

"Because of the inquest?" Mamma asked.

The constable shook his head. "No, a magistrate has ordered his arrest for murder."

Mamma swayed and grabbed at the desk. I clutched her arm as she spoke. "What? Why?"

"Nobody knows anything," I argued. "Why are they so fixated on my brother?"

"He is the link between the two dead girls," the constable said.

"They are the link between themselves," I said. "Twins. And what about John Griffith? He's a far more compelling suspect than Charles."

"John Griffith is right down the street, doing his work like an innocent man," the constable said. "It is your brother who has vanished. One can only assume he harbors a guilty conscience."

"He harbors a heart full of fear," Mamma said. "He's very young. Mr. Griffith may know how to act the part, but what does a boy of nineteen know?"

The constable brandished his paper. "You need to give him up, madam."

"I cannot," Mamma said, spreading her hands. They had sweaty circles of black ink on them. "I cannot help you."

"I know something." The words were out of my mouth before I could think better of it.

"What do you know, Miss Clairmont?" the constable asked.

I glanced at Mamma. Her frightened gaze compelled me to come up with a convincing lie, and fast. "I, er—"

"What?" Constable Wharton demanded again, losing his amiable air entirely.

I feared to be arrested myself. "I . . . we had another letter from him."

"Where is this letter?" he asked.

I straightened to my full height. "I burned it."

"Why?" He tilted his head.

"Because I was irritated. He is refusing to leave Bath."

"He is in Bath?" the constable asked, his wirelike gray brows folding together.

"Yes, we told Mr. Fisher when the first letter came." I glanced at Mamma. "Last week. A professor of natural philosophy sacked his assistant and hired Charles just before he went out of town."

"How convenient." The constable's tone had gone sour.

I bristled. "He couldn't stay here and be harassed by the authorities. You should go there and stop bothering us in London."

"Jane," Mamma admonished. "Constable Wharton is simply trying to do his job."

"It isn't very far," I said. "Mrs. Shelley comes and goes from there regularly."

The constable inhaled, filling out his scrawny old man's chest for a moment. "I will inform the proper authorities, but I am appalled by the lack of consideration the Godwin family has for the relatives of the dead girls."

"What relatives?" I asked. "We have heard of none. And have received no consideration from your persecution."

"Jane," Mamma snapped. "That is enough. Show the constable out."

I went to the bookshop door and gestured him through, then glanced at Mamma again. She shook her head at me, but what could I have done but lie? I couldn't tell the constable where Charles really was.

Chapter 14

Mary

In the early afternoon, Mary left Polly to finish the ironing and went upstairs to beg Papa for some coins for food.

"Shouldn't that come from Mamma?" he asked, scarcely glancing up from the translation on his desk. He was still working on *The Swiss Family Robinson*.

"I heard her having words with Jane earlier. I thought it best to leave her to her private thoughts." Mary shifted from side to side. "She would do well to have a good meal tonight, don't you think?"

Papa unlocked his desk and handed over a few small coins. Mary took that as agreement.

"A small joint of beef?" Papa suggested. "We have had a lot of ham and seafood of late."

"I will see what I can do." She hesitated. "It is difficult because we are behind on so many of the local accounts."

He unlocked his desk again and handed over a guinea. "If that can't clear an account, we are in more difficulties than I realized."

Mary smiled and tried not to snatch it too eagerly. Their household did tend to spread small amounts across many shops. "This will help a tremendous amount, I am sure. Thank you."

She went down and saw, from the landing, Shelley in the hallway, a golden nimbus around his hair from the sun streaming in through the window. Her pulse leapt at the vision. It suited his angelic nature. "What are you doing here, sir, so early in the day? I am going to the butcher shop." She ran down the stairs, then held out her hand to him in utter abandon.

He took it and gave her a gentle squeeze before carefully releasing her. "I'll come with you." He offered the secret smile, creasing his cheeks into near dimples, that he'd used to such devastating effect on her under the willows, after he had poured out all the secrets of his heart, emptied himself really. She'd never felt such pure tenderness for another creature, or such a desire to protect a tender soul.

She grabbed her bonnet and opened the door to another windless day, the sky a nearly uniform blue. He stepped out behind her.

"Are you sure?" she asked. "I know you cannot be comfortable in a butcher shop."

"The air in this area reeks of animal scents as it is," Shelley said. "It is not much worse in an actual shop."

"I am eager to get away for once and for all, as is Jane." Mary let her arm brush against his as she led the way, watchful for pickpockets. "Do you think Papa might send us away, like he did Fanny, if I profess my love for you?"

Shelley didn't laugh. "I think not. It would move the marriage forward all the faster, perhaps."

"I've seen no sign that Mr. Fisher can afford a license," Mary said. "He always wears the same coat, have you noticed? One wonders if he will be able to clothe me."

"From what I've heard, he does very well, not that it matters. You will not have him."

Mary heard his voice go tight. She had shown too much interest in Mr. Fisher for Shelley's taste. "No, he will not," she agreed, then peeked into the cheese shop window as they passed. She didn't recognize the girl behind the counter.

When they were some five minutes away from the house, Shelley stopped her. She leaned against the wall of a warehouse and looked up to him. "I can't be gone for long. Papa wants a joint."

"I just wanted to give you these. I know you've read your father's copies, but I wanted you to have ones of your very own. I've matured a lot since I wrote them, but still." He smiled at her, then pulled two small books from his coat.

The first, she saw, had her name printed on the calf binding. It was his *A Refutation of Deism*. The second was his *Queen Mab*. He'd written her name in pencil inside, Mary Wollstonecraft Godwin, branding it hers. And there on the flyleaf, she read, "You see, Mary, I have not forgotten you." Smiling, she flipped through the beloved text, noting the tiny printed hands that highlighted his most important footnotes.

She knew the footnotes by heart. He proposed that marriage should continue only so long as there was mutual love. Ideally, marriage would be abolished and, along with it, the notion of enduring relationships.

"'Love is free,'" she read. "'To promise for ever to love the same woman is not less absurd than the promise to believe the same creed.'"

She turned back to the dedication and saw the words he'd carefully inked, apparently at some time other than when he'd written to her, underneath the printed inscription to his faithless wife. She read, "Count Slobendorf was about to marry a woman, who, attracted solely by his fortune, proved her selfishness by deserting him in prison."

Mary's heart broke for him and the deception perpetuated on him by Harriet Shelley when he was ill, for all the conspiring her older sister had done with Mamma to get at his money.

Poor Shelley had been so betrayed. Harriet had married up socially, but doing so had cost her husband a healthy allowance from his noble family, causing her to fall back on her father and him to beg for the charity of friends.

"You can count on me." Her heart was full as she closed the books and held them protectively in front of her heart. "I will be true unto death, even."

He leaned in close to her ear, making her sensitive skin there tingle. "I long to kiss you again."

"If only," she whispered back, turning her head so that his breath dusted along her mouth. "I am desperate to be alone with you again."

His smile bloomed slowly along his lips. She recognized the intent behind the glint in his eye now.

"We will manage it. Jane is our good guardian," he said.

"She is such a child. She has no idea." Mary shook her head. They were so close that her bonnet brushed his cheek.

"I am glad of that. We will walk again soon." He winked at her, then stepped back so that they could continue on to the butcher shop.

He stopped in the street when they arrived. "Go in alone," he suggested. "It gives a better appearance of poverty."

She chuckled. The door opened, and out came a woman with a bonnet decorated with an overabundance of silk flowers. She glanced at Shelley and, clearly liking what she saw, glanced up and down him again with a carnivorous air. Mary blanked her expression and went in. Shelley would have no use for the dried-up face under the bonnet. The woman must be at least thirty.

Inside, she made her deal with the butcher and handed over Papa's coins. When she walked out again with her joint wrapped in paper and string, all that money gone for this small bit of meat, it mattered not, for Shelley was there, the sun shining down on his face, casting his skin in gold. His eyes creased with joy when he saw her, the emotion reflected in her brow, as well.

They walked beside each other without speaking, the fabric of his coat and her dress swishing against each other. Luckily, no boys came to try to knock the meat from her hands, for she was scarcely aware of anything but the beating of her heart and the heat brewing low in her belly.

When the bookshop came into view, she saw a streaming mass of children, like ants going into a hill, through the wide open door. "Business looks good," she gasped, blinking as if coming out of a dream.

"You'll have to have Polly mop the floor," Shelley said. "The dust is floating off of them."

Mary rubbed her nose, feeling the summer dust there, too.

"You are now, Mary, going to mix with many, and for a moment I shall depart, but in the solitude of your chamber, I shall be with you," he said solemnly.

"I wish I could go to my chamber and look over the books you have given me," she said.

"It's a poor gift. I know you've read it all before."

She stepped close to him, hoping to feel his breath on her lips again. "It is your heart you give me, your soul in the words from your pen. I prize them dearly." She smiled tremulously, then ran downstairs into the cooler recesses of the house with the precious meat.

When she arrived, she found the kitchen empty. Muttering with the irritation that quickly replaced delight, she opened her package, then rubbed the meat with butter and rosemary, before coaxing the kitchen fire to life. Even underground, it would be a hot afternoon with the fire going.

To amuse herself, she recited poetry. Despite her happy mood, a rather sad poem came to her as she staked the flesh of the unhappy cow over the fire: Lord Byron's poem "To Thyrza," from some three years before. As she went along, trying to remember it, the words slipped into her mind, and she found herself reciting it aloud.

> *Ours too the glance none saw beside;*
> *The smile none else might understand;*
> *The whisper'd thought of hearts allied,*
> *The pressure of the thrilling hand;*
>
> *The kiss, so guiltless and refined,*
> *That Love each warmer wish forbore;*
> *Those eyes proclaim'd so pure a mind,*
> *Even Passion blush'd to plead for more.*

Amazing that the poet had written words years ago that related to her life today so well. And Shelley... How did Lord Byron know a man he'd never met? Jane had had some scant interaction with the poet, and Papa knew him, of course, but Mary didn't think Lord Byron had met Shelley.

Poets truly had an immortal gift. Shelley believed so much in the community of like-minded souls that they would have to come upon each other somehow.

Once she had the meat roasting, she cleaned her hands and pulled a pen and a mostly empty bottle of ink from behind the tea chest on the shelf.

She sat down at the table and opened *Queen Mab*. There, as she stared at the endpapers, part of Lord Byron's almost prophetic poem came to her again. *Ours too the glance that none saw beside.*

Shelley's book, gifted to her, deserved something of herself. She inked her pen, and the words flowed from her.

> *This book is sacred to me, and as no other creature*
> *shall ever look into it, I may write what I please. Yet*
> *what shall I write? That I love the author beyond all*

powers of expression, and that I am parted from him. Dearest and only love, by that love we have promised to each other, although I may not be yours, I can never be another's. But I am thine, exclusively thine.

*By the kiss of love, the glance none saw beside,
The smile none else might understand,
The whispered thought of hearts allied,
The pressure of the thrilling hand.*

I have pledged myself to thee, and sacred is the gift. I remember your words. "You are now, Mary, going to mix with many, and for a moment I shall depart, but in the solitude of your chamber I shall be with you." Yes, you are ever with me, sacred vision.

*But ah! I feel in this was given
A blessing never meant for me,
Thou art too like a dream from heaven
For earthly love to merit thee.*

Tears stained the page as she wrote until she could manage no more, and the meat needed to be turned, besides.

The ceiling still sounded with running feet as she rose and went to the spit. She ought to help Jane with whatever was transpiring upstairs, but perhaps Shelley had gone to assist. Or Mamma. Or at least the porter.

She turned and basted the meat again. Upstairs, the footsteps had developed a rhythm, as if the children were playing a game.

Polly came in with a bundle of her own, then looked up and frowned. "What is that noise?"

"Lots of children upstairs," Mary said. "Where have you been?"

Polly untied her bundle. "Your mamma sent me off with a

letter to post for someone, and I was given potatoes and a cabbage in return. I'll make soup."

Mary nodded and returned to her joint. Polly muttered about the heat and the lack of beer in the house and a pain in her arm. Mary drowned her out, dreaming up one of her Gothic story ideas, this time with Shelley and Fisher in it.

Bysshe, the Pure; or, The Lover of Truth.

A Romance; in which is depicted the terrible trials of Bysshe, son of Nature, who was tormented and abused by the untimely betrothal of his true love to the monstrous and wicked Denarius. Upon watching Bysshe being forced to witness the wedding under the stern countenance of his love's bankrupt father, and the horrors of the wedding night, she expired from longing for his pure heart, and, after Bysshe went into the water to lay down his life in his despair, was kidnapped by a dastardly constable of the watch in order to multiply his suffering. Bysshe, too weak from his sorrow to fight, ready to die in his dungeon chains, until being rescued by the faithful sister of his love, who nursed him until his eternal rest, where his soul would be joined with his love.

Poor Shelley, to be tormented so by her troubles. She smiled to herself and began to edit the idea in her head. Why did the heroine have to suffer such deep troubles? Surely it was enough that Bysshe thought her in desperate straits. Perhaps instead of expiring after the wedding night, she could flee to a convent or a school or something and return at the end to cry beautifully over his grave, which, of course, would be a manly, erect monument, possibly with a statue of a weeping cherub standing guard.

"What have you got to be humming about?" Polly asked irritably. "Haven't I just been telling you that your mother is copying out letters for the sake of a few coins to feed this family?"

"Papa gave me more than a guinea for meat," Mary said. "Which one of them is playacting, I wonder?"

Polly gave her an unusually shrewd glance. "I am glad you

are wondering, miss. If we can play them against each other better, we might set a good table again. They never could stand their old cook's hysterics."

"So we need to be hysterical in order to serve delicious meals again?"

Polly put her finger to her nose. "They can find the coin to relieve their own suffering."

"It just drives them deeper into debt in the end," Mary reminded her. She wished she could look at Papa's books. He'd managed to terminate his most pressing debt not too long ago. How much was left, and how dire was it? No one, especially not Papa, would consider it any business of his daughters', no matter how much it affected the state of their bellies.

"I will be leaving soon," she said dolefully. "It won't matter to me much longer."

"We'll see about that, with you so unenthusiastic about your bridegroom," Polly said. "He might actually care, once he notices."

"If only," Mary said. "It would make my life simpler."

She left Polly to the dinner preparations and went upstairs, carrying a broom, to tidy the dining room. In the front hall, she heard a knock on the door and cautiously opened it.

On the pavement stood a man of middle years with a very prominent nose and an unshaven chin. "Mrs. Godwin, if you please, girl," he said.

"What is this about?" Mary asked.

He sneered. "As if I would tell the business of a lady of the house to a servant. Fetch your mistress and be fast about it."

Mary shut the door in his face and, still holding the broom, went into the bookshop. It must be some personal business for Mamma to be called a lady of the house rather than the proprietress of the Juvenile Library.

"Sweeping the bookshop?" Jane asked as she passed by.

"Dining room," Mary said.

"Give it here, then. I can do the floor." Jane moved from behind the counter and pounced on the broom.

"You must be bored. What happened to all those children?"

"Nothing but pencils. They were having a lesson about money. Enormous family."

"All one?" Mary said.

"No, there was some mention of cousins." Jane shrugged and went to the door with the broom.

Mary looked down as she crossed the bookshop. Crumbs and dust fairly littered the floor. A children's bookshop was not safe from children.

She knocked on the office door, then stuck her head in. Mamma looked cross and sweaty behind her desk, her plump arms shiny with perspiration. "You have a man waiting for you in the street. He wouldn't tell me what it was about."

Mamma stretched her neck, then stood.

"It is stifling in here," Mary said. "Should you work in the parlor?"

"That is never done," Mamma said. "The parlor must always be ready for guests."

"The scullery, then," Mary said, then laughed. "It is cool."

Mamma shook her head dispiritedly and walked out. Mary joined Jane, since she had the broom. Jane pointed to the floor, so Mary knelt and held the dustpan.

"I can't dump it into the street now," she said.

"Put it in Mamma's bin in the office," Jane said. "I'm going to listen at the door. Who is the caller?"

"A creditor," Mary guessed. "Not a nice sort at all."

When she returned from the office, she joined Jane at the bookshop door. Mamma had not taken the man into the parlor. In fact, she was talking to him through a crack in the front door. Rather odd.

"I think it's about money," Jane whispered.

"Isn't it always?" Mary whispered back.

Not thirty seconds later, Mamma slammed the front door shut, making the house shake. She turned on her heel and stomped back into the bookshop.

Mary and Jane jumped back as she came through the door.

Mamma stopped, her mouth working, then said, "Worthless daughters." She threw up her hand. "All the expense of worthless daughters, educated above their stations."

"Mamma," Jane cried. "Are we not both working?"

Mamma's eyes closed into slits. "I cannot wait for Mary's wedding. One less of you to deal with."

Jane's lips trembled. Mary snatched the broom. "I've never seen that man before in my life. What did he have to do with me? He had no idea who I was."

"A creditor, always a creditor."

Curiosity piqued Mary's interest. "Why did he ask for you and not Papa?"

"I borrowed the money for Charles from him, and now he turns up, suggesting you might need a dowry." Mamma barked a laugh. "Pulled me right out of my figures, and I have to get the bills done to send them out on Friday."

"It's almost the first of July," Mary declared. "The year is nearly half over."

"You'll soon be gone, and this household will be your trouble no more." Mamma grunted and stomped away.

"For your sake, I hope she doesn't take out a loan to pay for a cook," Mary told Jane. "I would not put it past her."

"The business cannot bear the expense. If she was to do such a thing, it would be to pay for a replacement for Charles." Jane swiped the broom, sending a few particles of dust under the counter.

Mary snorted. "Then the business would cease to be profitable, and her sense of business acumen would take a hit. No, she is all about comfort. As soon as Shelley has his loans taken care of, she will banish him to Bath, or the outer ends of the earth, and summon Fanny back to run the house."

"When will that be?"

"Probably after she marries you off, too, so she doesn't have to feed you."

Jane gasped. "You cruel thing! How dare you say something so mean to me."

"La, but you can talk about my marriage to a monster?"

"Mr. Fisher isn't a monster. He bought you cheese."

Mary shook involuntarily. "He wanted something to dine on when he was forced to come to this house, and it was a bargaining chip to get the Griffiths to talk. Come, Jane, you have more intelligence than you are displaying."

Jane's hands curled into fists. The broom dropped against the counter. Mary caught it before the handle could fall. When she turned back, Jane had already produced pearly tears in the corners of her eyes. Her face had gone red.

"Oh, Jane, no hysterics now," Mary said.

"I don't want to marry this summer. You turn seventeen in August, but I'm not seventeen until next spring. I'm too young. I could die in childbirth." Jane raised her fists, then lowered them again.

"No suitor is evident," Mary pointed out.

Jane raised her fists again, then opened them and scrubbed at her eyes with her fingers. She didn't even look sixteen. "I don't want to marry."

"You are safe until this business is done with Mr. Fisher." Mary lowered her voice. "You must know I will never actually marry the man. I have pledged myself to Shelley, body and soul. It's true love, Jane. I will never go to the altar with the Bow Street Runner."

Jane lowered her tear-stained face until her gaze was level with Mary's. "Then they'll make the trade. They'll make me marry Mr. Fisher."

"At least you're better suited to him, with your height. You're much sturdier than I am." Mary smirked. She was relatively sure that Mr. Fisher wouldn't do it. He had nothing to gain from marrying into the Godwin clan, quite the opposite, in fact. But she could not help riling up Jane, who took Mary's miseries and made them her own for dramatic effect.

"I won't." Jane stomped her foot.

"Calm yourself," Mary warned. "Or Mamma will come."

Jane whirled around. "I will never marry. I will have to find paid employment somehow."

"So will I, for Shelley has a wife. I shall be brought to ruin, but someone needs to run the bookshop."

"It will all fall apart now."

"Mamma and Papa have proven to be resilient. They will muddle through somehow, but they cannot manage here alone."

Jane rubbed her eyes with her arm this time. "I don't want to stay in this room year after year, growing old. I'll end up like our porter, feebleminded and bent."

"Better this room, where no one can take you to task for being sour. You couldn't do that in a school, and the hours for lady teachers are endless. One never knows what it will be like in a governess position, either."

"You can't do any of that work, either, and see Shelley again. You aren't related to him."

Mary stared. "You know I'm going to be a writer. That is never under discussion. I will write or die. It's as simple as that."

"What will it cost you? Look at Papa. Look at your mother," Jane said.

"Papa is happy upstairs in his library. He hovers over his books like a dragon with his treasure. He and my mother were happy. They each had their separate spaces to work. I must have that, whether I can live with Shelley or not."

"Would you? Live with him, I mean?"

Mary nodded. "If I am given the choice. I would walk at his side until the end of the earth."

Jane sniffed, her nostrils flaring, then grabbed Mary at her shoulders. "Promise me, if you ever leave, you will take me with you."

"You should stay," Mary said. "I expect the business won't fail. They will keep borrowing until they are dead."

"I have no more interest in the business than Charles does. Take me, Mary."

Mary sighed. "If I can. But that is up to Shelley."

"I will make myself indispensable," Jane promised. "Just you wait."

Chapter 15

Jane

On Friday before luncheon, Mary came into the bookshop and said Papa had given her coins for the butcher. He wanted another joint. I wished she'd see what cruelty that was for him to request it of her on a hot summer day, but she endlessly worshipped at his feet, an acolyte of the great creator of books.

Besides, she probably thought Polly would turn the spit for her.

"It will go faster if you get the kitchen ready while I go to the butcher," I said.

She raised her eyebrows. "The bookshop?"

I shrugged. "Very well. You'll have to stay in the bookshop, but I need some fresh air. Can I go to the butcher, please?"

"You are such a child." Mary sighed and reached for a shop apron.

I ripped off mine with a whoop and took the shillings she handed me, then fairly ran into the street, the strings of Mary's bonnet trailing behind my shoulders.

A group of about five boys, a little younger than Willy, loped down the hill toward me. I flattened myself against the bookshop windows, keeping the coins layered in my hands, so they couldn't knock me over and steal my money when it went flying.

One of them caught at my elbow, jerking me around, but I, wise to street urchins, spun with him and kept my fingers laced together. I saw Mary looking back at me through the window. She came up to it and shouted at the boys. One of them jumped in alarm, but another, hardened, stuck his tongue out at her. All five of them dispersed, though. Funny that reed-slender Mary behind a window was more frightening than taller, broader me on the street. I tied the bonnet strings into a bow and found a handkerchief in my pocket to knot the coins into, making them a little safer.

Shelley always seemed to pop out of nowhere when Mary went out, but I remained alone as I walked to the butcher's. When I passed the cheese shop, I looked into the window out of habit. Would I someday see the ghost of a murdered Davies twin waving back at me?

I lurched back when someone did wave at me. I put my free hand to my pounding chest. Then they waved again, and I realized it was only Cleda Griffith and not a ghost at all behind the rather wavy glass of the shop window. She gestured me into the cheese shop.

I swallowed hard and opened the door. "You startled me," I called. "How are you today, Mrs. Griffith? I'm afraid I'm not on an errand to buy cheese."

"Since you are out and about, I thought you could do me a favor. You're a fast walker, I've always noticed." Mrs. Griffith pulled up the corner of her apron and wiped her forehead.

"You need me to walk somewhere?" I asked.

Mrs. Griffith pulled a penny from her coin box and set it on the counter, then pushed a large round of cheese tied into a cloth toward me. "Can you take this to the St. Sepulchre rectory for me?"

"Of course." My mouth watered at the thought of being invited to Reverend Doone's table. But then what if he settled marital expectations on me, since Mary was no longer available? I forced a smile and took the cheese and the coin. She'd offered me no more than one of those street urchins would have received for the mission, but at least it was honest work.

"They'll give you payment at the door," Mrs. Griffith said. "Bring it right back. I know how much they owe me."

"I'll return soon," I promised, then retraced my steps to head to the rectory.

The housekeeper answered the door and seemed surprised to see me, but she handed over the coins after unwrapping the bundle and didn't invite me in.

I was sweating by the time I returned to the cheese shop. John Griffith had replaced his wife at the counter, unfortunately. Very businesslike, I set the coins in front of him. "For the cheese, Mr. Griffith."

"Did my wife pay you?"

I nodded. "A penny, sir."

He slapped another on the counter. "There's tuppence for you, then, my girl."

I made the coin disappear. "Thank you, sir."

He winked at me. "There's more where that comes from. Meet me at the back door tomorrow morning at sunup, and I'll make it worth your while."

"N-no, thank you," I stuttered. "I work in the bookshop, and I'm not looking for a new trade."

"I'll make it fun for you, you'll see." He leered. "You'll be begging for more, and I don't mean the coin."

I stiffened. "No, thank you, sir."

He reached out and stroked a finger down my bare arm. It jerked involuntarily. "You see, Miss Clairmont? Responding to me already."

I pulled my arm away, turned, and ran out, knowing from what I had seen in the past of his behavior that he'd just made an advance at me. I was no prostitute, willing to let him lift my skirt in an alley. With two parents living, I hoped I would never be so desperate as to make my daily coin in that manner. The man was a wolf. I'd have to make sure I dealt only with his wife in the future.

Or neither of them at all, given that he'd claimed his wife was a murderer. How many girls had been so abused by the consequences of having his child in their belly when his wife could not accomplish the same?

Starting up the street, I was nearly blinded by the sun in my eyes. It wasn't until I bounced off a lady's shoulder that I came out of my reverie.

"Miss Clairmont," said a sharp voice.

I tugged down the bonnet and looked up. "Oh, Mrs. Griffith, I didn't see you."

"It is bright. You need a better brimmed bonnet."

I nodded. "Yes, ma'am."

"I know you work in your mother's shop, but I can hire you to do more deliveries. I see you running around the streets enough with that sister of yours to see you know your way around the area."

"No, thank you," I said automatically.

"No? With your older siblings gone, I'd have thought you would need the help. Another place to go if you need it." She regarded me with those shrewd, small eyes.

"We'll be fine. Thank you." I didn't like a possible murderess looking at me with daggers in her eyes. "I . . . Well, if you need something delivered very close by, like to the rectory again, that would be fine." I bobbed, then ran up the street, holding my coins to my side so they wouldn't jangle.

My thoughts were careening against each other all that afternoon, like marbles in a circle. Could I earn honest coin from the cheese shop, or was Mrs. Griffith in collusion with her husband to turn me into his doxy? What game did they play between the two of them? She seemed much like Mamma, a tired, middle-aged lady of business, but how could she ignore the undercurrents in the shop? How many of the girls were under her husband's power? How many had turned up with full bellies? How many had died?

When the bookshop closed, I went down into the kitchen. "It's lovely and cool down here," I said to Mary.

She glanced up from her potato peeling. "Not when you are working hard."

"Not by the fire," Polly said irritably. "What sort of man demands a joint on a Saturday? Pure dangerous luxury, if you ask me."

"We can serve what is left cold tomorrow," Mary pointed out.

"I know what this household is," Polly said. "This is extravagance." Her arm muscles flexed as she turned the spit again. The coals spit as a drop of moisture hit them.

"You were happy enough of the meat before," Mary said. "I cannot understand how you can talk so about my family."

"Those who treat servants the way your mamma treated the cook will come to a bad end. Just you wait," Polly said darkly.

I hugged myself. The words had an air of prophecy to them and did not improve my mood. I drew Mary into the scullery to tell her what had transpired with the Griffiths; then, at her request, I took the largest water can I could carry outside to fill it.

Instantly, the heat made me feel sick. Where were the clouds? My head ached. I left the can by the cistern and went up to my room to lie down.

When I woke, I immediately sat up, disoriented. I heard a seam pop and realized I had lay down in my dress. After rolling off my bed to avoid further damage, I went to the window to open the curtains. From the way the sun hung in the sky, I suspected it must be time to eat.

With my water jug in my room empty, I went down with a mouth tasting of ashes. Even the sight of Shelley in his habitual seat at the table, making a face at the roast meat Polly had complained about, did not cheer me.

I sat stone-faced and ate what Mary placed in front of me. From the state of my hunger, I must have missed a meal.

Papa ate well under Mary's approving gaze, his color improving as he polished off a considerable portion of the meat. I hoped my hard-earned tuppence had been put to good use, though I should have saved it toward the purchase of a bonnet.

"What is it, Jane?" Shelley asked, his good-natured face full of concern.

"What?" I asked.

"You were moaning," Willy said, then giggled at me.

I rubbed my temples. "It is too hot. May I be excused?"

Papa nodded at me, and I ran out of the room. I did not want to face disagreeable Polly in the kitchen, so I went to hide in the parlor.

When the door opened a few minutes later, I did not move from my position facedown on the sofa.

"You are out of control," Mary sniped over me.

"Is she ill?" Shelley inquired. "Jane? A summer ague? With all those children running through the bookshop, it is no surprise."

It was no surprise Shelley expected an illness, for he often felt unwell himself and fancied invalidism for all his blooming health.

"I am not ill," I said, my voice muffled by the cushion. Lifting my head slightly, I added, "I am merely afraid I will be murdered next."

"Good heavens, why?" Mary asked rather coldly.

"Because I am mixed up in the cheese shop business now, and it's a very deadly place."

Shelley came over to the front of the sofa. I sat up so that he could join me. "Explain?" he asked.

I told him about my errand.

"You shouldn't have done it," Mary said.

"It helped me obtain a slightly larger joint," I pointed out.

Mary knelt in front of me. "Don't put yourself in the way of danger, Jane. Shelley cannot always be available to protect you."

"We must promise not to leave her alone," Shelley told Mary.

Mary sighed. "It is rare that we do."

He nodded. "Then we must pay better attention so that it does not happen again. Don't leave Skinner Street alone, Jane. Not until we know what really happened to the Davies twins."

On Monday, as soon as the porter returned from a standard set of deliveries that he made every start of the week, Mamma sent me out to the garden to help with the washing, muttering the entire time about how dreadful the linen had been the week before.

I thought she was coming along, since she walked out the front door right behind me, but instead she continued down the street, a reticule bobbing foolishly along the side of her skirt.

I knew Mamma to be formidable, but how did she think to be safe from pickpockets with it displayed so? I shook my head and went around to the back.

"It's just me," I told Mary. "Mamma has vanished to I don't know where."

"Hopefully, to the post office, to send a note begging Fanny's forgiveness and beseeching her to return by the next coach," Mary said.

I hadn't seen her without a line of perspiration over her lip for weeks. She handed Willy's soiled shirt to me so that I could scrub it and went to pour more water into the tub.

We worked hard under the sun, unwavering in our toils, until Mamma appeared. I noted that she still had her reticule. It appeared to be hanging even lower than before.

"Did you finish a translation or sell some more letters?" I inquired.

Her expression was largely shadowed by her enormous bonnet. "Where is my son?"

Mary blinked at her innocently. "Jane said he went to Bath. You know this."

"I have been to see that wretched Mr. Bryan," Mamma said. "He told me Professor Asquith has been blackout drunk in Limehouse for days. Charles is not working for him in Bath."

"He went there to make arrangements?" I said, knowing how foolish I sounded the second the words left my mouth.

"Go inside, Polly," Mamma ordered.

The maid didn't protest, just pulled a couple of pieces of the thinnest linen off the washing line and dropped them into the basket before leaving the garden with it.

"You've done something," Mary said after taking a shrewd look at Mamma.

Mamma gestured us closer. I left Mary's stained shift on the washboard and stood, stretching my back.

"I've taken out another loan to get Charles out of the country. How do I get the funds to him, girls?"

"Are you trying to get yourself thrown back into the Bow Street lockup, madam?" Mary inquired. "We cannot afford more loans."

"Your father cannot, but the business can," Mamma said. "You can't hide secrets from me."

Mary and I shared a look. I knew she was as horrified as me at Mamma's profligacy.

I could see it in her eyes. Mary would never escape the

kitchen. I wouldn't be able to sing. It had been so long since we'd seen Mr. Fisher that he'd probably lost interest. Had the banns been called the day before? I had no idea. Charles's difficulties would ruin us even faster than Papa's would.

We needed an escape plan.

"I cannot believe you, Mamma. To risk what is left of the family's safety? How can you think he will leave London?"

"By a privately hired coach," Mamma said. "It can easily be arranged. Closed body, curtains down. Leave at dawn."

Mary nodded. "Then I will tell you where he is, but if I were you, I would not go yourself. You'll lead the authorities right to him."

"Then what should I do, girl?"

Mamma must be desperate indeed to look at Mary with such hope in her eyes.

"Give the money to Shelley and have him make the arrangements. Charles is at a location our friend can visit without seeming out of place."

Mamma nodded. "I will speak to him at dinner tonight."

I put my hand on her arm. "We are sure one of the Griffiths killed the twins, Mamma."

She shook her head. "John Griffith is a defiler, not a killer. And Cleda isn't evil. You girls have wasted your time and attention on them. I don't know who killed the Davies girls, but it wasn't one of the Griffiths."

At dinner, Mamma was a very portrait of pleasing matronly solicitude. She had instructed Polly to cook turnips in butter for Shelley. I wondered if Papa knew about the latest loan. Admittedly, he had never treated us Clairmonts as any less his children than Mary or Willy, so if he objected, it wouldn't be because Charles was his stepson. Papa was a wonder, but a wife who took on additional debt could irritate even the mildest of men. Perhaps she was hoping Shelley's loans would come through before Papa knew about the debt.

"Shelley, dear boy, would you help me in the wine cellar? There are a couple of bottles I cannot reach, and you are the tallest of us all," Mamma said grandly as soon as he had polished off his turnips and bread.

Willy giggled. "Wine cellar?"

Mamma fixed him with a gargoyle stare. Shelley pushed back his chair without comment, despite the bizarre quality of the request. I knew she planned to do what Mary had suggested and ask him for help.

Papa reacted not at all, merely smiled genially at Willy and asked him what he'd been studying that day.

Mary glanced sidelong at me and began to gather the plates. I helped her, thinking we could get a nice long walk outside that evening since Mamma would be playing up to Shelley. The sooner the dishes were returned to the kitchen, the better.

Shelley patted his pocket as soon as we were outside.

"Do we go to Old Bond Street?" I asked.

"No, I will run the errand tomorrow," Shelley said.

"Will you try to make all the arrangements so he can go soon?" I asked.

Shelley narrowed his eyes at me. "The walls have ears, Jane."

"I thought Willy might like to go to the springs in Hyde Park tomorrow," I prattled to hide my mistake. "Do you think he would benefit from bathing his eyes there? I think they must be getting weak on account of all the studying he does."

"That does sound delightful," Shelley said thoughtfully. "We all might benefit from such a healthful practice."

Mary tucked her hand through my arm. "Where shall we go now?"

"St. Pancras, I think," Shelley said, with a smile in her direction. "We should consult with your mother about the best course of action. She went to the places we are discussing, after all."

I thought he meant France or maybe Scandinavia. I did hope

Charles would go to Switzerland, so I could visit him. But I didn't think that Mary's mother had ever been there. Hadn't she been denied entrance during the Revolution in France?

It didn't matter if he was confused. I had the soft evening breeze to delight me, cooling me despite the ugly old cotton bonnet of Fanny's I wore. We took ourselves to the fields around the St. Pancras burying ground.

"Have yourself a nice walk in the shade," Shelley said. "I want to consult with Mary on a letter I have to write."

"A letter?" I asked. "I can write nearly as neatly as she can."

"It's the subject matter," Shelley said. "A quotation."

"Very well, then," I said. "I don't want to hide under the willows, anyway. It is much too nice of an evening."

Mary's lips curved; then she walked away on Shelley's arm, brazen in her devotion when no one but the dead could see.

I walked out toward the marshes, wondering if I'd find anyone else fallen in, but I didn't see a soul except my own reflection in the water. I enjoyed the breeze, though, and the feeling of emptiness. No need to fear pickpockets or anything else. I listened to the air sing through the weeds, "*Wish, wish, wish.*"

I knew what I wished for. To go somewhere more exciting than this. I wanted to go with Charles. He would need someone to keep house for him. Who better than his sister?

"Have you turned to stone?" I turned at the voice behind me. Mary and Shelley both looked red in the face. Mary had her bonnet hanging down her back by the strings, though her hair was pinned neatly into a bun, with pleasant little waves of hair around her cheeks. Shelley seemed to be moving even more indolently than usual, but his smile was ever genial.

"What are we going to do about Charles?" I demanded. "We cannot wait for Bow Street to find him."

"More important, we cannot wait for Mamma to bankrupt

the business with plans to help him." Mary threw up her hands. "Charles hasn't even been consulted."

"He'll take any bit of money she offers," I said. "But then if Bow Street gets him, it will just go into their pockets."

"We need to solve the murder," Mary said.

"On my life," I said. "The gun case is the thing."

"Is there anyone who would know what is behind it?" Shelley tucked hair behind his ears.

"You were going to try to find that pink-and-red woman," Mary reminded him.

"Upon my soul, I clean forgot." He beamed at her.

"You aren't taking this seriously enough," I scolded. "What has entered into the pair of you?"

"I don't see why Charles should be the one to leave," Mary said, staring very intently at Shelley.

"You are deeply oppressed," Shelley agreed. "When Fanny was home, at least she shared in the work."

"I was still in school then and had my singing lessons," I reminded him.

He put his hands into his hair. "Things have grown quite dire. I do wonder if my promises caused dear Godwin to become a bit indolent."

"Big ideas take a dreadfully long time to germinate," Mary said, ever loyal to Papa.

He nodded. "Either way, you, with your own fine minds, don't deserve to suffer for his genius. More than that, I do not like to see what your mother does. I have seen the bruises on Mary's arms."

"We should run away with Charles," she said.

"That's what I was thinking!" I shouted. "I should go with him to run his household. He'll need me."

"We should all run away." Shelley hushed me with a gesture. "And form a community."

"Mamma didn't get a big enough loan for all four of us." I

doubted it could happen. Shelley was fairly cheap to feed, but four people was rather a lot.

"My post-obit loans ought to be finalized this month. I will tell Godwin that I will need half the money for my own purposes. After all, if I am keeping the pair of you, that reduces the strain on his household."

"You don't want to get a job?" I asked. "We'll be working awfully hard, Mary and me, to run our little household."

"Jane, my dear. My value is in my literary work, just like with your dear papa. There is no position befitting a nobleman. What would I do? Join the army? The clergy?"

"What a silly notion," Mary said. "Your birth has you in a sort of shackles, but at least it afforded you an education that allows you to benefit humanity."

Shelley nodded.

"I understand the value of your art and learning," she added. "I only hope that I can match you someday."

"I will develop a program of learning for all of us," Shelley said, throwing his arms open wide. "We will travel with nothing but books and consider how the French live now, since Napoleon is defeated. It will be as instructive as your mother's experience during the Revolution."

"What a notion." Mary clasped her hands together. "Yes, we will have much to say about it. I fancy we could keep a journal and any letters we write and publish them as Mother published her letters to Fanny's father."

Shelley grinned and took her hands, then danced through the mud with her. They cavorted madly, Shelley singing, Mary calling out, "Caution," when she stumbled. Shelley grabbed her; then somehow they fell into the grass, laughing.

"What about Switzerland?" I asked plaintively. "I want to go there instead."

They didn't appear to hear me.

"Are you really going to tell Papa you are keeping half the

money?" Mary asked, rolling away from Shelley and tucking up her hair again.

"I'll check on the loans tomorrow," Shelley promised, taking a pin from her hand and inserting it expertly into her hair. "I'll talk to him as soon as I have more information."

I whooped, realizing this might actually happen. We already had the money for Charles. Why, we might all be out of London by the end of the week.

Chapter 16

Mary

When Mary brought in the fish stew, she found Papa and Shelley already in the dining room. Papa poured wine, a vacant look in his eyes, while her love stood, staring out the window. Papa's color was not the best. Had he spent much of the day at the end of the garden again, with his stomach problems? Shelley cleared his throat in a sorrowful way, commanding her attention.

"What are you thinking of, Shelley?" she asked him as she set the bowl down, then pulled the ladle from the crook of her arm.

His gaze fairly crackled with electricity. "I am considering the boundaries of sacred friendship."

Mary smiled, given they'd been exploring this very topic to its utmost, then turned, careful to keep her reaction from Papa. Shelley had been thinking of her. A happy thing to hear, for she could think of little else but him, the sheer, carnal pleasure she found in his physical form. His gentle touch, the way he felt when he moved. The sounds, the smells, the sensations. How much clearer the romances she had read seemed now that she knew the mysteries of love. But at the same time, she herself hadn't seemed to be able to set pen to paper. He could write poetry for her while she seemed unable to summon a word.

Her inability to work might be because of the tension in the house. How exhausting it was to have to beg for a few coins every day just to feed the people who were withholding the money.

"Good evening," Mamma said, coming in, her words seeming too loud for the hush that had been in the dining room before.

Willy, trailing behind her, ran his hand over the wallpaper to the right of the door, leaving it shining with something.

"What are you doing?" Mary demanded, then went to wipe it with her apron. *Boys.* "Sit down."

Willy twirled, then darted to his seat. He pulled it back too roughly, and it toppled over. Laughing loudly, he uprighted it and dropped down. Mamma, taking her own seat with a groan, smiled at Willy's antics, but Papa didn't seem to notice at all.

Mamma spotted Shelley. Her nose quivered. She rose and stalked in his direction. "Is there any word?"

He regarded her mildly. "As to the course of action I have taken?"

"Have you seen Charles?" Mamma demanded.

He inclined his head. "I spoke to him, and arrangements are being made."

"When?"

Shelley tilted his head farther, his overlong sandy locks brushing his neckcloth. "He insists he does not want to leave the city just yet."

Mamma frowned horribly. "Why not? Give me some wine, husband. I thirst."

Papa glanced at Mary, but it seemed as if he looked right through her. Confused, she passed him a wineglass, and he filled it. When she leaned over the table and gave it to Mamma, all the older woman did was snort as she snatched it up.

Shelley took a deep breath. "Developments."

Mamma frowned. "Developments?"

"I have a name for the lady with the case."

"I don't know what you mean," Mamma snarled.

Mary's ears, though, perked right up. "The pink-and-red lady?"

"Caitlin," Shelley said, nodding his agreement. "An Irish lass, I'm told, plying her trade around the prisons. I don't have an address for her yet, but a first name is something."

Mary nodded. "It's a thread to pull."

"What is this all about?" Mamma asked, but then Polly came in with a platter of greens topped with potato balls, and Shelley turned back to the window, just as Jane danced through the door.

"The stew will get cold," Mary said, and everyone took their seats.

Mamma brought up the subject again as soon as her bowl was full. "Do you think this Caitlin is the real killer?"

"No," Shelley said. "More like part of the gang the twins were in. They had to have been mixed up in something serious."

Mamma continued to pelt Shelley with questions throughout the meal. Papa, unusually, said nothing. Jane glanced at him every time she attempted to say something charming, but he just put spoon to stew, or lips to wineglass, without speaking. Mary shook her head when Jane gave her an inquiring look. She didn't know what was wrong.

Shelley, on the other hand, positively hummed with some secret happiness. Mary found it hard to keep her calm mien when her constant glances at him brought her so much joy. Was it too much to think she might be the cause of his elation?

"Is there something sweet?" Mamma said. "I'd like to get the taste of that stew out of my mouth."

"It was much nicer than some we've had," Mary said defensively.

"You could make a pudding," Mamma suggested.

"I don't have the funds." Mary felt her blood start to boil. "You don't give me enough money for anything extra."

Papa stood abruptly. They all stared at him. Looking down at the table, he said, "Mary, come upstairs after you have cleared the table. I will be in my library."

"Yes, Papa," Mary said, very confused. But she glanced, for she could not help herself, at Shelley, and he gave her a quick wink.

Mamma rose. "Come, Willy. Let us see if I have any shortbread still in my tin."

As soon as they went out, Jane threw her napkin on the table with a flourish. "As if Willy needs shortbread. He's already as plump as a Christmas goose."

Shelley turned to her as she continued. "With Charles gone, there isn't anyone to take him for long walks."

Mary emptied her water glass. "Don't worry, Jane. He's at the age where he's about to sprout up a foot. Boys change so fast."

Shelley cleared his throat. "You probably want to know why Godwin was so out of sorts tonight."

Mary leaned forward. "Do you know?"

He pushed his hands into his hair, then pulled them out again, leaving himself looking like a lion. "I confessed all to him and disappointed him besides."

"What did you say?" Jane asked before Mary could demand the full news.

"I told Godwin that I love Mary," he said simply.

Mary put her hand to her chest, enchanted. How daring he'd been. "How did Papa react?"

"Not well." Shelley shook his head. "I also informed Godwin that half of the twenty-five hundred pounds I promised will not be coming to him, as I will need it to support myself and Mary."

"And me," Jane said. "You promised, and besides, Mary cannot run a household alone."

"We can afford a servant with those kinds of funds," Mary said.

Jane scowled at her.

"I am tired of being a servant myself," Mary pointed out. She knew Jane would be coming with them. As if they could manage to divest themselves of her. Besides, she didn't trust her stepsister to keep her neck out of a gibbet without Mary's watchful eye and Shelley's wise counsel. "Just now, I've been instructed to call upon Papa after I've cleared the table. Servant duties before family matters."

"It is likely to be a difficult interview."

Mary smiled at him. "You've basically ended my betrothal for me. How can I be anything but happy? You've informed Papa that I will not be marrying Mr. Fisher."

"But the banns were called, weren't they?" Jane asked.

"Mr. Fisher wasn't in town, and we didn't go to the church," Mary said, shrugging.

"You didn't need to be there," Jane said. "I suspect it is already in motion."

"It doesn't matter." Shelley, brazenly, put his arm around Mary's shoulders. "As long as the wedding doesn't take place. Now, do your best. I'll wait for you in the street."

Jane rose to follow him out, but he gave her a quelling look and left. Her lips turned down. Sullen, she returned to the table and helped Mary stack up the plates. "Hurry up," she urged. "It's hot in here."

"I have sweat trickling down my back," Mary agreed. "July is a difficult month. How will we be able to sleep tonight?"

"Just dream of Shelley," Jane advised. "Sleep will come easily enough."

Jane was such a child, to think that. Why, thinking of Shelley was utterly energizing.

Mary left Jane in the scullery a few minutes later and went to see Papa, holding a tankard of ale, which she thought might calm him. She put the cool surface to her forehead as she went up the steps, trying to calm her thoughts.

Shelley had said out loud to another person that they were going to live together. She'd scarcely realized he'd made plans. He must expect that they would all go together, Charles, Shelley, Jane, and her, all at once. They would be outlaws somewhere. France? Switzerland? How quickly everything had changed. That was the power of Shelley's name and fortune. He could spring into action when the likes of her could not.

Though her mother had managed it. She had demonstrated spirit, which Mary endeavored to emulate, and she had no ill mother's needs or violent father to hold her back, though she had sisters to consider, like her mother had.

She knocked on the door and started to go in when Papa said, "Come." She walked in, then set the ale on his desk.

"I thought you might like something to drink, Papa. Are you very well?"

"Well enough, daughter," Papa said, his bald head shining with perspiration. He picked up the tankard and took a deep drink. "This heat will dry us out down to the bones, which is something to desire."

"I am glad that the sun helps with the aches and pains," Mary agreed.

Papa didn't invite her to sit. Instead, he let her stand while he drained the tankard and gazed at the portrait of Mary's mother.

"Am I very like her?" Mary asked.

Papa kept his eyes averted. "No, not very much at all, Mary. She, unlike you, was a good, dutiful daughter."

Mary's mouth dropped open. Had she not come up here with the tankard sweating in her hands, thinking only of her father's comfort? Had she not cooked him his dinner, indeed, all his meals? Helped run his bookshop so that he had a roof over his head and clothing on his back? Had she not mended that very shirt? Well, probably Fanny had done it, but close enough.

She had so many things she wanted to say, and frankly, she had been trained to say them, yet the staring eyes of Papa looking into the immortal ones of dead Mary Wollstonecraft kept her silent.

"I am outraged at your conduct, Mary," Papa said, still not looking at her.

"I do not know what you mean," she said carefully. Shelley had not made it entirely clear what he had told her father.

"Shelley, a stain on this household, has revealed all," Papa said.

There was a leading statement if she had ever heard one. "If you feel that way, why was he at dinner?"

"He is not forbidden in this house. Indeed, he cannot be. Therefore, the change needs to be behind these doors."

"You do not find problems with his behavior, only mine?" she asked.

"You should know better!" He stood and pounded his fist on the desk, eyes blazing. "Young ladies are taught better than this. You know Shelley's ways. He has a wife. And there have been other entanglements. Look at what happened to your mother. You, of all girls, should know better."

Mary stared at him, feeling the cold steal outward from her heart to travel down her body. "My mother despaired. I would never throw myself in a river over a man."

"Your sister could have died on the streets, Mary, if your mother had successfully ended her life. How could you be so foolish as to run toward her fate?"

"Shelley's marriage is dead, and he loves me truly. He has promised to keep not just me but Jane. How is that dishonorable? I was not raised to believe in marriage. He will not betray us."

"He is on fire, Mary. Shelley is always on fire. But this nonsense is threatening to take bread out of your mother's mouth, your brother's."

"It also reduces the household," Mary said. "How can you talk of money when we talk about love? Shelley and I share the same intellectual pursuits. Mrs. Shelley cannot be to him what I am. I can help him be the man he will be, and he can help me be the proper heir to my parents. Don't you see that?"

"I see a young man who is going to blaze out young. A man in love with his aches and pains in the same way he loves anarchy, who will not eat properly or take care of his children." Papa took a breath. "A young man who roves this city, attaching himself from one household to the next, cultivating irregular habits, instead of a course of study that would bring out his genius."

"What good is getting old?" Mary asked. "Is not the best work done in youthful exuberance? Mother did not live to be old. You revise your old work as often as you create something new."

"I have to pay my bills. Revisions and new editions, and yes, translations, bring in money." Papa clenched his fist next to the wet tankard but didn't bring it down again.

"Shelley is keeping daily cares minimal, living the way he

does. Instead of spending his days choosing the best chair or needing to pay for the expensive wallpaper he has chosen, he thinks. He builds perfect societies in his head."

"He discards people, Mary. Women, children. You know this. He is a veritable Pied Piper of Hamelin and, in some ways, not my true disciple."

"He goes places and learns about them. He tried to help the Irish and the Welsh. Future generations will thank him for his ideas," Mary said.

"I agree with you," Papa said. "But I do not want you to sacrifice yourself to his ambition. I have given you a good life. I protected Fanny from his wiles, and now I see you are entrapped even more completely. I thought you more intelligent than this."

"Papa!" Mary cried. "It is his very intelligence, his purity of belief that attract me. I can learn under his tutelage and write work as sublime, I know it."

Papa gave Mother's painting a pinch-faced glare. "You are not to leave the house. You have two rooms full of books with which to educate yourself, and as busy as you claim to be, I know you have time for mischief. Therefore, you have plenty of time for your course of study. Every night at dinner we can discuss it."

"Shelley?"

"You are not to leave the house with him." Papa fixed her with a look, the one she'd seen him giving his creditors when they were not looking. "Be a good daughter, Mary."

Mary snatched up the tankard, gave him a sarcastic little curtsy, and walked out. At least Papa didn't seem to know or care that her love with Shelley was complete. They had given themselves to each other, body and soul. Papa would not be able to keep them apart. Destiny was at work.

She went upstairs. When she reached her room, she put her

hand on the door. Should she run right back down, out the door, and into Shelley's waiting arms?

She paced down the passage and back again, her better self reminding her that he was making arrangements for the carriage to take them all safely off together, a perfect little community like he wanted. They had Charles to think of. He was waiting for them to extricate him from his disaster. If she left this house tonight, Shelley would not be able to help Charles. Promises had been made to Jane, as well. What if Shelley made her turn back into the house because she had not included Jane?

Her hands went cold at the idea that he might choose Jane's happiness over her own. Or worse, be disappointed in her because she had not done so. Shelley, the mildest of men, unhappy with her? No, she could not bear it. She loved and respected Papa, but she was a woman now, destined to follow her mate. At least Papa had had the delicacy not to bring up Mr. Fisher. He was angrier about the loss of half of Shelley's money for Skinner Street more than anything. Because he would have to face Mamma with the news.

She went into her room and pulled her notebook from under her pillow and tore out a page. "Dearest Shelley," she wrote, tears welling in her eyes as the words went down in pencil. "Your Mary is entirely yours. Papa cannot defy us in this. Please make the arrangements as we have discussed, so that we can be together. I will not destroy Charles's future with too-fast actions, but I remain committed to our future together and long to see you. Until tomorrow, my love. Your Mary." She folded up the letter, wiped it with her tears, and went to find Jane.

Though she had hoped Jane would have gone down to the kitchen and helped Polly, instead she found her stepsister in Willy's room, lining up soldiers with him and giving the enemies silly French names.

"I, Jean-Claude-Marc-Querry François, will run you through with this saber, I do declare," she cried, shaking a little figure with an upright sword.

"And I, Captain Lord Smythe-Belly-Just, will take you down to hell with me!" Willy screeched, bashing his miniature soldier against Jean-Claude-Marc-Querry.

"I announce the captain lord the winner," Mary said. "Jane, Shelley is in the street waiting, is he not?"

"Waiting for you," Jane said.

Mary held out the damp note. "Take it to him, please?"

"Can't you walk?"

Mary shook her head, then glanced at Willy. "Just take it, please. I have to go help Polly. She's too lazy to have done the dishes without being instructed."

"You can't be serious," Jane said. "Surely she knows that most basic of her duties."

"I am afraid that as each day passes, she forgets her place and considers herself just another daughter of the house. It is not good to have just the one servant. I see Mamma's sense in that."

"There is no money for a new cook."

"It will not be my problem for much longer," Mary said. "Go."

"Who will Captain Lord Smythe-Belly-Just defeat next?" Willy asked.

Mary sat down on his bed and picked up a badly painted blue-coated figurine. "I, Le Duc du Septieme Voulez-Vous Me Tuer Maintenant, will run you through, Captain Lord!"

Jane cackled and walked out, shutting the door behind her. Mary sighed and went into battle. Polly and the dishes could wait a few more minutes.

On Thursday morning, Jane stopped Mary at the dining room door and took the napkin-wrapped coffeepot from her hands.

"I'll help you with this, then open the bookshop," she said, pushing Mary out the door.

"What is it?" Mary asked. She'd woken with a headache, probably because she'd polished off the remains of the wine in three glasses while she did the dishes. Normally, Polly would have drunk it, but Mary had been feeling savage and selfish after Willy had scratched her hand with one of the toy soldiers and then broken one of her fingernails to the quick with a miniature cannonball.

Jane went to the stairs and didn't speak until they were both on the landing, out of hearing of the dining room. "You are not going to believe where Shelley heard that pink-and-red female lives."

"He has learned something?"

Jane grinned. "He told me last night. She lives at the Polygon!"

Mary's eyebrows rose almost to her hairline. "Is she a French émigré?"

"Very possibly. Can you imagine, she lives where we used to? What if we know her family?"

Mary shook her head. "It will make it easier to learn what is going on with that gun case. Will Shelley find her today?"

"He is going to try."

A knock came on the front door. Jane handed the coffeepot back to Mary. "I'd better get it. What if it is a customer?"

Mary walked down behind Jane, wondering how Shelley would have time to do it all. Find Caitlin, order them a carriage, and do his work. Not to mention the matter of the loans.

"Good morning, Mrs. Griffith," Jane said after opening the door. She stepped back so that the cheesemonger could enter. "Were you in need of pencils or paper? I can set up an account for you."

"I admire your attempt to drum up business," Mrs. Griffith

said, wiping her forehead. "You are more like your mother than your stepfather, I see."

Mary cradled the coffeepot in her hands and resisted the urge to lash out. They could not trust the Griffiths and didn't need to give them a target.

"What can we do for you, then, Mrs. Griffith?" Mary asked. "As you can see, Jane is about to open the bookshop."

"I've seen you behind the counter, Miss Mary," the older woman said. "Could you run the bookshop today? I'd like to have Miss Clairmont help deliver cheese."

Jane tilted her head, looking confused.

"You remember the gold-decorated cheese?" Mrs. Griffith said. "I need some extra hands to take it there. I know better than to trust all the girls I have."

"No." Jane shook her head vigorously, dislodging a pin from her thick hair.

"Why not?" Mrs. Griffith asked. "I'm sure Miss Mary will do fine alone."

Jane turned to Mary and shook her head, her eyes wide. Mary recognized her fear. What if she found herself alone with John Griffith in the process? They couldn't trust him.

"You'd do better to hire boys," Mary suggested. "You need stronger arms than Jane's. I'm sorry Charles isn't here. Maybe we could lend you our porter?"

"What's all this?" Mamma asked, coming down the steps. They squeaked loudly since she didn't try to avoid the bad spots.

"I was offering your daughter a day of honest work," Mrs. Griffith said.

"She has work here, as you well know, Mrs. Griffith," Mamma said. "An errand or two is one thing, but she can't take a day away from our concerns."

Mrs. Griffith patted her chest with her knitted glove. "I

thought you'd be desperate enough for the coin, Mrs. Godwin. I suppose I'll have to find my ne'er-do-well stepson and make him help."

"Son?" Mary asked.

"He doesn't work in the business," Mamma said. "He went out on his own some time ago, as I recall."

"More than three years. Independent sort, that boy," Mrs. Griffith said. "Not like your children."

"Our business can support the family," Mamma said, with no hint of irony. "Please let us know if we can offer some other service. Warehouse room for your cheese, for instance?"

"We don't need it." Mrs. Griffith smirked. "It sells much too fast." She turned around and swept through the door.

Jane closed the door behind her. "Stepson?"

Mamma shook her head. "Don't you remember the fights between young Griffith and his father? They'd shout at each other in front of the warehouse."

"When was that?" Mary asked.

"Oh, the worst of it would have been when you were in Scotland. The lad ran off. I've seen him in Covent Garden since, but he's no one to know, if you get my meaning." Mamma took the bookshop key from the drawer, then took the coffeepot from Mary and went up, breathing heavily.

Mary stared at Jane. "We need to write to Charles and see what he knows about young Griffith. What if he is the twins' killer?"

"I'll write it at the counter," Jane offered. "Send Polly in to mail it."

Mary nodded. "As soon as the dishes are done. We finally have a reasonable candidate. An angry young man with a connection to the cheese shop."

Jane squeezed her arm. "This means that Charles might not have to flee London. What does that mean for us?"

Mary shook her head. "It means we can take Mamma's money and go to France ourselves. I don't care about Charles. We have to go, or I'll have to spend my life with Mr. Fisher."

"They can make you come back and marry him, anyway," Jane warned.

"I'll be so ruined in the eyes of the world that even Mr. Fisher won't take me then," Mary said. "And given the kind of company we keep, what I do has to be terrible indeed. I'm leaving with Shelley. I don't care what you or Charles do. I have to go."

Jane nodded. "I know, Mary, truly I do. Love must triumph."

Chapter 17

Jane

Something woke me just before dawn broke on Friday. I sat up, blinking, trying to figure out what it was, then stepped to the window. I couldn't see outside yet, but my mind started to work. Perhaps the front door had opened and closed.

Not hearing anything in the house, I worried less about someone having broken in downstairs. Could Charles have sneaked home? He must be desperate for fresh clothing by now.

I crept to my window and unlatched it, then leaned out. I recognized Mary's whisper before I could see her dark figure. Another person, taller and broader, separated from the shadows; then the two figures came together in a carnal embrace.

Shelley, it had to be. The man was too lithe to be Mr. Fisher; I could see that even in the dark. They were being too brazen, standing in the street like this. I leaned back from the window and paced my floor, not sure what I should do. The thought struck me. What if they were about to run away together and leave me behind? My heart raced. How cruel!

I was spurred into action. Still in my nightgown, I ran downstairs, the steps squeaking a discordant symphony. I jumped off the second to last step and dashed across the front hall's floor, then tore the door open.

"Don't leave me!" I cried. I ran between the figures and pushed them apart.

Shelley grabbed me by the arms. "What is this?"

"Jane?" Mary gasped.

I wrapped my fingers around the fabric of Shelley's coat. "Don't leave, please. You have to take me with you."

"Jane, Jane, now then," Shelley said gently. "What do you think is happening here?"

"It's early. Mary snuck out."

Mary took a fistful of my nightgown. "Are you mad? In the street like this? Go back inside, you idiot."

Shelley released me. I wiped my hands down my face. They came away damp with tears and snot. My breath whistled through my nose.

"I thought Charles had snuck in," I said. "And then I thought you were leaving me, Mary. What are you doing outside at such an early hour?"

Commotion sounded in the house. Mamma burst out of the door, breathing heavily, a cudgel in her hand. "Have they come to arrest me again?"

"You!" Mary cried at me. "What have you done?"

Mamma grabbed Mary by the arm and pulled her inside. The sun had come up just enough by then that she could recognize Shelley. Her mouth tensed, then fully dropped open when she saw me in my gown. "Get inside," she said in the sternest of tones.

I went to her, but she filled the door, so I had to face her, suddenly realizing how much my feet hurt. I must have cut the soles of my feet on the tiny rocks that were everywhere under the dust.

She backed away from the door. I ran downstairs to the kitchen to bathe my feet, but I wasn't out of earshot when I heard the sound of a slap. Mary didn't even cry out. She was too used to the blows, I supposed.

I stayed in the kitchen a good long time, soaking the debris out of my feet in a water-filled bucket, waiting for my heart to revert to its customary rhythm. When I finally went up, no one was in the front hall. I went to my room and dressed as best I could, a sour feeling in my stomach. It was much too early for breakfast, so I went through my room, packing up a little bundle of items to take with me. I should be ready in case they tried to flee without me again. Next time, I would be better prepared. I would not let Mary doom me to a fate she didn't want for herself.

When breakfast time came, I went to the dining room. It was still dim. I opened the curtains, allowing the July sun to blaze in. No sign of the usual morning preparations had occurred. I set the table and then went down to the kitchen. Polly stood over the fire, stirring porridge.

"Isn't Mary helping you?"

Polly turned an angry expression in my direction. "I don't know where she is."

"At least you don't have to make fires upstairs at this time of year." I took the wooden spoon from her. "Make the tea. I'm sure Papa and Mamma will want their breakfast."

Polly rolled her eyes and grabbed a rag so she could take the steaming kettle and pour the water into a teapot.

"What else are you going to serve? Is there any bacon? Toast?" I asked.

"What am I, our Lord Jesus himself, to create loaves and fishes out of nothing?" Polly demanded. "This is all we have."

"What would you have done if Mary had been here this morning?" I scraped the bottom of the pan to keep the porridge from burning.

"I'd have gone to fetch milk and butter and a bit of bacon at the market. But she didn't come." Polly put the kettle back on the hob.

"Can you go now?"

"It's too late."

"But you have the money for it?"

"No, your mother paid that account." Polly made a face.

"Help me bring the porridge and tea upstairs. Then go fetch what you normally purchase. We can have it at lunch, if nothing else. This is a poor way to nourish a household."

Upstairs, Papa was seated at the table, along with Willy. "Coffee this morning, I think, Polly," he said pleasantly.

"There's no milk, Mr. Godwin," she said with a quick bob.

"Why not?" Papa asked.

"She's going to fetch it now, right, Polly?" I said pointedly.

The girl bobbed in Papa's direction again, then left.

"I'm sorry there is only porridge," I said.

Mamma came in and sat at the other end of the table.

"Where is Mary? Bringing up the bacon?" Papa asked.

"We need to talk," Mamma said. "Jane, take Willy and go upstairs."

"I'm hungry," Willy whined.

Mamma spooned a steaming mound of porridge onto his plate. "Take this."

Willy made a face but, obviously sensing that danger was afoot, took his plate and escaped. I scooped porridge onto one side of another plate, then balanced a teacup on the other and went out much more carefully. We never ate in our rooms for fear of rats.

A table rested in the passage in between the dining room and the library. As soon as Willy had gone up, I set my plate on the table, picked up my teacup, and drank while I listened. Mamma had not noticed that I had left the door open a crack.

"Why is Mary not doing her duty this morning, Mrs. Godwin?" Papa asked in a rather dangerously neutral tone.

Mamma humphed. "I found Mary outside with Shelley this morning, when it was still dark. Jane woke me, making a scene, out on the street in her nightgown."

"Both girls were outside?" Papa inquired.

"Jane must have run after Mary," Mamma said. "Quite unprepared, unlike Mary, who was fully dressed. She has no sense. First, we lost Fanny to Shelley's attractions, and now both younger girls? What are we to do, Mr. Godwin?"

"Shelley has told me that he and Mary have made plans to live together," Papa said tersely.

Mamma muttered an oath. "Just he and Mary?"

My eyes widened. They had promised me, but then why would he tell Papa? I had to trust Shelley, even if I did not entirely trust Mary at times.

"You know he took his wife away from her school when she was sixteen, with the future Mrs. Shelley's sister helping him," Papa said. "He believed the girl was being oppressed. He seems to couch Mary's life in the same vein, now that she is banished to the kitchen and betrothed to Mr. Fisher." His tone remained pedantic.

"He can't say that about Jane. She's not doing a maid of all work's duties," Mamma said.

Papa cleared his throat. "Jane isn't going to school anymore. I know Shelley used to visit her there. And the singing lessons are done, too. I don't know that we can trust Jane's safety from him, either."

"Jane is still a wide-eyed child. Mary is the slatternly one, the one with all the men and boys alike after her. How are we to keep my daughter safe, Mr. Godwin?"

Papa rubbed his lower lip with his thumb. "Shelley has made it clear he wants Mary. I have not yet had an interview with her today, but I will do so now. Call her to my library, will you please, Mrs. Godwin?"

"I don't think we should give her the run of the house," Mamma said.

I frowned. If they kept her in her room, who would cook? Polly had no intention, or likely, any ability, to do everything herself.

"Then I will speak to her in her bedchamber."

I heard a chair scrape back on the floor. My eyebrows went up. Luckily, my teacup was empty by then. I grabbed my plate and darted up the stairs as quietly as I could before anyone came out.

I sat on my bed, plate in hand, door cracked. Hopefully, Papa wouldn't spot me, and I could hear everything. Luckily, the dear old thing didn't pay any attention to my door when he came up. He went to Mary's and knocked, then rattled the door. She must have locked it, or Mamma had locked her in.

"Open the door, Mary. It is your father."

"You never come here," I heard Mary say.

"Open," he instructed.

I heard the door rattle again. Mary must have been trying to open it. Why had Mamma locked her in? She and Shelley met all the time. I had just panicked due to the fraught circumstances with Charles. She'd have been better to lock me in instead, given the state of the breakfast we'd had. Who could run a shop with slightly scorched porridge and old tea leaves in their belly? I set my plate aside and went to watch from my door.

Papa ran his hand over the doorframe and lifted a key from the top. I was fascinated. I hadn't known it was there. He unlocked the door, then slid the key into a pocket, which was unfortunate.

"Your wife locked me in?" Mary asked in her coldest voice.

"You hadn't noticed?"

Mary didn't respond.

"Why were you out of doors in the dark?" Papa asked gently. "Were you looking for food?"

"I often forage very early," Mary said. "For berries or greens. But not in the dark."

"Does Shelley go with you?"

"He does, to keep me safe."

"Well, daughter, I am glad for that, but why was Jane so disturbed that she ran out of doors in her nightgown and woke up Mrs. Godwin?"

"She must have thought we were going to say our farewells to Charles without her."

"Is something afoot with him?"

"Mamma asked Shelley to make arrangements for him to leave town. I don't think they have been finished yet, but I can see why Jane would worry."

"Then Jane was not afraid that it was you yourself who was running off, with Shelley?" Papa said, still in the gentlest of tones.

"I know there is an issue of blackmail, and an issue of money that led to my betrothal," Mary said in careful tones. "But Shelley is a gentleman, and honest. Surely, he is a better bargain for me."

"He is married."

"You know his marriage is dead. His wife carries a child that is not his." Mary sniffed. "I won't marry Mr. Fisher. It is too late for him to hurt Charles. He doesn't know where Charles is."

"The banns have been called." Papa's tone held pure reason.

"That doesn't make it my sacred duty to wed him. I'd even say I'd rather marry Reverend Doone, but Shelley is my love, and . . ." She paused, then her voice rose dramatically. "My lover."

My eyebrows rose. How daring she was.

"He cannot have the money he has promised me, daughter," Papa said. "The family's future depends on it. You and your sisters will all be damaged if you leave and take those funds with you. He is not offering you a life that society will deem proper. All your prospects will suffer."

"How can the author of *Political Justice* say such things?"

"There is the world I want and the world that is," Papa said. "Your mother married me to give you a reasonable start in life, and Mrs. Godwin married me for the sake of a child who died. See what I have done, rather than what I wrote before you were born. I want what is best for you."

"I want Shelley," Mary said.

"Mary," Papa said more firmly, "until I can be certain of your return to good sense, you are confined to the schoolroom, since Shelley will not be forbidden from coming to Skinner Street for dinner and conferences about the loans."

My mouth dropped open. Oh, he wouldn't. What a devil Papa was being, in his imperturbable way.

He continued, driving me down to a lower level of hell. "Now Polly must be the cook and Jane the shopgirl. I will sack Willy's tutor, and you are to be in charge of your younger brother now."

"I am to tutor, sir?" Mary asked, with a note of hilarity in her voice. "Do I not have the least education in this house?"

"You with your nose perpetually in a book? You have sufficient knowledge, I am sure. But there is no reason why you can't educate both of you on subjects you find of interest. Chemistry, perhaps."

"Alchemy," Mary said sourly. "Surely I can discern what was in St. Leon's chest of implements."

"Something much more practical," Papa suggested. "I had best stop talking, or Jane will never get to work."

I winced. He'd known I was there. We were all going to suffer. Polly could not manage the household herself. Papa, secure from most domestic concerns, would learn that soon enough.

"Am I to go upstairs now?" Mary asked.

"Yes, go up, and send the tutor down to my library. I will have some callers for you to see later." Papa paused. "They will be sent upstairs. Jane can open the shop."

He turned, without making eye contact with me, and went down the stairs. Mary and I looked at each other from our respective doorways. Her bleak expression mirrored mine. Then she pressed her lips together until they quite disappeared, and went up to the schoolroom.

None of this would help fix the mess our household was in. We fed the tutor only one meal a day, despite his wistful demeanor and comments, and his salary was paltry enough. Papa was jousting with air, and Shelley was a creature of flesh and blood.

Besides, I could not resist either of them. They would use me as a go-between, since I was part of the plot, and who could blame me? It was my duty to help Charles, and he was sadly involved in this farce.

I had just finished sweeping the bookshop floor when two ladies entered. I recognized both of them. Pretty Cornelia Turner, brown ringlets fluttering about her cheeks, was the wife of one of Papa's disciples. Shelley had been quite close to her at one time, or had wanted to be, so the rumors said. Behind her was Shelley's wife, of all people, an attractive ginger-haired girl, not yet showing signs of the expectations she claimed to have.

"Mrs. Turner, Mrs. Shelley." I greeted them in something of a monotone, for I did not like to see either of them at Skinner Street. What if Mrs. Shelley took up with her husband again? It would break poor Mary's heart, and didn't she have enough to deal with?

My eye twitched. I pressed my finger to it and tried not to cry.

"Miss Clairmont?" Mrs. Turner asked. "I'm surprised to see you not at school."

"I would think you would know that very well," I said bitterly, for she was married to a disciple of Papa's. "What can I sell you today, madam?"

"Nothing. We are here at dear Godwin's request. Is he upstairs?" she replied.

I nodded and slowly took my finger away from my eye. It immediately twitched again, to my irritation. "He invited you to come today?"

"Yes, I had a letter," she said.

"So did I," Mrs. Shelley said, her expression sour. "Is my husband here?"

"I haven't seen him." My voice was curt.

"Do you expect him?"

"He often has his dinners with us." I couldn't resist. "You haven't joined him here in a very long time."

She blatantly put her hand to her belly and caressed it. "I can't live on turnips."

"Let's go up," said Mrs. Turner hurriedly, the last person who would want to debate subsisting on vegetables. She took Mrs. Shelley's arm and towed her out of the room.

Shortly thereafter, I could hear footsteps moving in the library over my head, then a large racket as everyone in the room departed. The roof shook, then subsided again, but they didn't come back down. They must be going up to the schoolroom. What an unusual day. Mamma spent so much of her energy on Charles, and Papa had now focused on Mary.

Which left me to do what I wanted. I warred with myself, but really, this was too important. As soon as the porter came in, I bade him take control of the desk and went up, hugging the wall.

As I suspected, the library was empty. In Papa's journal, I

saw the fresh update: *H S in town.* Papa was always so precise. I met Willy on the stairs when I went out.

"What are you doing?" I asked. "Isn't Mary teaching you how to pluck feathers from a chicken or to make a soup stock or something?"

He shrugged. "First, Papa makes Mary stay with me. Then he makes me leave the schoolroom. That is well enough. I'm going to go play by the church." He grinned at me and ran down the stairs, making so much racket that I was able to climb up them without stirring any notice.

I walked toward the schoolroom cautiously, but no one was looking in the direction of the door. Papa and his guests, lovely as muses, had their backs to me, intent upon Mary, who had her placid gaze fixed on Papa. It hardly mattered. She had the curious gift of exuding intensity even when she looked as still as a statue. I felt it when she and Shelley were in a room together, and I felt it now, when Papa was persecuting her.

"I know you will better understand the errors in your conduct after speaking to these married persons," Papa said. "They are able to give context and history to what you are experiencing."

He spoke of love as if it were nothing but another experience. Papa, so much older than us, might possibly be right, of course, but he'd never fallen in love with a beautiful and young creature like Shelley, nor had he fallen in love with anyone when he was hot-blooded and sixteen. He was over forty when he'd married Mary's mother, and she not so many years younger.

"Will you stay and hear it?" Mary said. Her lips twitched.

"I have business." Papa turned.

Quick as a flash, I jumped behind the door, shielding myself, but he kept his eyes straight ahead as he left, in all apparent eagerness.

"I have nothing to say to either of you," Mary said.

"I feel quite differently," Mrs. Shelley said. "How can you think to run away with my husband? He has a child. Do you think you are anything special, when he chose me at sixteen, too?"

"You married a man I can quote. 'A system could not well have been devised more studiously hostile to human happiness than marriage.' What better proof of that is your marriage, Mrs. Shelley? You have betrayed him."

"He has betrayed me," Mrs. Shelley said.

"Not until your marriage was thoroughly dead," Mary returned emphatically.

"You are wrong," Mrs. Turner interjected. "Not long before Shelley met you, he was attempting to entice me, Mary. With words and soft glances."

Mary snorted. "He is a poet."

Mrs. Turner pressed on. "Your family has known mine for years. I have no reason to lie to you. I don't want you to be unhappy. You are young, and this is a difficult time. I'm aware of the troubles you are laboring under."

"I am the happiest," Mary said. "For I can be sure of Shelley's love."

If I was an artist, I'd have been desperate for a brush to paint the scene. Mary, as pale and composed as a martyr, and the two slightly older matrons, stretching out their arms to beseech her. I knew they had no hope of persuading her. Mary had made up her own mind. Shelley was so compelling. True love would win. Most important of all from my point of view was Charles. We had to leave with him. He needed our support.

Mrs. Turner sighed. "Mary, let me read you some lines that Shelley left for me at my mother's home at Bracknell." She unbuttoned her reticule and pulled out a curled piece of paper, then read.

Thy dewy looks sink in my breast;
Thy gentle words stir poison there;

> *Thou has disturbed the only rest*
> *That was the portion of despair!*
> *Subdued to Duty's hard control,*
> *I could have borne my wayward lot:*
> *The chains that bind this ruined soul*
> *Had cankered then—but crushed it not.*

"What of it?" Mary asked coolly.

"He wrote those words for me," Mrs. Turner said softly. "My mother kicked him out of his refuge with us after she read the poem. He was quite obsessed with me."

"Did you respond in kind?" Mary asked.

"Of course not."

Mary nodded. "I did respond in kind. I love him, and that is the difference. Anyone might be rejected and move on to find love elsewhere."

"You speak of my husband," Harriet Shelley said in a choked-up sort of tone.

"You cannot expect to be under the same terms with Shelley after your betrayal of him. Why was he at Bracknell?" Mary asked. "He was ill, and you weren't caring for him? Think about that when you wonder why things broke down."

"You only see the situation from his perspective," Mrs. Shelley said. "There was a pregnancy, a baby, no money. I have done what I've had to do, and don't think your life will be any different from what mine has been."

Mary looked down her long nose at Shelley's wife. "We wish to live in the same manner. He was unable to ever come to a sort of agreement with you, and then there is the issue of your sister. I know she has schemed with my stepmother. *Poison* is what I would call her."

"You are never without your stepsister," Mrs. Shelley remarked very cattily. "Then there is the matter of your half sister. You have nothing to hold over my family, I assure you.

You claim my sister is scheming. Well, what about your father?"

"Shelley offered help out of the purity of his heart," Mary said. "The approach came from him, never my father."

"We revere *Political Justice* at Bracknell," Mrs. Turner said, her blue eyes full of tender emotion. "You know this. But think of how it will look if you run away with Shelley and your father receives funds from him? It will look as if he sold you to Mrs. Shelley's husband as a concubine."

"No one who knows my father, or Shelley, for that matter, will think such nonsense," Mary declared. She went to Willy's desk and sat behind it.

I thought she looked rather weary, perhaps because she was trapped inside. She was a girl who liked her walks.

"Think hard," Mrs. Turner advised. "You are simply the latest young girl he's become infatuated with. He isn't well, Mary. He spends much too much time in laudanum dreams."

Mrs. Shelley nodded. "I have no doubt that half of what he tells you is utter fiction."

"I've seen you with other men," I said, stepping boldly in where I didn't belong. "He isn't telling fiction about your behavior."

Mrs. Shelley didn't react. "What of his? What of his principles, that would state I have done nothing but follow his own philosophy? We are still closer than you expect, and always will be."

I could see that Mary remained resolute. I wondered if these two young wives knew anything about Charles or about the tyrannical behavior of Mamma toward Mary. Mary really was desperate.

"I am sorry that you felt the need to waste your time by coming here," Mary said blandly. "Truly, my only immediate concern is my stepbrother's situation under the law because of the murdered Davies girls."

Mrs. Turner spoke, surprising me. "That John Griffith is a foul creature, and I would not be surprised if he murdered a girl who refused him."

"How do you know him?" I asked.

Mrs. Turner's gentle expression hardened. "I've been to that shop. He was so rude to me after I told him to stop making advances toward me that I never returned."

"We thought he preyed only young girls," Mary said. "Was this after your wedding?"

Mrs. Turner's curls danced as she shook her head. "No, just before. It has been some time."

"Then he is consistent, at least," Mary said, as if to herself, then lifted her gaze. "Do you know anything about his son?"

Mrs. Turner shook her head. "I didn't know the Griffiths had a son."

"It is odd," Mary said. "The current Mrs. Griffith is not his mother. How old is he that none of us seem to know he exists?"

"He might have been sent away to school," Mrs. Shelley suggested.

"A cheesemonger's son? It seems unlikely," Mrs. Turner said.

"Mrs. Shelley was sent," Mary snapped. "And me, besides."

Mrs. Shelley put her hand to her belly. "It is not always the best thing, for it leads to estrangement."

Mrs. Turner put her hand on Mrs. Shelley's arm, clearly attempting to stop any further commentary that might lead to harsh words.

"You are a prideful creature," Mrs. Shelley said, shaking Mrs. Turner off. "The fact remains that he is my husband."

"You have enough education to know how little that matters to me," Mary said. "He is the other half of my soul but is much too good a creature to cast you off entirely for your mistreatment of him. He will remain in the life of you and your daughter."

"Insolence," Mrs. Shelley hissed.

"We've done all we can," Mrs. Turner said gently. "Let us give Mary space to think. She is an intelligent girl and may yet come to her senses."

Mary snorted. "Like either of you did? One of you married him, and the other had him run off by her mother."

"Think like a parent instead of a girl, then," Mrs. Turner said. "I know this household well enough to know that you have had to mother yourself, Mary."

"My mother loved a married man," Mary said, her lips twisting. "And ran off to a revolution with a broken heart. How can I make a safe choice with a parent like that?"

Mrs. Turner shook her head in such a tight motion that her curls did not dance again. She merely took Mrs. Shelley's arm and towed her out of the room, nearly bumping into me.

My eyes met Mary's from the doorway. My stepsister stared me down, then shut the door in my face.

I started down the stairs, moving faster when I heard voices in the hall. Mrs. Shelley and Mrs. Turner must have greeted Mrs. Griffith, who stood there. Did they know she was the spouse of the loathed Mr. Griffith?

"Is your mother here, Jane?" Mrs. Griffith asked, squeezing her hands together.

"She'll be in her office. Come," I invited, opening the shop door.

I found Mamma behind the counter, attending upon a young mother with a large infant in her arms. Mamma dropped coins into the cash box and told me to wrap up a copy of Aesop.

I winced. Where had the porter gone? But Mamma had thankfully spotted Mrs. Griffith before she lashed out at me. She nodded at our neighbor while I fussed with old newspaper and string. I helped the customer set the book into the basket on her arm, and then she went out.

"What can I help you with, Mrs. Griffith? I'm happy to trade our goods for yours."

"We have three girls out missing today," Mrs. Griffith said. "I thought maybe you could spare Jane to mind my counter, since you have another daughter?"

"They are good girls, not allowed to leave the house," Mamma said. "They have plenty to do here."

Mrs. Griffith rattled her skirt. Coins clinked, reminding us that she had ready money, which we never seemed to possess.

"Why are your girls missing?" Mamma said, coming back to herself after a vague moment brought on by the jingling.

"Passed a summer ague around in the dairy," Mrs. Griffith said. "My poor husband has a bit of it, too. Ran a fever last night, though it's gone today."

"Hmmm," Mamma said.

"A shilling extra if she can come right now for the afternoon," Mrs. Griffith said coaxingly.

"Jane can bring back some cheese with her?"

"I'll pay her in it, if it pleases you."

Mamma held out her hand, and a shilling was dropped into it. Sad, I watched the money disappear, but perhaps I'd be able to eat some cheese when no one was looking. Without saying anything, I followed Mrs. Griffith out.

"Mind your reputation," Mamma called as we departed the house. "Don't talk to any unfamiliar men."

Mrs. Griffith frowned as we went into the street. "You may have to talk to men, if they are customers."

"I have no idea what she is worried about," I muttered. Unfamiliar men weren't our problem. It was the familiar ones who put us at risk.

At the shop, Mrs. Griffith showed me a ledger and the cash box; then she sent the girl she'd left at the counter to run for the facilities behind the shop and went back into the dairy herself. "The price list is inside the cover," she said from the doorway.

"If you don't find the name, they don't have an account and need to pay before they leave."

I stared at the cheeses around me, which were all labeled for the customers' convenience and, therefore, my own, as well. The milky smells around me made my stomach growl, but at least there was no dust to tickle my nose. I preferred our own bookshop, though, where I could read anything I liked when Mamma wasn't looking.

Four hours went by quickly, with lots of women, mostly local maids, coming in to fetch cheese for their masters' evening meals. The Griffiths managed their supply in tune with the neighborhood. Earlier in the day, they must have estimated what was likely to be purchased, and cut cheese into the right amounts. I didn't have one chance to cut portions from a larger block and take a bit for myself in payment for the labor.

Just as I was starting to wonder how long I would have to remain at the shop for nothing but a shilling, John Griffith came in through the front door.

He did a double take. "Why, if it isn't Jane Clairmont! What are you doing here?"

His eyes had a reddened look, and the rest of his face had the pale hue of an invalid. I hoped he would not try to get too close to me. I did not want the ague.

"You have three girls out ill," I said. "Your wife begged my mother for my assistance."

He nodded. "A wise woman, Mrs. Griffith. We have found it increasingly difficult to attract the right sort of girl." He leered at me, but even with my lack of experience, I knew the effort was half-hearted. Rightly so, for he would not want to cross Mamma in a full temper.

Ignoring his haggard appearance, I said, "May I leave now? Mrs. Griffith said she would pay me in cheese. I've been here these four hours." I pointed to a small round, hoping he would be generous.

Instead, he sniffled. I thought he was going to sneeze, but instead, he squeezed his rheumy eyes, and fat tears dripped down his cheeks.

"Whatever is wrong?" I asked.

"T-that was Miss Davies's favorite cheese. We bring in the sheep's milk to make it. To think she will never steal a sliver again when she thinks we are not looking." He pulled out a handkerchief, quite stiff with the results of his cold, and wiped his entire face.

"Winnet Davies is a sad loss indeed," I agreed. "My brother was her friend."

Mr. Griffith leaned toward me. I held my breath, not wanting to breathe in his illness. "I know there are rumors he was more than a friend."

I shook my head. "Only by those ignorant souls who did not know of his attachment to Branwen Davies."

"Precisely," he said, exposing his yellow-rooted teeth in his verbal precision. "Winnet was my little love, and mine alone."

I fought to keep a serene expression, in the manner of Mary. "That must mean the unborn babe was yours?"

He nodded, tears welling again. "And much wanted by me, for Mrs. Griffith is barren. I was going to set up a nice warm room on the other side of St. Barts for Winnet and the babe. I had such plans."

"What went wrong?" I whispered.

"Someone was jealous of her good fortune," he said. He stared over my shoulder. "Someone punished her for it."

"Like a dairy rival?" I guessed. "Or your wife, as you've said before?"

"Even the women here are strong," he said, then sneezed loudly into his handkerchief. Behind him, the door opened, but the woman in a smart gray gown heard the sneeze and shut the door again, then hurried down the street.

I could not believe he was the killer, regardless of Mrs. Turner's opinion of him. He had wanted the child. Mrs. Griffith, though, might have felt differently, or even one of Mr. Griffith's other lovers.

He patted my arm, but I didn't jump back, as I might have on another day. "You tell your brother to stay strong. The killer will be found, and we'll see him again at the warehouse."

I smiled at the kindness, no longer afraid of him. "Thank you, sir. Now, about that cheese?"

Chapter 18

Mary

Mamma sent Polly up to the schoolroom with blankets and a meager meal of bread and cheese on Friday night. The room held all the heat of the house, it seemed. Mary slept very poorly that night, revenge brewing in her heart for the way she was being treated.

On Saturday morning, after Mary had already been awake for at least an hour, pacing the dusty floor, Polly came in with a bowl of oatmeal and a teapot. She took Mary's chamber pot without a word and departed again. Mary called out behind her, "I need a jug of water." No response was offered.

She ate her breakfast, then paced around the room, muttering stanzas of Shelley's poetry to herself.

"'Behold the chariot of the Fairy Queen!/ Celestial coursers paw the unyielding air;/ Their filmy pennons at her word they furl,/ And stop obedient to the reins of light,'" she recited, then fancifully went to the window, just in case a rescuer would appear there. In the street below, she saw men walking around, intent on their daily routine, and an occasional maid with a basket. Carts were pushed down the hill, and even a trap went by now and then, as she rested her nose on the glass. No traffic came toward the bookshop. "Shelley," she whispered. "Where are you?"

She heard footsteps in the passage, then laughed because for a moment, she thought she had summoned him with an incantation. But he was not such a fae creature as to be conjured out of nothing but air.

Jane came in with a jug, then collapsed into one of the hardback chairs, all the schoolroom offered for comfort. She stared up at Mary with quite a stupid look on her face.

"What?" Mary demanded.

"Polly and I cannot do everything," Jane said, a staccato bounce to each word.

Mary shrugged and paced again. "None of this is my fault. Does your mother not recognize that locking me up will only prevent Shelley from rescuing Charles? She is hurting her own son with her intransigence."

"Charles will have to help himself," Jane said. "Why couldn't you have met Shelley away from the house?"

"This is your fault," Mary snarled. "You are the one who ran into the street in your nightdress. That is what Mamma is incensed about. She's just taking it out on me. You should be the one locked up in here."

"I'm locked up in the house just the same. What's the difference?"

"The difference is that you get to fetch water when you want it, and I have to ask for it." Mary's stomach clutched. "Do you think they'll let me into the garden?"

"On Monday, probably, for the washing," Jane said. "I have to go down to the bookshop now."

"What am I to do?" Mary went to the jug.

"Willy will be up here soon. Work on your French," Jane advised. "We'll need it for when we escape."

"Do you still believe we can?" Mary asked.

Jane smiled at her. "There will be a moment when Shelley will strike. You'll see. This amount of romance will elevate his sensibilities to new levels."

Mary went to a history book and pulled out the note she'd written late the night before. "Get this to Shelley, will you? I'm sure he'll come into the bookshop at some point."

Jane took it and tucked it down her bodice. "I will, Mary. You can trust me."

Mary wiped perspiration from her cheeks. "I need the chamber pot. Polly took it."

"I'll tell her to bring it back up," Jane said, then went out the door.

Willy eventually came in, but he wanted only to talk about wars and kings. Mary read a French primer in a corner of the room and fanned herself while he set up the Battle of Agincourt with his soldiers.

For luncheon, Mary had only oatmeal again. What were they eating downstairs? She'd periodically gone to the window, and she'd seen a couple of people coming in. Surely, they had a few coins in the box?

"Go down and fetch me a bucket and some rags," Mary said, getting tired of hearing him describe soldiers being run through in the belly. "We really need to clean this floor."

Hours passed. They cleaned the floor and even wiped marks from the tables and walls. Mary read Shelley's notes on a vegetable diet and considered how Harriet Boinville, Cornelia Turner's mother, had encouraged him into it.

She watched from the window as Jane went out and hurried out of sight, holding a basket. Would she be able to give Shelley the note? She'd written him to find an answer to their troubles.

"Can I go now?" Willy asked.

She waved him out. Jane had told her she was absolutely certain that Mr. Griffith was crushed by Miss Davies's death, even though he'd stolen her money. She'd indicated sentiment had been behind it. If that were true, how could they trap Mrs. Griffith into a confession? Leaving aside the mysterious matter of the gun case. It might have nothing to do with the dead girls.

She pondered that. Mrs. Griffith had likely tolerated her husband's bad behavior for years and had not killed her employees. What had changed? The seriousness of the amours? The pregnancy? Why would the murdering have continued on to Branwen Davies?

Mary's thoughts fixed on that. No, Mrs. Griffith did not seem a likely murderer for two girls who were killed the same way and in the same place. Mary struck the wall next to the window in frustration. She left a dent in the damp plaster.

Someday they would never wake up because the walls of this decaying mess would collapse on top of them. She turned away. Not her problem.

Shelley was the key and answer to all these matters. He had to find the gun case. He had to arrange passage for Charles. She could do nothing here, and her brain was descending into the mush that she'd been given to eat.

Movement in the street caught her eye. She saw Shelley coming up the street rapidly, no hat, bent to an angle as his long legs made strides. Jane hurried behind him, burdened by her basket.

They didn't see her, but the house rocked when he pushed open the door so hard that it hit the wall. She imagined plaster drifting to the floor like snowflakes.

The house gasped and groaned as he bounded up the steps. A cacophony of squeaks followed his progress. Jane's steps resounded behind him. Voices rose as the rest of the house was aroused from the sleepiness of the summer afternoon. Mary wiped the sweat from her face. Was he going to kidnap her like the hero of a novel? Her pulse leapt in expectation.

The schoolroom door opened with the ferocity of a soldier bayoneting another.

"Mary!" Shelley cried in tones of sweet desperation.

She expected him to rush her, to hug her. She held out her arms, faint with excitement. Instead, he turned when Mamma came in the door, followed by Polly, her cap hanging down over one ear.

"Mary," he cried, an expression of utter anguish on his face. He hadn't shaven, and dots of brown stubble, darker than his hair in the summer, covered the taut line of his jaw. Reaching into his coat, he pulled out a small brown bottle and handed it to her.

Mary took it, her hands feeling strangely apart from her. "What is this, Shelley?"

He pulled out a gun. As Jane screamed, he began to recite Shakespeare.

> *Why art thou yet so fair? Shall I believe*
> *That unsubstantial death is amorous,*
> *And that the lean abhorrèd monster keeps*
> *Thee here in dark to be his paramour?*
> *For fear of that I still will stay with thee*
> *And never from this palace of dim night*
> *Depart again. Here, here will I remain*
> *With worms that are thy chambermaids. O, here*
> *Will I set up my everlasting rest*
> *And shake the yoke of inauspicious stars*
> *From this world-wearied flesh!*

"What are you talking about?" Mary cried. "Why are you reciting Romeo's death speech?"

"Drink the laudanum," Shelley urged. "There is no way forward. Drink. It will be an easy death, and then I will shoot myself in the head. We will lie here together for eternity."

> *Eyes, look your last.*
> *Arms, take your last embrace. And, lips, O, you*

The doors of breath, seal with a righteous kiss
A dateless bargain to engrossing death.

Shock sank low into her belly. Why did he despair when she'd been true? "No, Shelley, no!" She had wanted him to come here, to rescue her, but not like this. What had gone wrong? Ignoring the cries of the other women, she spoke softly. "My love, my only love."

"It is lost. It is all lost," Shelley moaned. Still holding the gun, he raised his hands and tore at his hair.

"All is not lost. It is not." She reached out to him, fingers trembling, ignoring Mamma's indeterminate hiss.

Jane started to speak, but Mary threw the little bottle in her direction. Instinctively, she knew the only way forward was for Shelley to focus on her.

"We have to die," Shelley said, rocking back and forth.

"Then kill me with that gun," Mary said, forcing her voice to remain calm. "Put it to my breast and stop this heart, which beats only for you. Meditate on my bloodstained form as you reload the weapon and destroy that brilliant brain of yours." She lifted her rib cage and pointed her index fingers to her chest.

"No, Mary," Mamma cried.

Mary stayed resolute, looking only at Shelley. "You are, and will always be, my only love. If you were to die before me, I would pluck out your heart and keep it next to me."

"No," Shelley whispered, his gaze unfocused, the blue seeming to have dimmed to gray.

"Yes," Mary said stoutly, hoping she was reaching him. Did she not know sadness? Her mother had tried to kill herself, and now her lover was intent on the same destruction. Why did she court darkness? "I would. If you want to kill me, do it, and keep my heart with yours, to make yours all the stronger." She held out her arms, exposing her chest to him. "See, my love? Do what you will. This body exists only for you."

He swayed, his hands dropping to his thighs, the gun loose in his fingers.

Mamma gave a little desperate gasp. Jane's footsteps sounded. Mary saw her going to Mamma. Jane kicked the bottle of poison to the wall and hugged her.

"I don't know how to fix this," Shelley moaned.

"You don't have to, not tonight," Mary assured him. "Some news will break. Something will change. But, Shelley, I want you to be alive tomorrow. The world needs you."

"Yes," he whispered.

She nodded and daringly wrapped her arms around his waist. Never had she been so close to a loaded gun. In her house, words were weapons, not cold metal. "Tomorrow you will wake refreshed and full of ideas. I will wake and tell Willy how brave you were. You are his hero, you know. Everything you've done, in Ireland, in Wales . . . I know it has left a cruel mark on you, Shelley, but you must go on, for the world, for me."

"For me," Jane added.

Shelley took his gaze off Mary and looked at Jane. His entire being seemed to sag a little. He licked his lips and put the gun to Mary's cheek.

She went even more still. Would she have to die? Had his reason departed? She kept her eyes open, wanting to imprint his tortured face on her eternity. All he did was caress her cheek with the backs of his fingers, the cold metal scraping her. She smelled the tang of the metal.

"I have failed you," he said. "I cannot find the gun case. I cannot save Charles. I cannot save myself."

He turned, dropping his hand, and passed through the line of Jane and Mamma, then went heavily down the stairs.

Mary ran to the window, Mamma and Jane behind her. They watched Shelley leave the house a minute later and walk into the street, his attitude that of a man with a thousand cares. He still had the gun.

"He is going in the direction of his rooms," Jane reported.

"He should not be alone," Mary said, still shaking. "He has lost the light in his heart. He needs hope."

"You will not follow." Sweat trickled from Mamma's temples into her dark hair. "How would your papa feel if he lost you?"

Jane picked up the laudanum bottle. "Shelley left the bottle."

"I will not take it. If I die, he will have to watch," Mary responded.

Mamma plucked the bottle from Jane's fingers and left the schoolroom, moving slowly.

Mary and Jane stared at each other. "How desperate do you have to be to want to die? Even cooped up here in this room, I don't want to die. I understand him, I do, but what has made him lose hope? Has something gone wrong with his plans?"

"He is a creature of dark moods," Jane said, equal question in her voice. "He needs us to be his light."

"And the animator of his intellect. He's done nothing but spin his wheels with us trapped in the house." Mary clutched Jane's arm to center herself. "I think he'd be better off with Harriet and Ianthe than alone."

Jane nodded and put her hand over Mary's. "He probably forgets to eat and sleep."

"Something has to change," Mary said with a cry. "When you see him next, you must tell him that the only answer is for us to flee together. I don't give him a week of sanity in the present circumstances. What if he uses that gun?"

Jane squeezed her shoulder. "If I see him, I will tell him that. I think you are right. My bundle is ready."

"Take my things into your room," Mary urged. "My writing box, please. It has all my papers in it, and various letters."

"I will," Jane promised.

On Sunday, Mary watched from the window while Jane and Willy left for church. Mamma had refused to let her go, for fear of Shelley appearing somewhere along the path. Mary hoped he did. She wanted proof of life, having passed an anxious night fearing for him. Surely if he put the gun to his temple, the thought of her face would stop him?

Just after breakfast time, Mary had had enough. Polly had not come up with any food for her, and her stomach rumbled. She'd had nothing since an oatcake the night before. Death from a gun held by her lover was one thing, but starvation was unacceptable.

Resolutely, she marched down to the dining room, but if they had eaten there, the remains had been cleared. She debated her chances. Papa would never beat her, and Mamma struck at her randomly regardless of her actions. A little pain did not matter when her belly had command of her.

She did not hesitate but went down to the front hall, intent on the kitchen. Maybe she had missed Mamma going to church herself, or she and Papa were paying calls.

As she crossed the boards, a knock came on the front door. She tore the door open. A bright green coat demanded attention.

"Mr. Bryan?" she said, recognizing him. "What are you doing here?"

"I require an immediate consultation with your father, if you would be so good, Miss Godwin." The man rubbed his gloves together, then laced his fingers.

"I don't know where he is," Mary said.

To her right, she heard the noise of the opening parlor door. Her body screwed up tight. She wanted to flee but stood her ground. She was caught either way.

Papa stood in the doorway. "I thought you were to remain upstairs."

"I am starving, Papa. No one fed me today."

He frowned and came forward, addressing the interloper rather than her. "Mr. Bryan?"

"Please, sir," Mr. Bryan said, wringing his fingers together in earnest. "I need shelter."

"That is rather dramatic, sir. Are you in need of new employment?"

"If I may." The conjurer's assistant stepped boldly in and shut the door behind him. "Are we alone, sir?"

"Alone?" Papa looked flustered. "Near enough. Why? The bookshop is not open today."

Mr. Bryan let out a little cry of anguish. "Oh, good sir, we have been so betrayed."

Mary's stomach gurgled, reminding her of her own betrayal. "By whom?" she asked.

The man lowered his voice to a confidential whisper. "Professor Asquith is going to try to kill the Duke of Wellington at the Carlton House fête on July twenty-first."

Mary's eyebrows rose in tandem with Papa's.

"Stuff and nonsense," Papa blustered.

"It is not," Mr. Bryan insisted. "We have four days to save a man's life."

"How was it that you came to work for such a man?" Papa's eyes creased. "My own son is with him now."

"It was a lie about Charles," Mary said, patting Papa's arm. "He is not with the professor in Bath. That was one of Jane's little fibs, but it has served to keep him safe."

"He is with the professor?" Papa asked, his brow creased in gentle confusion. "Here in London?"

"No," Mary assured him. "Charles has nothing to do with the man at all." She kept her counsel as to where exactly Charles was, however. They could not trust this Mr. Bryan. Desperate for money, he might divulge Charles's whereabouts to the magistrates for a few coins.

"How come you by this information?" Papa asked, ignoring Mary again.

"I knew the professor had business matters beyond that of

natural philosophy," Mr. Bryan said. He clutched his stomach. "Please, may I have some food? I am dreadfully hungry."

Mary fixed him with a glare. "Story first, sir. We cannot set the table we did when we first met you."

Mr. Bryan took off his hat, exposing the greasy circle inside. "The professor is the last of his family. He lost his brother at Mysore fourteen years ago, when the duke ordered soldiers against the insurgency there, and his only son at Talavera five years ago. When his wife died in the spring, I think the last bit of sanity snapped. He has become secretive, alchemic."

"How do you know of this plot? Why is it important now, today?" Papa asked.

Mr. Bryan rubbed his eyes, then put his hat back on. "We toured the north. He had meetings there. I was in a tavern in Cheapside, trying to get work, when I saw one of the associates he had met at a low place along the River Mersey. The man had no business being in London."

"Why is he important?"

"He lost an eye and a hand at Talavera," Mr. Bryan explained. "He hates the duke as much as the professor does. He is unforgettable."

"Come upstairs," Papa said. "I will write a letter and send it to the Home Office."

"Will they listen?" Mr. Bryan asked.

"I do not know what else you could ask of me," Papa said, then gestured the man upstairs. He turned to Mary and said, "Quickly, bring some food to the library. Then return to the schoolroom."

"Yes, Papa," Mary said, intent on doing that, anyway.

She went down and found the kitchen cold and empty. Polly must have gone to church, as well. Half a loaf of bread was in the box. She cut off a moldy corner and sliced the loaf, then generously buttered the slices. After she tucked half of them into a napkin and hid them in her apron, she put the rest on a plate and brought it up to Mr. Bryan, along with the weak cup of tea she'd made from the leftover leaves in the pot.

"Is this all?" he asked, his gaze surprisingly hostile, given that she'd warned him.

"Yes," Mary said.

Papa blotted a piece of letter paper and folded it intricately, then reached into his desk and pulled out a few pennies. He set them on the letter. "Deliver it, though I do not know who you will be able to find on a Sunday."

"Who do you recommend?" Mr. Bryan asked.

Papa snorted. "I am not the man to ask. Go to St. James's Palace and ask around."

"They might arrest me."

"Play the fool. Deliver the letter. Then go," Papa said. "Use your good sense, sir."

"I could take it," Mary suggested. "And buy food on the way back."

Mr. Bryan's hand closed over the pennies, and the letter disappeared into his coat.

"Return to the schoolroom." Papa's tone allowed for no immediate disobedience.

Mary went up, glad for her mouthful of tea and pocket of bread and butter. Her mood had restored, somewhat. Did they mean to starve her into submission? At least she'd have good experience to recall when she worked Isabella the Penitent's suffering into her book.

Mary had been continually shocked all that Monday by Mamma's adherence to Papa's dictate that she stay in the schoolroom. While she attempted to teach Willy his kings, his mythology, and his Latin, she'd watched Mamma, Jane, and Polly struggle around the back garden with the laundry.

What she hadn't expected was Jane and Polly being sent up with baskets of clean linen and the iron on top of the firebox, ready for her to occupy herself through the night.

"Am I not to sleep?" Mary asked, dumbfounded, as Polly spread a clean sheet of linen over a long deal table in the schoolroom so that she could iron.

"It will give you some exercise other than pacing," Jane said, staring doubtfully as Polly left. "There's more. We caught up on everything."

"Because you never stopped to iron." Mary felt close to tears and near feverish from deprivation.

Jane shrugged. "It's just cold dinner tonight, but the ham is good, I think."

"Bring me some. Did you see Shelley at all today?"

"He took a walk with Papa instead of with us, can you imagine? He looked miserable, nearly as bad as that Patrick Patrickson. He is here for dinner. And Mrs. Boinville called with another friend. I expect she is not happy about her daughter getting mixed up into this."

Mary ignored all the prattle. "Do you still want to leave Skinner Street?"

Jane nodded. "This is no adventure, and we have Charles to think of."

"When you see Shelley again, send him my love." Mary's voice caught on the final word, but she didn't want Jane to go downstairs emotional. Mr. Patrickson was such a watering pot that Jane's tears would send him into a tizzy, poor boy.

Jane nodded. "I'll bring you up whatever is left." She shut the door behind herself when she exited.

No key turned in the lock, but what did it matter? Enough people were in the house that she wouldn't be able to creep downstairs alone. Had they banned Shelley from dinner now?

Mary sighed and went to the table, then pulled out the first shift. The very clothes she might wear to run away might be in this pile, so she ought to take care of them.

She spread the fabric across the linen protecting the table from the heat and picked up the iron with a rag and started to flatten the cloth. By the time she finished with the first basket,

Polly came up with a plate of odds and ends of ham and bread, along with a sour expression.

"When will this nonsense end?" Polly asked. "I cannot do everything."

"I cannot help you," Mary said. "Please take that first basket down to Jane. She'll know where the clothing goes."

Polly muttered something under her breath and went out. Mary choked down the disgraceful bits of food, wondering how she would treat a daughter of her own in similar circumstances. She could imagine being a mother to a tiny baby, but to someone her own age? Impossible. That would be like trying to be a parent to Jane.

Mamma came up as the watch called eleven. Mary had steadily ironed on for the lack of anything better to do, sweat collecting in every place it could find, though the iron did not heat up much anymore, given that the coals in the firebox had turned mostly to ash.

"You've done a lot," Mamma said, after she rummaged through the basket. "We've caught up on a month of work."

"Where's the mending?"

"In the basket with the broken handle."

"If you bring me my sewing box, I'll start on it," Mary said.

Mamma looked at her curiously. "Don't you want to sleep?"

"It's too hot up here."

Jane appeared in the doorway with a jug of water. Without speaking, she picked up Mary's chamber pot. She made a face and covered it with the rag Mary had been using to handle the iron.

"Bring up Mary's sewing box," Mamma said.

Jane left the room at a trot, holding the pot in front of her.

Mary wanted to dump the water over her head, but she settled for filling her glass and drinking her fill, then opened the window. She folded up the linen sheet on the table and put the iron on the box, then lifted the mending basket onto the table and spread out the little projects. Willy's shirts always needed repair. Jane had a hem loose. Papa had three socks in danger of disintegrating.

Mamma sat in one of the schoolroom chairs across from Mary. When Jane appeared to put the chamber pot away and handed Mary her box, Mamma said, "Bring me some wine, girl, and my box, as well. Then you can go to bed."

Jane had shadows under her eyes. She didn't even nod, just went out numbly.

Mary opened her box and put her thimble on her finger, then threaded a needle. Mamma flipped Willy's first shirt inside out.

"You are usually an intelligent girl, Mary. Why won't you listen to Mrs. Turner and Shelley's wife?"

"Shelley's wife is dishonest. It's a fact, Mamma. There's no need to discuss it. She has laid waste to Shelley's life."

A long pause ensued. Jane came back, then left again. Mamma sipped her wine and made no effort to open her own box. When Mary set the first shirt aside, neatly folded, and picked up the second, Mamma said, "What of Mrs. Turner?"

"Shelley finds Italian very alluring. I expect her attempts to teach him Italian set him on a little flurry of romance. He admitted as such, at a time when he was ill and his spirits were low. It had nothing to do with Mrs. Turner, whatever her charms."

"Really," Mamma said tersely.

"He's a very attractive man, besides. Who can say?" Mary asked.

"You bend yourself into knots to defend him, Mary," Mamma said.

"As I ought to," Mary said. "He is the best of men. No one would defend any act of Shelley's more than Papa, and it is he whom I look to for guidance."

"What about me?" Mamma said tersely.

Mary thought about that, but surely anything that Mamma

had ever done to be kind, like trips to Ramsgate, had come at Papa's direction. Besides, she only had to think of Eliza Westbrook and her plotting with Mamma to know that Mamma was as much of a deceiver as Shelley's wife. There could be no trusting this woman, not even at a quiet hour like this.

The street had gone still as midnight approached, but Mary swam up from the depths of her mind enough to recognize that outside noise had picked up again. She heard someone running, and voices.

"What is that?" Mamma asked.

"I do hope Charles has not tried to sneak home for a visit, with the watchhouse so close by," Mary fretted. She stuck her needle into Jane's hem and went to the window.

"What do you see?" Mamma asked as Mary wiped her breath from the window and attempted to pierce the darkness.

"I don't know." Mary cupped her hands around her eyes. "Wait. It is two, well, men running. They are coming straight to Skinner Street."

"They may not stop here."

"I think they are. Listen!" Mary craned her neck and just then was rewarded by a pounding at the door.

She flung the schoolroom door open, heedless of the consequences, and ran downstairs. If it was Charles, where could they hide him from the watch? Under a bed? In Mamma's clothes press? In the water butt in the kitchen?

She reached the front hall before Mamma's heavy treads had even descended a floor, then picked up the lamp from the table and unlocked the door.

She didn't recognize either of the young men she saw in front of her. One had the look of one of Shelley's friends, someone with family money to pay for the newer tailcoat and polished boots. The other had a youthful but more weathered appearance of a person who had spent their childhood mostly out of doors, and his hands were visibly roughened, rather than ink-stained like those of the first.

"We seek Mary Jane Godwin," wheezed the slim poet type.

"It is an emergency," the other added in a local accent.

Mary remembered when the watch had called for Mamma before and arrested her, but neither of these had that look. "Where are you come from?"

"Hatton Garden," they said together.

Mamma reached the foot of the staircase just as the church bells tolled midnight. With the door open to the street, the sounds echoing across the city were impossible to miss.

"Why do you call me there?" Mamma asked, coming up alongside Mary.

"It's Shelley," the poet type said. "He has taken too much laudanum, and he may die."

Cold sweat broke out on Mary's torso. She swayed, then dug her fingernails into her hand to keep herself oriented. "No! Not the gun?"

The rougher man shook his head. "Not the gun, miss. He didn't have any bullets."

Behind them, Mary heard Jane coming down the stairs. Her sister put her hand on Mamma's back and her chin on Mary's shoulder. Predictably, she'd forgotten to put on a dressing gown, and her appearance was utterly inappropriate.

"What am I wanted for?" Mamma asked in a manner much more resigned than angry.

"Someone needs to keep him awake while the drug runs its course, Mrs. Godwin," the poet type said. "Shelley, he asked for you."

"Better you than his wife," Jane said brightly. Mary threw a shawl over her sister's shoulders to protect her decency. "What is going on?"

"Go back to bed and don't leave the house, either of you, girls," Mamma said. "Mary, hand me my cloak. Jane, run down and fetch me a bottle of wine and some bread, whatever we have."

Jane ran down the hall, ghostly with her white linen flowing out behind her.

Mary stood dumbstruck, until a pinch on her arm brought her back to herself. She stumbled to the pegs and helped Mamma with her cloak and bonnet and gloves. "He will live, won't he?" she asked the men.

"Probably," the rougher man said. "These poets are always trying to harm themselves. We had one who half slit his throat last year. Lived, but oy, what a scar."

"Faith." Mary's hands dropped away from Mamma. She remembered that little bottle of laudanum that Shelley had thrust at her. Did he mean for her to hear this news and join him in death? But no. Her mother had been of such a temperament and had survived herself twice. She could not, in this terrible way, be like her mother. Her art was worth living for. She deserved to live out her own promise, whatever the cost of it. The end was worth the means.

"Tell him to live," Mary begged Mamma. "Can I please go with you?"

Mamma shook her head, a hint of compassion seeming to swim in the depths of her dark eyes. "This is a job for a woman, not a girl." She nodded briskly at the two men. "Take me to him."

Mary closed her eyes as the night wind hit her face. It seemed to call her name—"*Mary, Mary*"—like a tide ebbing and flowing. She could follow it to her destruction on this night, when no jailer watched her, but she would not. Tonight was meant for words. She shut the front door as soon as Mamma left with the provisions Jane brought.

Her feet took her up to her own bed, forbidden or not. Papa would do nothing, with Shelley incapacitated. She picked up her pencil and pulled a notebook from under her pillow, then wrote a letter of support. When she read it over, she wasn't sure if it had been written to Shelley or maybe to the ghost of her mother.

Before she could turn the page, Jane entered.

Jane set her candle down and settled down next to Mary, searching her face. "Is he going to die?"

"In front of Mamma?" Mary laughed. "No, she won't let him. The loans will never happen if he dies now."

"That's right," Jane said, as if to herself. "The never-ending matter of the loans."

"Help me with my clothes, won't you?" Mary gestured. "I'd like some fresh linen."

Jane sighed and helped her undress. Mary changed her shift, then pulled back her bedclothes and slid in. "I'll need to wake with the dawn, but this is so much more comfortable than the pallet on the floor upstairs."

"And nearly cool, with the window open." Jane jumped in next to her before she could protest.

Mary woke near dawn. Jane didn't stir, so she gathered the rest of her clothes and took them down to make Polly help her. Polly wasn't aware that Mamma had departed, despite Jane coming down the night before. They made breakfast together; then Mary took her portion up to the schoolroom, not knowing when Mamma would return.

The morning passed quietly, then the afternoon. She prayed as much as she could around lessons. How could she go on without the light of Shelley to lead her? Jane came in about four, after Willy had long since ceased paying attention to Mary's attempts to conjugate verbs in Latin.

"Papa has gone out to see Mr. Ballachey about the possible partnership," Jane reported.

Acid bubbled in Mary's stomach. "Does that mean bad news about Shelley?"

"No, he said he would call on Shelley after, then try to take him over to the Hookhams' to cheer him up."

Mary blinked. Shelley must be better, even if Mamma hadn't returned. "Does he know that Charles is in hiding there?"

"I don't think so, but this may be when he finds out."

"Then Shelley is alive?" Mary persisted.

Jane nodded. "You love him so. Wouldn't you feel it if he had expired?"

Mary put her hands to her heart. "I would hope so."

Willy made a face at her.

Mary shooed him away. "La, child. Go play outdoors."

He broke into a run so quickly that his feet skidded on the floor. Grabbing for the doorframe, he pulled himself through and pelted down the stairs.

"What energy five more years of living has cost us," Mary said.

Jane snorted, then looked to the window when a banging started on the front door, resounding all the way up to the schoolroom. "We'd better go down."

Mary shook her head. "Mamma will come soon. I will remain for my own safety."

Chapter 19

Jane

I opened the front door, the pleasant odor of fresh linen drifting around me as I moved. Nostalgia for the way things had been in the spring, when all the women of Skinner Street had been here after Mary had returned home from Scotland, filled my heart.

In the street, Denarius Fisher stood, legs spread, massive arms folded over his chest. How could Mary safely birth the child of this giant? She could not. Because of our poverty, there would not even be a painting of her left to hang on the wall.

"What news?" I asked after a long, rude pause. I did not think he could do much more to ruin Mary's life.

"There is much," he said. His eyes narrowed as he took me in, but I could not discern what he observed about me. "I am calling on Miss Mary. Can she spend a few minutes with me in the parlor?"

I shook my head. "She cannot. She has taken over the role of tutor to our brother and is not allowed out of the schoolroom."

"What happened to the cooking?" he asked, with an air of suspicion, which came naturally to such a man.

I bowed my head and said nothing.

"Are you the cook now?"

I laughed. "No, I am still mistress of the bookshop counter."

"Can't she come down just for two minutes? I would like to set eyes on my betrothed." His rough-hewn face creased into an expression of animal longing.

I shook my head. "My parents have forbidden her to do anything but tend to Willy."

"There is something you are not telling me."

I moistened my lips. "Our parents' rule is law."

He put his hands on his hips. "Why don't you take me up to your father's library, then? I'd like to say a few things to him."

"He isn't here. Nor is Mamma," I said quickly, before he could ask that of me, as well. "I can't break their rules."

"I've never thought of either of you as the dutiful sorts." He moved quickly and centered himself in the doorway before I could even draw back in alarm.

I startled in fear. "What?"

"Please, Miss Clairmont. What do I need to do to win Mary? I want to possess her heart. You know a marriage will go better if a woman feels kindly toward her husband." He shook his head. The breeze caught at his bicorne hat, waving it around and making it look like a collapsing sausage.

"I do not see that she can be won," I answered honestly.

"I promise to help Charles leave the country if she does. Learn to love me, I mean," he offered.

I wanted to retort and say that Shelley had already promised that, and without any demands being made, but then what of Shelley? He'd tried to kill himself. Would we ever have his help again?

"I can see by your expression that you are distraught. You want your brother and stepsister to be well and happy, don't you, Miss Clairmont?" He pressed his lips together, causing the flesh at the sides of his harsh mouth to bulge.

"I want Charles to come home," I whispered.

Mr. Fisher took a step toward me. I stumbled back, not eager for his touch. He closed the door behind him. "I have news. I found the prostitute who took the gun case."

"Never," I exclaimed, shocked. "I had given up hope."

"Yes, I interviewed her. The woman said she took the gun to a natural philosopher for research."

I was immediately struck by that. "Did you get a description?"

He gestured. "It is rather generic. Tall, of middle years."

"It could be Professor Asquith," I exclaimed. "Even so."

"But that means your brother is with him. With the gun case, just like he must have been when the Davies sisters were alive." He pointed a cylinder of finger at me. "He is the common link."

"Dash it," I muttered, caught in my own lie. "Why is this gun so special? Charles knows nothing of arms, I assure you."

Mr. Fisher inhaled a breath through his enormous nose. "According to the doxy, it is a long-distance rifle with a special bent stock to increase accuracy."

I winced at his crude language, but then the import of his words struck me like a body blow. I bent forward. "Then he is going to try to kill the Duke of Wellington with it!"

"What?" Mr. Fisher exclaimed. He pulled off his hat and furiously scratched at his scalp.

I saw it then, the way to get rid of him right away, before Mamma or Papa came home and took him up to see Mary. Mary, who might proudly reveal herself to be Shelley's paramour and receive a beating as a result. I had to get this lovesick fool out of the house. "You must go after Professor Asquith to get rid of him."

"What? How can you be certain?"

"Listen," I said and began to lie my heart out. "He is planning to kill the duke this very day." It was scheduled for forty-eight hours, in truth, but who knew how long it would take to find the man? "There is no time to plan. Go!" I made a shooing motion.

"Where to?" he asked.

"Whatever the, er, prostitute told you." I shooed some more. "Where did she hand over the gun? Go there. Apprehend him."

"What about your brother?"

I widened my eyes into a theatrical near outrage. "We can't let the duke die. He's a national hero."

He nodded. "It's very brave of you, Miss Clairmont. Please pass my regards on to Miss Mary, and I will find the villain. The bounty will pay nicely for new furnishings for your sister's marital apartments." He flourished his ugly hat at me and went out without another glance at me.

I sagged against the front hall table when he had gone. "A near miss," I muttered. "How many times must I get rid of the beast?"

I stood there for a long moment after he left, opening and closing my hands in mute shock. Turning in a circle, I wondered if I should go back to the counter. When I heard light footsteps, I looked up and saw Mary coming downstairs.

"It may not be safe for long," I said, shaking a finger at her.

"I'll just run down and get a bite to eat," she promised. "I saw you rid us of Mr. Fisher. Is there any word about Shelley?"

Did she think of no one else? "No. Nothing from Mamma, either." I followed her down the kitchen steps. "Mary, this is such a mess."

"Yes, I cannot imagine how Shelley became so depressed," Mary said, misunderstanding me. "His wife again, I suppose. He cannot quite stop caring about her, no matter what I have become to him."

"No, I meant about the duke," I corrected.

"What?" Her tone was absent.

"Professor Asquith is going to try to kill him," I said patiently. "I lied about the timeline to Mr. Fisher in order to get him away from us."

"Did you tell him to look for the professor too late to stop him?" she said over her shoulder as she walked into the quiet kitchen.

"No, too early."

"I don't think Mr. Fisher is such a fool. Capturing a murderer before the murder is to be committed should be good enough." She centered a bowl on the table and took her wooden spoon from its holder.

"But it's Wellington. Surely, he is worth our best effort to save him?"

"Shelley is out of commission because of his overdose," Mary said. She started pulling canisters from side shelves.

"What are you going to make?"

"Bannocks," Mary said. "See if there is any milk or cream or eggs anywhere."

I went into the scullery and checked Polly's hiding places. I had no idea where the dratted girl had gone. Luckily, I found an egg and an inch of cream in a bottle that still smelled somewhat fresh.

I stirred up the fire for Mary while she made the dough. She heated the griddle with some oil and started to fry up her concoction.

"We really must find out what is going on," Mary said.

"But we want to stay away from Fisher," I added as she dropped a hot bannock onto my waiting plate.

"Right. Let's go see Charles."

"Papa said he was going to take Shelley to the Hookhams' if he felt up to it."

"We'll avoid the public rooms, then, and just go right to their private abode. Charles will be lurking there."

I nodded as I forked up a huge bite. "If you're willing to risk a beating, I'll go with you."

"It will all be over soon enough," Mary muttered.

"Not if Shelley dies."

"All the better for him to get a glimpse of me, then. It will give him hope and remind him that he has much to live for."

Upstairs, I heard the door. Mary looked alarmed. "Go into the scullery," I whispered. "I hope it is a customer, even this late."

I ran up and saw Mamma, swaying as her fingers fumbled with her apron strings. Rushing toward her, I took charge and undid a knot, then helped her balance against me as she removed her half boots. "I have never seen you so tired."

"Shelley took a great deal of nursing, but he has the drug out of his system," she reported.

"Did you have to walk with him all night?"

She nodded. "All the friends that young man has, but they came to Skinner Street in a crisis. I wonder why?"

Mary, I suspected, but she could not have tended him. Mamma was at least sturdy enough to keep him upright as they fought to keep him breathing through laudanum's soporific effects.

"Did Papa come?"

"Yes, which gave me a reason to leave. I am going to bed now. Fetch me some bread and butter and bring it upstairs, Jane."

I listened anxiously as her footsteps ascended, but they faded off before the top floor, where Mary was supposed to be. I ran down to the kitchen and poured some dried lavender into a pot, then added boiling water and fixed the bread.

Mary peered out. "Is it safe?"

"You can't go back to the schoolroom. Mamma went to her room."

"Good. Let's sneak out to Old Bond Street."

"She's much too tired for vigilance. Meet me in the street in ten minutes."

She nodded and helped me set up a tray. When I came downstairs again, the front door was cracked open and Mary was around the corner, out of sight of the bedroom windows.

She swung her arms widely as we walked. "How good it is to feel a breeze again. It was so stuffy upstairs."

We avoided the Hookhams' bookshop and went up to the private rooms. I paced back and forth along the patterned floor in the front hall while the maid went to fetch my brother.

Eventually, she admitted us to a small, closed-up study. Mary looked outwardly placid, but she smelled different. Sweat from the heat and an inability to wash, but also there was an underlying scent of fear there, too.

"There he is," she said, unsmiling, as Charles appeared.

I noted that his wardrobe had improved, with a borrowed shirt and striped waistcoat. How did the Hookhams manage to live so much better than us?

"You were banished to the schoolroom, Mary. Why are you out?" he asked.

"I think the Duke of Wellington's life is worth a little disobedience from me," she said.

Charles's brow furrowed. He had lost the hint of sun on his skin and seemed fleshier. "What do you mean?"

"You know what I mean. Your lover must have started this dreadful business somehow. We have to end it."

"I don't understand." Charles made a helpless gesture, then collapsed into a leather chair next to a lamp in the corner of the study. He didn't even invite us to sit.

"Papa innocently invited to dinner one night some men whom he had met on the street," Mary said. "A Professor Asquith and his assistant, a rude creature named Bryan. Little did Papa know he was inviting associates of your Miss Davies into the house, or that they were part of a plot to murder the Duke of Wellington!"

"Worthy of a Bow Street Runner," I murmured after her delivery.

"Branwen had nothing to do with it," Charles said.

I stared at him. "You knew about all this? And did nothing?"

He shifted uncomfortably, looking like the schoolboy he had been until recently. "It was nothing to do with me, Jane."

"Explain," Mary demanded. "I don't have much time. Mamma might wake from her nap and come to check her jail. Not to mention, Papa is probably downstairs in the coffee room."

"In this building?" Charles said, alarmed.

"This very one," I confirmed.

Charles bared his teeth. "You remember the troop review in Hyde Park?"

"How could we forget?" I asked. "That was the day we met Miss Davies."

"We were arguing," Charles said.

Mary nodded.

He slicked his lips. "It was because Winnet was Professor Asquith's mistress."

"How did that come to be?" I asked.

"Their father was at the Battle of Seringapatam in seventeen ninety-nine. He lost his life in the confusion of that night battle," Charles explained. "Their mother never forgave their father's commander for his part in the disaster that night and raised the girls on poisonous thoughts."

"So Winnet and Branwen wanted the duke dead?" Mary suggested.

Charles nodded. "Winnet went to work for the Griffiths because they provided cheese to the upper classes, which meant she could access their kitchens. Professor Asquith was the mastermind. They had quite a gang, which I realized after Winnet was murdered. She always pushed for more."

"Someone must have forced Branwen to act in her place after Winnet was killed, or perhaps she chose that?" Mary asked.

Charles bit his lip and looked down. "She would not have done it willingly. She gave her sister money for the cause but didn't participate. She was with me, not with one of that group, after all."

"I do wonder how some girls like the Davies sisters could have so many lovers when I cannot even manage to see even one," Mary said gloomily.

"They didn't have a father," Charles said. "You are properly supervised, like a young girl should be."

"Gently reared above our class," I said, mocking him with Mamma's tones. "Maybe you should look higher yourself for a wife."

"I don't want to be with a girl of strong beliefs again, that is for sure. Both of the twins are gone, and the duke is still out there, unperturbed."

"Who killed them?" I asked.

"Professor Asquith fell into the pay of the French in order to fund his obsessions." Charles tugged at his cravat.

"What were his obsessions?"

"Alchemy, to be sure, and also his own reasons for hating the duke. He believes himself to be the duke's half brother."

"What?" I said with a gasp.

Charles leaned forward. "The father was a profligate composer, you know. It's said he romanced an Irish serving girl with his talent on the violin, then deserted her when the inevitable occurred. He offered her not so much as a coin in aid upon the news, and she never saw him again."

"What a tale," Mary said in more animated tones. She leaned against the desk and folded her arms. "These people hated the duke or his family for personal reasons, and Napoleon's spies found them and funded them."

"And killed them," Charles added.

"Why the girls, and not the professor and his assistant?"

"They are destroying the evidence as they go." Charles swallowed hard. "I'm sure they will kill the men, too, when their usefulness is at an end. Winnet must have made demands for more money and paid the price. I don't know why Branwen died. I have to get out of London, girls. They might come for me, too, even though I was nothing but an innocent bystander. I argued that day with Winnet, trying to persuade her to sever ties with the professor."

"Do you think she listened?" I asked.

"I'll never know." Charles dropped his head into his hands. "Maybe I don't care if the duke dies. You would not believe the misery his family has left behind them."

"That is always the case with great men," Mary said softly.

My thought went to Shelley and his wife. Of course, the situation was entirely different, as she was quite evil, but what of their daughter, Ianthe? Would she suffer for the sins of her parents?

"If you know the names of these French spies, you should tell Mr. Fisher," Mary said. "Are they Englishmen?"

"I know absolutely nothing," Charles said, lifting his head and speaking strongly.

"You can tell us the truth," I coaxed.

He rubbed his nose. "I expect you might know some of them, too, or at least Mamma. I believe the spies live among the French community near our old house. Branwen took me there sometimes, to Somers Town. But who is friend and who is spy, I cannot say."

"I'm going to go home," Mary said just after a clock on the desk chimed the hour. "I value the skin on my back more than anything else, and I must be home and upstairs before Mamma wakes."

"But the duke?" Charles asked.

"You should tell someone," I said, ignoring his wince. "One of the Hookhams."

"When Mr. Fisher returns, I'll tell him what I know, but I won't be allowed to see anyone else," Mary said. "Really, Charles, you need to take some sort of action."

"You can't pin it all on me," I said when she glanced in my direction. "I've got to work in the bookshop tomorrow. I don't know if I'll even have time to eat."

"Where is Mr. Fisher?" Charles asked.

I fluttered my arms. "I sent him to Bath, to keep him away from Mary. I didn't know we were going to need him."

Charles rubbed his nose again, staring blankly at the curtains covering the window. "I'll tell someone when I can."

"We'll talk to Mr. Fisher," Mary said. "He's sure to turn up again, since he still believes we are to wed."

On Wednesday morning, neither Mamma nor Papa kept to their regular schedule. Willy and I were in our seats when a pouting Polly arrived in the dining room with porridge and toast, along with a plate of sausages, which I knew had made it to the table only because a street seller had come to the door. They were probably full of sawdust and horsemeat, which was meant to be sold for cat food, not for human consumption.

Still, Willy tucked right in and said they were delicious. I enjoyed the admittedly enticing smell of them but stuck to toast with extra butter.

I opened the bookshop on time, a good thing because a mother came in right away with a crying child, saying his father had cast his Aesop into the fire during a drunken fit the night before. The mother was very white around the mouth as she counted out her coins for the new tome.

"I saw it was the last one," I said, "but don't worry. I'll send the porter to the warehouse for more copies."

"I'll hide this one," she said grimly. "As this is, it's coming out of his meat budget for the month."

"Why would anyone object to Aesop?"

"Too much fancy. He's a banker. Believes only in facts."

"Whimsy is so important, though," I said. "Life is grim enough."

As the woman departed with her now beaming child, I heard Papa's morning shuffle above me in the library. Hopefully, the sausages wouldn't send him running for the garden, but I didn't have time to warn him, because two gentlemen came in, looking for travel memoirs. I pitched Mary Wollstonecraft's brilliant *Letters Written During a Short Residence in Sweden, Norway, and Denmark*, but they wanted novels by Laurence Sterne and the admittedly very interesting *The Antiquities, Natural History, Ruins, and Other Curiosities of Egypt, Nubia, and Thebes*.

Some forty minutes later, the morning rush had ended. I'd gone through the scanty post and sent the porter off with two packages that had been ordered locally, with instructions to collect payment immediately if at all possible. My stomach already rumbling, I had dreams of a better class of sausage for tomorrow morning. We'd had sales enough.

I debated swiping a guinea from the cash box so Polly could take it to the butcher, but then I heard Mamma's tread on the stairs. She didn't come down right away, but I couldn't risk it.

I had just finished directing a hopeful author to better-heeled publishers in St. Paul's Churchyard, rather than the Juvenile Library, when I heard a knock at the front door. I frowned and started out from the counter, but then Mamma came out and opened the door.

Voices murmured low. It was never a good sign when people didn't walk right in during business hours. Nervous energy made my palms sweat. A minute later, Mamma came in with two gentlemen behind her. One looked familiar, but it took a few seconds to place him. He was a clerk at Bow Street, and we'd spoken to him when we went to visit our old cook, who'd been in the lockup in the spring. I recognized the faded red curls peeking out from his top hat.

The other man was no clerk. He wore beautifully shined boots, and his breeches were tightly fitted. A starched white cravat was tied in a rather complex fashion around his neck.

My heartbeat drummed a warning, but they didn't have a local constable with them or a Bow Street Runner. Surely, I wasn't being arrested.

"Miss Godwin?" the gentleman asked.

I shook my head. "Miss Clairmont. Should I fetch Miss Mary Godwin? Miss Fanny Godwin is out of town."

The man glanced at Mamma. "Get her," she barked at me.

I was all confusion as I ran upstairs. Mary had been upstairs or with me at all times. What trouble could she be in now?

"Come," I said, nearly breathless as I reached the top of the house, already unpleasantly warm in the continuing July heat wave.

Mary sat down her pencil, which she'd been poking into a Latin grammar in front of Willy. "Both of us?"

"Just you." I put my hand to my chest and drew in a breath.

She smoothed her favorite loud tartan dress and followed me after telling Willy he could play marbles while she was gone. I whispered in her ear as we went down.

"Two men to see you. One is from Bow Street. I don't like this, Mary."

"It must be about the gun case," Mary said, "though they ought to talk to Shelley, not me."

I frowned. That didn't sound right. I could not imagine what they might want with her.

When we stepped into the front hall, Mamma was ushering the men into the parlor. Mary clutched my hand, showing her first hint of sensibility, and wouldn't let me return to the bookshop, so I went in with her.

The men stood in front of the fireplace, watching us enter.

Mary walked forward, then lifted her chin. "I am Mary Wollstonecraft Godwin."

The clerk stared very hard at her. "Miss Godwin, we have come to take you to the bedside of Denarius Fisher."

I gasped as Mary said, "Bedside, sir?"

"You are his betrothed?" the gentleman said.

"I—" She glanced at Mamma's stony face, then nodded. I knew she wanted to declare her independence from him but judged it a poor time.

"I am Courteney, from the Home Office," the gentleman said. "I am sorry to say that during the fulfilment of his duties, Mr. Fisher was shot and is dying."

"But I—" I stopped. I had sent him on a wild-goose chase, not toward his death. Had he been fulfilling some other commission and ignoring what I had said? "Where was he found?" I asked.

"On the road to Bath. He managed to crawl into a coaching inn. They brought him back to London by cart, but infection has set in, and the doctor says it is only a matter of hours now."

Mary's lips trembled. "He wants to see me?"

"It is his dying wish, Miss Godwin." The clerk lifted his hat and swiped at a cowlick. "I am sorry."

"Some refreshments?" Mamma asked. "Jane?"

"No." The gentleman shook his head. "We must go, Miss Godwin."

"I should go," I said. "I must go."

Mary had yet to let go of my hand. "Please," she said.

The gentleman nodded. We followed him to our bonnets. Mary, in a daze, didn't protest as I tied the ribbons under her chin and pulled her gloves over her unresisting hands.

I thought they would hand us into a carriage, the man from the Home Office being such an exalted sort of person, but instead they led us into the street. I quickly realized they were taking us to Barts. I cried as we walked, holding Mary's hand. I hadn't meant to send a man to die.

Less than fifteen minutes later, after walking through a maze of hallways, we arrived at Mr. Fisher's bedside. The massive body was not fitted to the hospital bed. His feet splayed off the mattress. His skin had gone gray, and he held his belly in a pose of agony.

"Oh," Mary cried and let go of my hand to rush toward him. She touched his face.

I had not known she could offer a man she loathed such tenderness, but now she handled him like a child. She dipped her handkerchief into a bowl of water and tenderly wiped his face. "You poor dear," she murmured. "Is the pain very bad?"

"I failed," he whispered.

"No, no," she protested. "You wanted to save the duke. It was a noble fight, Mr. Fisher."

"Denarius," he wheezed. "Say my name, Mary."

"Denarius," she said immediately. "My poor Denarius. Is there no hope for you?"

His eyes fluttered closed. "Stay safe, Mary. That Asquith, he has murdered me."

I gasped, the truth unassailable. I had sent this man to his death. He really had been rather kind and sweet when he wasn't blackmailing Mary. But who was I to claim a greater morality than him? We had both done bad things to get what we wanted. But now I stood, healthy and strong, and he was on his deathbed as a result of my lies. How could I bear this?

"I cannot believe he ever dined at Papa's table," Mary said. "We will avenge you, Denarius."

"Let Bow Street take care of that," he rasped. "You stay in your house."

"I must make this right." Mary wiped his forehead again.

His hand moved slowly, agonizingly to his breast. He patted himself there. "Take this."

Mary reached under his coat as gently as she could and pulled out a knife in a sheath.

"Keep this close by. It's deadly sharp. I only wish I'd been close enough to use it on the scoundrel. That gun is powerful."

Mary took it. "You will be avenged."

"I will see you in Heaven, sweet Mary," he said in broken tones.

She went back to wiping his brow with a damp cloth. A man came in, wearing a bloodstained apron. He took Mr. Fisher's pulse and shook his head gravely.

The Bow Street Runner did not speak again. Shortly after I heard the bells tolling midday, his breath rattled, then stopped. His features relaxed, still that awful shade of gray. I could see he was dead, but Mary kept wiping his brow.

Gently, I took the cloth from her and spread it over his face. The lines of it had softened, making him look gentler. "He is gone."

She seemed to snap out of her reverie then. We had been left alone in the room. She took one last look at the oversize frame, slack now, then pulled me into the corridor, where our companions waited.

"A good man has perished," I said.

She shook her head but said nothing, her lips pressed tightly together.

The three men crowded in at the bedside when we went back into the death chamber. The doctor nodded after taking the dead man's pulse again. The Bow Street clerk look devastated, and the Home Office man's eyes narrowed in anger.

"We do not even know who killed him," he said, striking one fist into his palm.

"Not true," Mary said. "He told me. Professor Asquith, who is plotting to assassinate the Duke of Wellington."

The gentleman's eyes widened. "He said this?"

Mary nodded. I nodded with her. "I heard it."

"Asquith?" the gentleman inquired.

"Hubert Asquith," I said, recalling his full name. "A professor of natural philosophy."

"The real kind or a charlatan?" asked Mr. Courteney.

"Charlatan, I would think," I said.

"Description?" the clerk asked.

I gave it to him and described Mr. Bryan, as well, grateful my brother's involvement had been nothing but fiction.

"Shall we escort you to your house?" the clerk asked.

"No, we know the way," Mary said. "I would like to seek spiritual counsel from Reverend Doone first."

"Is St. Sepulchre Mr. Fisher's parish?" the clerk asked.

Mary shook her head. "No. He lived in Covent Garden. Do you need my family's help with the arrangements?"

"No, miss. Bow Street will care for him."

"Tell me. Please tell me where he is buried," Mary said. She put her hand to her eyes.

"Of course."

I took Mary's arm and escorted her out. She didn't look back. Every step I took out of the building felt like it added weight to my heart.

"I wanted him gone from my life, but not gone from this earth," Mary said when we had reached the dubiously fresh air of the busy courtyard. We crept alongside the building, hoping to stay out of the way of the horse traffic.

"Of course you didn't," I soothed.

"He was not a good man, but not a terrible one. He behaved no worse than we have at times."

"We've met more terrible men," I agreed.

"I owe you for my freedom," Mary said. "But I thought you were lying to get him away from me. How is it that he went to his death?"

"I must have sent him to the right place without realizing it. He must have mentioned Bath, and I didn't remember." Tears welled up, and my voice strangled. "I'm sick over Mr. Fisher's death."

"He is Marguerite from Papa's novel *St. Leon* reborn, a victim of love and misfortune," Mary said in eulogistic tones.

"Did he love you, or did he just want to possess you?" I asked.

"It all comes to the same in the end, in this case," Mary said.

She took my arm and directed me to the rectory where Reverend Doone presided over his excellent table.

His housekeeper did him justice, as always, but Mary and I couldn't eat very much. The plum jam he offered looked too much like the stains on the sheet over Mr. Fisher to be appetizing.

We didn't stay long, though the wealthy curate was very kind about Mary's suffering and didn't even offer himself as a replacement husband this time. Mary, all defiance leeched out of her, went right up to the schoolroom when we arrived home, forgetting even to remove her bonnet.

The churchman had insisted we return home with a basket of his housekeeper's best jellies and beef tea. Feeling emboldened by the tragedy, I also begged a loaf of fine bread from her, to make toast for Mary, since our maid was a poor shopper.

Mary barely touched the broth or the bread, though, when I brought it up on a tray for dinner. Sir Charles and Lady Aldis came to the meal. A surgeon, he discussed Mr. Fisher's death with Papa in the parlor after the meal. After they left, I paced the parlor, feeling most restless.

When it was nearly dark, someone knocked on the front door. I flew to it, as if I'd been waiting for someone to call. I was desperate for news of the murderous professor and of Shelley, who had not come.

At the door, I found the same two men as earlier, the Home Office man and the Bow Street clerk.

"What evil news comes now?" I asked, wringing my hands.

"Is your father at home?" Mr. Courteney asked, not enlightening me.

I nodded and ushered them in, too anxious even to ask permission before taking them up to Papa's study.

"What is it?" he asked, pulling off his glasses and rubbing the bridge of his nose as he stood.

I gestured toward the men, words failing me.

Mr. Courteney nodded at Papa. It was rather odd to have someone from the Home Office here when Papa was rather an enemy of his because of his philosophy.

"Can I help you?" Papa asked, replacing his spectacles.

"I wanted to inform you personally that Professor Asquith has been taken into custody outside Carlton House. Shall I inform your daughter, or would you like that pleasure?"

I put my hand on his sleeve, unthinking. "Did he have his gun with him?"

"No," Mr. Courteney admitted. "We'd have liked to recover the murder weapon, but unfortunately, he was unarmed."

"Are you sure it was him?" Papa asked.

"We'd like you to identify him personally," the clerk said. "But he had cards with that name in a carrying case, and he matched the description your daughter gave us earlier."

"I think the gun is very important," I said. "It's a special kind, a real killing device. You need to find it."

"We have constables combing the area," the clerk said. "If it is nearby, we will find it."

I was afraid a person had it, rather than a stray bit of ornamental greenery. But who? Why had the professor been by Carlton House without his special weapon?

Chapter 20

Mary

Mary felt quite her old, determined self when she shook Jane awake at dawn on Thursday. She needed to shake off her oppression for a few hours at least, and today was the day for it.

"What is it?" Jane yawned. "We still have some bread and jam from Reverend Doone for breakfast."

"Let's sneak out to see Charles early, before Mamma rises."

"I do not think I can tolerate her wrath today." Jane rubbed her eyes.

"All will be forgiven if we bring back some good meat," Mary said. "What good is imprisoning me going to do now? My unchosen betrothed is deceased."

"They locked you up because of Shelley."

"He is still recovering, no? Papa said he was pale and listing on his feet when he forced him to walk to Old Bond Street." As sorry as she was for his suffering, he would not have been at Skinner Street at dawn. "Come, let's go there ourselves and tell Charles what is happening. He must have some notion of where the gun might be."

"Mr. Bryan has it," Jane said. "Who else but his faithful assistant?"

Mary nodded. "I have thought of that, as well, but I do not know where we could find him. Besides, he said he was no longer employed."

"With the French. At Somers Town?" Jane guessed. "I expect he lied to us."

"We need better direction from Charles," Mary urged. "He'll know better than us, and then we can tell them at Bow Street where to go. I couldn't sleep for thinking of it. Besides, I cannot sit upstairs all day thinking of that terrible scene at Barts. I will go mad."

She helped Jane dress, and they crept down, hugging the walls. Jane insisted on wrapping a shawl around herself. "It might be July, but it's too early yet to be warm."

When they went into the street, Mary could hear drovers coming with their fly-ridden animals. She grabbed Jane's hand, in readiness to flee the area. A shadowy figure peeled away from the wall as they went around the corner. Jane shrieked, but then a strong hand grabbed Mary, and they saw it was Shelley.

Mary stopped, incredulous, but Jane flung herself into his arms. "You are well," she cried. He put his hands over her ears and grinned at Mary.

"You are well?" she asked in the gentlest tone she could muster. He had to be; she needed her savior. "Not doubting us any longer?"

"No." His eyes held the purest light of sanity, and she believed him. The moment of madness had passed.

Jane pulled away. "Come with us."

"Always." He took both their hands, and they went swiftly down the street toward Fleet Prison, away from the drovers. When they were clear, they hopped on the back of a cart of oranges heading for Covent Garden.

The house had not yet risen, but Shelley had a key to the Hookhams' private residence from his time there. After they entered, he left them in the front hall and went to the chamber that Charles inhabited. Mary paced the floor, trying to remember a time before Denarius Fisher or, barring that, one of the precious times she'd been with Shelley under the willows.

A few minutes later, with some form of peace restored to her heart, she saw Charles, half-dressed in breeches and shirt. He made a face when he saw Jane.

"I'm sorry about Mr. Fisher," he said to Mary.

"It is very sad," she agreed. Saliva pooled in her mouth, nausea rising at the remembrance of horror, but she forced it down. "But we have no time for mourning. You know the duke is supposed to be murdered today, and while the professor has been captured, the gun has not. You must have some idea of who Professor Asquith would have passed the gun to."

"I think Mr. Bryan has it," Jane announced.

"You are probably right," Charles said. He put his finger to his lips, then led them up to his small bedchamber. "Who else would have been trusted with it? What news?"

Jane quickly caught Charles up to date while they arranged themselves around the square room, Shelley in a relaxed pose against the fireplace along the outer wall.

"Were there not others in the gang?" Shelley asked when Jane was finished. In the front hall's light, he had a sickly green cast to his skin. His overdose might have affected him more than Mary had originally realized. They had to be together. Neither of them would survive otherwise.

Charles frowned. "That prostitute will be impossible to find again."

"What about the French? Can you direct us to their lair in Somers Town?" Mary asked.

"Didn't you tell the Home Office about that? The neighborhood will be crawling with the king's men by now."

"What do we do?" Mary asked. "Mr. Bryan is so nondescript. No one will recognize him but us, and we cannot be sure he has the gun."

"Who else could be involved?" Shelley asked.

"The bonnet thief?" Jane suggested. "He did have the gun case at one time. He's part of the gang."

"Then there is the Griffiths' mysterious son," Mary added.

"Maybe he is my thief," Jane said. "We saw him just around the corner."

"That doesn't mean he's the same person." Charles scratched his chin.

"He's tall and thin like Mr. Griffith, and dark-haired." Jane gestured to her own dark locks.

"She might be right," Shelley added. "It is undeniable that the cheese shop is at the center of the plot."

Mary paced on a narrow strip of braided rug while Jane sat down on Charles's bed. "We need to go to Carlton House. That's where the professor was caught."

"There are supposed to be twenty-five hundred people there tonight at the fête for the duke," Charles said.

When Jane gave him a confused stare, he shrugged. "They bring up the papers to amuse me."

"Then that is where the killer will be." Shelley pounded one fist into the other with a hint of his old fire. "At some point this evening."

"When will the duke arrive?" Jane asked.

Charles scratched his chin. "I know the main events are going to be in the garden. Come with me."

They went downstairs to the study and spread the morning newspapers over the grand desk in the room. Though there were a lot of books, tidy on well-dusted shelves, Mary thought the room not half so fine as Papa's monument to literature.

"Nine in the evening," Jane read, spotting a pertinent bulletin right away. "And the queen to come at ten with her daughters."

Shelley shook his head. "There are going to be so many people there, all to amuse the overgrown bantling, Prinny. It will all be overthrown like Rome, mark my words. This is all more than barbaric as it is."

"You're right, of course, Shelley, but we cannot allow the duke to die if we can prevent it. The people would be heartbroken. How do you think the gunman means to sneak in?" Mary patted his arm.

"There will be some kind of ticket for this ludicrous magnificence," Shelley mused. "There are gates, though as we saw in eighteen eleven, the crowds can overwhelm security."

"There will be dancing," Jane read. "Maybe he'll pretend to be a musician?"

"What will we be to get in?" Charles asked.

"Are you coming with us?" Mary looked at him, surprised.

"What if there is something only I can recognize?" Charles asked. "I don't want our country falling to Napoleon any more than the next Englishman."

"The war is over," Jane said.

Charles shrugged. "I don't think Napoleon will stop as long as he lives."

"How ghastly." Jane shivered.

"I have a ticket," Shelley said unexpectedly. "I'll fetch it from my rooms. Then we will head to Pall Mall. Charles, disguise yourself as best as you can. It puts us in danger to bring you with us, so make sure to melt away if you see anyone we know."

Several nerve-racking hours later, the four of them joined the multitudes thronging around Carlton House, filling both Pall Mall and the Haymarket with a crush of sweaty summer bodies. Shelley's ticket allowed them admittance through the gates, though it was a slow process. Jane made faces at Mary several times for her choice of dress for the evening.

"Isn't it better to look like one is wearing their best?" Mary asked. "Rather than like a drudge? I burned the bodice of the gray dress I was wearing earlier with a stray spark." She looked far more distinguished than Charles, with his ancient, formless hat meant as a disguise.

"You are rapidly turning into Thérèse," Jane said sourly. "Take my shawl, at least, so you're less visible."

"I like the dress," Shelley said. "It's original, and I never see that pattern without thinking of her."

Mary grinned at Jane. Her true love always came to the rescue. Charles, on the other head, couldn't seem to focus on anything. His gaze jumped from one place to another.

Shelley took them straight toward a waterfall. Mary followed in his wake, scarcely having time to glance at an array of statues, what looked like an observatory, and a temple. The grass was largely protected by matting, which also helped save the ladies' slippers and the polish on gentlemen's boots. When they had to venture off it, the grass was rather damp.

The covered walks were decorated more finely than the Skinner Street parlor, with fresh flowers adorning painted trellises. Every so often Mary caught a glimpse of herself in looking glasses, which served to make the spaces seem even more enormous. Beyond that, trees were everywhere. Anyone might be lurking around the trunks or up in the summer-dense, leaf-laden branches. Meant to be festive, in Mary's opinion, the scene had taken on a macabre hue.

"We'll have to find the duke," she urged. "It's the only way. He will have a cluster of important people around him, men in their best uniforms. We're never going to spot the killer in this crush."

"Two thousand souls," Shelley muttered. "Waiting for Nero to play."

Jane made a face at Shelley. "I think it's nice that we are celebrating. To think this party could be for Napoleon instead of the duke."

"Never," Charles said, paying attention for once. "Our army never would have allowed it."

Mary shushed him and took the newspaper they'd brought from Jane. "Listen to this. Prinny has a polygonal building set up somewhere in the garden. It's brick, one hundred and twenty feet, and the roof should look like an umbrella."

"Very nice," Charles said. "Couldn't we stop at one of the supper tents first? I haven't walked so much in ages. My stomach is eating itself."

"Not a supper tent," Shelley said. "Look at the crowds. But there will be simpler tents for refreshments, as well, and it does not take so long to acquire drink. A glass of wine would help me a great deal."

Mary thought something must be done to bring color into Shelley's pale face. But even though she could scarcely see Charles's face between his high-tied cravat and his tilted hat, the unshaven jaw, and the overgrown curls, he still seemed perfectly recognizable to her. "We shouldn't risk it. Let's refrain from getting too close to anyone."

"No one will know me at Carlton House," Charles said rather sourly.

Behind them, Mary heard, "Shelley!" She gave Charles a look of alarm, then turned.

Shelley was swept into a manly embrace between two young gentlemen about his age. Mary and Jane pressed against Charles, though Mary quickly realized these were old schoolfellows of Shelley's, who soon began to retell each other the tale of what Shelley had suffered for refusing to play servant to an older boy at Eton. Charles hadn't gone to the upper-crust schools like Shelley.

She lost interest, having heard the woeful story before, and scanned the crowd.

"Should we look for Mr. Bryan or the Griffiths' son?" Jane asked, leaning into her face. "Or will the killer be too disguised?"

"The gun case," Mary suggested. "It will be noticeable. How would he even get it through the gates?"

"It could have come in under a serving table or in a box of food," Charles said. "This place is like an anthill."

"It's swarming," Mary agreed. "Let's make our way to that brick building I read about. We've got hours until the duke comes, but it will be even worse once it's dark. We've got to find the killer now."

Jane gave her a nervous glance. "What if he doesn't bring the gun case? He could just hide the gun under a cloak or greatcoat."

"That would be more noticeable," Mary said. "In this heat, even you are overdressed, I'd look at you askance."

Jane straightened her shawl pin. "It will be cold later, when the wind picks up and it's dark. Mark my words."

The three of them left Shelley to his friends, since they could hardly make themselves known to the men, and strolled the periphery, attempting to stay near the tree line without drawing any attention to themselves. Every time Jane started to speed up, Mary slowed her to a sedate stroll. She smiled randomly and nodded at people to seem less odd.

"You girls look like servants," Charles fussed. "We do not belong here. It's embarrassing."

"You are wanted by the law," Jane snapped back. "And there are plenty of maids around."

"Maybe we should look busier," Mary suggested, secure in the knowledge that in her tartan dress, she did not look like a maid. People would probably look at them and think Jane was there to serve her.

"If we held glasses of punch, it might look like we were delivering them to our betters," Charles said hopefully.

An open-front tent was set up just to the left of them, in fact, doing a brisk business in cups of something. "Very well," Mary grudgingly agreed.

Jane grabbed her arm and stopped her. "Look up ahead. I think that's the building from the newspaper."

"Perfect," Mary said when she caught sight of bricks. There was no sign of a foundation, a dead giveaway that the building was a temporary design.

Jane bounced on her feet. "Let's get two cups each. Then we can circuit the building, looking like we're waiting for our masters."

Charles took rapid strides to the tent. Mary and Jane followed. Mary was too thirsty to protest that she wouldn't fit their disguise. They waited in line so long that sweat ran from her hairline to the small of her back, but eventually she had her two glasses of punch for "my lady" and Charles had managed to get something stronger for "his gentleman." Irritatingly, the barman didn't even react to her claiming to be a servant.

Jane, the last of them, turned away from the drink purveyor and bumped into the man just behind her. "Excuse me," she said. Then her eyes went wide.

Mary stopped, barely holding on to her glasses. It was Mr. Bryan, in his green coat! In a flash, he had tightened his fist around Jane's arm and dragged her toward him, spilling the punch, his careworn face contorted with a snarl.

"I say . . . ," Charles started, one of his glasses near empty already, then looked at Jane's face and stopped.

Mr. Bryan backed out of the tent, pulling Jane along. Mary and Charles, just a couple of feet away, followed them. He didn't stop until they were at the side of the tent, out of the flow of traffic.

He let go of Jane and snatched the cups from her fingers. As she massaged her wrist, he tossed back the contents of each of them. Charles did the same, a wild look in his eyes, then clutched the empty cups in his fists, as if thinking to use them as weapons.

Before Jane could try to edge away, Mr. Bryan had dropped his cups to the grass and, with a flick of his wrist, made a knife appear from under his sleeve.

Mary realized then that he held the gun case in his other hand, though it had been somewhat altered. The leather had been painted white, and he'd attached a fake or real strap to it to make it look like a street vendor's tray, the kind that hung from a person's neck.

"Don't hurt me," Jane begged.

"I don't want to hurt you. I want you to get away from me," Mr. Bryan said. "All you three have to do is leave, and nothing will happen to you."

Charles slid his empty cups under Mary's full ones and took them from her hands. They clinked slightly, but Mr. Bryan was so focused on Jane that he didn't notice.

"But you have a . . . a knife," Jane said with a sniff.

"To show you I mean business, Miss Clairmont," he said. "Walk away now and don't look back."

"What are you going to do?" she asked, her troubled gaze bouncing from Mary back to the assailant.

"I want the bounty payment from the French for the duke's death. None of you care anything for the Duke of Wellington any more than I do." His tone was oddly monotonous.

"But he's a national hero," Jane protested.

"Otherwise," Mr. Bryan's upper lip twitched. He continued, as if she'd said nothing, "there is nothing but the poorhouse for Mr. Bryan, and that won't do. You see that, don't you?"

Mary didn't like that he'd spoken of himself as if he wasn't Mr. Bryan. He sounded quite deranged. Next to her, Charles gently rattled the cups. Could he do anything with them to stop the man? "Were you supposed to be here at all? We thought the boy conjurer would be here."

He brandished his knife. "I already took care of the Griffiths' boy, same as the twins. The French payment is mine alone."

Mr. Bryan moved toward Jane with the knife. She stepped back, sliding along the side of the tent. Instead of telling her to run away again, it seemed that he drove her back in a ghastly dance, moving her steadily into position near the brick building, where the duke would eventually be honored.

Mary and Charles followed, as if attached to him by leading strings. Mary tried to signal to Charles with her eyes, to tell him to throw the pottery cups, but he shook his head in return. What was he afraid of? If the authorities came, surely, once the situation was clear, Charles would be cleared. Only Shelley remained to save them, if he could escape his friends.

The sounds of the crowd seemed to recede as they reached the building, too early in the evening to be of use.

"What ho!" she heard from behind her. She turned slightly, just enough to see Shelley ranging toward them, his long legs eating up the grass.

Jane shrieked. Mary turned back to see Mr. Bryan close his hand around her upper arm and push her roughly against the bricks. His expression drew tight with anger at the sight of their tall, well-muscled friend.

Shelley reached them. Mary saw the instant he spotted the knife. His boots skidded on the grass; then he came to a stop. His hands in fists went to his temples, his features distorting. What was this doing to Shelley? He'd been depressed enough to want to die, and now he had to see Jane's life under threat?

Mary had to do something before her love collapsed. She motioned to Charles in order to rip the cups from his useless hands. She'd throw them at Mr. Bryan. But then her arm rubbed against something hard in her pocket. The memory of Mr. Fisher's final moments flashed in her mind's eye like lightning. She reached into her pocket and pulled out his knife, a gift that at the time had seemed to offer less utility than cheese and fowl.

Her fingers found the indentation along the blade as her determination grew. She pulled it open. Jane and Shelley needed her to act. "You let go of my sister!" she shrieked, running at Mr. Bryan.

The world seemed to slow. She picked up speed. He was only a few steps away. Her half boots slid in the grass. They hadn't yet put matting around this building. Mr. Bryan stood transfixed directly in her path. He started to raise the gun case, as if to use it as a shield, but Mary flung herself or slid or levitated. The knife sank into his chest. She collided with him, bounced off his body, lost her grip on the knife. His knife dropped to the grass, but Mr. Fisher's remained in his chest. They both stared at it.

Mr. Bryan staggered back, and his head fell against the brick. Blood darkened his waistcoat. Jane screamed and ran to Mary. Charles caught her, dropping the cups, and covered his sister's head with his hands.

Slowly, the bleeding man dropped to his knees, his eyes fixing on some spot in the distance. He fell forward and lay over the gun case. Not one word more passed his lips. His green coat covered any sign of damage, making him seem only awkwardly asleep.

All seemed still at that moment. Even Jane was inaudible, to Mary at least. Mary opened her hands and looked at them. They were her regular hands, rather pink in spots from new fire burns and rougher than they had been from kitchen work. Not the hands of a killer, though. "To die so miserably," she whispered. "So close to his evil goal."

Shelley came up alongside her, his expression set now instead of tormented. He stared at her chest. She glanced down, following his eyes, and saw the terrible dark stains down the front of her beloved tartan dress.

He put his hand to her cheek. "We need to leave."

"What about the gun? Do we take it to the authorities?" Mary asked, her hands fluttering above her bosom. She couldn't bring herself to touch the mess. Just a hint of the falsely decorated case peeked out from under the right side of Mr. Bryan's body.

"It is best we not touch it." Shelley cleared his throat, but a rasp had developed in his voice. "If someone in the Home Office, or some other authority, gets wind of this and we are seen, we could be killed on sight. He's known to be part of a foreign gang."

Mary nodded. "You are right, of course, Shelley."

Charles let go of Jane. She stumbled against Mary; then her eyes went wide as she saw the stains, still damp. Jane unpinned her light shawl and wrapped it around Mary, hiding the bloodstains as much as she could. Their brother walked to the exposed side of the case. He considered for a couple of seconds, then kicked it three times. The body rocked, but then the case was hidden underneath it.

"The sun is lower on the horizon," Mary reported.

"Go home for now," Shelley said. "Like nothing ever happened. Forget these disgusting splendors and what we have had to do tonight."

"What about me?" Charles asked.

"You need to return to the Hookhams' and pray no one ever knew you'd left," Shelley said. "You need to be known to be elsewhere, as do we. I will spend the evening getting loudly drunk in a tavern. Mary needs to return to the schoolroom, and Jane should stay close to your maid."

Mary clutched Jane's hand. "We'll go into the trees. Keep your head turned away from other people at all times."

Jane nodded. "What about the knife?"

Mary's lips trembled. "It was put to its ordained purpose. Mr. Fisher would surely have saved us with it if he'd been here."

"It was Fisher's?" Shelley asked, very alert. "Does it have any markings? Any initials?"

"What if it does?" Mary asked. "He's dead."

"It can be tied to you, Mary." Shelley had gone white around the mouth. "We need to leave the country."

Charles squeezed Shelley's shoulder. "Hold, man. We need to leave this party first. I'm not digging the knife out of his chest. If we have to deny something later, we will. It has to be enough."

Mary's eyes were nearly blinded by tears as she and Jane turned. She resolved to put the sight out of mind as quickly as possible. Nothing mattered but returning home, and no one could see the tragedy etched on her face. They had managed a heroic deed, saving the Duke of Wellington, but no one could ever know about it.

When Mary and Jane crept into the house, the house was as quiet as if it were midnight. It seemed that Mamma and Papa had suffered from the effects of dealing with Shelley more than he had, rough though he had looked.

Mary went directly up to the schoolroom. Jane came in a few minutes later with a jug and helped her change out of her ruined dress.

"What are we going to do with it?"

Jane stuffed Mary's beloved tartan into the jug. "Burn it, so that no one can tie to you a mortal bloodstain."

"Where?"

"I'll do it in the kitchen fire tonight. Polly has gone off somewhere."

Mary handed her the basin full of bloodstained water. "Be careful not to spill."

Jane sighed, looking much older than sixteen in that moment. "Pour as much as you can over the dress so that I'll spill less."

Mary spent Friday with meandering thoughts, mourning her beloved Scottish dress, and jumping every time she heard the door open and close. Willy complained about how often she ran to the window. It didn't help to settle her nerves that every time she caught a glimpse of those going in and out, they weren't constables or Bow Street or mysterious gentlemen from the government.

On Saturday, Willy refused to study. Mary gave him freedom to run out and play after they'd eaten the ham sandwiches Jane brought up, wondering if Mamma would abuse her for letting Willy outside, but her stepmother never ascended to the schoolroom. Willy had brought her porridge in the morning, and Polly brought her dinner that night, muttering under her breath about ill treatment.

Mary was sunken too low in her thoughts to snap back that Polly had surely managed to eat three meals while she'd had only two. She mustered her energy sufficiently to pace some two hours back and forth in front of the window, ruminating over the events at Barts and the garden party, those bloodstained memories that would not leave the center of her thoughts. Shelley was right; they had to run. Could he make the arrangements in time? She forced herself to sit. Travel had never agreed with her, and she didn't want to start her escape while feeling weak.

Jane came in with a basket of yarn just as the first gust of evening wind came through the open window. "I know it's too hot, but winter will come before we know it, and we need socks."

Mary wiped perspiration from her forehead. "Is this what I am to do tonight? Sit up here knitting?"

"I'll stay with you. I'm not allowed to leave the house, either."

Mary screwed up her mouth. "I haven't seen Shelley come in."

Jane set the basket on Willy's desk. "I hope he's busy making arrangements. It's more important than ever that we go after what happened yesterday."

"At least no one can think Charles had anything to do with the Davies girls' deaths now."

Jane pulled out a skein of white wool and stared at it. "Do you think the authorities are as clever as we are? What good is a dead body who can't explain? We left the gun there. Anyone might have taken it."

"They would have to have rolled the body over first. Made a mess."

"There were so many people. There's been nothing in the papers, Mary. It's like it never happened."

"We shouldn't speak of it, either," Mary said, reaching for a pair of knitting needles. She preferred decorative work, but at least this would keep her hands busy. "Shelley will save us soon. I just hope we don't run out of time."

On Sunday, she watched from the window as Jane and Willy left for church. Another sort of household might have lifted Mary's imprisonment so that she could attend to her religious duties, but not Skinner Street.

Later that afternoon, she saw Mamma and Papa walk out together. Other than Polly, she was alone in the house. She ran downstairs to the kitchen and bathed in cool water from the kitchen butt, then fixed herself bread and butter.

After that, she went into the bookshop and stole a couple of the newer books to read. She lingered by the windows, hoping Shelley would appear, but she didn't see anyone she recognized, so she passed the time reading on a chair she'd set next to the schoolroom window. She hadn't realized she'd fallen asleep until the door opening startled her upright. A book fell to the floor, and she had to grab the windowsill to keep herself upright.

Mamma picked up the book. Her thick fingers pressed into the spine. "Where did this come from?" she demanded, then smacked Mary's shoulder hard with it.

Mary's skin flushed hot and cold as she rocked and fell back. Her head hit the floor plank, and she saw stars. She had not thought to be caught with the proceeds of her adventure through the house. *Shelley, come!*

She turned to the side, trying hard not to cry, and stood up from the chair as far away from her stepmother as she could. But then Mamma set down the book and picked up the knitting needles with a couple of inches of a knit circle on them.

"Jane brought you some work, I see," she said.

Mary nodded. Jane could be blamed. She was safer than Mary ever was.

"Enough of this," Mamma pronounced, dropping the knitting back into the basket. "I want a hot meal tonight. Polly will be back with a roast soon. Go down and help her, but make sure to be back up here at dusk."

Mary curtsied and ran out the door, holding her sore head, before Mamma could change her mind. The kitchen sounded like a blessed change, though it might not be any cooler with the fire going.

When Monday arrived, Mary rose from her schoolroom pallet as soon as she woke and limped downstairs, thinking Mamma might not stop her if there was a hot meal ready in the dining room. When she reached the front hall, she saw a small pile of letters on the table, ready to go out, and noticed Shelley's name on one of them. Why had Papa written to him instead of expecting him to call?

She snatched up the letter and took it downstairs. Polly was just stirring as Mary poured water into the teakettle and stirred the fire.

"Should you be down here?" Polly asked, sitting up.

"She sent me down last night. Why not today, too?"

"There's no roast and pudding to make," Polly said and yawned hugely. "Just potatoes and porridge."

Mary poured more water into a bowl and scrubbed a pound of potatoes while Polly went to the outhouse. As soon as the kettle began to steam, though, she used it to help her pry up the wax seal Papa had dripped over the folded paper, then stood at the window with the letter as soon as she had it unfolded.

Tears filled her eyes as she saw the shocking contents. How dare he call Shelley capricious and deceitful! Shelley had ever been honest, even when she'd been uninterested in hearing the truth of his feelings for her. She'd thought to marry another, but all men other than him had betrayed her. He was the only one who'd been true. Yet Papa honed his cunning pen to heap cruelties on her perfect angel? When she heard Polly's footsteps coming in from the garden, she quickly restored the paper into its intricate folds and did her best to stick down the seal again, then went back upstairs, breakfast forgotten, her body still aching from Mamma's attack.

Oh, they had to leave. Papa would never soften toward them. She could see it clearly. Any latent hope she'd had that he would change his mind was gone now that she'd seen the vitriol of his pen.

She did her best to help Willy with his lessons, though her thoughts circled back to Shelley over and over again all of Monday, as she was worried how he would react to such cutting words from his mentor. He never appeared, and Mary was mostly left alone, until Jane struggled up with a big basket of ironing for Mary to do from her Monday laundry labor.

Mary didn't recognize anyone coming to the door until teatime the next day. Mrs. Topping, a French émigré they had known for years, came to call.

Why had Papa asked her to come? Was it possible she had some ties to the men who had paid the professor and Mr. Bryan? Mary's desperate curiosity was not answered, though, for Mrs. Topping left after less than an hour.

The next person who came to call made Mary's blood run cold. She recognized the gentleman in the street as the man from the Home Office.

"Go downstairs," Mary told Willy. She pushed her feet into the slippers she'd been avoiding to keep cool. Crossing her arms over her chest, she went to the window. No one else stood in the lane. She would have thought more men would come, and maybe a cart or trap, if they were going to arrest her.

She heard the steps groaning as people began to move through the house. Not ten minutes later, Jane burst through the door. "That man from the Home Office is here," she announced.

"I saw Mr. Courteney."

"You're wanted downstairs."

Mary nodded. Was this how Queen Marie Antoinette had felt when she'd had to face the guillotine? She pulled back her shoulders and walked downstairs very slowly, following Jane.

"Go into the parlor," Jane said when they were in the front hall, and gave her a little push. "Be brave, Mary. You're a heroine."

In the parlor, sun streamed in through the open curtains, dust visible in the rays. The house showed more and more signs of inattention with fewer hands to keep it clean. There was visible dust around the fireplace, too, and the sofa had divots from unplumped cushions.

Papa stood in front of the fireplace, his hands behind his back. Mary looked at him, love and disappointment warring in her heart. Mamma sat in a chair. She gestured to Jane to stand next to her.

"These are my daughters who are in town," Papa told the man. "They have been locked in the house for days."

Jane opened her mouth, but Papa put up his hand to silence her. "They have duties to this household, and we have a maid to do the marketing. They have not been in the streets."

"I last saw these young women at Mr. Fisher's deathbed,"

Mr. Courteney said. "They made claims about a Professor Asquith and his assistant, and now we have found three dead men, one with Mr. Fisher's knife in his chest."

Jane gasped theatrically. When the gentleman looked at her, Jane poked Mary's arm. "He was cruel to her, sir. Mr. Fisher, I mean. My sister dropped that knife in the street. It never came home with us."

"You were not in possession of the knife on Thursday last?" the man said.

Mary shook her head, grateful for Jane's easy lies for once. "No, sir. He had threatened my poor brother, you see. He said I had to marry him to protect Charles, and so I agreed." She put her hand to her eyes. "What else could I do? It is the duty of a sister."

Jane nodded several times. "Once he was dead, she didn't want anything of his."

"He seemed quite tender to her when he was dying," Mr. Courteney remarked.

"No man wants to be remembered unkindly, no matter what he'd done," Mary said. "But he could not make his amends to my heart. He was a blackmailer, sir."

"In any case," Papa said, "they can have nothing to do with Mr. Bryan's death. They have not been allowed to leave since attending at Mr. Fisher's bedside."

The gentleman stared at them very hard in turn. "Where is Charles Clairmont?"

"I have no idea," Papa said. "But I had our old friend Mrs. Topping here for tea today, and she gave me these names." He pulled a piece of paper from his coat and handed it to the gentleman. "These are probably the men who smuggled that gun into London for the attempted assassination."

"Who is this Mrs. Topping?" Mr. Courteney asked.

"She is part of the French community in exile. A good woman, but of course, there will be a bad element in that crowd," Papa said.

"You think one of these Frenchmen killed the three men and Branwen and Winnet Davies?" the gentleman asked.

Papa nodded. "It seems quite certain. There, I have done your work for you."

"I have seen this name Jacques de Longe before," the gentleman said, stabbing his finger into the paper. "Godwin, I doubt you are any better than him, but never say the law is unfair in our country. I will have these men picked up for questioning."

Without looking at Mary or Jane or even Mamma, the man walked out. They all stayed as still as wax figures until the front door closed and the gentleman passed by the window.

Papa moved then. He went and closed the window and locked it, then pulled the curtains closed.

"The light, Mr. Godwin," Mamma protested.

"Light?" Papa snapped. "I have had enough of you women. If they don't toe the line, I will keep all three of you locked in the house until the day I die."

"Mr. Godwin," Mamma said in a shocked voice.

"Yes, Mrs. Godwin," Papa said. "I know you let Mary out of her prison because you wanted your meals to improve. Well, you had better find the money to hire a new cook, because Mary is not allowed to leave the schoolroom again."

"Papa," Mary said in a voice very similar to Mamma's. "I have done nothing but try to help—" She stopped, recognizing Papa could never know what she'd done. He'd spent his adult life under too much suspicion as it was.

"Go upstairs with Jane. She can determine the state of your hygienic supplies. Jane, you are not to leave the premises."

They both curtsied and went upstairs, united in the knowledge that protest was futile.

Tears streamed down Jane's face by the time they closed themselves into the schoolroom. Mary, on the other hand, felt that all moisture in her body had dried up. "I am nothing but a husk."

"We cannot survive without him," Jane said. "That man wasn't even allowed to interrogate us. Papa is angry, but he protected us."

"We have to be free," Mary said. "I am in prison. How is this any different than when Mamma went to the Bow Street lockup?"

"You know that is worse." Jane looked utterly miserable. "And Mr. Fisher is dead. There is no one at Bow Street to protect you."

"What way do we have to be free of this? We've seen how easy it is for women to be incarcerated, whether in their houses or in the Bow Street lockup. I can't live like this. I'll be dead before winter comes again." Mary rubbed the back of her head. "Why hasn't Shelley called? Is he so angry with Papa that he's forgotten us? Is he ill again?"

"I'll think of a way to contact him. I don't know why he hasn't called," Jane said, wiping her eyes.

"I know why. Papa wrote him a very nasty letter." Mary crossed her arms over her chest. "Shelley will probably not give him any money now. It was so vile."

"Shelley is a gentleman. He would not go back on his word."

"He also promised to rescue us." Mary hugged herself, refusing to let doubts grow. "But he doesn't know how desperately we need it."

"Tomorrow," Jane said. "I will figure out a way to get a letter out."

"There is paper up here at least. I will prepare our inquiry." Mary nodded. Jane looked so miserable that Mary gave her a hug. "Shelley will save us like he promised. Oh, I do hope Papa's letter didn't make him ill."

On Tuesday, Mary woke at her now customary early hour. She took paper and ink to the chair by the window and used the sill as a desk to write out a precise history of the past day for Shelley. "I cannot make it any clearer," Mary wrote, "that Jane and I must leave. I believe Charles has been saved by Papa's discovery of some names of Frenchmen. In any case, my stepbrother's name was scarcely raised by the Home Office. Jane and I, though, we are in peril, for reasons I cannot put into writing."

She was ready when Jane came with her porridge.

"What are you going to do?" Mary asked, trading the folded letter for the bowl.

"I will slip it to the porter for delivery. He has to take some books to Old Bond Street. Papa must have made some sort of deal with the Hookhams when he called on them with Shelley. It will not be so difficult for him to get the letter to Shelley's rooms."

"Will the porter tell Mamma?"

"I do not think he has the sense to consider it. Why would he think I was doing anything wrong?"

Movement came on the stairs. Jane straightened and hid the letter in her pocket, then went out.

On Wednesday, Mary woke with the light again. Was this how her days would pass, with no difference in them but the changing of the season? She loathed the inaction of it. Was there nothing she could do for herself? Had her letter reached Shelley? She had full confidence in him, if only he could know what was happening.

Willy came in a couple of hours later. He seemed to have an odd gray light about him, as if she and her little brother did not exist in exactly the same room. She reached through the light and gave him a hug, feeling that they would soon be parted forever. But she had to make the sacrifice to be free, and she would do it willingly. She was nothing but a decaying corpse here and must be reanimated elsewhere or die forever.

A few hours later, she sent him to take a walk. It seemed like it had been days since she'd seen Polly. The maid did not come that day, either. Jane had been designated her turnkey.

Her heart skipped a few beats when she saw Mr. Courteney arrive just a couple of hours after noon, but she was not called downstairs, and he left alone not very long after.

Her stepsister came in at teatime with a bounce in her step, which had been missing.

"What is it?" Mary asked, returning sluggishly to the schoolroom from a history of ancient Rome.

Jane handed her a letter. "I never saw him, but a boy handed it to me at the door."

Mary snatched the paper. It had no writing on the outside. She unfolded it and recognized the large, untidy handwriting. For a moment, she could do no more than clutch it to her breast.

"Mary," Jane urged.

Mary scanned the contents, reading at half her normal speed. Had the world slowed down, or was it just her? She spoke in a whisper. "Here is my darling's reply. Shelley is planning our escape and says we will settle in Uri, Switzerland, for your sake."

Jane reached for Mary's shoulder and clutched at it. Mary squeezed her hand. "Now that the moment is here, is it the right thing to do? To leave Papa?"

Jane chewed on her bottom lip. "That Home Office person came again."

"I saw. Do you know what happened?"

"There was some tumult in Somers Town last night. I believe some Frenchmen perished."

Mary blinked. "The Home Office killed them instead of arresting them?"

Jane worried at her lip again. "I could not listen at Papa's door. I had to be in the shop. I only heard what was said when Papa escorted him back downstairs."

"Did they say anything about Charles?"

"That he was lucky," Jane reported. "I expect that means he'll be coming home. Another mouth to feed again. More laundry." She sighed. "Mamma said she will not be hiring a new cook."

"Then you must leave." Mary noted the circles under Jane's eyes.

"Yes, I want to see Switzerland. We will be safe with Shelley."

Mary smiled. "And blissfully happy, I know it. It's just, well, leaving Papa."

"You'll never be able to return here," Jane said. "It is the end."

"We're to meet Shelley at dawn," Mary said after glancing at the letter again. "He'll have a carriage. The plan we had for Charles. Do you want to get word to him?"

"No. I think he's safe, and if he comes along, he'll spend Shelley's money, and we'll have to wait on him. I'm tired, Mary, so tired." Jane wiped her eyes.

"He's never been at all grateful for anything we've done."

"You literally killed a man for him, and he didn't thank you," Jane said.

"Right." Mary nodded. Charles would be no benefit for Shelley's community. "It's going to be warm. Bring up my black silk dress tonight, when you come to fetch my tray. Wear yours, as well. Shelley says we'll need to travel fast and light, but we need to look our best."

"I will," Jane said. "It is too bad this isn't Monday. You would have had the laundry up here. We could have taken more."

"It's no use worrying about it now," Mary said, though her head was full of nothing but. To never see Papa again? Or the bookshop? To commit to Shelley completely, for the rest of her life? That didn't frighten her like the rest. Where was her angel? The sight of him might have reassured her, yet she had not seen him for nearly a week.

"What about money? Shelley never seems to have much," Jane said.

"It is a worry." Mary handed her the letter. "Take this. Maybe you can reply and ask about the practical matters. This might just kill Papa. It has been so hot this month, and he is unwell."

"And you are dying in a prison. A slave," Jane said emphatically.

"I know." Mary put her hand to her head. Dark spots danced before her eyes. "Bring me water, please. I have to think."

Chapter 21

Jane

It frightened me to see Mary's face so pale, her gaze so distant. Could she persuade herself not to flee, after all? Had too much of her intellectual reserves been drained by saving Charles and not herself? Had Mamma battered her body worse than I knew? I had to persuade her that this was the only step to take. I did not want to go into debtors' prison with Papa or, worse, have to stay here all alone and manage the bookshop and the house. Mary had not seen the machinations with creditors while she'd been locked upstairs.

I was staring at the letter, trying to decide what to do, when I heard the front door open. I folded it up quickly and tucked it into my apron pocket, but a figure appeared in the bookshop doorway while a corner still poked out. I shoved it down, hoping I wasn't creasing it overmuch.

"What is that, Miss Godwin?" asked the gentleman from the Home Office.

"Returned to us so soon, sir?" I asked. "Is there some further news about the dead Frenchmen?"

"I believe you sell your stepfather's books here?" Mr. Courteney said.

I froze. "This is a children's bookshop, sir."

"Yet from all reports, rather a great deal of young men do business with you," he said, acid etching his voice.

"A great deal of young men are tutors," I replied. Had all this business brought Papa back under the eye of the Home Office? I knew Shelley actively feared them, but Papa was hardly young. Why, everything he wrote these days seemed to be an attempt to diminish his youthful fervor.

The gentleman began to wander, running his fine gloves along the bookshelves.

"Why, sir," I said, my body quivering at a fine hum, "you will do the dusting for me."

"Hmmm," he replied and went out of sight.

I remembered, against my better will, the body Mary had found, knifed on the floor, not but a few short months ago. How did it feel to be her, a girl who had ended another man's life in similar fashion? How could she find the will to run after all she had been through? I had to be strong for her.

He came back into sight a couple of minutes later, volumes in his hands. He slapped Papa's *St. Leon* on the counter.

"I—I'll have to charge you for it," I said. "We need the trade, as I'm sure you know."

He smirked and pulled out the guineas. When he set them in my hand, I felt the fineness of the calfskin and shuddered.

"What is wrong, Miss Godwin?"

"What do you want with that book?" I asked.

"Your family is trouble," he said. "I don't know which of you is worse. The father, an atheist. The mother, a mannish woman of business. The son, despoiler of women. The daughter, claiming a fine Bow Street Runner blackmailed her, or you, Miss Clairmont. What horror lies behind those pretty dark eyes?"

He stared at me, his face coming closer to mine. Or maybe I imagined it, because when I blinked, he was on the other side of the counter and turning away from me, and in his hand, Papa's book about a man with terrible secrets who spent his life running from one source of trouble to another while wanting only to help people.

I didn't want that. I wanted to be free. It would be a long night, but Mary and I would meet Shelley at dawn and climb into that carriage and be on the way to Switzerland, where I belonged.

"It is only a matter of time before Papa is arrested," I told Mary over a single candle flame. Just minutes would pass until the bells tolled midnight. She wore only her shift, though I was already in my black silk. I had attached a pocket to hold the franc coin Willy had found in Covent Garden. I would use it to buy my first bite of French food. "I am afraid Shelley's funds won't be good for a second rescue, if we don't leave now."

Mary tapped two letters she'd spent the evening writing to Papa, even though I had advised against it. I hadn't been able to supervise her very much, for I had to do all the work downstairs. Now, though, the house was quiet.

"Do you not think I should confess the facts about Mr. Bryan's murder to Papa? He can tell the Home Office what happened, and maybe they won't persecute him."

I heard footsteps in the street. I saw the shadow of a man passing between torchlight emanating from passing carriages. "We are being watched."

"I must see Shelley," Mary moaned. "I haven't seen him in so long."

"He'll be waiting for us around four. A boy came at dusk." I brandished the note.

"What do we tell Papa?"

"Leave the note that doesn't talk about Mr. Bryan's death. Please, Mary. We'll never be able to come back to London if you confess it." I snatched the letter from her hand and held it to the candle flame.

She mewled in protest but didn't attempt to rip it from my hand. Instead, she dressed. "I'll leave alone first as a test, to see if I can get past the watcher."

"You won't desert me?" I asked, afraid.

"I will return, I promise. I just want to make sure Shelley isn't walking us into a trap."

I wanted to faint with gratitude when I heard her words. I took her box of precious writings, her novel, letters of her mother's and father's, and a few books downstairs, and the second letter, and paced the front hall while she slipped out to test the escape plan. She melted so cleanly into the shadows that I could not have testified the direction in which she went.

When she returned, silent as a burglar, she gave me a determined nod over my candle flame. "He's going to the stable. He'll be at the corner any moment."

"We can leave?" I felt breathless. My heart pounded in my chest, while she seemed calmer than before.

"There's no one outside watching now. Maybe it's too close to dawn. Or you imagined shadows into men." She bit her lower lip. "We have to go before the cattle are driven past. The carriage will be stuck otherwise."

She took the letter from my hand and went upstairs very quietly. When she came back, she did not have it.

"What about Charles?" I asked. "I thought he'd be home by now. I want to say goodbye."

"Do you want to go or not?" Mary asked. She put her hands to her head and squeezed the straw of her bonnet.

I saw shadows in the street again. Traffic was picking up as it grew closer to dawn. "We go now." I handed her the box of her things, and took my own off the table in the hall.

We waited in front of the door until we saw no one, and walked out as noiselessly as possible, leaving the door unlocked behind us, because we had no further use for the key.

Shelley's carriage awaited not far away. Mary climbed in first, directly into Shelley's arms. Once I was inside the carriage, I leaned back, too tense to relax against the squabs, hoping we had made our escape.

As we went through Covent Garden, I peeked out of the window, directly in the eyeline of a man I recognized as being in business with Papa. He tilted his head, confusion crossing his face, as he recognized me, but then we were gone, heading to the road to Dover, aiming for the English Channel and France, then ultimately Switzerland, leaving Charles, Willy, Mamma, and everyone else behind.

Epilogue

From the diary of Shelley and Mary

In Shelley's handwriting: *The heat made her faint. It was necessary at every stage that she should repose. I was divided between anxiety for her health and terror lest our pursuers should arrive. I reproached myself with not allowing her sufficient time to rest, with conceiving any evil so great that the slightest portion of her comfort might be sacrificed to avoid it.*

At Dartford we took four horses, that we might outstrip pursuit...

In Mary's handwriting: *On arriving at Dover, I was refreshed by a sea-bath. As we very much wished to cross the Channel with all possible speed, we would not wait for the packet of the following day (it being then about four in the afternoon), but hiring a small boat, resolved to make the passage the same evening, the seamen promising us a voyage of two hours.*

The evening was most beautiful; there was but little wind, and the sails flapped in the flagging breeze; the moon rose, and night came on, and with the night a slow, heavy swell and a fresh breeze, which soon produced a sea so violent as to toss the boat very much. I was dreadfully sea-sick, and, as is usually my custom when thus affected, I slept during the greater part of the night, awaking only from time to time to ask where we were, and to receive the dismal answer each time, "Not quite half-way."

The wind was violent and contrary; if we could not reach Calais the sailors proposed making for Boulogne. They promised only two hours' sail from shore, yet hour after hour passed, and we were still far distant, when the moon sunk in the red and stormy horizon and the fast-flashing lightning became pale in the breaking day.

We were proceeding slowly against the wind, when suddenly a thunder squall struck the sail, and the waves rushed into the boat: even the sailors acknowledged that our situation was perilous; but they succeeded in reefing the sail; the wind was now changed, and we drove before the gale directly to Calais.

In Shelley's handwriting: *Mary did not know our danger; she was resting between my knees, that were unable to support her; she did not speak or look, but I felt that she was there. I had time in that moment to reflect, and even to reason upon death; it was rather a thing of discomfort and disappointment than horror to me. We should never be separated, but in death we might not know and feel our union as now. I hope, but my hopes are not unmixed with fear for what may befall this inestimable spirit when we appear to die.*

The morning broke, the lightning died away, the violence of the wind abated. We arrived at Calais, whilst Mary still slept; we drove upon the sands. Suddenly the broad sun rose over France.

William Godwin's diary entry for 28 July says only, *Five in the morning. Macmillan* [one of Godwin's printers, based in Bow Street] *calls. M J* [Mamma] *for Dover.*

Acknowledgments

I want to thank you, dear reader, for picking up *Death and the Runaways*. We authors live and die by our book reviews, so thank you for reviewing *Death and the Runaways* and anything else I've written, especially *Death and the Sisters*, the first book in this series, and *Death and the Visitors*, the second book.

Thank you to my beta editor, Elizabeth Flynn, and I appreciate the emotional support provided by the Columbia River Sisters in Crime chapter. Thank you to Barbara de Boinville for the biographical information on Cornelia Boinville Turner. Thank you to my agent, Laurie McLean, at Fuse Literary. Thank you to my editor, Elizabeth May; my copy editor, Rosemary Silva; and my communications manager, Larissa Ackerman, along with many unsung heroes at Kensington.

While the Godwin family and the larger Shelley circle are real people, my plot is entirely fictitious. Recollections of this time period are different depending on the witness and the era, and I have done some compressing of the events as they appear in William Godwin's journal to move the story along. I found it fitting to end this trilogy with these accomplished writers' own words. A tremendous amount of material is available about this period in London, and I encourage readers to pick up some nonfiction on the topic.

While we cannot truly know what motivated Mary, Jane, and Shelley to do what they did the summer of 1814, the consequences of their actions affected every one of the people in their lives. *Liber librum aperit.*

BOOK CLUB READING GUIDE for

Death and the Runaways

1. We've been building up to July 28 1814 for this entire trilogy. Did you come to these novels knowing what Mary, Jane, and Shelley decided to do?
2. What echoes of Mary's visionary masterwork *Frankenstein* do you see in this novel?
3. How do you feel about Denarius Fisher after reading this book? Do you feel Mary and Jane were justified in how they treated him?
4. The notion of how a father fits into a household has changed a lot over the centuries. How do you feel about William Godwin's role in his family?
5. William Godwin revised his philosophical work multiple times over his long lifetime, softening his earlier opinions. Why do you think Shelley and the younger generation continued to hold on to his 1790s interpretation of marriage and his other ideals?
6. Alchemy is an intensely secretive process, covered under layers of symbolism and esoteric notions. What do you know about the agelong search for turning base metals into gold?
7. Have you read any of the books of this era that are mentioned in this series? Mary Shelley's work? Percy Bysshe Shelley's work? William Godwin's?
8. What is your feeling about mysteries featuring real historical figures? It has become quite the subgenre, with amateur sleuths from the famous to the famous adjacent.
9. It is said that the hardest thing about being an adult is figuring out what you are going to eat every day for the rest

of your life. How much more difficult was that in Regency England?

10. Are you curious to follow Mary, Jane, and Shelley to France? What will change when they are in a foreign environment?